CHAMPION

Niccolo laughed huskily. "Why did you kiss me, milady?"

Aurora shrugged, but a deepening blush gave away her excitement. "Because your countenance is pleasing, knight, and because I was curious about kisses."

Niccolo was charmed by her honesty. "And now, milady? Are you more curious still?"

She wiggled nearer, eyeing him boldly. "Mayhap a little."

Enchanted to his soul, Niccolo slowly shook his head in mock reproach. "Oh, milady. You should not tease a man so."

"And why not?" she inquired saucily.

All at once, Niccolo could barely breathe. He had never expected such unabashed temptation from her. "You may not have come here to meet a lover, milady . . . but you may find one ere long," he whispered.

CHAMPION

by

Fabio

in collaboration with
Eugenia Riley

AVON BOOKS ◆ NEW YORK

CHAMPION is an original publication of Avon Books. This work has never before appeared in book form. This work is a novel. Any similarity to actual persons or events is purely coincidental.

AVON BOOKS
A division of
The Hearst Corporation
1350 Avenue of the Americas
New York, New York 10019

First Avon Books Printing: November 1995

AVON TRADEMARK REG. U.S. PAT. OFF. AND IN OTHER COUNTRIES, MARCA REGISTRADA, HECHO EN U.S.A.

Printed in the U.S.A.

RA   10   9   8   7   6   5   4   3   2   1

I dedicate this work to those selfless individuals around the world who have devoted themselves to making a difference in the struggle against abuse, violence toward, and exploitation of, women. I diligently support the eradication of these examples of the oldest scourge of the battle of the sexes.

Fabio gratefully acknowledges
the contribution of Eugenia Riley,
without whom this book would not
have been possible.

Acknowledgments

Special thanks to my friend and partner Eric Ashenberg and all the people at Global Entertainment Management and Celebrity Management, Inc., who help me with all of my business and legal affairs, both personal and professional, and whose support keeps my life manageable.

Thanks as well to my devoted fan club president, Bonnie Kuhlman, whose management of the Fabio International Fan Club, P.O. Box 827, DuBois, Wyoming 82513, has been extraordinary. She has computerized an international group of thousands of fans who correspond in over fourteen languages. Her tireless efforts are greatly appreciated.

Many thanks to Ellen Edwards and all the wonderful people at Avon Books. It's been a pleasure to work with all of you, and I greatly appreciate our association.

Special thanks to all my fans for their support and kindness.

ONE

Venice
Late fifteenth century

"I SEEK THE WORLD'S GREATEST KNIGHT," THE stranger said. "And bless Saint Mark, I think I may have found him."

Standing in the night shadows on the upper colonnade of the Palazzo Ducale, Niccolo Campioni overheard this tantalizing remark, spoken by one of two men who now emerged from the doge's lavish *sala* to stand before him on the balcony and stare out at the *Piazzetta* amid the pageantry of the Ascension celebration. Niccolo noted that the man who had spoken was a robust, elegantly attired foreigner who stood in the company of his own good friend Vincente Dionzetti, who was a successful silk merchant and revered member of the Doge's Council. The two men sipped Marsala wine in bronzed, bejeweled chalices long ago captured by Venetian crusaders in Byzantium.

For a moment they fell hushed, evidently unaware of Niccolo covertly observing them as they watched the festivities spilling over San Marco, the carnival atmosphere of trade booths, acrobats, and wandering minstrels, the crush of pilgrims and Venetians noisily

1

intermingling amid the glow of torches and the splendor of the barge-lined lagoon beyond. To the north
loomed the Turkish majesty of the Basilica, its glittering statues and soaring cupolas backlit by the smoky,
luminescent skies; to the south along the waterfront
stretched the Molo, where public executions where
held. Niccolo was aware that even now, the head of
a Venetian galley captain turned traitor to the Turks
was exhibited on the *Pietro del Bando*. Sometimes Niccolo swore he could actually smell the metallic odor
of blood that had oozed into the stones of the *Piazzetta*
over the centuries; that haunting essence, as well as
the scent of the sea and the odor of opulent decay,
filled the cool spring air.

As a burst of fireworks illuminated the foreground,
sending shards of light dancing across the colonnade,
Niccolo caught a better glimpse of the two men. In
appearance they shared little in common; Niccolo's
friend Vincente was tall and rangy, while the newcomer was short and barrel-chested. Unlike Vincente,
who wore the red robe and matching cap of the *scar-
latti*, the portly visitor was arrayed in an extravagant
floor-length cape of silk brocade and a bejeweled
chaperon turban.

"The world's greatest knight," Niccolo now heard
Vincente repeat. "Quite a novel undertaking, my
friend. Why would you seek such a champion?"

"To save my fair niece," the stranger replied solemnly. "She is a princess who is trapped in her castle
back in our homeland, the Kingdom of Falconia."

"Ah, a damsel in distress," murmured Vincente. "A
most intriguing predicament." Vincente paused,
scratching his bearded jaw. "I have heard of this Falconia. Does she not lie to the north across the Alps?"

"Yea," the stranger concurred. "Falconia is a picturesque little kingdom, where life was once very
good for us all. Unhappily, for the past two years, our
state has been under siege by the rival Kingdom of

Ravenia. Basil, King of Ravenia, seeks to conquer Falconia and force my niece, Princess Aurora, into wedlock. Aurora is heir to the throne, you see, and I do not wish her wed to a villain such as Basil. That is why I have embarked on this critical mission. If only I can find a knight great enough to rescue Aurora and defeat Basil, then I shall reward this man with her hand in marriage—as well as her dowry, a fortune in gold and jewels."

"My, what a fascinating account," observed Vincente. "Setting this matter to rights will require the skills of a great champion."

"Yea, so it will."

A smile lit Vincente's bearded face. "As fortune would have it, I know of such a man."

"Do you?" inquired the stranger with interest.

Vincente spoke with great zeal. "His name is Niccolo Campioni, and he is grand master of the esteemed Venetian knightly order of *Cavalieri di San Marco*. I wish you could have seen him perform at the state tournaments after he was awarded his first *condotta*. He is *magnìfico*. For years Niccolo has distinguished himself for the Republic, as captain general of our forces in battles against the Turks, and as the doge's emissary in the delicate negotiations that have reopened the sea lanes between here and the Far East."

"Ah, he does sound like a mighty warrior and an astute statesman," acknowledged the stranger.

"*Sì*, Niccolo is an intelligent strategist as well as a ferocious fighter." Vincente sighed and stared out at the Piazza. "But he is also a man who has been plagued by tragedy on both a personal and financial plane."

"How is this so?"

As Niccolo waited tensely, Vincente hesitated. "I really cannot say more without violating a confidence," he said at last. "I would only assure you that Niccolo

Campioni's ruthlessness in defending your niece would be unparalleled. Otherwise, I would ask that you defer to him for further details."

"Mayhap I shall," murmured the stranger.

Niccolo was cynical enough to find this particular cue irresistible. "*Sì*," he agreed as he stepped out of the shadows. "When one is dealing with the devil, one must give him the chance to speak his own mind."

Amid Vincente's startled curse and the stranger's gasp, both men turned to confront the giant of a man who had materialized like a ghost to join them. Dressed in a brocaded dark tunic and pale hose, Niccolo Campioni towered head and shoulders above the other two. A shaft of moonlight outlined his noble face and sternly set features, the deep-set eyes that gleamed, cold and ruthless, beneath straight male brows, the fair hair spilling down about his broad shoulders.

"Niccolo," cried an astonished Vincente, "we did not see you there, my friend!"

"Obviously," mocked Niccolo as he joined the other two at the railing. He regarded the foreigner, and found himself staring into a round, fleshy face, an inscrutable countenance accented by dark, beady eyes, protruding lips, and a thin black mustache. He smiled. "You must introduce me to your friend, Vincente."

"But of course," Vincente replied. "Niccolo Campioni, I present to you one of the doge's esteemed guests this fine eve—Artemas of Falconia, Count of Osprey. The count does trade in iron ore with our merchants in the Rialto."

"Ah," replied Niccolo, bowing to Artemas. "I am honored to make your acquaintance, signore *il conte*. I do hope you are enjoying our fair city?"

"Verily, I am," replied Artemas. "I have never encountered such splendor as in the Palazzo and the

Basilica. The magnificent architecture, the mosaics, the paintings of Mantegna and sculpture by Donatello . . . Our little kingdom of Falconia seems backward by comparison."

"Do not believe him," chided Vincente to Niccolo. "My friend Don Forenzo Vasari has traveled to Falconia, and reports that the royal castle is a marvel of architecture."

"You are too kind, my friend," said Artemas modestly.

"You are under siege, signore?" inquired Niccolo. "Forgive me, but I could not help but overhear."

"Alas, the situation is most grave," concurred Artemas. "That is why I have embarked on this journey throughout the Christian world."

"Artemas is searching for the world's greatest knight," said Vincente.

"Truly?" Niccolo encouraged.

"I seek a man who is Christian, upstanding, as well as English-speaking," explained Artemas. "You see, English is now our state language, in honor of my sister, the dear departed Queen Lyris, who came to Falconia from our homeland of Lancaster in England." He paused to cross himself, then brightened. "I note that the merchants and galley captains of Venice are proficient in many tongues."

"*Sì*, so we must be, given our travels to diverse regions of the world," said Niccolo. He frowned thoughtfully. "I heard you mention to my friend that you may have found this great knight you seek."

"Yea, the Duke of Milan has told me of a great warrior," replied Artemas with relish. "He is Genoese, a member of the Figliosi family."

"Genoese!" scoffed Niccolo. "Genoa has been a second-rate power ever since our war galleys decimated hers at Chioggia."

"Ah, but is Genoa not still a bitter trade rival of the Republic?" asked Artemas wisely.

"The Figliosis are no better than pirates and conscienceless mercenaries," argued Niccolo. "They are beneath contempt. You are most ill advised, signore, to entrust the future of your kingdom—and your niece—to such a company of scoundrels."

Artemas chuckled. "You speak as if you seek to champion her cause yourself, signore."

Niccolo flashed a bitter smile. "I am no one's champion, signore, nor am I the knight to go rescue damsels in distress. I would simply warn you not to be fooled by charlatans such as the Figliosis."

As the three men stood in the tense aftermath of Niccolo's remarks, a distant bell rang, summoning the guests to come dine at the doge's sumptuous table. Artemas nodded stiffly to the two other men.

"*Scusi*, signores," he murmured. "I have neglected my host, the doge, long enough."

Watching Artemas amble off toward the doge's apartment, Niccolo offered Vincente an apologetic look. "I beg your pardon, *amico mio*. I seem to have insulted your guest."

Vincente merely shrugged. "The count is not my guest but a friend of the doge's whom I was showing about the Palazzo at his request. Nevertheless, I would have expected you to show more interest in his dilemma."

Niccolo stared out at the lagoon, watching a dark, magnificently carved state galley glide by under oar power, the banner of the Republic waving from its foremast, a great lantern gleaming on its aftercastle. "And why should I be interested?"

"Perhaps because I saw the Bondi brothers inside searching for you."

Niccolo groaned. "And doubtless seeking to leave here this eve with my tunic and purse."

"They are merely bankers seeking to turn a profit," pointed out Vincente gently.

"*Sì*, and I owe them more than my soul."

Vincente scowled. "That is why I must wonder at your spurning what Artemas of Falconia might offer you."

Niccolo hesitated. "There is something about the man that disinclines me to trust him."

Vincente appeared perplexed. "Pray, explain."

Niccolo offered an open-handed gesture. "I cannot say, for it is just a feeling . . ." He glanced at his friend. "Do you think the count is honorable and legitimate, or merely some arrogant braggadocio?"

"He is a friend of the doge's. Surely that commends him."

"If we trust Cristoforo Moro."

"Do you trust anyone, Niccolo?" asked Vincente ironically.

For a long moment Niccolo stood silent, staring grimly at the lagoon. When at last he turned to his friend, his hands were curled into fists, and his words poured forth with hoarse bitterness. "Do you mean can I trust after my wife committed adultery with my cousin while I was off defending the Republic? Can I trust after my cousin bankrupted the family enterprises and killed my wife in a fit of jealous rage? After he committed suicide? After I returned home to face heartache, ridicule, and bankruptcy for myself and my family? *Sì*, my old friend, trust should come easily to a man with so little tragedy to overcome."

Vincente stared into Niccolo's blue eyes, vivid eyes filled with the gleam of bitterness and hatred. He laid a hand on the other man's tense shoulder. "Niccolo, my friend, three years have passed. I would see you happy, that is all."

"Happy wed to some princess in a benighted Alpine kingdom?" scoffed Niccolo. In an angry undertone he finished, "Happy knowing my mother and Caterina will soon lose everything?"

Dropping his hand to his side, Vincente implored, "But, my friend, if you win this princess's dowry, you can save your family's fortunes and your shipping empire, no?"

Niccolo sadly shook his head. "There is nothing left to save. All our galleys are gone now, forfeit to our creditors. There is only our small exchange left in the Rialto—"

"But what of your estate on the mainland—the home of your mother and sister? What of Caterina's dowry? Young Filippo Travola will not wait forever to wed her."

Niccolo gave a dismal nod, his fingers tensely clutching the balcony railing. "*Sì, amico mio,* you speak the truth. But how can I ever hope to secure the five thousand ducats for Caterina's dowry when I owe ten times that amount to the Bondis?"

"That is why I argue that you must not ignore the stroke of fortune offered by Artemas of Falconia," implored Vincente.

"Perhaps . . ." murmured Niccolo. "But I am still not sure I trust the man."

Gently Vincente suggested, "Mayhap you cannot trust him due to the tragedy of your own circumstances, *amico mio*? Some matters must be accepted on faith."

Niccolo's sardonic laughter rang in the night. "I have no faith. You of all people should know that."

At the blasphemous comments, Vincente automatically crossed himself. "But if you do not trust someone, how else can you rescue the fortunes of your family . . . or yourself?"

Niccolo expelled a heavy breath. "Myself, I do not care about. My family is another matter altogether."

"Then do not allow your pride to defeat you."

Niccolo glowered at his friend.

Vincente stepped closer and spoke in a tense whisper. "Earlier, as we spoke, the count told me he yearns to see some of our mainland estates owned by the esteemed Venetian families. I will invite him to my home this night. Come with us later as we cross the lagoon. Perhaps an arrangement can still be made."

Ruefully Niccolo shook his head. "You are determined to save me, are you not, old friend?"

"*Sì, amico mio*," replied Vincente sadly, "because I see much that is worth saving."

TWO

The long, sturdy gondola glided across the silvery lagoon. Vincente sat at the prow beyond the
oarsmen; Niccolo and Artemas were seated at the
stern. Behind them loomed the dramatic domes,
spires, and tiled roofs of the city; beyond them twinkled the lights of the mainland estates. The night had
grown colder, but the air still bore the tangy scent of
the sea.

Niccolo was lost in thought, remembering his conversation with Vincente, and wondering if he should
offer his services to the Count of Osprey. He knew
Vincente had stationed himself near the bow to offer
him a chance to converse privately with Artemas of
Falconia.

If he did not speak up soon, his chance would be
lost. Yet Niccolo still felt doubt. Given the agonizing
betrayal he had suffered previously, he was reluctant
to trust anyone, especially this enigmatic foreigner.
And the prospect of rescuing a trapped princess
grated badly on his pride and sense of manhood; as
a man bereft of both faith and chivalry, he had for
years scorned such gallant pursuits. Nor was he eager
to take a bride—the proffered prize in this question-
able venture. He was tempted to keep his silence—

Yet, as Vincente had wisely pointed out, if this prin-

10

cess's dowry was substantial, he might well be forsaking his one chance to rescue the fortunes of his family and secure a prosperous future for his mother and sister. Certainly he would be taking a gamble, but surely Mamma and Caterina's future would be worth the risk. The very thought of his mother being cast from their villa to satisfy their creditors, his sister being left unwed and brokenhearted due to the lack of a dowry, brought a dark scowl to his face . . .

"Do you live near your friend, signore?" Artemas asked, breaking into Niccolo's thoughts.

Niccolo nodded. "*Sì*, our family estates adjoin, and Vincente and I have been friends since childhood."

The count's dark eyes glittered. "It was kind of Vincente to offer me the hospitality of his home—but I sense a hidden purpose behind his overture."

Niccolo chuckled; Artemas of Falconia was clearly no one's fool. "Actually, Vincente thought you and I might benefit from an opportunity for further discussion."

Artemas raised a dark, thin brow. "Indeed. In what regard, signore?"

Niccolo drew a bracing breath. "Vincente feels I should offer my services to rescue your niece—Princess Aurora, is that not her name?"

"Yea, that is her name." Artemas frowned in perplexity. "Now you say you desire to rescue her, signore? Did you not earlier state that you are no one's champion?"

Niccolo drew himself up with pride. "I have distinguished myself well as captain general for the Republic. I have defeated Turkish marauders in the Adriatic and have beaten back Ottoman attempts to claim our Greek island possessions. Moreover, I am grand master of my knightly order. I would say I am eminently qualified."

"Perhaps," conceded Artemas. "But did your armies not lose Constantinople to the Turks?"

"Even the most skilled legion cannot resist truly overwhelming numbers," Niccolo countered vehemently. "Yet Venice is well on her way to reestablishing sea supremacy, a feat I have fought long and hard for. Indeed, I recently escorted into our harbors six state galleys filled with Byzantium silk, so you cannot argue the Turks have truly impeded us."

Artemas nodded. "Mayhap you are qualified, signore. But I must wonder . . . what has brought about this change of heart?"

Niccolo gazed at Artemas sharply, musing that a very shrewd mind lay behind the count's fleshy face. "I will speak frankly, signore. Due to family and other obligations, I covet the prize you offer."

Moonlight glinted off the count's small white teeth. "Ah . . . you are a frank man. As for the prize . . . I presume you speak not of my niece?"

Niccolo fought to repress a grin. "How sizable is her dowry?"

Artemas chuckled. "The hills of Falconia are rich with iron ore and silver. Over the centuries, we have traded this commodity for priceless jewels and gold. Suffice it to say, my niece's coffers are full, and the income from her tenants and vineyards is also sizable. Aurora needs but a powerful champion to marshal her forces and defeat Basil decisively."

"I could easily perform this feat," boasted Niccolo, thinking of how he could repay the Bondis and secure his mother and sister's future with the princess's dowry.

Artemas nodded slowly. "From what I hear from Vincente regarding your fearsomeness, I have no doubt you could defeat Basil. But what could you offer my niece in return?"

"You are inquiring of my own marital portion?"

"Yea."

"I would offer the traditional dower of one third of

my earthly possessions," answered Niccolo forth-rightly.

The count made a sound of contempt. "According to both you and your friend, such an offer is largely meaningless. A portion of naught is yet naught."

Niccolo chafed at this assault on his pride and honor. "I will bring your niece my protection and good name."

"Doubtless. But the fact remains that I have found the Genoese knight I wish to dispatch to rescue Aurora."

Disappointment sagged Niccolo's spirits. "You have contracted with the Figliosis?"

"Nay, signore. But the Duke of Milan has already transmitted his written endorsement to the Figliosis on my behalf. To withdraw at this juncture would cause a serious loss of face for the duke—"

"I care not if Francesco Sforza loses face!" burst out Niccolo. "Have you forgotten that Genoese brought plague among us? As for Sforza, he is no better than a ruthless soldier of fortune."

"Regardless of whether or not the duke may be considered a mercenary, I have an obligation to the man," stated Artemas firmly. He continued with greater tact. "Although I do realize, of course, that relations between the Republic and the Duchy of Milan are strained . . ."

"Forces of the Duchy killed my father when our countries were at war," interjected Niccolo heatedly.

"My sympathies, signore. But we in Falconia are involved in trade with Milano. There are sensitive political considerations hanging in the balance."

Niccolo fell silent, brooding. He had not anticipated this much resistance from the count. "You will not consider dispatching another knight to rescue your niece?"

"Not precisely, signore," replied Artemas eva-sively. "I am saying it is a most delicate matter, appeasing the honor of the Duke of Milan, and potentially severing my obligation to the Figliosis."

"I will serve you better than any Milano knight," declared Niccolo.

Artemas's thick lips curled with amusement. "Mayhap. I must say you are an astonishingly confident man. You eagerly defame the Figliosis, but argue I should trust you instead?"

"*Sì.*"

Artemas frowned. "Vincente tells me you are a man who has been plagued by tragedy."

"This is true," Niccolo admitted warily.

"If we are to consider doing business together, I must know the type of man I am dealing with."

Niccolo fell coldly silent.

"Signore?"

Niccolo hesitated for another long moment, then stated harshly, "You are dealing with a man who has known betrayal of every kind—the heart, the mind, the spirit. You are dealing with a man who could have allowed those betrayals to destroy him. Instead, he has used those treacheries to temper him like the strongest, coldest steel."

For a moment, the count appeared speechless, his corpulent mouth hanging open. Then he asked carefully, "This betrayal of the heart . . . ?"

"I am a widower."

"And this makes you a suitable bridegroom for my niece?" posed the count skeptically.

Passionately Niccolo retorted, "I am a man of experience in many regards, signore, a man who will prove himself utterly devastating against your niece's enemies. As for my obligations as her husband, you may be assured I will do my duties both to protect her—and to get an heir on her."

The count's beady eyes widened. "You are a bluntly spoken man."

Niccolo smiled slightly. "It will take such a man to defeat your enemies, no?"

"Mayhap so." Artemas gazed off at the mainland. "I am impressed by your frankness, signore, and tempted to accept your offer. However, there is still the troubling matter of my obligations to the Figliosis and the duke . . ."

At last Niccolo began to pick up on the Count's broadly dropped hints. "Then let us address your qualms with equal candor," he replied cynically.

Well past midnight, Niccolo finally arrived back at his family estate. After bidding Vincente and the count farewell at the jetty, he quickly made his way up the hillside, passing the crumbling Oriental pavilion where his parents had entertained friends during better times, wending his way through the formal gardens with their familiar scents of moist earth and tangy junipers. His footsteps rapped in counterpoint to the croaking of tree frogs, the hooting of an owl, and the tinkling of water in the stone fountain. Guided by the light of the moon that glittered over bronze statuary, he approached the marble front steps of the palatial Roman villa.

His mind teemed with doubt regarding the devil's bargain he had just made with the Count of Osprey. He could not believe he had actually agreed to pay the man a bribe in order to gain the *privilege* of rescuing the count's besieged niece! Even by his standards, paying an inducement to secure a marriage contract was dishonorable and beneath his dignity. He would surely have to mortgage his family estate in order to secure the needed five thousand ducats. But he was a desperate man making a final gamble to save his family's fortunes. Once he secured the princess's hand in marriage as well as her immense dowry, he could repay the Bondis, provide for Caterina's marriage, and ensure lifetime security for his

loved ones. If he had to sacrifice himself in the proc-
ess, through wedding some anonymous princess who
might well possess the countenance of a swine and
the temperament of a donkey, then so be it.

Creaking open the heavy oaken door, he walked
quietly through the vast, marble-floored vestibule and
down a wide, darkened corridor. He paused by his
sister's door, which was slightly ajar. He called her
name softly, and heard no reply except for a low
mewling. A moment later he felt something soft and
furry brushing against his calf. Smiling, he leaned
over, picked up Caterina's old tomcat, Tito, and then
tiptoed inside her room.

He spotted his sister sleeping, the covers pulled up
to her chin, and his heart welled with tenderness at
the sight of her, lying there so young, innocent, and
beautiful, her long fair hair spread about the pillow
and catching the silvery light. He and Caterina shared
the same blond hair and blue eyes, and were blessed
with their mother's striking, aristocratic features. But
Niccolo well knew he and his sister were alike only
in appearance; her outlook on life was guileless and
hopeful, while his was cynical and jaded. He was now
a man of thirty-two years, she a young woman of sev-
enteen; he had missed her growing-up years while he
was off fighting. But he could make things up to her
by ensuring her marriage to Filippo Travola.

Stirring slightly, she blinked sleepily. "Niccolo? Is
that you?"

He stepped toward the bed. "I did not mean to
awaken you, Caterina. I heard Tito mewling and did
not think you would want him roaming the house all
night."

Yawning, she sat up, the covers pulled up to her
neck, the moonlight spilling over her lovely face.
"Will you bring him to me, please, brother? He is so
blind now that he gets lost in the darkness and over-
turns the spittoons and chamber pots."

Niccolo chuckled and started toward the bed. "*Sì,*
he raises one devil of a clamor, and will surely send
poor Benita on another tirade when she comes to
clean the chambers." He set the cat down next to his
sister. "But you will take good care of your faithful
old friend, no?"

"*Sì.*" Caterina gently petted the old cat, and the animal responded with a harsh, grating purr. "Where
have you been, Niccolo?"

"Out plotting a way to secure your dowry, *cara,*"
he teased.

"Truly?" she asked. "And now I shall be able to
wed Filippo?"

Eyeing her young, eager countenance, Niccolo
found he could not bear the thought of dashing the
exquisite hope etched there. "Of course, sister."

She cuddled the cat and beamed up at him. "Oh,
Niccolo, you are my champion!"

Grinning, he leaned over and kissed her brow.
"You shall have the grandest wedding the Basilica has
ever seen, and you shall be the envy of every young
lady in the Republic. I shall see to it. Now you must
both sleep."

She nodded happily. "I knew you would find a
way. I cannot wait to tell Filippo. I am so proud of
you, Niccolo."

"Goodnight, *cara.*"

Niccolo slipped from her room and proceeded
down the corridor, praying he would be able to fulfill
the promise so rashly given his sister. He noted light
spilling from beneath his mother's door. He sighed.
Julieta Campioni had not slept well for so many years,
ever since Niccolo's father had been killed in the war
with Milano. He rapped at her door.

"*Avanti!*" she called.

Niccolo stepped inside to see his mother sitting on
the four-poster bed, dressed in a brocaded dressing
gown, a handsome, open text of Petrarch's *De Vita*

Solitaria lying in her lap. Julieta was a graceful presence with her gray-streaked black hair spilling about her shoulders; and although her long, thin face was heavily lined, her features still reflected a noble beauty. She reposed like an aging gem in the fabulous setting, her chamber filled with priceless Byzantine figurines, silk tapestries, carved Roman furnishings, and a dozen huge, carved bronzed candelabra providing light.

"Niccolo!" Spotting him, she smiled.

He strode to her bed, took and kissed her frail hand. "Mamma. I had hoped you would be fast asleep by now."

"Sleep will become my good friend soon enough," she replied solemnly. "How was your evening, my son?"

"Most absorbing."

"Indeed? I had hoped the Bondis would not dog your steps again."

"As my friend Vincente says, they are only bankers trying to turn a profit."

"They are rapacious in the extreme."

"Spoken like a loyal mother," Niccolo replied with a smile.

"Why did you find your evening so diverting, son?"

Niccolo slowly shook his head; his mother knew him so well. "Mamma, I think I may have found a way out of our dilemma . . . a way to save our fortunes and secure Caterina's dowry."

"Truly?" she inquired with rapt hope.

Niccolo spoke earnestly. "Tonight I met a stranger—Artemas of Falconia, Count of Osprey. He needs a great warrior to rescue his niece, a princess, who is under siege in her castle in the Kingdom of Falconia. I think I have convinced him to dispatch me as her savior."

Julieta went pale, a slim hand fluttering to her

heart. "No, Niccolo! You will not contract as a *condottiere*! I will not lose you as I lost my dear Vettor. You will not sacrifice your life for us!"

He laughed. "Mamma, the situation is far from dire. I have not contracted as a mercenary, but rather have agreed to rescue the princess in exchange for her fortune—and her hand in marriage."

Julieta frowned. "But to marry a woman you have never met . . . whom you do not love . . ."

"Mamma, you well know that I will never love again," Niccolo chided bitterly. "This is the best—the only—solution for us all. And think how pleased my faithful squire will be to see me championing a cause once more."

Julieta still regarded her son with a mother's worried frown. "I am not so certain. For one thing, we may never see you again."

"But of course you will," he reassured her. "The little kingdom is but a fortnight's journey over the Alps. Besides, I would never miss Caterina's wedding."

At last his mother forced a smile and reached out to squeeze Niccolo's large hand. "You are too good to us."

He leaned over and kissed her cheek. "You are deserving of much more."

"When will you go?"

"Soon—mayhap on the morrow."

"Niccolo!"

He patted her hand. "Do not fret. We will discuss this when we break our fast. Sleep now, Mamma."

Yet he knew her troubled gaze followed him as he strode to the door . . .

Niccolo proceeded to his own chamber. Inside, he spotted his thin, elderly squire asleep in a leather Spanish chair near the fireplace, and smiled at the sight. With his head lolled back, Lorenzo's curly silver hair caught the gleam of candlelight. His gaunt, wrin-

kled cheeks, broad brow, and large nose were etched
in repose; his thin lips hung slightly open as he
snored softly, and spittle streaked his long beard. Still,
there was an almost childlike innocence about the old
squire, a man who had lived a life of utter humility
and service to others, a man Niccolo much admired.
Guilt often needled Niccolo because Lorenzo should
have retired long before now; but the squire stubbornly clung to his duties in order to see his master
settled . . . and reformed. Lorenzo was dressed in his
typical, modest uniform of gray wool tunic and dark
hose. In his lap lay Niccolo's shield with its colorful
coat of arms; in one of his gnarled hands was gripped
a polishing cloth.

As Niccolo crossed the stone floor, the old man
jerked awake, set down the shield and cloth, then rose
unsteadily to his feet.

"Signore," he mumbled, yawning, "I have awaited
your return so we may attend to our prayers together."

Niccolo merely raised an eyebrow at his squire and
friend. For three years Lorenzo had awaited him
nightly to say their prayers; for three years Niccolo
Campioni had not prayed.

Niccolo removed his cape and handed it to the old
man. "My friend, your prayers may soon be answered. We shall shortly embark on a mission together."

"A mission, master?" echoed Lorenzo.

"*Sì*, and you will be pleased. We shall rescue a
trapped princess. Her castle is under siege."

"You are accepting this noble undertaking, master?" inquired the squire, clearly confused.

"*Sì*. I accept this noble undertaking because I shall
be handsomely rewarded for my services—and shall
gain a bride."

Lorenzo's fine gray eyes went wide. "A bride? You
are referring to the princess, signore?"

"A lamb to my slaughter," mocked Niccolo.

Lorenzo was aghast. "Signore, a holy knight must never speak of a lady in such a disrespectful manner."

"We both know I am not holy," sneered Niccolo.

"You are a knight, and you have taken vows," scolded the squire.

Niccolo waved a hand. "Pray, do not lecture me."

"But a lady must be treated with grace and chivalry," admonished Lorenzo. "She must be protected, honored, and revered." Placing his hand over his heart with an air of tragedy, he finished, "Oh, for the chance to kiss once again the hand of my beloved Marta."

Niccolo gave an ironic laugh. "Not all women are saints like your dear departed wife, old man. Plenty of them are about as endearing as scorpions."

"Master, for shame!" chided Lorenzo, shaking a finger. "What of your mother, your sister?"

Niccolo blinked in sudden fury. "You know of whom I speak!"

"*Sì*, I know," acknowledged the old man sadly. "And she is still with you, my son, eating you up inside—"

"She is not!" declared Niccolo.

"You must regain your faith and give up this bitterness that will destroy you."

"Mayhap I have reason to be bitter!" Niccolo gritted back. "More to the princess's pity."

The two men confronted each other for a long, tense moment. At last Lorenzo shook his head and implored, "Master, why speak so cynically of this princess we are to rescue? Why judge the lady before you have even met her?"

"Because I shall never give my heart again to any woman, and you well know it," came the adamant response.

Lorenzo heaved a great sigh. "Oh, master. You torment me terribly. You have made my life such hell. *Il*

Dio has entrusted to me the task of seeing to your redemption, and yet my mission seems hopeless. You have taken up a noble cause, but with malice in your heart. You are an infidel, a man without faith or chivalry. Your soul is corrupted, my son. What am I to do? I am but a poor old squire, so feeble, so very tired. I should be spending my days in prayer and reverence, preparing myself for the call from *Il Signore*. But I cannot leave this world and rejoin my dear Marta until my mission is completed."

"Your mission is doomed, old man," stated Niccolo, a vein jerking in his temple in betrayal of his emotion. "The faith I once embraced only made me vulnerable and left my heart open to unspeakable betrayal and hurt. Never again, do you hear? Never!" Breathing hard, he leveled a fierce glance at the squire. "And try as you will, you will *not* make me feel guilty for keeping you alive!"

Lorenzo nodded wearily. "When do we depart, master?"

"On the morrow." Niccolo strode to the window, threw open the latticed panel, and stared out at the glittering lagoon. "Before all is said and done, the lady shall doubtless rue the day of her salvation."

Lorenzo stared at his master in keen disappointment, then crossed himself and trudged off to attend to his prayers.

THREE

"WHAT IS THE MEANING OF ALL THIS CHAOS?"
asked Niccolo.

"*Dio* alone must know, signore," replied Lorenzo.

A fortnight had passed by the time Niccolo and his
squire approached the outskirts of the village of Osprey, which a peasant had informed them was near
the royal castle of Falconia. Niccolo was mounted on
his magnificent black courser, Nero; Lorenzo rode a
gray palfrey and tugged along the hack loaded with
their supplies and Niccolo's polished and carefully
wrapped plate armor. The men had ridden hard from
the mainland over the snowy Alps, sleeping in flea-
infested inns or on the ground in the pine and fir forests, and paying the steep tolls prescribed by the
cantons along the mountain passes.

Now they navigated their way down a potholed
mud street lined by thatched cottages and thronged
with burghers and serfs. Monks and craftsmen mingled with housewives and small children, cotters, and
barefooted peasants. Niccolo found his senses reeling
with the jumble of children laughing, peddlers hawking raw chicken and fish, dogs barking, pigs squealing, and geese honking. Even on this crisp spring
morn, the combined odors of the offal strewn in the
streets, along with the smells of the tannery and the

butchery, were sickening, and even the potpourri of more pleasant aromas drifting up from the gardens—spring nectar mingling with mint, spices, and herbs—could not compete with the unholy stench.

Niccolo tensed as a peasant collided with Nero, causing the stallion to rear. He quickly controlled the spirited charger with soothing words and subtle pressure from his muscled thighs.

The filthy, bearded peasant jerked back and gaped up at the tall visitor on his black steed. Niccolo scowled down at the peculiar little man, noting to his confusion that the villager wore his tunic inside out, and several cloves of garlic were strung about his dirt-encrusted neck.

"Your pardon, milord," said the peasant, bowing deeply. "I did not mean to harm your steed."

"No harm done," replied Niccolo irritably. "Tell me, man—why is there such tumult in the village today?"

As several shrieking children raced past them rolling hoops, the peasant sidestepped the youngsters, then grinned, revealing crooked and rotting teeth. "Why, 'tis a holy celebration, milord—the Sacred Day of the Turtle."

Niccolo glanced at Lorenzo, who shook his head in disbelief. "You are jesting, man," he scoffed to the peasant.

"Nay, milord." The man pointed down the street. "Look yon and you will see the procession."

Shielding his eyes with a hand, Niccolo stared ahead at the odd parade wending its way about a corner and moving toward them. First came a priest sprinkling holy water, followed by jongleurs with lutes, jugglers wielding bowls and spoons, and tumblers doing handsprings. Next came six burly peasants bearing a platform similar to a carrying chair on which had been mounted a crude wooden cage that housed a large snapping turtle!

"Lorenzo, tell me my eyes are deceiving me," muttered Niccolo.

"Nay, signore, the spectacle is quite real," replied the equally amazed squire.

Niccolo watched children throw bits of fish and bread at the passing chaise, while the turtle snapped at the tidbits. "But why would they worship a turtle?"

"Milord, in the last century, 'twas a turtle that frightened away a coven of witches in the Falconian forest," answered the peasant.

Niccolo eyed the man skeptically. "Quite a feat for a mere turtle."

"Yea, milord. All turtles are revered in both Falconia and Ravenia. The last housewife who made turtle soup was hanged."

After the man moved on, Niccolo and Lorenzo exchanged a mystified look. They navigated their way through the crush of celebrants, Niccolo glowering his irritation when a couple of giggling peasant wenches showered him with rose petals.

Over his shoulder, Niccolo murmured to Lorenzo, "What an odd fellow I spoke with—wearing his clothes wrong side out and garlic cloves strung about his neck. Yet methinks he is no more peculiar than the rest of these people—worshiping turtles."

"The people fear witches, milord," answered Lorenzo. "I have spotted rosemary growing near cottage steps, and iron crosses on the doors."

Glancing about the area, Niccolo realized Lorenzo was right as he spotted additional talismans to ward off evil spirits: crescent moon shapes carved on shutters, forks of rowan wood standing in gardens, salt-cellars placed on front steps of dwellings, and swallows' nests up in the eaves. He shook his head. These were curious people indeed.

The two at last made their way to the edge of town and paused before a picturesque Gothic church with distinctive pointed arches, flying buttresses, and stained-glass windows picturing various saints. Beyond the church loomed the gray stone walls of a monastery, and in the distance stretched a vineyard where several monks labored among the vines.

As the men paused their mounts, a tall, thin priest emerged from the church and walked toward them. Dressed in an alb, chasuble, and liturgical cap, he wore an ornate silver crucifix around his neck.

"Good morrow, my sons," the priest greeted them pleasantly. "Are you pilgrims, come to Falconia for the sacred celebration?"

"Good morrow, Father," answered Niccolo. "We are men-at-arms, not pilgrims. We seek the royal castle. 'Tis our mission to rescue your fair princess who is trapped there, under siege."

"Ah, then you had best await nightfall, my son," answered the priest. "The enemy forces lay siege to the castle walls with each dawn, and flee with every sunset."

"And why is that?" questioned Niccolo.

"King Basil's forces fear the darkness due to a long-ago massacre of their knights at the witching hour."

"The peoples of Falconia and Ravenia seem to suffer from numerous superstitions," commented Niccolo.

"Ah, but 'tis wise to fear the forces of the devil," admonished the priest. "Would you care to join us at the noon mass, my son, to help ward off the legions of evil?"

With effort, Niccolo repressed a cynical smile. "Thank you, Father, but we must press on. How may we get to the castle?"

The priest gestured toward the village. "You must first pass back through Osprey, then ride north through the royal fields and vineyards."

Niccolo groaned at the thought of trying to make their way through the carnival-packed streets again. "Is there not another way?"

"Yea, though 'tis farther." The priest pointed to the
west. "Follow this path to where it ends at the lake.
You will spot the castle from there, but you must circle the entire lake to attain it."

"Thank you, Father."

"And beware the gnomes in the forest," the priest
added ominously. "If they come upon you unawares,
they will hack you to death with their axes."

Niccolo glanced askance at his squire, who rolled
his eyes, and nodded soberly to the priest. "We shall
be forever on our guard against the wily little fellows."

Evidently missing Niccolo's attempt at humor, the
priest crossed himself. "May God guard your journey,
my sons."

The two men rode past the vineyard and continued
through foothills into a verdant forest of pines,
birches, and magnificent dark firs. Soft drifts of needles muffled the sounds of the horses' hooves, and
the scent of conifers laced the air. Rabbits and squir-
rels frolicked about in the dappled light beneath trees
where warblers flitted about, sweetly singing, and
tree creepers scavenged for insects.

Soon Niccolo could hear the distant thud of a battering ram, the whoosh of a trebuchet releasing its
stones. As the priest had predicted, the road ended
near the lake; Niccolo and Lorenzo dismounted, un-
packed their horses, and released them to graze. On
a small boulder, Lorenzo set out a meal of water,
bread, and fish; Niccolo took his dried cod and crust
of bread and walked out to view the lake; Lorenzo
followed, pausing just behind his master.

Beyond the vast, mirrorlike expanse of water
stretched a field cluttered with war machinery, archers, and knights on horseback. Beyond the field rose
the castle, with a guardhouse and moat shielding its
gates.

The splendor of the mystical palace startled Niccolo; built of fine white stone, 'twas a Gothic master-piece of soaring towers and swirling turrets, its oriels and parapets looming high into the mist that cloaked the majestic snowcapped mountains rising behind it. Colorful banners flew from its high spires, and ravens swirled about its battlements. The magnificent structure graced the landscape in proud and perfect symmetry, and Niccolo felt a thrill of pride at the prospect of becoming lord to such a grand domain. With such a magnificent prize dangled before him, he was willing to tolerate even an ugly and obnoxious bride.

But the serene opulence of the castle was jarred by the sight of the attackers with their ram in its penthouse, the archers shooting flaming arrows, the men-at-arms on scaling ladders, the ballista spewing huge spears. High up in the parapets, the Falconian knights repelled the siegers with arrows and projectiles of their own.

Niccolo took in the scene with the practiced eye of a knight who had seen many battles. "They have neither cannon nor petards," he scoffed to Lorenzo. "The attackers wield arrows and scaling ladders, while the defenders spew back iron, hot sand, and boiling water. We have landed in another century, my friend."

"*Sì*, I fear we have arrived in Dante's *Inferno*," answered Lorenzo. "I do not understand these peoples, master. While the princess is besieged, her villeins celebrate the Sacred Day of the Turtle."

"Rather reminiscent of Nero when Rome was burning, eh?" Niccolo sighed. "I suppose we had best wait until nightfall before attempting to enter the castle—and we must pray the gnomes do not hack us to death as we sleep."

Glancing warily about the landscape, Lorenzo crossed himself. "I will stand guard while you slumber, master."

"Nonsense," chided Niccolo. "You need your rest more than I. You know when you become unduly tired, you are prone to sinking spells." He smiled grimly. "Besides, I sleep lightly. If any gnome should be foolish enough to provoke us, I shall cheerfully skewer the little fellow and roast him alive for our supper."

The old man actually chuckled. "Master, you are ruthless. Methinks the princess will be relieved to learn her uncle has dispatched such a fierce warrior to save her."

"Ah, but will she be happy to take me as husband?" posed Niccolo cynically.

The old man wagged a finger ominously. "Not until you find grace within your heart, milord."

Niccolo frowned. "Finish your meal, old friend, and take your rest. I have a feeling we will both need our strength ere nightfall."

"*Sì*, signore."

As his squire trudged away, Niccolo turned back to observe the battle, hearing the distant screams of several knights as their scaling ladder was deflected from a turret, and watching a wounded archer tumble off the parapets and fall into the moat.

And somewhere behind those walls was trapped his future bride. Niccolo shook his head. "We have arrived in the kingdom of the mad," he muttered.

FOUR

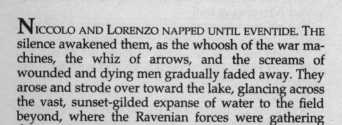

Niccolo and Lorenzo napped until eventide. The silence awakened them, as the whoosh of the war machines, the whiz of arrows, and the screams of wounded and dying men gradually faded away. They arose and strode over toward the lake, glancing across the vast, sunset-gilded expanse of water to the field beyond, where the Ravenian forces were gathering their casualties and fleeing on horseback, tugging along their loaded palfreys and wheeled catapults.

Niccolo shook his head at the sight. "The priest spoke the truth. The enemies of our princess fear the darkness."

"And you do not, milord?" asked Lorenzo.

"The forces of darkness might well fear me," answered Niccolo cynically.

With a cool dusk rapidly falling, the two men packed, mounted up, and slowly navigated their way around the lake, passing through the dim forest where owls hooted and an eerie evening breeze stirred the conifers. Spotting shadowy movements ahead of them, Niccolo strained in his saddle and grasped the hilt of his sword. He scowled at the sight of several small, cloaked figures scurrying through the dusky trees.

"Look, master! Gnomes!" gasped Lorenzo from behind him.

Squinting in the dim light, Niccolo was amazed to discern the obscure forms of half a dozen small, bearded men crossing the path ahead of them. Although it was difficult to see many details, all of the gnomes seemed to be wearing pointed hats, and to be carrying backpacks as well as tools or weapons of some kind. Niccolo could have sworn he could hear the jingle of bells, and the high-pitched sounds of the little men's laughter.

He smiled in bemusement. "So the priest did not lie. There truly are gnomes in the forest. I wonder what they are about."

"No doubt, the devil's mischief," intoned Lorenzo ominously.

Squelching a smile, Niccolo clucked to Nero and maneuvered the charger through the trees. "This is an enchanted place indeed. Blessedly, the gnomes appear to be heading away from us, toward the mountains. They will not molest us. Moreover, should they prove so reckless, I will eagerly lop off a few heads."

The two men proceeded in silence, save for the neighing of the horses, and the sounds of their hooves plodding over the soft forest floor. Niccolo again found himself wondering what his future bride, the Princess Aurora, would be like. In Greek mythology, Aurora had been the goddess of light, he recalled. Would his princess be fair or dark? Beautiful or plain? Clever or dull-witted? Whatever her qualities, she was surely doomed to be betrothed to a man such as himself, a man who had not a spot of warmth or tenderness left in his heart. But such was the price she must pay for his protection. And such was surely the bounty he deserved for committing his life and future to her!

They emerged from the forest, briefly skirting the narrow perimeters of the royal fields, orchards, and

vineyards that curled back toward the village proper.
At last they arrived on the darkened green, which was
littered with spent arrows, spears, and chunks of iron.
The odor of blood still hung in the air. They galloped
steadily toward the castle, its high, rounded towers
and gleaming turrets outlined in the incandescent ra-
diance of the snowy Alpine pass. From somewhere
along the high parapets, Niccolo could hear a nightin-
gale's plaintive song, a striking counterpoint to the
life-and-death struggle just concluded.

They halted before the tall, square guardhouse with
its raised drawbridge and lowered iron gate forbid-
ding access to the moat. Staring at the murky waters
beyond and watching an alligator glide past, Niccolo
smiled grimly as he remembered the man who had
earlier fallen from the walls to his death.

"Who goes below?" called a voice from high in the
stone tower.

Both men gazed overhead to see several sentries
with armed crossbows scowling down at them from
the bartizans.

Lorenzo answered, "Pray, admit Sir Niccolo Campioni of Venice, grand master of *Cavalieri di San Marco*.
Sir Niccolo has been dispatched by your princess's
guardian, Artemas of Falconia, to rescue your lady
and become her prince."

Upon completion of the squire's portentous an-
nouncement, Niccolo was astounded to hear the
sounds of hearty laughter spilling down from the
tower. He stared at Lorenzo in consternation, and his
squire responded with a mystified expression and an
open-handed gesture.

"Ah, so we have another *prince* among us," called
down a scornful voice, "seeking to save our fair
lady."

"Giles, raise the gate and lower the drawbridge,"
called another, "and, Owen, pray inform our lady's
seneschal that her salvation has arrived."

Amid the screech of the gate as it was raised, and the creaking of the drawbridge as it was lowered on its chains, Niccolo was perplexed to hear the sounds of additional mirth spilling down from the bartizans. He and Lorenzo guided their steeds through the guardhouse, the horses' hooves clanging on the stone floor. They traversed the narrow, creaky drawbridge over the fetid, smelly moat, then passed under the raised portcullis and into the bailey. Cantering Nero across the vast, walled ward, Niccolo spotted a large haystack and several newly sown gardens, as well as the shadowy shapes of a blacksmith's forge, a barracks, a stable, and a chapel. The cool, moist air was scented with the odors of manure and freshly turned earth. Across a courtyard loomed the magnificent keep with its high roofs and soaring turrets.

They halted their horses just beyond the barracks as four men strode toward them from the keep. A tall man in an elegant black gown and rounded cap led the group, followed by a burly peasant in stable hand's garb, and two more sentries armed with broadswords.

The tall one paused to bow before them. Niccolo noted that he possessed a thin, intelligent face, dark eyes, and a hawk nose.

"Visitors, I bid you welcome," he said in a high, nervous voice. "I am Mortimer, seneschal to our princess. How may I serve you?"

"I am Niccolo Campioni, and this is my squire, Lorenzo. We have been dispatched by your lady's uncle to secure her safety and defeat her enemies. We must see your lady at once."

The seneschal squinted at Niccolo warily. "The sentry tells me you have come to wed milady."

"Sì, I have a proper marriage contract from her uncle."

As the guards chuckled, the seneschal appeared distressed, a muscle jerking in his thin cheek. "How

we wish the count would not put us in these dire
predicaments!"

"What are you saying, man?" demanded a puzzled
Niccolo. "Did the count misrepresent himself to me?
And why are all your lady's sentries mocking us?"

"You had best judge for yourself, sir knight," be-
moaned the seneschal, wiping his brow with his vel-
vet-cuffed sleeve. "If you and your man will
dismount, the stable hand will see to your steeds, and
the sentries will escort your squire to your quarters. I
shall take you to the princess, signore."

"Very well," muttered Niccolo.

He and Lorenzo dismounted, and the seneschal motioned for Niccolo to follow him toward the donjon.
Niccolo trailed the man up a flight of steep stone steps
and around a corner, to a portal where the frail man
struggled to open a heavy oaken door. Inside the
darkened corridor, the wan light of torches winked
out at Niccolo from the stone walls, and a dank smell
of mold, mingled with the acrid scent of smoke, as-
saulted his nostrils. The two men proceeded down the
winding passageway, emerging in a great hall.

Niccolo blinked at the brightness of many torches
affixed to the pilastered walls. Magnificent Gothic
arches vaulted the high ceiling, the hammer beams
hung with colorful banners emblazoned with coats of
arms. Brilliant tapestries, depicting various prophets
and saints, battles and hunting scenes, lined the paneled walls. Rushes covered the stone floor, and a huge
fire blazed in the grate.

The sounds of male laughter drew Niccolo's attention to the center of the hall. At a long trestle table
sat five lavishly clad men, attired in an array of silk,
velvet, or brocaded tunics, elegant black hats deco-
rated with brooches or plumes, and pale hose. The
men were breaking bread and sharing ecuelles of
soup, platters of mutton, and bejeweled goblets of
wine. They laughed together and tossed scraps to

three large, rangy gray wolfhounds that bounded about, sniffing the rushes. A minstrel strolled about the table, strumming his lute and softly singing a ballad.

Who were the men? Niccolo wondered. The princess's knights? Or royal visitors? From their opulent and varied attire, Niccolo suspected the latter. The presence of the men made him uneasy.

Glancing to the front of the room, Niccolo noted the royal dais was deserted. He turned to the seneschal. "Where is your lady?"

"I see she has already retired to her chamber following the repast," replied the seneschal. He snapped his fingers to a nearby steward. "Inform milady we have a newly arrived guest, Signore Niccolo Campioni of Venice, and beseech her to greet the newcomer, if it pleases Her Highness."

"Yea, Seneschal." Bowing, the steward rushed from the chamber.

Mortimer gestured to Niccolo. "Come. I will introduce you to the others."

As Niccolo followed him to the table, the men grew silent and stared at him curiously.

"My lords," began the seneschal, "a new visitor has joined your ranks, Signore Niccolo Campioni of Venice."

The nearest man, who was spare but handsome, dark-haired and dark-eyed, spoke up to Niccolo. "Signore, are you the grand master of *Cavalieri di San Marco*, the champion who scuttled three Turkish galleons after Constantinople fell? The Duke of Burgundy has lavishly sung your praises."

"I am the one," acknowledged Niccolo proudly. "And who am I addressing?"

The man deferred to the seneschal, who announced, "Signore Campioni, I present to you Sir Gilbert of Burgundy, of the Order of the Golden Fleece. Sir Gilbert is a nephew of Charles the Bold."

Feeling bemused and wondering what a Burgundy knight was doing here in Falconia, Niccolo nodded to the man. "I am honored to be in your esteemed presence, sir knight. I have heard wondrous tales of the prowess of your company in Alsace and Lorraine."

Sir Gilbert bowed his head.

The seneschal introduced the others, gesturing toward each man in turn. "I present Sir Edgar of York, grand master of the Order of the Garter. Next to him sits Sir Olaf of Norway, and Sir Baldric of Bavaria."

Niccolo nodded to each man, noting that Sir Edgar was of middle years, with fine features, hazel eyes, and a graying beard; Sir Olaf was a fair-haired, clean-shaven Viking; and Sir Baldric a husky, brown-haired Hun. His sense of disquiet deepened. Why had these knights come here from various parts of the world?

Then his gaze settled on a small, dark-eyed Italian sitting at the end of the table. The man bore a striking resemblance to one of the Figliosi brothers he had once met in Rome. *Dio*, could this be the scoundrel Artemas had mentioned? If so, why was he in Falconia? Something was *very* amiss!

"And who have we there, Seneschal?"

"Signore Cesare Figliosi, of Genoa."

Niccolo sneered at the knight. "What is your purpose, Figliosi?"

The Genoan smiled back, revealing small, even white teeth. "What is yours, Venetian?"

To Niccolo's irritation, all of the knights burst out laughing. He paused until the guffaws died down. "My purpose is to rescue the princess and wed her," he stated coldly, gritting his teeth as new chuckles poured forth.

"And do you seek to claim her dowry as well, sir knight?" asked the clearly amused Hun.

"*Sì*, so I have arranged with the lady's uncle."

The other knights only laughed louder, fueling Niccolo's outrage and indignation.

"And what immense sum did you outlay to her uncle for the privilege of saving the princess, sir?" asked the Englishman.

Although by now Niccolo had the sick feeling that he might have been played the fool, he regarded the man with contempt. "I am certain I do not know of what you speak. I did not try to buy the princess. I am not a woman who must entice a husband with her dowry."

Even as mutterings of derision greeted Niccolo's words, a lyrical feminine voice called out, "Methinks you lie, fair knight."

A flood of ire assailed Niccolo at the spoken slur to his honor. But as he turned with the others to view a young, beautiful woman gliding through the archway, his anger soon faded into awe. The lady's regal bearing and lavish dress at once bespoke that she was the royal princess. She wore a gossamer silk gown shot through with gold threads that glittered resplendently as she moved; her garment was low-necked, fitted to the hip, and embellished by a bejeweled girdle. She was trailed by a flaxen-haired lady-in-waiting who carried her train.

A trumpet sounded out, and a young, blond page stepped forward to address the men. "Harken all, your princess is here!"

The chamber fell utterly hushed. The knights ceased their swilling and solemnly rose to their feet. The minstrel fell silent, and even the dogs paused to sniff the air.

Niccolo was stunned to find the presence of the princess emotionally staggering. So this was Aurora, he thought dazedly, raking his gaze over her. Indeed, there was a luminous aura about her. Even though her hair and eyes were dark, she truly was a goddess of light; she seemed to radiate life, beauty, and vitality. Her face was fair and perfectly formed, with a smooth brow, high cheekbones graced by a rosy flush, a straight nose, wide mouth, and brown eyes that gleamed with secret merriment beneath delicately arched brows. A dramatic widow's peak accented her smooth, high brow. A swath of thick, raven hair was bound by a diaphanous wimple into a smooth chignon at her nape. Her figure was pleasing to behold, her shoulders proudly set, her firm breasts pushing against the glimmering gold of her gown, her waist trim, and her hips nicely rounded.

With her lady-in-waiting lingering just beyond the portal, the princess glided farther inside the chamber, pausing not far from Niccolo and regarding him with bold impertinence. Although he returned her scrutiny with a scowl, Niccolo felt a grudging admiration for the lady's spirit. She was a plucky one, he thought, to greet her future lord with such impudence—a disrespect he would quickly divest her of!

So this was his bride . . . He did feel relieved to discover that Aurora was neither ugly nor repulsive, and yet he also felt oddly threatened by her ravishing beauty. He knew he would enjoy claiming this young woman's wealth, and especially her body; but despite the almost magnetic pull of her loveliness, he vowed he would keep his emotions safe from her. Breathtaking though Princess Aurora was, Niccolo had long ago learned his lesson about love. He would touch this princess's body, but never would she touch his heart . . .

Even as Niccolo stared at the lady, Princess Aurora, heir to the throne of Falconia, found her own gaze riveted to the tall knight who had just arrived at her castle, for he radiated a power, virility, and magnetism that at once drew her to him. Aurora did not doubt she was staring at the latest cavalier dispatched by Uncle Artemas to "rescue" her. None of the five champions who had arrived at Falconia Castle thus far had really intrigued Aurora, but she sensed this newcomer was different. Could he be the one she had waited for, her one true love who could at last free her from the ancient curse that had plagued her family for so long?

Her squire had told her the stranger's name was Signore Niccolo Campioni of Venice. She studied him eagerly. Niccolo was a giant of a man, blond-haired and blue-eyed, with handsomely chiseled features—a broad brow, deep-set eyes, a beautifully formed nose, thin but sensual lips, and a strong chin. A tunic of vibrant blue wool draped over the sculpted perfection of his broad shoulders; a wide, bejeweled scabbard with sword encircled his trim waist. Thick, pale hose molded over powerful thighs, stretching tautly past well-shaped knees before disappearing into soft leather boots. He wore no hat, and his long, thick blond hair caught the light as it spilled down about his shoulders.

Verily, this knight was fair as daybreak, and yet there was something about him . . . an arrogance and intensity in his confident stance, a darkness and ruthlessness radiating from those fire-bright blue eyes. Aurora had always been immune to fear, and yet she realized this man definitely daunted her—and excited her even more!

Belatedly she remembered she had just called her guest a liar. Mayhap *that* was what put the fearsome glower on his handsome face!

She swept closer. "Greetings, milord. I welcome you to Falconia Castle, and offer you the hospitality of my keep."

Raising an eyebrow, he inquired sardonically, "You welcome the knight you just called liar, milady?"

Chuckles broke out around them, and Aurora's eyes twinkled with merriment. "Mayhap I spoke in haste, milord."

As the two stared at each other tensely, the seneschal rushed forward. "Princess Aurora, I present Signore Niccolo Campioni of Venice."

"Yea, I have been informed of his name," replied Aurora with some impatience.

"Your uncle has dispatched him—"

"To rescue me and wed me?" she cut in, extending her hand toward Niccolo.

At her cue, Niccolo went down on one knee before her. He took her hand and kissed her soft skin, secretly thrilling when her fingers trembled in his. The scent of her enveloped him—the enticing aroma of roses mingling with the duskier bouquet of woman, a well-remembered essence that unexpectedly stormed his senses like a potent aphrodisiac. Drawing his intent gaze up her sultry curves to her face, he wondered if she used rouge to affect that lovely, high color.

At last, holding her gaze raptly, he replied, "Yea, milady, I have journeyed here to defeat your enemies and become your husband."

Niccolo finished his ardent words, only to burn in indignation as the insufferable knights behind him erupted yet again in laughter. What ailed the *idiotas*? Did they mock him for their own diversion? He shot to his feet and glared at them.

"Why are your guests so amused, milady?" he demanded. "And why are you entertaining these others at your table when you have been betrothed to me?"

"She has been betrothed to many," jeered the Hun.

Now deeply alarmed, Niccolo turned back to the princess, who still appeared secretly amused. "Explain what he means. I am the man who has been dispatched to save you and claim your hand in marriage."

Dimpling mischievously, she strolled away from him. One of the dogs bounded over to her, and she gently scratched its ears. "I am afraid I have dire news for you, sir knight."

"And what is that?"

She turned to him with features impishly set. "You are not the knight who will rescue me and claim my hand in marriage. You are only one of many who will try . . . and likely fail." Fighting laughter, she finished, "Methinks you are a fool as well as a liar, sir knight."

As the others roared with ridicule, black rage assailed Niccolo at the audacious, shocking insults from the lady. Princess or not, she was one fresh wench. She deserved to have her saucy mouth scrubbed with lye soap—and her backside thrashed! No man worth his salt had to accept such grievous insults from a female.

Aggressively he stepped toward her. "I will thank you to guard your tongue, Princess. You are a lady, but my patience is not without limit. Malign my honor at your peril. Furthermore, we are betrothed. No matter what you or these other fools may claim, I have in my possession a document that brings you under my complete control—and you will be wise not to mock your master."

Undaunted, she smirked at him, and Niccolo could have cheerfully throttled her. "You will never master me, knight."

His eyes glittered with determination and affronted pride. "Do not tempt me to demonstrate, Princess."

With an air of boredom, she turned away to pet the dog again. "Furthermore, I have no interest in matrimony . . . and certainly not with you."

Over the howling amusement of the others, Niccolo countered furiously, "I have a document that obligates you otherwise."

"As corrupt, I presume, as the man bearing it." Brazenly she met his enraged countenance. "You are here under a ruse, sir knight. The document you describe is meaningless. It is fraudulent and I shall not honor it."

"There is nothing fraudulent in the document or in my mission!" he declared.

"You are saying you did not bribe my uncle for the right to rescue me?" she taunted.

Guilt needled Niccolo, for he knew his paying an enticement in order to champion her cause had been dishonorable. He caught the other knights staring at him with skepticism or even pity.

Nonetheless, he responded tightly, "I do not know of what you speak."

She gestured toward the table. "Then mayhap the others will refresh your memory." She inclined her hand toward the English knight. "Sir Edgar, pray enlighten our visitor, if you will."

"As you wish, milady," he replied solemnly, and turned to Niccolo. "Sir knight, it pains me to inform you that you have been duped like the rest of us."

"Duped in what manner?" snapped Niccolo.

"You have been defrauded, sir, your pockets picked by the Count of Osprey." With a self-effacing grin, the Englishman admitted, "Indeed, 'twas more than a king's ransom I proffered by the time I was done with the princess's wily uncle."

Even as Niccolo regarded Edgar belligerently, the German knight spoke up. "I sacrificed more than my republic's papal taxes for the honor of being defrauded."

"How many ducats did Artemas purloin from you, Venetian?" demanded the Genoan. "My father paid him ten thousand florins to secure the perfidious agreement."

Niccolo glanced from the Genoan to Aurora. "What perfidious agreement?"

When she merely smiled coyly, the Burgundy knight answered. "We are saying, knight, that we have all been deceived and cheated, that we all paid handsomely for the *privilege* of rescuing the princess and wedding her."

Niccolo swung his angry gaze to Sir Gilbert. "This

is not possible. I have a signed *contratto di matrimonio*."

"We *all* have signed contracts," sneered the Viking. "I paid for mine with a chestful of Moroccan gold. Now I find the promises made to me by the Count of Osprey are worthless."

Niccolo regarded the others in fury. "You are telling me Artemas of Falconia has lied to us all, that he dispatched *six* potential husbands for the princess?"

Five male heads bobbed in agreement.

"But why?" cried Niccolo.

"To pad his own purse," answered the Genoan.

"And to bring his fair niece an army of bridegrooms," added the Hun.

As all the men fell into bawdy laughter, Niccolo turned to Aurora, and her guilty smile quickly sank his hopes. "Is this true, milady?"

"Yea, milord," she responded with an air of tragedy, "I am afraid my uncle has a terrible failing of greed. Unbeknownst to me, he has traveled far and wide, selling the right to my hand to every nobleman with a fat purse—and leaving me to face the consequences of his mischief. To be frank, I have gown weary of dealing with so many disgruntled suitors."

"They seemed not disgruntled to me," scoffed Niccolo.

"You did not see each when he first arrived," she answered peevishly. "They all acted much as you have, knight, as churlish as badgers caught in a lair. 'Twas most burdensome trying to appease one and all."

"Was it, milady?" he asked with an undercurrent of violence in his voice.

Offhandedly she continued, "To make matters worse, my uncle has promised all of you a dowry that does not even exist."

Niccolo went pale. "You are lying!"

The Viking waved a fist at Niccolo. "Heed who you call liar, Venetian!"

"Yea, Venetian, guard your tongue!" yelled the Englishman.

Niccolo placed his hand on the hilt of his sword and glared at the two.

The princess merely shrugged a slim shoulder. "I tell the truth, sir knight. Aside from my lands and the rents from my tenants, there is no royal treasure. Thus all of you have been defrauded by my uncle ... but mainly, you have been seduced by your own greed."

Niccolo stared hard at the unrepentant princess, murderous thoughts billowing in his mind like poisonous black smoke. He could not believe this was happening to him! He turned back to the table and the amused knights.

"Has the princess spoken the truth?" he demanded.

Nods and "Yeas" greeted his question.

"Then where is your outrage?" ranted Niccolo. "Are you men, or merely fools?"

"We are fools," admitted Sir Gilbert cheerfully, raising his cup, "as you shall be, ere long, Venetian."

"You shall be dead ere I'm a fool!" exploded Niccolo.

"We are besotted with the lady," explained the grinning Englishman, "and we have all taken up her cause, hoping she may favor us with her hand."

"You are idiots!" scoffed Niccolo. He advanced on Aurora, his hand gripping his sword hilt. "Enough of this babble, milady. I have a signed contract from your guardian. It *is* binding and you *shall* honor it, or face consequences you shall find ... most unpleasant."

"Are you threatening me, knight?" she asked softly, raising her chin a notch. "Do you dare tell me, royal princess and heir to the throne of Falconia, what I shall do?"

"*Sì*," replied Niccolo nastily, "I do."

Her dark eyes sparkled with defiance. "And what if I say nay, that you shall leave this keep post-haste?"

Niccolo smiled ruthlessly and drew out his sword, only to flinch as he heard a great clamor of curses, and the crash of benches being overturned. Within seconds, he found himself surrounded by five wrathful knights wielding sabers.

"Stand down or I shall disembowel you!" ranted the Englishman.

"Threaten our lady and die, knight!" shouted the Hun.

"Retreat or rot in hell!" cried the Viking.

Realizing his powerlessness in the face of five skilled swordsmen, Niccolo angrily sheathed his weapon. "You are worse than fools, all of you!" he shouted in disgust. "Do you not realize what has happened here? We have all been deceived and defrauded by both the princess and her uncle!"

Sir Edgar frowned. "What are you saying?"

Niccolo flung a hand outward in exasperation. "Think, you simpleton! Is it not patently clear the princess was a part of her uncle's nefarious scheme?" He turned his contemptuous gaze on Aurora. "Just look at her standing there, smug as a well-fed cat, totally without remorse. She clearly conspired with the Count of Osprey to increase her own fortunes. And she is the one I hold accountable."

"Bah!" scoffed the Englishman. "I shall not hear our princess maligned."

"The princess had no part in this," agreed the Genoan. "Threaten her at your peril."

"Yea, we believe our lady," stated the Viking. " 'Tis not her fault her uncle is a greedy liar. We are pleased to stand by her."

Niccolo glared ferociously at the smirking princess. "Then have her, all of you, for I am done!" he roared.

With Aurora's lady-in-waiting darting out of his

path, Niccolo charged from the chamber in the wake
of the knights' insufferable laughter, haunted by an
image of Aurora's smiling face as she watched him
leave . . .

Moments later, Princess Aurora left the great hall,
accompanied by her lady-in-waiting with her train.
Both women were trailed by Aurora's anxious seneschal. Mortimer wrung his hands and dogged the
women's steps as they swept briskly up the darkened
staircase toward the royal solar.

"Princess, I fear this Venetian who has come here
in the night," fretted Mortimer. "He threatened you,
milady. Let me have him cast from the keep post-
haste."

Aurora merely laughed. "Sir Niccolo has already
sworn he will soon leave. I see no reason to cast him
out in the darkness. He shall surely be gone on the
morrow."

"And I say you must not trust him to remain for
even one night," argued the seneschal. "His heart is
filled with black thoughts, and for all we know, he
may try to murder you in your sleep."

Arriving on the stone landing, Aurora paused and
slanted her retainer a look of patient indulgence. "I
am well guarded, Mortimer, and I do not fear him.
Indeed, I find Sir Niccolo different from the others—
mayhap, even diverting."

"You would risk your life for the sake of frolic, milady?" cried Mortimer, aghast.

She smoothed down a silk sleeve. "You present the
matter in too dire a light."

"But, milady, he has sworn to gain satisfaction for
what he perceives as your betrayal."

She stifled a yawn. "He is merely angered by Uncle
Artemas's trickery, as the others were at first—and I
cannot say I truly blame him. I, too, have lost patience
with my uncle's intrigues. Methinks when Sir Niccolo

recovers from his anger, he may even prove himself an able warrior . . . should he choose to remain."

"True," conceded the seneschal, "but I still believe you are imprudent to trust him."

She touched his hand. "You have spoken your mind, Seneschal, and I have made my decision. I must now bid you good night." She winked at her companion. "Lady Flora and I have much to discuss."

Watching the two giggling ladies sweep toward the solar, the seneschal could only shake his head.

FIVE

"I SHALL SLAY THE WITCH! I SHALL!"

In a stone-floored cell in the barracks, Niccolo paced in a terrible temper, his fists clenched, his eyes glittering with rage. A bewildered Lorenzo watched him from a crude wooden chair resting near one of two cots dominating the small, austere chamber.

"Master, pray explain again what has transpired," beseeched the squire. "You are ranting so that I do not understand of what you speak."

Niccolo paused in his tracks, heaving infuriated breaths and glaring at Lorenzo. "I have been duped—betrayed by Artemas of Falconia and his conniving niece, the princess. The marriage contract I signed in Venice was an instrument of perfidy, a sham I secured through paying the uncle a hefty bribe."

"You bribed Artemas of Falconia?" gasped Lorenzo, wide-eyed.

Gesturing passionately, Niccolo continued to pace. "*Sì*, I mortgaged my family estate to the Bondis—"

"You did *what*, master?"

" 'Twas the only way I could secure the five thousand ducats needed to convince the scoundrel to let me champion his niece's cause."

"*Dio mio!*" cried Lorenzo, crossing himself. "I cannot believe you have stooped to such a sacrilege. To

48

pay a bribe, signore, dishonors both yourself and your family—"

"Do you not understand, man?" Niccolo cut in heatedly. "I was desperate, gambling all to save the fortunes of my mother and sister. Now, thanks to the perfidious princess, my family and I stand to lose everything. I have arrived here only to discover that the dowry I have been promised does not even exist, that the princess has no intention of ever wedding any man—and that her uncle contracted her hand in marriage to no fewer than six knights."

"Six!" exclaimed Lorenzo.

"*Sì*, the lot of us have been defrauded and deceived on the grandest possible scale."

"And what of the other five knights, signore? Are they also at the castle?"

"*Sì*, they all arrived before me."

"What are their feelings regarding this treason?"

"They are fools!" declared Niccolo. "A bunch of doltish cowards who are already besotted with the princess and have sworn to champion her cause despite her perfidy. It falls to me alone, then, to hold her accountable . . . which I shall do, and gladly."

Lorenzo shook his head in horror. "But, signore, has the princess admitted to being a part of her uncle's plot?"

"Do you think she is dim-witted?" scoffed Niccolo. "No, she is a wily little vixen if I have ever seen one. Certainly she has not confessed her treason, the scheming little liar. But I have no doubt as to her complicity."

Lorenzo's mouth fell open. "Signore, you have no proof!"

"Proof!" shouted Niccolo. He angrily pounded a fist against his chest. "I am the proof, man, along with the five other cretins who sat swilling wine and drooling all over her tonight!"

For a moment the squire sat in stunned silence. "What will you do?"

Vehemently Niccolo replied, "I will make her suffer for ever deceiving me. I will find a way to wound her as badly as she has injured me—to make *her* lose all, just as she has taken all from me!"

Lorenzo shot to his feet, his eyes wild with pleading. "No, signore, you must not! You have surely become possessed of a demon! I know you suffered grievous and long over the betrayal dealt you by Cosimo and Cecilia—"

"Do not mention their cursed names, old man!" Niccolo exploded.

"I am merely contending that their treachery makes this wrong seem so much more shameful," pleaded the squire. "But that is no cause to harm the princess—"

"I just stated reason enough!"

"But you are condemning her without proof," implored the squire. "Moreover, a holy knight and a man of honor must never harbor such evil, unchivalrous thoughts in his heart, and never toward a lady."

"Bah! The princess has proven herself no lady!"

Lorenzo frantically crossed himself. "Signore, you are plotting your own doom. You will burn in hell if you follow through with this iniquity. You must go to confession at once and repent of your evil ways."

Niccolo's features were clenched with anger and determination, his eyes gleaming with violence. "You should know by now, Lorenzo, that I am beyond redemption. I am no longer a man of honor, and the princess will rue the day she betrayed me!"

"Blessed saints!" cried the squire abjectly. "I must pray for you!"

Even as Lorenzo sank to his knees, Niccolo swore savagely, then stormed out of the chamber. Outside, he paced the darkened courtyard, his mind whirling with black thoughts and a grim obsession for revenge.

How could he have been such a fool, allowing himself to be duped again, just as Cosimo and Cecilia had betrayed him? To make matters worse, he had conspired with Artemas of Falconia against his own better judgment. He had distrusted the man from the outset, yet he had recklessly gambled away his family's entire future.

Well, he would gain his revenge, and the princess would bear the brunt of it. He shook his head as he recalled Lorenzo arguing that perhaps she had been unaware of her uncle's plot. The squire's pleadings had caused guilt to nag him, but had not weakened his resolve. In some demented corner of his mind, Niccolo doubted he even cared whether or not Lady Aurora was guilty of involvement in Artemas's perfidy. He had been betrayed, by damn! Lady Aurora had become the instrument of that treachery, and *she* would pay the price!

Aurora sat in her solar not far from an open latticework window. She loved her vast, fanciful chamber with its gold frescoed ceilings, its paneled wall murals picturing troubadours courting fair ladies, and its magnificent bed of carved oak, with blue velvet hangings and coverlet.

Behind Aurora stood her maid, Martha, who was brushing her lady's thick raven hair. Beyond her at a carved chest was bent Lady Flora, selecting the princess's garments for the morrow.

Flora, who was flaxen-haired, with a pretty, round face and pale green eyes, turned to Aurora and held up a red velvet gown trimmed with ermine. "Will this do, milady?"

"Yea, 'tis fair enough," Aurora replied. "Pray, set the garment aside, Flora, and come keep me company."

Flora laid down the garment and crossed over to

sit on a stool at Aurora's feet. Martha moved away
and began tidying the chamber.

"Your mind is on our latest visitor, is it not?" asked
Flora conspiratorially.

Aurora laughed. "You know me well. I am pleased
you were present in the great hall tonight, for I can
always count on you to be an apt observer of my life's
little dramas."

"Tonight's performance was hardly a minor tragedy, milady," quipped the lady-in-waiting.

"Verily, 'twas not," agreed Aurora. " 'Twas more
like the miracle play of Judgment Day we viewed last
autumn."

Flora smothered a laugh.

"What think you of our latest arrived knight, Niccolo Campioni?"

Flora slowly shook her head. "He is wondrous fair,
milady, but frankly, the sight of him put a shiver
down my spine."

"And mine," admitted Aurora ruefully. "I have
never seen a man like him before. That deep voice . . .
those bright eyes . . . the sheer size of him . . ." Her
voice trailed off, and she blushed.

"Yea, milady, he is quite different from the others—
in many respects. And so full of himself."

Aurora giggled. "You noticed that, as well?"

"Yea." Worry lines wrinkled Flora's smooth brow.
"Methinks he will not accept his plight with chivalry,
as have done the others."

"He certainly has not so far," concurred Aurora
drolly. "Sir Niccolo strikes me as having much pride."

"Yea, and you will do well to be rid of him, milady,
just as your seneschal has warned," Flora continued
soberly. "Were I you, I *would* cast him from the castle
this night."

Aurora shook her head. "Nay, I find him amusing."

"Amusing as he plots your ruin?"

"He has no time to plot," argued Aurora. "As you

are aware, he has vowed to leave. Surely he will not linger past the morrow."

"Mayhap, but I still do not trust him. He has a thirst for revenge in his heart, that one."

Aurora bit her lower lip. "If he lingers, I shall ask my half brother's advice once he returns from his mission—mayhap on the morrow."

Flora brightened. "You miss Christian, do you not?"

Aurora winked at Flora. "And you pine after him, eh?"

A blush stole up Flora's fair cheeks. "No doubt we shall both rejoice at his homecoming ... and he will advise you to be well rid of Niccolo Campioni."

Aurora fell silent. She knew Flora had spoken with wisdom. Niccolo Campioni frightened her, intrigued her, and stirred her in a new and daunting way. But, like Flora, she did not trust him, not at all ...

All at once she was roused from her thoughts by the sounds of a horse neighing, and a loud banging, coming from the bailey below. Curious, she rose and went to stare out at the courtyard amid shadow and silver. She gasped as she spied a solitary rider there, and realized someone else shared her restive state—

'Twas Niccolo Campioni, with lance in hand, charging his destrier at a quintain! The magnificent steed leaped through the night; Aurora winced as Niccolo's lance crashed against the shield hanging from the crossbar, setting the entire mechanism spinning.

"Flora, come look!" she called softly.

Flora joined Aurora at the window, and both women gazed down at the fearsome knight, watching him expertly turn his horse, raise his lance, lean forward slightly in his saddle, and ruthlessly storm the quintain again. Flora made a soft clucking sound. "Verily, milady, he looks angrier than Lucifer with his tail set on fire. His horse is wearing grooves in the green."

"Yea," admitted Aurora drolly. "And his aim is deadly, even in the darkness."

The two women regarded each other conspiratorially, then giggled.

Aurora glanced back at the bailey, her gaze riveted on the daunting tension and restless energy in man and beast as Niccolo charged his target repeatedly, his splendid steed pounding the earth with furious hooves. Even from this distance, the Venetian was formidable. She stifled a shudder at the thought of all that angry menace being unleashed on her!

"Verily, who can blame him if he hates me now?" she asked quietly.

"You did bait him terribly, milady," agreed Flora with a nervous laugh.

Aurora smiled guiltily. "Sometimes a devil seems to possess me when I am around arrogant men—and tonight Niccolo Campioni brought that devil out."

"But he was terribly fresh, milady, insulting your royal dignity and calling you liar," soothed Flora.

"Indeed." Aurora stretched forward slightly to see him better. "But I understand his frustration. Sometimes I am tempted to curse my uncle for putting me in this position—defrauding so many honorable men, and leaving me to appease them."

"Yea, but it has turned out for the best, has it not, milady?" inquired Flora. "So far, five of the knights have taken up your cause, even without a promise of your hand."

"Yea, but 'twas inevitable that sooner or later, a dark knight would appear, a warrior without honor. Now he appears to have arrived . . . yet he is the one who intrigues me most."

Flora went pale. "Take care, milady. He is a devil knight!"

Aurora merely shrugged, a fatalistic light glimmering in her dark eyes. "If I remain true to my heritage, I will not linger long in this world. I have no time for fear, Flora, and must gain what diversion I can."

Touching Aurora's arm, Flora implored, "Oh, milady! You trifle with your very life if you tempt that one! I shall pray that the morrow finds him gone!"

Still studying Niccolo, Aurora mused, "Mayhap I should seek the counsel of my ancestors."

At this frank admission, Flora thrust her fingers to her mouth, while behind them, Martha, who had been folding back the bedcovers, paused, wild-eyed, to cross herself.

Flora stepped closer to her mistress and spoke in urgent tones. "Do not speak of such madness, milady! 'Tis heresy! Even the servants are afraid to whisper of your ancestors, and the royal curse. If you do not take greater care, you could be burned as a witch."

Aurora glanced sadly at her companion before turning back to the window. "Do not fret, dear friend. We both well know that I am likely doomed in any event."

SIX

NICCOLO AWAKENED EARLY THE NEXT MORNING, AF-
ter spending a fitful night on his lumpy cot in the
barracks. By the wan light drifting in from the cell's
single small window, he glanced over at Lorenzo and
saw that the old man still slept. He could hear the soft
sounds of his snores.

He arose and performed his toilette quietly and ef-
ficiently, washing and shaving, then donning yellow
hose, soft leather boots, a linen doublet, and a wool
tunic of forest green. The passage of darkness had not
improved his temper—

Nor had his restless activities last night. He had ridden angrily about the moonlit courtyard, tilting at a
hapless quintain. After rubbing down his horse in the
stables, he had almost throttled an unfortunate sentry
who had dared to question him on his way back to
the barracks. This morn he remained every bit as enraged toward Princess Aurora, and just as determined
to make her suffer.

Her betrayal brought back to mind all the wrenching hurt, the agonies he had suffered at the hands of
Cosimo and Cecilia. He had struggled all night long
to keep his demons at bay, but the perfidious princess
had definitely unleashed them. He felt emotionally
raw, as if scores of sharp lances had been driven into

56

barely healed flesh, so devastating were the memories of the heartbreak and humiliation he had suffered three years past.

Nothing in Niccolo's life theretofore had prepared him for such emotional ravagement. His youth in Venice had been largely idyllic. As a boy, he had spent much time hunting and fishing with his father, while being tutored by monks at a nearby monastery. At the age of sixteen, he had left for the university at Naples, returning four years later to join his father's shipping business in the Rialto.

Back then, the Campioni enterprises had flourished; for centuries the venerated family had successfully imported spices, silks, and wines from the Orient, and had exported glassware, furniture, jewelry, and works of art. Niccolo had prospered in his family's business, and like his father before him, he had joined the knightly order of *Cavalieri di San Marco*. At the age of twenty-two, Niccolo had married Cecilia, the daughter of another prominent Venetian merchant; even though he and Cecilia had been betrothed as children, Niccolo had loved his bride throughout their seven-year marriage.

Like Aurora, Cecilia had been dark and beautiful, quick-witted. Like the princess, she had been flirtatious, but in a more haughty, cool, and manipulative manner. Yet Niccolo had found Cecilia's coquettish ploys enticing. Back then, he had been naive in the ways of women. During his youth, he had taken his Catholicism, and later his knightly vows, most seriously; thus, he had come to the marriage bed chaste, and he had assumed his wife was also virginal. Their wedding night had been a disappointment, due to his wife's lack of response and his own fumbling, short-fused performance. Niccolo had blamed his own inexperience; yet afterward, as much as he had tried, his wife had still failed to respond to his lovemaking. It was not until many years later, when he, a jaded

widower, had seduced a Greek virgin on the isle of
Corfu, that he had realized his wife had not been
chaste on their wedding night. Only after bedding numerous ladies in many ports of call, had he realized
his wife had never truly given of herself in their marriage bed, that she had never felt gratification during
their lovemaking. Before then, he had only known
that his wife's failure to participate had often ruined
their moments in bed for him.

Nonetheless, Niccolo had tried endlessly to please
Cecilia, even when she had lain largely unresponsive
beneath him. He had also taken great pride in his
lovely bride, in having her grace the glittery world
they shared. When her smiles had strayed toward
other men, he had made allowances, deciding she was
merely being gracious, refusing to believe she could
be false. And he had prayed endlessly that *Il Dio*
would bless their union with a child to fortify the
bond between them.

He and Cecilia had been married three years when
his father was killed during the territorial dispute
with Milano. Niccolo's anguish over Vettor Campioni's death was magnified by his wife's seeming in-
difference to his suffering. Still, he had made excuses
for her emotional remoteness. When the Turks had
taken Constantinople, Niccolo had felt duty-bound to
accept the baton of captain general offered to him by
Doge Francesco Foscari. Naively hoping a separation
might improve his marriage, he had left his family's
enterprises in the hands of his cousin, Cosimo, and
he had commanded an expedition of state galleys. He
had fought long and hard to reestablish the sea lanes
to the Far East for the Republic.

He had seen terrible things while off at battle—men
eaten alive by Greek fire, impaled by arrows, their
heads blown off by cannon. But the thought of returning to his bride had sustained him. He had
dreamed of finally conceiving a child with Cecilia

when he returned home, for surely she would welcome him then.

After two years on the high seas, he had at last sailed back to Venice, only to have his mother distraughtly inform him of the devastating events that had transpired shortly before his return: how his trusted cousin had allowed the family enterprises to languish and deteriorate; how his faithless bride had committed adultery with Cosimo; how Cosimo had killed Cecilia when he found her in bed with her gardener; how he had then turned the knife on himself . . .

Niccolo's trust, his faith, had been utterly shattered. His every waking moment had become a torment, as he had endlessly envisioned his wife and cousin betraying him, fornicating in his very bed, treating him with utter contempt even as he had risked his life for the Republic!

Niccolo had felt as if his heart and soul had been ripped out of him with a blunt instrument. The wounds still festered to this day, ripped open anew by the betrayal he had just endured. And Princess Aurora would hardly become the second woman to tear out his heart and rend it asunder—

No, he would wound her even more grievously than he had been hurt. He would stay and determine a course for her ruin . . .

Niccolo left the barracks and crossed the courtyard. The crisp morning air, the smells of earth and manure, greeted him. Three cackling chickens and a squealing pig skidded across his path. Niccolo spotted several peasants working garden plots or throwing corn to livestock, and he walked past a laundress tending a huge, smelly vat of sheets. He felt bemused to note that the woman wore a huge iron cross about her neck and was singing a dirge as she turned the steaming laundry with a stick.

He climbed the steps and reentered the keep, pro-

ceeding down the smoky, torchlit corridor. As he
turned the corner into the great hall, he practically
collided with a short, stocky servant who was backing
out of the archway with a huge, porridge-encrusted
pot in hand. Niccolo stepped aside in the nick of time,
almost gagging at the odor of the man's garlic necklace. He glanced askance at the servant's clothing,
which was worn inside out, in the style of the Ospreyans.

Spotting Niccolo, the little man bowed nervously.
"Your pardon, milord," he muttered, still backing
away.

"Why do you leave the chamber backwards?" demanded Niccolo.

The little man's eyes darted about with fear, and he
solemnly crossed himself. "Milord, I dare not say."

"Why? Are you afraid you will turn into a pillar of
salt if you do?" scoffed Niccolo. "And why do you
wear your clothing wrong side out?"

"Milord, I dare not say," repeated the little man,
genuflecting and frantically backing away.

Shaking his head, Niccolo strode inside the chamber to view the same five knights seated at the long
table, eating porridge and drinking whey. The lavish
costumes of last night were absent; like Niccolo, the
knights wore serviceable wool tunics and thick hose.
A couple of stewards attended the men, and the familiar wolfhounds were also there, bounding about
sniffing for scraps. Again the princess's dais was deserted, and Niccolo wondered what Lady Aurora was
about. No doubt she was plotting a new way to torment and defraud them all!

"Good morrow, Sir Niccolo," called Sir Gilbert,
waving a hand.

"Good morrow," called back Niccolo with ill humor.

"Come break your fast with us," invited a jovial Sir
Edgar. "There is not a moment to spare, as the enemy

may arrive at the castle gates at any moment."

Scowling, Niccolo strode up to the trestle table and sat down next to Edgar, picking up a spoon and taking a bite of porridge from the bowl he shared with the English knight. "Tell me more of this enemy."

Sir Edgar replied, " 'Tis Basil, king of the state of Ravenia, which lies over the hills beyond the Valley of the Boulders."

"Why does Basil attack our princess?" asked Niccolo, sipping his whey.

This time the Genoan, Sir Cesare, spoke up. "Because she refused to wed him."

Niccolo all but choked on his whey. "Ah," he murmured cynically, "yet another disgruntled suitor."

Chuckles greeted his comment. A grinning Edgar explained, "Yea, the war commenced two winters past, methinks, when the princess declined Basil's suit."

"And now he attacks every day?" Niccolo pursued.

"Yea, and flees with every sunset," answered Sir Baldric. "Basil and his company fear the darkness . . . which leaves all of us free to woo the princess."

The knights grinned at one another.

"But Basil's strategy makes no sense," protested Niccolo. "A siege must be continuous to be successful. After all, is not the purpose of such a blockade to slowly starve and wear down one's enemies?"

"Yea, 'tis true," admitted Sir Gilbert. "But Basil seems to prefer a course of harassment."

"He charges like a wild boar, then retreats to play in the mud, methinks," commented Sir Olaf.

Several men snickered.

Breaking off a piece of bread, Niccolo asked, "And who does the princess have to defend her?"

"The Royal Guard," answered Edgar.

"And all of us," added Sir Olaf.

"There is no other male relative, aside from the perfidious Artemas?" pressed Niccolo.

"There is a half brother, Christian, who is now riding about the countryside, raising additional forces for our princess among her villeins," replied Sir Baldric. "He is expected back most any time now."

Absorbing this information with a scowl, Niccolo glanced up and down the table. "I am curious. How long have all of you lingered here, and why have you not demanded satisfaction from the princess on account of the fraud committed by her uncle?"

The knights glanced at one another, then deferred to Edgar.

"Sir Gilbert and I arrived in Falconia first," explained the Englishman, "almost three fortnights past. As luck would have it, we met on the very same day, in Osprey at the public house, while awaiting sunset and the end of the daily besieging. We drank ale and told tales of our various campaigns. But when we realized we both had contracted to marry the same princess"—a slow grin spread across the Englishman's bearded face—"we all but slew each other."

Laughter rumbled over the table.

With obvious relish, Gilbert continued the story. "At sunset Edgar and I both rode up to the castle to demand an explanation from Princess Aurora. As you might imagine, we stormed about this very chamber like madmen and questioned her most aggressively. But when we realized she had no knowledge of her uncle's arranging the marriage contracts, we both acknowledged 'twould be dishonorable to hold her accountable."

Edgar took up the tale. "Then, seeing her plight and observing the continuing siege, we were compelled to offer our knightly services. As you are likely aware, the code of chivalry demands we protect those who are defenseless."

"Especially fair ladies," concluded Gilbert.

Restraining the urge to voice a cynical comment,

Niccolo glanced down the table. "And the rest of you?"

"I have been here three weeks," confessed the Viking. "Like Edgar and Gilbert, I was enraged when I first discovered I had been duped. But I, too, soon adapted to my fate."

"My story is much the same as Olaf's," stated Baldric, "except I have been here for a week."

"I arrived just two days before you, Venetian," finished the Genoan.

"And none of you remains angered over the princess's duplicity?" demanded an incredulous Niccolo. "Where is your honor, men, your sense of moral indignation?"

Dark scowls greeted Niccolo's question as the knights consulted one another. Again Sir Edgar spoke for the group. "As we have readily admitted, we were all vexed at first." He winked at Niccolo. "Then as we became acquainted with the princess, we became as giddy and befuddled as you soon will be, sir knight."

The others howled with mirth and beat their fists on the table.

"Bah!" scoffed Niccolo. "There is no mortal woman I will ever slobber over like a lapdog."

"But the princess is not a mortal woman," argued the Genoan.

"Nay, she is an enchantress, mayhap a witch, who has beguiled us all," admitted the Viking. "You will see, Venetian. You will not be safe from her."

"On the contrary," stated Niccolo coldly, "she will not be safe from *me*."

The knights responded with more rollicking comments, seemingly oblivious to Niccolo's serious intent. He continued questioning the others—gaining as much information as he could about Princess Aurora, her enemy, Basil, and the ongoing war—while inwardly plotting a way to use the information to ensure the princess's downfall . . .

SEVEN

Carrying a torch, Aurora walked gingerly down the darkened, slimy secret passageway, heading toward the sally port that led to the forest behind the castle. As far as she knew, only she and her half brother, Christian, were aware of the hidden tunnel, dug long ago to offer the royal family of Falconia an escape route during siege. Two years past, a fever had taken Aurora's beloved mother and father, the king and queen, and now the secret of the corridor was held by her and Christian, who was two years her senior and had been born of their English mother's first marriage. Aurora loved and missed her half brother, who had been gone for two days in the countryside, trying to raise additional forces to combat their enemy, Basil.

Aurora rounded a corner and, in the dim light, spotted a fat rat darting across her path. Stifling a shudder, she hurried on to the scarred oaken door at the end of the corridor. She deposited her torch in a bracket on the earthen wall and creaked open the heavy panel. A sweet, crisp breeze swept in to greet her, and lovely dappled sunshine spilled into the dank cavern.

Stepping outside and shoving the door back in place, Aurora climbed lichen-encrusted steps, then crouched behind a large hawthorn bush that hid access to the port. She glanced overhead to make sure no sentry was passing above her on the parapets. Confident she could pass undetected, she moved aside several branches and emerged on the mossy ground behind the castle curtain. She quickly crossed the narrow open area and entered the forest. Safe at last in the dense, sheltering trees amid the honeyed coolness of morn, she heaved a sigh of relief. She heard a willow warbler singing in a nearby birch tree, watched smoky spikes of light filter through the lofty branches of firs, pines, and birches, and filled her lungs with the fresh spicy scent of the conifers.

Morning was Aurora's favorite time, when the day was as yet sweet and unsullied. Feeling unfettered, exhilarated, and invigorated, she hurried on toward the forest shrine, eager to play with her fawn and converse with the spirits of her ancestors.

Climbing the hillside, she was delighted to spot her friends the gnomes making their way through the trees, about to cross the trail ahead of her. The troupe of six stocky, bearded little men marched briskly along, humming a droll little tune, the bells on their hats and shoes jingling. Looking as similar as brothers with their stout torsos, stubby arms, skinny legs, and knobby knees, all six wore colorful green jackets and yellow tights, pointed hats and shoes, and carried backpacks, tools, bows, and arrows.

The leader of the gnomes spotted Aurora and screeched to a stop, raising a small hand. "Halt in the name of the princess, men!" he commanded in his shrill little voice.

Pressing her fingers to her mouth, Aurora stifled laughter as the leader's attempt at dignity quickly disintegrated into chaos. She watched wide-eyed as the rest of the gnomes, attempting to stop, crashed into one another and their leader. In the noisy melee that followed, heads bumped against heads, shovels and

axes collided, fists were raised, and curses spewed
forth. Aurora giggled as she watched one of the little
men box another's ears, while a third kicked a com-
rade in the shin, causing him to clutch his calf and
hobble about, howling in pain.

"I said, come to attention, men!" yelled their exasperated leader.

The gnomes at last jerked themselves into a recog-
nizable line, grumbling all the while, their grumpy,
gamin faces twisted into sullen frowns. The leader
marched forward, removed his cap, bobbed into a
bow, and grinned up at Aurora. "Good morrow, Princess. I apologize for the manners of my comrades."

Aurora smiled at the little man, with his wrinkled,
pointed face, beady dark eyes, balding pate, and full
beard. "Good morrow, Francis." She nodded in turn
to each of the others. "And Farley, Findley, Finn,
Fiske, and Frey."

"Good morrow, Princess," crooned the others in a
chorus as they, too, removed their hats and dipped
into bows.

"And what are all of you about this morn?" asked
Aurora pleasantly.

Francis cupped a hand around his mouth and whispered conspiratorially, "Why, we are about the royal
business, as we have been for centuries now. Where
are you bound today, Your Majesty?"

"On my daily walk to the shrine," she replied.

Farley wagged a stumpy finger at the princess.
"You must be careful, Your Majesty. Your enemy may
be about these hills."

"Yea, we often spy King Basil approaching your
fortress with his men-at-arms," remarked Frey.

The other gnomes nodded grimly and mumbled
ominously to one another.

"But Basil will not venture into this forest,"
laughed Aurora. "He is frightfully superstitious and
fears all of you. Did you not once slay three of his

comrades whom he sent to spy in our woods?"

The little men elbowed one another and grinned in pride.

"Yea, 'twas our pleasure to slay your enemies, Princess," boasted Fiske.

"We were only doing our duty to protect the royal family," bragged Finn.

"And you perform your duties so well," Aurora commended.

Amid a plethora of new, smug grins, Farley announced, "Yesterday when Basil came to attack, Francis and I ran out of the woods with our bows and arrows, and we spooked a score of your enemy's horses. A dozen Ravenian knights were unseated and went tumbling into the meadow."

All of the gnomes cackled and slapped their knees.

"Good for you!" cried Aurora, clapping her hands. "How can I fear, with the royal gnomes to defend me?"

All six of the little men beamed their happiness.

"Take care, now, Princess," said Francis, saluting her.

"Oh, I shall."

The little men respectfully waited for Aurora to pass before they trooped on. Glancing back at them, she smiled. The peasants of both Osprey and Kestrel feared the gnomes, not understanding the odd, grumpy little men who lived in huts in the forest. The villagers were convinced the gnomes were evil and mean-spirited. But Aurora had known the gnomes all her life; although they could be crabby and temperamental, they were essentially kindhearted as well as fiercely protective of the royal family. Indeed, without the gnomes, Aurora suspected that she and her forebears never would have known such prosperity.

The gnomes knew of her daily visits to the forest shrine. They doubtless also knew she conversed with her ancestors there, although she had never actually discussed the spirits with Francis and the others.

She continued on into the foothills, wending her way through a tangle of bramble, holly, hornbeam, and wild rose. At last she entered the bower, a secret copse hidden on a wide shelf on the hillside. As always, the beauty of the grotto enchanted Aurora; majestic and private, it was crossed by a mountain stream that fed into a tranquil pond, and sheltered by the entwined, protective arms of huge oaks and birches. Iridescent light flitted over the landscape, and a pinkish gold glow permeated the scene. Vibrant wildflowers carpeted the ground—purple morning glories, yellow daffodils, blue cornflowers, red roses, white day lilies, orange amaryllis. Bees and hummingbirds buzzed about, drinking nectar, and a rabbit munching on grasses paused to eye Aurora, wide-eyed, before hopping away. In the foliage, colorful finches flitted about and sang a lilting chorus, while a spotted woodpecker drilled away in the shadows.

The bower had always been Aurora's favorite place, a magical, mystical retreat where time stood still and the spirits of the ages were free to speak. 'Twas truly an enchanted spot—and yet she could risk telling no one, beyond a trusted few, that she came here—if she were so foolish, she would surely be damned a heretic or burned as a witch, just as Flora had warned.

Aurora gathered a bouquet of wildflowers, then strolled on to stand on the steps before the shrine. As always, she felt awed at the sight of the small temple. Inside an ornate stone niche with Ionic columns and Greek cornice reposed the magnificent bronze statue of the Angel of Wisdom. With a slight dusting of mold and heavy layer of tarnish only adding to her ageless appeal, the angel smiled down at Aurora and clutched a heavenly lyre.

At the angel's feet rested a brass urn with withered flowers. Kneeling down, Aurora discarded the dead blooms and replaced them with her fresh bouquet. She then crossed herself and said a silent prayer for the souls of her parents and her ancestors.

A wet nose nudging her cheek startled her from her supplication, and she turned to see her little fawn standing beside her. The dappled animal was precious with its spotted back, cottony tail, and large brown eyes. Aurora had adopted the fawn as her pet four years ago, and she often wondered why the animal had never grown up. 'Twas miraculous, just like this place.

"Tansy, I have missed your sunny company," murmured Aurora, stroking the fawn's soft ears. "I wish I could keep you at the castle with me, but then mayhap you would grow old, ere long. Have you guarded my ancestors well while I was gone?"

As if she understood, Tansy glanced up at the altar and perked up her ears, her fluffy tail standing at attention.

Sensing a slight shift on the air, Aurora rose and gazed around her, tuning her senses to the wisdom of the spirits. Usually she could *feel* their presence; for years she had heard their voices, their dire rhymes oft repeated, warning her of the ancient curse that had plagued the royal family for a century now. Sometimes Aurora swore she could see the air stirring as the spirits spoke, but she had never actually glimpsed the specters.

"Spirits, are you here?" she whispered.

For a long moment, there was only eerie silence. Then the familiar, spooky wind whistled through the copse, rustling the tree leaves and fluttering the flowers, and at last towing along on its wake a haunting, barely audible voice:

Harken close, the truth to know,
The course of love is filled with woe.

Aurora smiled, recognizing at once the source of the phantom voice, and the grievous greeting so oft heard. "Good morrow, Great-Aunt Beatrice," she called pleasantly. "As always, your verse brings such joy to my heart. Have you brought along Aunt Phoebe and Cousin Chloe this morn?"

A new voice, this one even more shivery, grimly intoned:

> Listen well and heed the morrow,
> The course of love is lined with sorrow.

'Good morrow, Aunt Phoebe," responded Aurora with a smile. "You truly are a prophet of cheer, as always. And Cousin Chloe, are you near, as well?"

A third voice, deeper and more ominous than the first two, answered:

> Hear our warning, dire and brief,
> The course of love will end in grief.

"Good morrow, Cousin Chloe," said Aurora brightly. "You are forever such a ray of hope. And have you all now finished with your glad tidings?"

Great-Aunt Beatrice, never one to hastily conclude a lecture, ominously added:

> Choose well in love, for pity's sake,
> Do not succumb to our mistake.

The wind grew hushed, the spirits fell silent, and Aurora ruefully shook her head. She had sought the solace of the shrine almost all her life. Her parents had first introduced her to the holy bower when she was quite young; as children, she and Christian had made the copse their secret refuge, a place to laugh and cavort. But only since the advent of her fertility had Aurora heard the spirits' voices. Previous to that,

she had oft wondered why a number of her female
ancestors had died so young, within a year of their
marriages; in her family's chambers, she had seen the
portraits of these tragic young women—including
Great-Aunt Beatrice, Aunt Phoebe, and Cousin
Chloe—who were taken from life so prematurely, so
cruelly. On a few occasions, she had heard servants
at the castle whispering about a royal curse. Then,
when she had first known her woman's courses four
summers past, she had begun to hear the voices in the
grotto.

At first she had been frightened, afraid to believe
the spirits were real, even more terrified that the
phantoms might bring her harm. Gradually she had
come to accept the unseen specters as tragic though
benevolent ghosts, who were trapped here in the Falconian countryside, having succumbed to the ancient
curse.

Soon Aurora's curiosity had prompted her to seek
her mother's counsel regarding the hauntings. Queen
Lyris had gently explained about the curse to her
daughter, and Aurora had at last learned the truth of
her own daunting legacy.

Many generations ago, one of Aurora's ancestors,
Princess Sybil, had chosen to marry for greed instead
of for love, and had rejected her one true love, Sir
Alaric. Sybil's husband, jealous of Alaric, had sent
him into the front lines in battle, and he had died,
cursing the woman who had spurned him, and cursing all her female descendants to die within one year
of marriage until one of them wed for true love alone.
Sybil did die within a year of marriage, after produc-
ing only one offspring, a son. Thereafter, although
males in the royal lineage could sire many heirs with
wives acquired from outside families—just as Aurora's father had wed Queen Lyris—every female descendant with royal blood had been afflicted with the

curse, and all had died within a year of marriage, having chosen poorly in love.

Aurora, only fourteen years old at the time, had been very disheartened to learn of the heavy burden she carried. Indeed, both her parents had urged her never to marry, rather than risk the near-certain vengeance of the curse. After she had lost her mother and father, when Basil had first pressed his suit, she had rebuffed him, knowing he was not her true love, even though guilt nagged at her because her refusal soon caused war with Ravenia. Still, she had managed to cling to her determination. As the last remaining blood descendant in the royal line, Aurora knew she was her family's only hope for breaking the curse. If she did not find her one true love, she would be doomed forever to haunt the countryside with her disgruntled ancestors.

In his will, her father had left to her uncle Artemas the task of finding her a husband. But now her uncle had woefully complicated her life by sending her so many suitors—including the brooding, masterful Venetian who had set such a fire stirring in her blood, although she did not trust him for a moment.

She considered her dilemma. She knew Basil was arrogant and stubborn and would not soon give up his mission to force her into wedlock. She needed the protection of the knights, and eventually might even be forced to choose a husband to defend her, and shield her kingdom from Basil. But how could she know she was making the right choice? Would she find happiness, or merely succumb to the curse like the others?

Should she seek the counsel of her ancestors? Certainly the spirits had been telling her for years of their own mistakes, and warning her that she must not follow in their doomed footsteps. Mayhap they could offer some wisdom now.

Should she tell them of Niccolo Campioni? But how

could she, when she could not yet fully describe her feelings for this newly arrived knight? Yet she somehow coveted the new, unsettling emotions he stirred, holding them close to her heart . . . Mayhap 'twas best for now to describe her predicament in more general terms.

Once more, Aurora knelt by the shrine, and solemnly she spoke. "My ancestors, I have come to seek your counsel. My uncle has sent me many potential suitors, and methinks more shall shortly arrive. How can I know which one of them I should take to husband, which one is my true love? How can I be certain I shall not succumb to the curse like all of you?"

There was a long silence, as if the spirits were deliberating. And then the wind surged again, bringing the chilling, ominously spoken words.

As always, Great-Aunt Beatrice spoke first:

My choice was Stephen, fair of hair,
He trothed his love and brought despair.

Aurora groaned as Aunt Phoebe added her own, oft-heard portent:

My love was Harry, pure of face,
He promised joy and brought disgrace.

Aurora struggled to maintain her patience as Cousin Chloe repeated her own familiar words of gloom:

My mate was William, sweet of breath,
He pledged delight and brought me death.

"Yea, yea, I have oft heard the warnings," replied Aurora with some impatience. "I know all of you chose badly in love. Now you are all doomed to haunt the countryside until the curse is broken. You do not

wish me to repeat your mistakes. You are determined
I select my mate wisely, and thereby free you all from
your torment. I know these things. But tell me, how
may I best choose my one true love—and thereby lib-
erate you?"

Another silence ensued, long and eerie. Aurora began to despair of ever receiving her answer. Then, to
her surprise and delight, Aunt Beatrice spoke:

>   Fling thy gauntlet, toss thy glove,
>   Test thy champion, find true
>   love.

Aurora's eyes lit with joy, and she clapped her
hands. At once she understood what the spirits
meant, and the prospect greatly appealed to her ad-
venturous spirit.

"You are saying I must stage a contest?" she cried
raptly. "That the knight who proves himself my
champion will be my one true love?"

Again Aunt Beatrice responded:

>   Yea, my dear,
>   Test thy cavalier.

At last Aurora had her answer, and it filled her
heart with new hope and a delicious thrill of anticipation.

EIGHT

In the great hall, Niccolo had listened to the other knights with interest, learning much more about the ongoing war and the princess's enemy, Basil. The warriors were now discussing their strategy *du jour*, how best to combat the Ravenians when they arrived for their daily besieging. Sir Edgar argued that they needed to station more archers in the bartizans, while Sir Olaf contended that they must gather much larger rocks and boulders to hurl from the parapets. Niccolo only half listened, his own thoughts still focused on revenge; he felt more determined than ever to remain here in Falconia until he found a way to plot the princess's ruin.

"Good morrow, sir knights," called a lyrical voice.

As had happened the previous eve, the sound of Princess Aurora's voice cut short the men's discourse, as well as halting Niccolo's musings. With the others he turned to view the princess entering the chamber, dressed in a red velvet, ermine-trimmed gown, and flanked by three ladies-in-waiting. Even at a distance, the sight of the regal beauty dazzled Niccolo. Following the lead of the other knights, he stood.

She swept toward the men's table, eyeing the warriors with a slight smile curving her full, red lips, and mischief gleaming in her dark, bright eyes. Niccolo mused that she was surely plotting some new duplicity.

Sir Edgar dashed around the trestle table to pull out a bench. "Good morrow, Princess. Will you join us?"

Flashing him a saucy smile, she replied, "Methinks I shall."

Edgar gallantly seated her and her ladies, while the other knights watched in irritation.

Smoothing her skirts about her, Aurora gestured regally to the men. "Pray, all of you must sit down and finish your repast."

"Thank you, Princess," said Sir Gilbert, and he and the others resumed their seats.

Stewards quickly made their rounds, depositing bowls of porridge and tankards of whey in front of Aurora and her ladies. Sipping her whey, Aurora glanced curiously at Niccolo. "Why, Sir Niccolo, I see you are still among us. I thought you planned to leave."

Observing the impish smile on the princess's face and hearing the knights chuckling, Niccolo fought back his annoyance. Although Aurora's remark rankled, he feigned his most charming tone. "Mayhap I spoke in haste this time, Princess," he replied, and again everyone laughed.

"Did you, milord?" she taunted, laughter gleaming in her eyes. "Have you reconsidered your harsh words of last eve?"

He gazed back at her and replied evenly, "Mayhap I have . . . but only because I have a debt to collect, Princess."

Aurora's lips twitched, but she did not comment directly. "Sir Niccolo, I do believe you have not met my ladies-in-waiting."

Niccolo glanced briefly at each. "No, I have not had the pleasure."

Gesturing to each lady in turn, Aurora announced,

"I present Lady Flora, Lady Violet, and Lady Iris."

Niccolo nodded politely, noting that the ladies appeared much like sisters, all with round faces and fair eyes—except that Lady Flora's hair was flaxen, Lady Violet's black, and Lady Iris's red. Each woman was dressed in a gown to complement her name—Flora in yellow, Violet in purple, Iris in blue.

"My ladies," he murmured, smiling.

"A lovelier bevy of flowers, we have never seen," declared Sir Baldric.

"We pray they may forever favor us with the bloom of their smiles," intoned Edgar gallantly.

While Niccolo stifled a groan at the knights' unabashed flirtation, the ladies giggled and a passing servant also snickered as he refilled the goblets of the women.

Niccolo frowned, watching the man back out of the room. "Princess, why do your servants go through doors backward?"

She laughed. "You are very observant, sir knight."

"Observant!" he scoffed. "Thrice now the bumbling fools have all but knocked me off my feet as I have attempted to walk through portals. They look not where they go, the dimwits!"

Amid renewed chuckles, the princess explained. "Only the Ospreyans follow the custom. They are badly superstitious of doorways, ever since one of their number died when he met the devil at his door. Now they believe if they go through doors backwards, they will keep the devil at bay."

Niccolo was flabbergasted. "Surely you jest."

She smirked at him. "Will their practice keep *you* at bay, sir knight?"

Hearing shouts of male laughter, Niccolo felt his face darkening by shades, and his hands once again itched to throttle the impudent princess. Aurora was plenty crafty and clever, he mused darkly. He might indeed have to apply soap to her acid tongue before he was done with her, but he could ill afford the luxury at present. With this conniving little vixen, he would need all his skills to exact his proper revenge. And for now, that meant he would have to reign in the raging anger she so skillfully stoked.

Flashing her his most dazzling smile, he replied, "The devil may sometimes be kept at bay . . . if he is given his due."

Grins of admiration replaced the jeers, and even Aurora nodded her approval at Niccolo's adroit rejoinder.

Niccolo regarded her with a thoughtful scowl. "I am curious, milady. Why have you deigned to join us mere mortals this morn? Do you not normally break your fast on your royal dais, or in your solar?"

Aurora glanced down the table at each of the knights. "Actually, I am pleased you are all present, for I do have a matter to discuss."

"Then by all means, speak out, milady," urged Sir Edgar.

"Do favor us with your royal thoughts," agreed Sir Baldric.

Aurora nodded, and began in dire tones. "Truth to tell, sir knights, I have been beset by turmoil. Indeed, I have felt so troubled by my uncle's abuse of your generosity that I could not sleep at all last night."

All of the knights, save Niccolo, appeared stricken.

"Milady, we are abjectly sorry for any harm we have done," declared Sir Gilbert.

"*Sì*, we would all gladly perish ere see you lose a second of sleep," insisted Sir Cesare.

As other fawning knights expressed their concern, Niccolo ground his jaw, tempted to add a comment of an entirely different nature—that he hoped the princess's dreams were haunted, her mattress lumpy, her slumber negligible. This little schemer was not the least bit remorseful—not after the way she had mocked his fate last night!

"You are so chivalrous, so kind," remarked Aurora to the others, batting her eyelashes demurely.

"We are eager to serve you in any way, milady," said Gilbert.

"We would gladly risk death just to see you smile," announced Sir Cesare.

Aurora did smile—brilliantly, Niccolo noted with ill humor. "Splendid," she said. "Then I must tell you I have come to a decision regarding your presence here, sir knights."

"We are your captive audience, Princess!" exclaimed Sir Olaf.

She beamed at the Viking. "Since 'tis true I am under siege by my enemies, and I will need the protection of a husband, I have decided that the knight who most distinguishes himself for me in combat against the Ravenians will be rewarded with my hand in marriage, and control of my castle and lands."

All of the knights appeared amazed.

"You are suggesting a contest, milady?" asked the Genoan.

"Yea, I am tossing my gauntlet," she replied gaily. "I shall have the captain of my Royal Guard, as well as my brother, Christian, observe all of you in battle to help me decide who is the greatest warrior. Do you accept my challenge, sir knights?"

Sir Edgar glanced down the table; after a brief hesitation, several heads bobbed in agreement. "Yea, milady, we accept gladly," he informed Aurora. " 'Twill be an honor to defend you to the death. And the knight who proves himself your greatest champion shall win your hand."

"Hear! Hear!" added several of the others, lifting their goblets and cheering.

"And, milady," added the dark-eyed Gilbert, flashing her a winsome grin, "may we assume we can conduct a contest of the heart, as well?"

As all the knights waited expectantly, Aurora nodded happily. "Yea, you will be free to pay court to me. 'Twill prove marvelously diverting, I am sure!"

Five of the knights grinned their delight.

Aurora turned to Niccolo, who had been silent, scowling darkly. "And you, sir knight, what say you? Will you join the contest?"

His mind humming, Niccolo absorbed the stares of so many watching him intently. All his instincts urged him to take up the gauntlet, then find a way to use the lady's contest to defeat her.

"Yea, milady," he replied soberly. "I accept."

A great cheer rose from the knights. Shoulders were pounded as several warriors wished one another good fortune. But the celebration abruptly ended as the thud of a battering ram and the whoosh of a petrary could be heard from the front castle walls. The knights began to murmur anxiously to one another.

Sir Mortimer raced into the chamber, trailed by several sentries. "Milady!" he cried, wringing his hands. "The enemy has arrived at your gates!"

Sir Edgar stood, his fist raised, his visage filled with fire and determination. "To prayer, men! And then to arms!"

The knights charged out of the room, save for Niccolo, who lingered, calmly sipping his whey. Aurora and her ladies watched him in astonishment.

At last Aurora spoke. "You have accepted my challenge, knight, but you will not rise to defend me?"

Niccolo laughed. "I shall defend you, milady, but I shall not go to chapel beforehand and grovel in prayer."

The ladies-in-waiting gasped at Niccolo's casual blasphemy, while Aurora appeared fascinated. "You are a knight without a soul, Sir Niccolo?"

For once, he responded in all honesty. Staring Aurora square in the eye, he spoke with soft menace. "Yea, milady, I am a knight without a soul—a warrior without mercy. You will do well to remember that."

NINE

Niccolo returned to the barracks to find Lorenzo there, praying by his cot. The old man appeared utterly guileless, kneeling with his eyes closed, his gnarled fingers clutching a rosary as he mumbled in singsongy Latin under his breath. The sounds of the siege—the scream of arrows and bang of the ram—seemed to have no effect on him.

The sight of his faithful friend so piously occupied bedeviled Niccolo with guilt, reminding him once again of the faith he had abandoned. Following the betrayal of Cosimo and Cecilia, he had been adamant in his decision to renounce both God and the church, yet the religious teachings of his childhood and youth were still heavily ingrained in him, rising up to keep him constantly at war with himself. He was a man who hesitated at little, but he could not bring himself to disturb his squire at prayer. Thus he paced the narrow cell as his man finished his supplications.

Finally Lorenzo opened his eyes and stared up at his master. "The siege has begun once more," he muttered.

"*Sì*, and you have at last taken note," replied Niccolo cynically. "I must go to the parapets to reconnoiter the battle. Kindly fetch my hauberk, squire."

Grimacing, Lorenzo pushed painfully to his feet.

"You will not wear your armor, master?"

Niccolo laughed. "And tumble to my death while climbing to the battlements? The white armor is light and flexible, but it is not suited to rigorous climbing. The chain mail should be ample protection for now, methinks."

Lorenzo went to fetch one of the parfleches in the corner. "You have decided to stay to champion the princess's cause?"

Niccolo hesitated, not wanting to admit to Lorenzo the black thoughts raging in his heart.

With the hauberk in hand, the squire turned, his gaze now filled with reproach. "Master?"

Niccolo groaned, the admonishment in his squire's eyes filling him with self-loathing. "Why is it I can never lie to you? Are you squire or father confessor?"

Lorenzo chuckled. "Mayhap a bit of both, my son. Methinks you are unable to prevaricate because beneath all your hatred and anger, and the deep wounds of your betrayal, lies a pure heart."

"Bah!" scoffed Niccolo, pulling off his wool tunic and exposing his linen doublet underneath. He tossed the garment on his cot. "You are sadly deluded."

"Then why are you preparing for battle, milord, if you are not defending the princess against her enemies?" Lorenzo inquired.

"Because I would not have her know my true designs," admitted Niccolo.

"And what are they, milord?"

"You do not want to know, old man!" Niccolo retorted.

"But I do, signore," insisted Lorenzo quietly.

The two stood tensely confronting each other, Niccolo with fists clenched and eyes gleaming, Lorenzo regarding him in righteous challenge.

At last, in a burst of anger, Niccolo spoke. "Very

well, squire, hear the truth if you must. You will not like it."

"I will hear it nevertheless, master."

"So be it." Drawing himself up with pride, Niccolo declared, "I have decided we shall stay, but only so I may conjure a way to ruin this princess. I will bring injury on her that will be tenfold the devastation she has heaped on me! Then I will leave her disgraced. If I can find a way to ransom her to her enemy, I will do that, as well."

Lorenzo was so horrified, he actually dropped the hauberk, which hit the floor in a loud rattling. "No, master, say 'tis not true!"

"You have demanded the truth and now you have it!" snapped Niccolo.

Lorenzo wildly shook his head. " 'Tis the devil's work you are about!"

"And at last you recognize with whom you are dealing!"

"No!" His expression crazed with dread, Lorenzo crossed himself. "Say a prayer at once, my son, and go to confession. Otherwise, you are surely condemned to hell for your perfidy!"

"I am doomed already," snarled Niccolo.

"And you would destroy the princess with yourself?" Lorenzo implored. "*Dio mio*, I must find a way to protect the lady!"

Niccolo shook a finger at his squire. "I would remind you, old man, that you are bound by oath of fealty to guard my confidences and not to plot against me!"

Lorenzo regarded Niccolo in terrible disbelief. "Then you leave me in unbearable torment, milord."

" 'Tis you who have chosen to join me in my hell," Niccolo replied coldly, leaning over to grab his hauberk.

Yet, after confessing his sinister designs to Lorenzo, he again felt tortured by guilt.

* * *

Niccolo stood high on the allure behind the parapets, in the company of Sir Edgar and Sir Galen, who was captain of the Royal Guard. On either side of the three knights, archers with crossbows were positioned along the high walkway behind the crenellations; their lethal arrows whizzed through the air with brisk precision.

Niccolo and the others were observing the battle amid the sounds of screams, the whoosh and bang of missiles, and the thump of the battering ram. In the foreground, the enemy's men-at-arms were scrambling over the moat on scaling ladders, then attempting to scale the walls, all the while being pelted by arrows and chunks of iron from above. Another group was pounding the castle gate with their ram even as hot sand was poured on them from the parapets. Amid the chaos of battle, alligators prowled the moat, snapping at the hapless knights who tumbled into the fetid waters, and a few intrepid ravens roved the bank, picking at fresh carrion.

Off in the distance awaited Basil's mounted knights, at least threescore in number, the warriors resplendent in their bright armor, their lances and shields gleaming. Nearby, the enemy's trebuchet and ballista cranked out rocks and propelled huge iron spears toward the castle curtain. From questioning Sir Galen, Niccolo had determined that each side had about three dozen knights and at least twice that number of men-at-arms.

Yet Niccolo found the besiegers every bit as inept as the defenders. "The castle is poorly designed," he commented to his companions. "The moat is too narrow, affording the enemy passage over it on his ladder or ram, and the bank of earth on the other side is merely a convenient point for him to embark or disembark."

Sir Galen, a large, brown-haired man with craggy,

blunt features, scratched his jaw. "Yea, but what would you have us do, sir?"

Niccolo pointed. "Deepen and widen the moat, carving away as much of the shelf of earth as possible. Plant thistles in the remaining space."

Sir Galen nodded and scowled.

"An inspired suggestion," commented Sir Edgar. "Our castle in York rises straight from a deep, wide moat. 'Tis practically impregnable."

"Yet our enemy's knights have yet to breach our walls," argued Sir Galen. "They must first bring down the guardhouse."

Niccolo made a sound of contempt. "I do not know why they have not already defeated you. A few well-placed petards at the guardhouse or beneath the castle walls would bring Basil's knights straightaway inside your bailey."

"But they have no petards, sir," answered Sir Galen. "And neither have we."

"I have noticed," replied Niccolo. "You have no petards, or cannon, or pistols. You also allow your enemy to besiege you daily."

"What would you have us do, sir?" posed Galen with a frown.

Niccolo waved a hand in exasperation at the slow-witted man; so this cretin would assist Princess Aurora in choosing the most able knight! "Be a soldier, for pity's sake—plan some appropriate strategies rather than waiting like lambs to your enemy's slaughter. This is a benighted place indeed. I am surprised you do not fight in coats of mail rather than plate armor."

Sir Galen's face darkened in embarrassment. "Mayhap our weapons are outdated, sir, but I will have you know that our courage and fearsomeness are without parallel."

Niccolo snorted a laugh and stepped up to the edge of the crenellation, easily kicking away a knight on a scaling ladder, sending him screaming and tumbling into the moat. He turned back to the other two men, both of whom were grim-faced. Yet Niccolo's attitude was every bit as dispassionate as if he had just whisked away a bothersome insect.

"If you were truly fearsome, you would ambush your enemies ere they arrive here—or discharge Greek fire on them as they scale your walls. That would make quick work of the jackals."

The two knights appeared appalled.

"But, Sir Niccolo," protested Sir Edgar, "to pour Greek fire on them would roast them alive, and they would die horribly."

Niccolo smiled sadistically. "That is our ultimate goal, no? Would you have them invade the bailey, storm the keep, and make *us* die horribly?"

Sir Galen spoke up. "Princess Aurora says that in time, Basil will grow weary of the siege and quit assaulting the castle."

"Princess Aurora is no soldier," replied Niccolo. "However, considering the ineptitude of her enemy— who attacks by day and flees like a frightened baby with every sunset—she may in this instance have spoken with some wisdom."

Once again, Niccolo strode up to the edge of the parapet and shoved off another hapless knight attempting to breach the crenellations, sending the man shrieking into the moat. Sir Galen and Sir Edgar were left to shake their heads as Niccolo calmly turned and descended the battlements.

TEN

THAT AFTERNOON NICCOLO WAS STRIDING ABOUT THE ward when he spied Princess Aurora in the distance. With two gray wolfhounds flanking her, she was heading toward the little stone chapel at the end of the bailey. With groined vault, flying buttresses, stained-glass windows, and ivy climbing its masonry facade, the chapel much resembled the little church Niccolo had seen on the outskirts of Osprey. A short, rotund priest emerged from the edifice, and Aurora spoke with him briefly; then the two went inside together, the hounds hunkering down on the steps to wait.

Niccolo tarried out of sight behind a large garden cart piled with earth, hoping he might steal a few moments alone with the princess. He felt rather depraved to be lying in wait for her outside the chapel, but he knew he could not afford to allow the fact that she was devout to sway him from his goals. After all, she had betrayed him terribly. He must learn more about her and her enemy in order to better defeat her.

He must be charming, woo and seduce her . . . He groaned at the very prospect, remembering the days when he had courted Cecilia, seeking her favors like a groveling lapdog, plying her with gifts and flowery compliments in the fervent prayer that she might grace him with one of her cool, glittery smiles.

His pride revolted at the thought of demeaning himself that way again. Yet he knew he must do whatever was necessary to win the princess's trust. For he had already decided the ultimate betrayal would be to seduce her, then leave her disgraced. She was comely, and he would take great pleasure in deflowering her—and in his own revenge. If he could also manage to ransom her to Basil, then her humiliation and ruin would be complete.

Nothing less would bring *him* satisfaction!

Then a doubt nagged him. What if she conceived? he asked himself with an unwelcome twinge of conscience. Would it be fair to visit his revenge on an innocent child? Yet even this troubling possibility could not sway Niccolo from his dire plan. After all, Cecilia had never bred during their marriage; it was possible the impediment had been his, that his seed was infertile, and he would never father a child.

After some moments, the princess emerged from the chapel, petting the dogs as they bounded up to greet her. Niccolo tried not to think of the fetching portrait she made as she eagerly stroked the animals—how the wind toyed with her raven hair, how the sun shone on her smooth, fair countenance, how her ermine-trimmed gown clung to the lovely curves of her body. After a moment, she headed back toward the keep, the dogs scampering after her.

Niccolo emerged from behind the cart, stalked the princess, and quickly caught up with her. She glanced at him curiously as he fell into step beside her. The dogs also noted his approach, their expressions turning fierce as they glided protectively closer to their mistress. Niccolo kept half an eye trained on the huge hounds.

"Good afternoon, Princess," he began pleasantly. "Have you confessed your sins?"

She gasped, her brow knitted, her features a picture

of righteous indignation. "You were spying on me, knight!"

He chuckled, for she looked so pious. "I am here to protect you, Princess. How can I watch over you if I turn my back on your charming person?"

She dimpled prettily and shook a finger at him. "Ah, you are a devious one, knight. You likely need to confess your sins more than I."

Again he laughed. "So my elderly squire keeps informing me."

She smiled in pleasant surprise. "I believe I must have spied him praying at the altar as I went into the chapel with Father Mark. Is he quite ancient and frail, with a long beard?"

"Sì, that sounds like Lorenzo," replied Niccolo drolly. "He will doubtless wear a groove in the aisle of your chapel ere long."

Fighting mirth, she slanted him a chiding glance. "At least he does not snoop on my affairs as you do."

"I am only fulfilling the duty of my oath to protect fair ladies," he responded gallantly.

She paused in her tracks, turning to face him with an air of perplexity. The dogs also halted, panting with their tongues hanging out, appearing tense and wary.

"Ah, so now you are devoted to the cause of chivalry, are you, knight?" she taunted, meeting his gaze boldly. "What has happened to the vengeful warrior who threatened me last eve?"

Niccolo shrugged. "I was merely angered by your uncle's trickery, as were all the others when they first arrived."

"Yea, but the others did not menace me as you did."

Niccolo felt irritation rising at the princess's skilled goading. "We already spoke of this when we broke our fast. Why do you belabor the subject? I am really not so terrible a fellow." To demonstrate, he reached out to pet the nearest hound, and both dogs growled, baring huge, sharp teeth.

Aurora giggled. "Take care, knight. Bruno and Bink are fiercely protective of me."

"So I see," he replied grimly. Despite the threat from the hounds, Niccolo kept his hand steady while boldly holding Aurora's gaze. "They will soon discover they have nothing to fear from me, that I, too, am here to protect you, Princess—to prove myself your champion and win your hand."

And with the princess looking on in wonderment, the dogs ceased their growling and approached Niccolo. He petted both and grinned his triumph.

Aurora slowly shook her head. "You have a treacherous way about you, knight. 'Tis in your words . . . and in your touch."

At the unconscious invitation in her voice, Niccolo glanced at her intently and moved closer. He caught a whiff of her intoxicating scent, and wondered if she bathed in jasmine and rose petals. A tantalizing image arose, of bathing her himself in nature's potpourri, caressing her ripe nipples until they puckered, touching her everywhere, and afterward taking her to his bed, rubbing her down with almond oil, and then . . .

Wrenching himself from his decadent thoughts, he stared lazily into her dark eyes. "How do you know about my touch, Princess?" he whispered.

She must have seen the wanton images swirling in his thoughts, in his eyes. For once, the self-possessed lady became flustered. Color flooded her cheeks and her gaze darted away from his. "I—I am speaking of your way with the dogs."

"I have a way with ladies, as well," he murmured huskily.

"No doubt," she agreed, her voice quivering.

He edged even closer, and boldly gripped her chin with his fingertips, tilting her flushed face toward his.

He felt greatly pleased by the widening of her eyes, her rapid intake of breath. "Shall I demonstrate, milady?"

Appearing extremely discomfited, she backed away from his touch. "I—I must return to the keep."

He touched her arm. "Are you afraid to be alone with me, Princess?"

Her eyes focused on his huge hand, she proudly denied, "Nay!"

"Then tarry a moment, pray."

"Why?" she demanded.

Releasing her arm, he said casually, "I would have you walk with me. I would know more of your situation, Princess—if I am to help you defeat your enemy."

Chewing her lower lip, she seemed to waver. Finally she nodded. "Very well. We will stroll about the bailey for a time. But bear in mind I must meet with my seneschal and constable ere long."

"I promise to release you shortly, Princess," he replied with mock gallantry.

They roamed the bailey, laughing at the antics of a peasant chasing a pig, watching children play with balls and sticks, strolling beside furrows where serfs were busily planting vegetables and grains. They neared the front walls of the fortress, where the sounds of the ram and the catapults boomed out.

"What would you know, knight?" asked Aurora. She gestured toward the battlements above them, where several archers were busily shooting off arrows. "Everything is here for you to see."

"*Sì*, I went to the parapets this morn—'twas not a pretty sight."

"I would expect war never is," she concurred.

He took her elbow and led her away from the clamor. "How long has this conflict been going on?"

"For the past two winters."

"And it began when you refused King Basil's hand in marriage?"

She nodded. "Basil and I were once childhood friends, years ago when our kingdoms were at peace. He was a shy lad, not handsome, but with a pleasing manner. We used to go hawking together, and he taught me how to catch fish in a basket, to hunt with a bow and arrow. But when he grew to manhood, becoming Crown Prince, then King, of Ravenia, the power intoxicated him. He became arrogant, his manner toward me aggressive and unseemly. Where before he had been homely, his belligerence made him repellent to me. I began to regret ever having been his friend. When I tried to avoid his company, he grew more obstinate than ever, often riding up to the castle uninvited, and demanding I receive him." She caught a deep breath. "The crisis between us occurred two years past, when a malady took my dear parents—"

"My sympathies, Princess," Niccolo interjected gravely.

"Thank you." Her gaze darkened with turmoil. " 'Twas then, when I was so consumed by my grief, that Basil decided we should wed and combine our two kingdoms under one rule. I was opposed to his scheme from the outset, for I knew his design would have desecrated the memory of my parents, who wanted nothing more than for Falconia to remain a free state. Nevertheless, Basil was determined to win my hand and join our two countries. As much as I tried to discourage him, he stubbornly continued to court me, and tried to convince my uncle to choose him as my prince."

"Obviously Artemas was not persuaded," remarked Niccolo wryly. "Indeed, the count seems to have extreme difficulty in making up his mind."

She glanced askance at him.

"And what of you, Princess?" he pursued. "Considering the consequences and everything at stake, why did you not simply accept Basil's hand to save yourself from this war? You could not have found him that repulsive."

She drew a heavy breath. "Ah, but I did. Basil was a most unappealing suitor. You see, his wit is slow, his breath foul, his manner crude. At times he belches and farts worse than a pig."

Niccolo laughed heartily, totally unprepared for such coarse, outspoken descriptions from a lady. Despite himself, he felt charmed by her spirit. "So he displeases you mightily. Tell me, is his character as vile as his manly form?"

She shrugged. "Basil is not really an evil man . . . only a man who had the misfortune to fall in love with me."

Misfortune indeed, thought Niccolo, while plotting a way to use the information to his benefit. Aloud he mused, "Still, I must question your reluctance, Princess, given all you have suffered . . ."

"You mean you wonder why I would not sacrifice myself to save my kingdom?" she inquired rather defensively.

"Sì."

She thrust her chin high. "Then I will tell you, knight. I shall not wed Basil because I *will* not wed for less than true love alone."

Niccolo scowled at the haughty princess, mightily intrigued by her unexpected though fervent declaration, and the determined set of her features. He also quickly realized her stance was contradictory. "You say that, Princess, and yet you have offered your hand to the knight who proves himself your champion."

A coy look softened her features. "Yea, because I have learned my champion will *be* my one true love."

Niccolo was puzzled. "How can you know that, Princess?"

She tossed her curls. "I shall not say. I have no ob-

ligation to tell you the secrets of my heart. I have revealed enough to you already, knight. To disclose
more will give you unfair advantage over the others.
'Tis your task to conjure the rest.''

  And so I shall, thought Niccolo darkly.

So the princess naively believed the greatest knight
would be her true love? He could not believe his own
good fortune! Would it be so easy to beguile her—
simply by proving himself the most ferocious in battle? This he could easily accomplish ... and then her
defeat would be ensured! She *would* be like a lamb to
his slaughter. Furthermore, he could think of no
greater revenge than to ransom her to the enemy who
so repulsed her!

"Are you finished with your questioning now,
knight?" she continued impatiently, tapping her slippered foot. "I must meet with my retainers."

"I am hardly finished with *you*, Princess," he teased
back.

She sharply sucked in her breath. Watching a pout
pucker her lovely mouth, even as color again bloomed
in her cheeks, Niccolo found himself unexpectedly
tempted to grab and kiss her. 'Twas unnerving to feel
the potent urge that might distract him from his true
purpose.

He quickly steered the subject to safer ground. "Before you leave, Princess, I would know why you have
not acquired more advanced weaponry—cannon and
pistols, gunpowder and petards."

"We are not a wealthy kingdom."

"So you have informed me. But have you not rents
you have collected, some sort of state treasury you
can use for war matériel? With a few cannon and
some loads of Greek fire, I could make quick work of
those dimwits trying to scale your walls."

"What is Greek fire?" she asked.

" 'Tis expelled through tubes and explodes when it
hits the enemy," he explained. "When I fought the

Turks in the Black Sea, our Venetian fleet decimated several of their galleys through use of it and the cannon—though we were too late to save Constantinople. Still, 'twas satisfying to watch the Turks roast alive on their galleys."

Her mouth fell open. "You would use such devices on Basil and his knights?"

His smile was pitiless. "Gladly, Princess."

"Would it not be cruel to so abuse them?"

Annoyed by her naïveté, he grasped her by the shoulders. "Cruel?" he asked in disbelief. "What do you think warfare is about, Princess? 'Tis about *winning*—and have no doubt that I shall!"

For a moment both were silent, staring at each other tensely, reeling with the force of Niccolo's intentional double meaning.

Then the princess spoke through gritted teeth, albeit a telltale flutter revealed her agitation. "Release me, knight."

He at once dropped his hands to his sides, but spoke obdurately. "Consult with your seneschal. With a suitable sum, we can dispatch a patrol to Venice or Milan, to buy cannon and gunpowder."

"Nay, we shall not," she denied scornfully. "I have no interest in such wholesale slaughter of the enemy forces."

"Then you have made this war into a game, Princess," he retorted in disgust.

"And you take this war on too personal a level, knight."

"Indeed I do," Niccolo replied fiercely. "I take this war, and the actions of your uncle, most personally. And you had best remember that your little game is over now, Princess. With or without your cooperation, I intend to win."

For a moment Aurora angrily confronted his determined visage. Then, her own mien proud, she turned and walked away.

Niccolo stood staring after her with fists clenched. He cursed himself as he realized he had given away far more than he had intended, and he blamed the princess for stirring such passions in him. He was a man accustomed to icy self-control, and he knew losing that tight rein on his emotions could well impede his goals. Indeed, when he had been close to Aurora, touching her, 'twas all he could do not to haul her close and kiss that pout off her ripe red lips. He had even allowed himself to succumb to sensual images of bathing her and taking her to his bed! How could he even imagine pampering the treacherous creature who had put him in this dire predicament in the first place? He could not afford to succumb to tender images that might well weaken his resolve for revenge. He must concentrate only on causing her pain, on leaving her as devastated as he had once felt at the hands of his cruel wife.

The princess was a temptress, and also too willful for her own good, he decided darkly. But she had met her match in him. From now on, he would be forever on his guard. He would redouble his efforts and not be dissuaded from his plans until he ruined her . . .

Aurora rushed up the steps to the keep, not daring to look back at Niccolo. His demands had provoked and unsettled her; his touch had stoked fierce yearnings inside her.

He could not be her one true love, for he was ruthless and bloodthirsty in the extreme! He would roast her enemies alive in Greek fire—he would clearly resort to *anything* to defeat her adversaries and win her hand. There was surely no love or tenderness in such a man—he would bring her naught but grief!

And yet, if Niccolo was not her true love, why did his nearness stoke such potent yearnings in her? He exuded such incredible power and virility; the intensity in his bright eyes all but left her gasping. When he had touched her, she had trembled, her pulse racing. When they had argued, her voice had quivered, her insides had quaked. She had even hungered to have him take her in those strong arms and slant that hard, ruthless mouth over her soft lips, even knowing he was strong and violent enough to break her in two. To her shame, the aura of danger he exuded only excited her all the more. Indeed, never before had she responded to *any* man in such a wanton manner!

Niccolo Campioni frightened her. She knew he had the power to destroy her. And yet she felt inexorably drawn to him.

ELEVEN

THE SIEGERS WERE REPELLED BEFORE SUNSET, WHEN A sudden, chilling rain drenched their enthusiasm and made the prospect of scaling the walls treacherous at best. That night when Niccolo joined the others for the meal in the great hall, he found the atmosphere festive. A huge fire snapped and crackled in the open grate, taking the damp and chill off the room. Minstrels circulated, strumming lutes or harps and singing ballads; stewards bore silver trays laden with boars' heads and pheasants cooked in their own feathers, colorful dishes prepared mainly to feast the eyes.

Niccolo sat with the knights at their long table, sharing his wine goblet and soup tureen with the royal constable, Sir Ignatius. Before the meal, Sir Galen had introduced Niccolo to the obsequious little man with gray, bushy eyebrows, large nose, prominent wart on one cheek, shifty dark eyes, and sly smile. Niccolo already disliked the fellow, who had babbled at length about how untrustworthy peasants were, how he had caught them stealing flour from the larder and hay from the royal stores. Niccolo sensed the constable pontificated regarding the sins of others in order to cover his own vices.

The table where Niccolo sat was filled with both the princess's men-at-arms and the six knights dispatched by her uncle. The lavish meal included copious amounts of wine, a pheasant brewet, fish soup, and a main course of leg of lamb with braised vegetables.

On the royal dais, beneath a brilliant tapestry picturing knights battling fire-breathing dragons, were seated members of Aurora's royal staff—priest, seneschal, bailiff, physician, and three ladies-in-waiting. Aurora had moved to her throne chair at the edge of her dais and sat with the hounds dozing at her feet. Sipping wine from a bejeweled chalice and occasionally sampling a plum, an almond, or a bit of lamb proffered by one of the stewards, she watched the activities in the hall with eyes alight with wonder. Near the princess, one of the jongleurs had paused to sing a picaresque ballad, and several pages-turned-acrobats were doing handsprings, leaps, or rolls for their lady's diversion. The princess laughed gaily and clapped her hands when two of the lads collided while attempting a double tumble.

As the embarrassed pages retired, the jongleur, a handsome, bearded fellow in tights, velvet tunic, and plumed hat, strolled even closer to the dais to ply the princess with song. Several of the knights scowled as the man paused before Aurora, knelt on one knee, and soulfully sang:

"I sing to the glory of my lady fair,
To win her smile is my most fervent prayer."

Watching Aurora beam at the minstrel at the conclusion of his song, Sir Edgar stood and cleared his throat. "Milady," he called sternly, "methinks your troubadour oversteps his place."

The minstrel, appearing taken aback, quickly retired to the side of the hall. Aurora smiled at Edgar. "If you think the troubadour too bold, milord, why do you not best him by plying me with verse yourself?"

As several knights chuckled, hot color stole up Sir Edgar's fair face. Nonetheless, he appeared rather pleased, and bowed from the waist. "Milady, 'twould be my honor."

"Then by all means, come forward," urged Aurora.

Edgar was striding toward the dais when Sir Olaf popped up, a scowl creasing his rough-hewn features. "Milady, 'tis not fair."

As Sir Edgar paused to hear the exchange, Aurora asked patiently, "What is not fair, Sir Olaf?"

Olaf gestured to the other men. "You promised all six of us an equal contest, both in the field and to win your heart. But now you allow the Englishman to court you first."

Impishness gleamed in the princess's lovely, dark eyes. "You have made a sound point, sir Viking. Why do you not draw lots, then, for the privilege of paying court to me?" Dimpling prettily, she glanced at Sir Edgar, who appeared perplexed. "Is that agreeable, sir knight?"

At first Edgar glowered at the others who had dared to interfere with his amorous pursuits. Then, as his innate chivalry won out, he nodded resignedly. "Yea, milady. We shall draw straws, and let the man with the longest length be first, the shortest be last."

"Yea, that is eminently fair," agreed Aurora.

Niccolo watched with ill humor as Sir Edgar strode back to the table. Leaning over and plucking a few rushes from the floor, he broke off bits of straw and extended them to the others, who quickly drew lots. When offered his pick, Niccolo merely shook his head. The others tensely compared their lengths. Realizing he had drawn the longest straw, Sir Baldric leaped up, shouting his triumph and waving a fist. With his companions watching in dour silence, the Hun stepped forward before the royal dais, dipped to one knee, and soulfully pronounced:

"My every thought is of my lady's face,
I would die content would she look on me with
     grace."

All of Aurora's ladies sighed ecstatically, and Aurora appeared so charmed that Niccolo could have
sworn he heard a tiny "Ah!" escape her, a sound that
had him irrationally grinding his teeth. Then the princess whispered something to the Hun and held out
her hand to him. Grinning his triumph from ear to
ear, Sir Baldric gently took Aurora's hand and slowly
kissed her fingers, while the other knights watched in
smoldering silence.

Niccolo drummed his fingertips on the tabletop.

After Sir Baldric retired, Sir Cesare, who had come
in second in the drawing of lots, came forward to bow
before Aurora with hand over his heart, and soulfully
intoned his own courtly lines:

"Milady's beauty is sublime and grand,
I would know a thousand torments just to touch
     her hand."

Niccolo groaned, watching Aurora regally extend
that same coveted hand, watching the despised Genoan kiss it. Oh, the little coquette! he thought darkly.
She was every bit as shameless as Cecilia had been!
Feeling his gut rumble, he frowned. What was this
bile boiling up in him? It could not be jealousy! He
had once allowed his own feelings to defeat him, and
he would never again allow this to happen!

At his side, the constable smiled slyly and spoke
behind his gnarled fingers. "Sir Niccolo, you seem to
be missing an opportunity here. Were I you, I would
be wooing the lady with the others."

Niccolo sneered at the man. "I do not play such
games."

Sir Ignatius raised a bushy brow. "Games, signore?
Then you do not fear being outmatched?"

Niccolo shrugged, but his gaze was hard as he watched Sir Gilbert go forward to ply the princess with verse. "The others are no competition."

"Verily?" queried the constable. "Even though they are all winning the princess's smiles?"

Observing the lady's latest smirk, Niccolo retorted with asperity, "She shall still wed her champion. And there has never been a doubt as to *that* man's identity."

Although the constable's expression was droll, he merely lifted the cloth to wipe his thin lips and did not attempt to argue further. Several more knights came forward to woo Aurora with flowery compliments, a few of her own men-at-arms joining in the fun. Aurora laughed gaily and flirted with each suitor, whispering secret encouragements or batting her eyelashes at the giddy cavaliers, while Niccolo sat silent, brooding, again wondering why the sight of the princess playing queen of the May should put him in such a foul temper . . .

Presently everyone became distracted as a horn blew and a page stepped forward to call out, "Harken, all! Sir Christian has returned."

Niccolo turned with the others to watch a tall, slender young man enter the room. The lad possessed a long face with handsome, sharply etched features, and thick, dark blond hair that was cropped neatly about his jaw. Wearing a forest green tunic, tan hose, soft leather boots, and a cloth cap, he bore a fierce-looking falcon on his wrist, its bells jingling as he moved. He was followed by a band of at least twelve men who were ill kempt and coarsely dressed, and appeared to be peasants.

Aurora's reaction was amazing to behold. Joy lit her eyes, and a happy cry escaped her lips. Even though Sir Galen was bent over her, kissing her hand, she bounded off the throne and down the dais, rushing over to the young man.

"Christian! You are safely home!" she cried, hugging him, while the falcon screeched and flew off to its perch on the royal dais.

Christian grinned at his half sister. "I am pleased to see you are well, sister, and have not suffered overly from the continuing siege." He gestured toward his company. "All of these fine men have volunteered to help you defeat Basil. I have offered each a small benefice in exchange for his service to the crown in our hour of need."

Aurora turned to the peasants, all of whom were eyeing her, awestruck. "Welcome to Falconia Castle, men. You will all be well cared for in appreciation of your efforts."

Niccolo watched as, one by one, the bedazzled velleins came forward to pledge their fealty to the princess, bowing before her, placing their hands between hers, and repeating their oath of loyalty. Once the formalities were done, Aurora summoned Sir Galen to escort her new men-at-arms to the barracks. She then took Christian's hand and led him to the knights' table.

"Brother, two more knights have arrived since your departure to raise forces." She gestured toward Niccolo and the Genoan. "I present Sir Niccolo of Venice and Sir Cesare of Genoa." Ruefully she finished, "Both were dispatched by our enterprising uncle, and have agreed to join our cause."

Christian nodded soberly to each man. Returning the greeting, Niccolo noted that Christian shared his sister's fair skin and dark brown eyes.

"Welcome to Falconia, knights," Christian said. "As I am certain my sister has already done, I must apologize for my uncle's perfidy in bringing you here. But you have undertaken a most noble mission, and I praise you for your chivalry and courage."

"We are happy to serve our lady," said the Genoan gallantly.

An awkward silence fell as all waited for Niccolo's response. At last he said in measured tones, "We are here, and will be of what service we can."

"Splendid," replied Christian.

By now, Aurora's ladies had moved over to join the others. The flaxen-haired Lady Flora eyed Christian wistfully. "Sir Christian, pray sit and break bread with us. You must be famished following your long journey."

Christian bowed before the pretty lady. "I am amply refreshed just to feast my eyes on your lovely countenance, Lady Flora."

Flora glowed with happiness, and behind her, Lady Violet and Lady Iris tittered.

Christian, Aurora, and her ladies joined the knights at their table, Christian sitting between his sister and Lady Flora, who continued to eye him with longing. Christian said grace before breaking his bread, then regaled all with tales of his exploits along the countryside, relating how he had prevailed in a nasty encounter with a wild boar, and had also triumphed in a brush with two of Basil's knights. "We locked swords in a small copse, and I would have brought back the scoundrels for ransom except they fled like cowards," he explained.

Amid appreciative murmurs from the others, Niccolo asked, "Why did you not pursue and slay them, Sir Christian?"

An audible gasp rippled over the table, and Christian stared at Niccolo in perplexity. "But, sir knight, 'tis not chivalrous to slay an enemy, even one who proves himself craven."

"Sì, but 'tis expedient," replied Niccolo.

A hush fell over the gathering, the tension relieved when Lady Flora smiled at Christian and encouraged, "Pray, tell us more about how you gathered your forces."

Christian nodded eagerly. "I chose one poor fellow

because he was a strong woodsman. But when his wife learned he would serve the royal cause, she chased us both with his ax."

Mirth rocked the table.

"Oh, milord, how terrible for you," sympathized Lady Flora.

Christian only shrugged. "Actually, 'twas amusing to see the female charging about like an enraged badger. Then another peasant vowed he would gladly cut off his hand to serve our princess." He winked at his sister. "The man's goodwife said, 'Take his worthless hand! I'll boil up the rest of him for supper.' "

Amid additional merriment, even Niccolo found himself feeling grudgingly amused by Christian's exploits. The wine flowed freely as the lad continued to enthrall everyone with his lively tales. Aurora appeared so fascinated by her brother's yarns, her expression so raptly innocent, that Niccolo again felt his gut clenching at what he planned to do to her.

Frustration raged within him, anger at himself for once again allowing her feminine wiles to affect him so. He could not afford to be fooled by her as he had been by Cecilia!

Yet how could she appear so guileless when he knew her to be so guilty?

Christian exuded that same lack of corruption, he noted. Niccolo beheld the young man, so full of high thoughts, chivalry, and joie de vivre, and felt a tightening in his chest as he recalled his own former self at Christian's tender age, and thought of all he had lost . . .

TWELVE

Later that night, Aurora and Christian strolled the allure behind the parapets, looking out at the misty forests and mountains of their kingdom, the wan lights of the small village of Osprey nestled in a dusky hollow. A sentry stepped back and saluted them as they passed along the high passageway, which had been a lifelong favorite haunt of both siblings.

"I am so relieved to see you safely home, brother," Aurora said feelingly. "When you go on your forays into the countryside, I never know if you will return to us. And Lady Flora fretted overly for your welfare."

"Did she, now?" he asked, grinning his pleasure. "Certainly I regret causing you or her the slightest worry. Both of you must remember that I shall always return, for we have right on our side. Besides, gathering more men-at-arms was a necessity, if we are to defeat Basil."

Aurora sighed, her expression turbulent as she remembered her discussion of the ongoing war with Niccolo earlier that day. "Sometimes I wonder if I should not simply give myself over to Basil, and end this travail for us all."

Christian stopped in his tracks, touching Aurora's

106

arm. In a hoarse whisper he urged, "Sister, no, you must never think that! Were you to do so, you would surely succumb to the curse!"

Morosely Aurora nodded. Although much of Falconia knew about, and feared, the curse, dreaded even speaking of it, Aurora was careful to discuss her onerous legacy only with three living souls—Christian, Flora, and Uncle Artemas. Fatalistically she remarked, "I shall likely succumb to it no matter what I do, brother, and we both know it."

He sighed heavily. "I do not agree. In any event, you should do nothing to hasten your own death. If we take care, there is always a chance for you."

She smiled at him. "You are forever the hopeful one, are you not, Christian? I remember how, even when we were children, you were always nursing wounded animals or trying to revive drooping daffodils. Sometimes I wish I did not have to take a prince at all, that you could rule in my stead."

"We both know I cannot," he replied, "for I do not carry your father's royal blood."

"And not having royal blood, neither do you carry the burden of the curse," she replied.

He eyed her with concern. "What has brought about all this dire talk? Was it Uncle Artemas sending you so many suitors?"

She laughed. "With his usual wily genius, our uncle has placed me in a precarious position, to say the least."

"Indeed he has," agreed Christian with a scowl. "How has it gone, with all the knights vying for you?"

"Actually, the prospective bridegrooms have continued to prove helpful in repelling Basil's forces, as well as a pleasant diversion for me." Dimpling, she admitted, "Tonight I had them all playing troubadour, worshiping me with poem and song."

Christian chuckled. "You always were skilled at playing the coquette, sister."

More seriously she replied, "Yea, and we are both well aware of why I must be so elusive."

Christian nodded soberly. "What of these last two Uncle Artemas has dispatched from the Italian city states? What do you think of them?"

"The Genoan seems of noble birth and respectable character. But the Venetian . . ." She paused to shudder.

"Ah, so you have noticed it as well, sister. He seems unchivalrous, to say the least."

Aurora fell silent, remembering how Sir Niccolo had merely watched the others tonight instead of courting her himself, recalling how his blue eyes had smoldered with an emotion she could not quite name. She could not deny that she had felt disappointed by his aloofness.

"Yea, I fear you are right," she admitted heavily. "Sir Niccolo may well be unscrupulous. For one thing, he has no faith."

Christian's mouth dropped open. "A devil knight? Then why do you allow him to linger here?"

"I am not certain," she confessed. "Mayhap I need a man who is ruthless like him to defeat Basil."

"Ruthless, he seems," agreed Christian. "But how do you know he will not turn his savagery on you?"

She laughed. "I have developed a strategy to prevent that from happening."

"You have?"

"Indeed, the spirits have helped me."

As another sentry marched past, Christian pulled Aurora aside and tensely motioned for her to be silent. Once the man was out of earshot, he whispered urgently, "Sister, take care when you speak of the spirits! You know how superstitious all Falconians are! I shudder at the prospect of seeing you damned a heretic or burned as a witch."

She flashed him an apologetic look. "You are a loyal brother to believe the spirits exist, when only I have heard them."

He regarded her solemnly. "Well, I may not have heard the specters, but I am acquainted with the gnomes—indeed, we encountered Francis and his troupe hammering rocks on the hillside not far from the castle. They frightened your poor peasant volunteers half out of their wits."

Aurora giggled.

"Thus, sister, I am quite aware that not everything in our mystical little kingdom can be readily explained," Christian confessed with rueful humor.

"Verily, I am still surprised you do not consider it your moral duty to turn me over to the judgment of the Church," she teased.

He paled, then quickly crossed himself. "Aurora, you must know I would never divulge your secrets. I would sooner die myself. I have always believed in the spirits . . . and believed in the curse." He forced a smile. "Now tell me what the spirits have done to ensure this Venetian does not betray you."

She drew a heavy breath. "The spirits have suggested a contest for the knights. They have told me that the one who proves himself my greatest champion in battle will be my true love. Thus I have challenged all six of the knights, and they have taken up the gauntlet."

"You have agreed to wed the greatest knight?" he demanded in horrified tones.

"Yea. And you must assist me, brother. I need you to observe them all carefully in battle to help me determine who is the greatest."

Christian was blinking rapidly in betrayal of his distress. "Dear God, sister, what if you choose wrongly? You will have signed your own death warrant!''

Aurora stared out at the countryside, at the loveliness of the velvety night enfolding the dusky forest and the gleaming Alpine passes. She turned back to Christian, her eyes luminous with tears. ''Sometimes I think you are right, Christian, that 'twould be better if I never wed.'' She shivered with emotion. ''But then I think, to never know love, never suckle a babe at my breast, never even try to free my poor, doomed ancestors . . . That seems a much greater sacrilege.''

''Oh, sister.'' Christian gently hugged her, his voice cracking with emotion. ''You were always such a brave, noble girl, placing the good of others above your own welfare. But I fear your courage and self-sacrifice may prove your undoing.''

She pulled back to stare up at him searchingly. '' 'Tis wrong to be brave and noble, brother?''

'' 'Tis wrong to let your bravado make you foolhardy,'' he admonished. ''What if this Venetian proves himself your champion? You will be bound by your word to wed him—and you will surely die for it!''

Regarding her brother's impassioned face, Aurora bit her lip. ''Think you he is the wrong one?''

''We both know he is, sister!''

They fell silent. Aurora again stared out at the night, wondering if her half brother had spoken the truth. Logic argued that Christian was right. She remembered walking with Niccolo in the courtyard today, how even when he had tried to woo her, his manner had also put a shiver down her spine—his ruthlessness, his remoteness, the aura of danger he radiated. She remembered him tonight—remaining at the table, regarding her with such arrogant conceit, refusing to ply her with verse as had her other suitors. And her captain-at-arms, Sir Galen, had told her how

Sir Niccolo had cruelly kicked two siegers from the parapets today.

She shuddered to think how such a man might behave as her husband. There would be no tenderness in him, no mercy. He would likely attack the marriage bed as he had charged the quintain, riding roughshod over her body, her feelings, her pride.

And yet as much as she felt leery of Sir Niccolo, she could not deny that he stirred feelings in her—especially today, when his large hands had gripped her shoulders, when his brilliant blue eyes had probed straight through her. He was virile, unmanageable, merciless. As Christian had said, a devil knight. Aurora was accustomed to controlling the men around her, just as she had skillfully manipulated most of the knights this eve. But Niccolo Campioni was a man she could never control, and yet 'twas perhaps his untamed quality that excited her most of all.

How could she feel so frightened, so daunted by him, and still crave him so much? She realized Christian was right. If Signore Niccolo Campioni proved himself her champion, her own cause might well be lost . . .

THIRTEEN

Niccolo fell into a routine at the castle. He arose before dawn and broke his fast with the other knights in the great hall. By the time the knights were finishing their meal, the bang of the battering ram could be heard at the front of the castle. The warriors, save for Niccolo, would dash off to mass while Niccolo would go directly to the parapets to help the Royal Guardsmen repel the siegers.

At nightfall, after Basil's forces fled, Niccolo joined the others in the great hall as they courted the princess. He watched with a jaundiced eye as his competitors made fools of themselves, wooing the princess with flowery verses and extravagant compliments.

Certainly Niccolo was forever charming while in Aurora's presence, but he refused to grovel before her as did his comrades. On one occasion when the Genoan, Sir Cesare, knelt to kiss the rushes as the princess passed, it was all Niccolo could do not to burst out in scornful laughter.

The princess herself obviously relished being the object of so much male adulation, and she preened nightly up on her dais like a lazy, content cat. To Niccolo's irritation, Aurora began to invite one or two knights to share the dais with her during supper, and

he grew even more affronted when it became apparent she would not invite him. If Aurora noticed his
agitation, she gave no sign as she gaily flirted, toyed,
and laughed with the others. Niccolo's humor grew
increasingly dour as Aurora's coquettish behavior
continued to remind him of another conniving female—his cruel departed wife. Yet even though he
was wise to Aurora's wiles, he still found he lusted
after her, longing to seduce and master her, to compel
her to shine the bright sunshine of those dazzling
smiles on him alone. He continued to fear his desires
would defeat him, weakening his own resolve.

He did chuckle one evening during dinner when
the seneschal ushered in a tall Spanish knight. The
handsome Castilian entered the chamber in full plate
armor and bearing his shield with the red coat of arms
of the Order of Calatrava. Behind him strode a squire
bearing an ornate, heavily carved bronze chest whose
sides were emblazoned with oil paintings depicting
scenes of courtly love.

"I present Don Rafael of Spain," announced Mortimer.

The gathering grew hushed, the others watching
with interest as the man awkwardly crossed the room,
his armor creaking. Waiting until his squire set the
fabulous chest down on the dais near Aurora's feet,
the Spaniard knelt before the princess with a loud
squeak of hinges.

Dramatically the newcomer intoned, "Milady, I am
Don Rafael of Castile, grand master of the Order of
Calatrava established by our magnificent King Sancho
III. I have distinguished myself in battle against the
Moors in the name of our honorable King Henry. I
bring you tribute, milady, a bride's chest made by our
finest artisans in Seville. I come to rescue you from
your enemies, and to claim your hand in marriage."

As snickers erupted in the background, the Spanish
knight glanced toward the knights' table in bemuse-

ment. Fighting laughter, Aurora replied, "Greetings, sir knight, and welcome to Falconia Castle. I thank you for your fabulous gift. Although your countenance is unknown to me, I must wonder why your words sound so familiar."

A split second later, the dignified Castilian was left to glower as all of the knights roared with laughter, while Aurora and her ladies giggled. Even Niccolo found himself chuckling.

Don Rafael rose with as much dignity as possible given his badly creaking armor, and glared formidably at the knights. "Who are these boors daring to make jest of my valor?"

"We do not make light of your courage, sir knight," called out Sir Edgar, "but rather, we question your sagacity."

"And our own," added Sir Gilbert.

The newcomer frowned. "What is the meaning of your mockery, señores?"

"You have just been admitted to the Order of the Witless," answered Sir Olaf.

"Yea, the Witless and the Bedazzled," put in a grinning Sir Baldric.

In alarm, the Spaniard turned back to Aurora. "Princess, I demand an explanation. Who are these dimwits and why are they ridiculing me?"

Aurora's dark eyes sparkled with merriment. "Sir knight, I think I shall allow the dimwits to explain for themselves."

Don Rafael turned back to the knights and glared. "Pray explain, señores, before I challenge the lot of you!"

Edgar spoke up. "I am afraid, señor, that you have become betrothed to a lady who already suffers from an wealth of potential bridegrooms."

"A wealth of bridegrooms?" gasped the Castilian.

"Yea, and a dearth of the dowry you have been promised," answered Sir Gilbert.

With the knights continuing their jocularity, the Spaniard appeared predictably mystified. During the long, confused discussion that followed, Niccolo observed largely a repeat performance of his own first moments at the castle, with Don Rafael first learning the details of Artemas's intrigue, then railing out at his fate, and finally grudgingly accepting his plight and agreeing to join in on the contest. Aurora assuaged Don Rafael's wounded pride when she invited him to join her on the royal dais and again lavishly praised the gift he had brought.

Watching her cajole and tease the Spaniard, batting her eyelashes and offering him wafers and wine, Niccolo was not amused. Thus the knights vying for Aurora rose from six to seven.

Niccolo's biggest frustration became his lack of opportunities to maneuver Aurora off alone. He remained determined to seduce and ruin her, to ransom her to Basil if possible, but he knew of no way to accomplish his designs as long as she was surrounded by so many knights.

He did notice she disappeared for long periods each day. Observing that after the morning meal, she normally returned to her solar, he tried to track her. But he was able to follow her to the doors of the royal chamber only once, as two sentries barred his way and gruffly questioned him regarding his business. When he told them he was inspecting the keep for vulnerable points, they reluctantly accepted his explanation and sent him on his way. But given the vigilance of the guards, he knew he could not venture upstairs again without arousing undue suspicion.

Niccolo wondered how Aurora spent her days; he doubted she languished away in her solar, since she did not seem the subdued, retiring type who might spend hours spinning or embroidering, praying or reading a book. He began to wonder if she did not leave the castle at times, and this possibility intrigued him. When he was not occupied with the siege, he roamed the grounds hoping to catch a glimpse of her, and he also explored the bowels of the keep, wending his way through dark, cold subterranean corridors past the dungeons and stores, the kitchen and well, searching for a secret passageway or sally port that the princess might use to leave the keep in secret.

Finally, one afternoon, outside one of the dungeons, he was groping his way down a clammy stone passageway when he found a wooden wall panel where no door should be. Setting his torch in a wall bracket, he rubbed his palms all about the inset until he released a spring clasp. Creaking back the heavy door, he retrieved his torch and illuminated a long, narrow passageway. He grew elated. He had found the sally port!

Ducking down, Niccolo started down the dank corridor, which was smelly and slippery, covered with a nauseating layer of wet slime. He kicked at mice and rats that scampered across his path. Finally he reached the end of the tortuous passage and spotted a door. Then he spied a motion—

The end panel was creaking open!

Niccolo ducked back behind the door and doused his torch in the slime. Motionless, barely breathing, he stood pressed against the wall as a furtive figure entered the passage, the person also bearing a torch. Was it Aurora?

Nay, 'twas her constable, Sir Ignatius! Niccolo at once recognized the little man's bearded face, his hunched shoulders, his traditional black robe and matching cap.

But why was the man here?

Squinting into the darkness, Ignatius stepped stealthily inside, shut the panel, and then started off cautiously for the dungeons.

Expelling a relieved breath, Niccolo decided not to follow the constable. Instead, he groped in the darkness until he found and opened the panel Ignatius had just shut. Thin spikes of sunshine threaded their way into the dank cavern. Flinging open the door, Niccolo stepped outside and climbed lichen encrusted steps, pausing behind a large hawthorn bush at the top that had obviously been planted to shield the exit. Hearing the shuffling sounds of a sentry passing above him on the parapets, he hesitated until the footsteps faded away. Then he emerged from behind the bush and crossed over into the forest, blinking at the bright sunshine that filtered down through the trees and taking deep breaths of the crisp, bracing air.

He smiled in grim satisfaction. He had found the sally port, all right, and he suspected the princess knew about this secret exit, as well. Now he, too, had a way to leave the castle in stealth, mayhap even to journey to Ravenia and conspire with Basil.

Was that what Ignatius had been about? Was the princess's constable a traitor? Niccolo had suspected, ever since meeting the sly little man, that he was untrustworthy. Of course, since it was yet daytime, the siege still ongoing, the constable might have been stealing out of the castle on some business for the princess.

But Niccolo suspected otherwise, that Ignatius might well be conspiring with Aurora's enemies. He wondered why this possibility angered him, when he intended to betray her himself. He rationalized that he was surely annoyed because he wanted to be the man who engineered her defeat, and he would not allow some crafty constable to surpass him there.

He had best watch the man carefully, he decided. Indeed, if he caught Ignatius committing treason and turned him over to Aurora's justice, this would surely increase his esteem with the princess, would ensure

she would trust him. And after she came to trust him,
seducing and betraying her would become easy!

He would keep a trained eye on the sally port, mon-
itoring Ignatius's—and possibly Aurora's—comings
and goings.

FOURTEEN

Niccolo CONTINUED TO HAUNT THE NETHER REGIONS of the castle during his free moments. Twice again he spotted Ignatius coming in or out of the secret passage, but he did not follow the man, wanting instead to concentrate his efforts on waiting for Aurora to possibly appear in the subterranean chambers. He had reason to anticipate her presence there, for one day, closely examining the slime in the passageway, he thought he discerned the imprint of a woman's footsteps.

A week after he came to the Kingdom of Falconia, he at last made his breakthrough. He was in the cellar near the well when he heard footsteps. He snuffed out his torch and crouched behind the well. A moment later, he spied Aurora sweeping past him, her lit torch illuminating her smooth features.

Grinning in private triumph, Niccolo crept after her. As he could have predicted, she went directly to the entrance to the secret passageway, springing open the panel. He waited a moment, then entered the passage himself, groping through the darkness, following the distant pool of light from her torch.

He emerged outside soon after she did, and followed her from a safe distance. He watched her glide through the trees, the sunlight gleaming in her raven hair and the strands of gold that shot through her gossamer apricot silk gown.

Where was she going? To be alone? To meet a lover?

After a time, she paused beneath the branches of a birch tree, looking up and watching a willow warbler flit about from branch to branch. Then she began to whistle, to sing with the bird!

Niccolo felt stunned, enchanted despite himself. He tried to remember the last time he had paused to watch a bird cavort, and he could not. The realization saddened him.

He trailed Aurora as she continued on through the woodland. Then, to his mystification, she paused again—this time when a troupe of gnomes crossed her path! From the look of the quaint little fellows, 'twas the same band he had spied on the night he came to Falconia. Niccolo hid behind a tree and peered about the trunk to see. He shook his head in awe as Aurora chatted with the odd little men in their green jackets and yellow tights, their pointed hats and shoes. Studying the gnomes' backpacks, their picks and axes, bows and arrows, he again wondered what they were doing in the forest—and why Aurora was speaking with them. But the little men were obviously having a grand time visiting with the princess, from the sounds of their high voices and shrill laughter.

Finally Aurora parted company with the gnomes and continued on. She moved into a large copse, a sheltered grotto crossed by an Alpine stream and filled with vibrant wildflowers. Behind her, Niccolo stopped in his tracks and stared about him. The beauty of the bower unexpectedly enthralled him; the air was sweet with nectar, alive with the sounds of birds singing and bees buzzing about the flowers. Niccolo could not repress a grin as Aurora paused to pick several blooms and stick them in her hair. He observed her movements, entranced, as she ap-

proached a stone shrine with a bronze statue of the
Angel of Wisdom. Not far from its steps, she paused
as a small spotted fawn approached her. She knelt
and petted the little animal, which nuzzled her cheek.

A knot tightened in Niccolo's belly. He suddenly
felt like a terrible intruder, his resolve threatened. The
last thing he would have expected was to see Aurora
in a secret forest shrine petting a fawn. He was much
more intrigued, mesmerized, and moved by her than
he cared to admit.

After a moment, she arose, the fawn trailing behind
her, and went to kneel before the altar. She crossed
herself and fixed her hands in an attitude of prayer.
Niccolo thought he could hear her murmuring. Intrigued, he went to observe her from behind a nearby
tree.

Still, he could not make out her words! He perked
his ears, listened with all his might, and at last heard
her murmur, "Spirits, pray, give me an answer!"

That particular cue proved irresistible to Niccolo.
He stepped toward her and said solemnly, "I am here,
milady. Am I your answer?"

Aurora clambered to her feet and turned, her eyes
huge, her mouth falling open. Her little fawn went
wide-eyed, then bounded away.

"You!" she cried.

Grinning, Niccolo stepped toward her. "I have
shocked you, milady?"

"You have followed me!" she accused.

"*Sì*, of course I have," responded Niccolo arrogantly.

"You . . ." Gulping, she asked, "Then you found the
secret passageway?"

"You so conveniently led me to it, milady."

"Oh!" she exclaimed. "I have never heard of a more
dishonorable ploy!"

"Mayhap," Niccolo conceded, stepping closer to
her, "but I am not nearly as dishonorable as you are

reckless, Princess." He gestured about them. "You should not go off on your own this way, milady. Should Basil capture you, he would make quick work of your virtue, methinks."

Her eyes blazed with indignation. "You are crude, knight!"

He chuckled, shaking a finger at her. "And you, milady, are surely into mischief to venture out of the castle unguarded."

"I am not afraid!" she asserted, lifting her chin high. "Basil's knights fear these woods."

"Because of the dreaded gnomes?" he teased.

Her expression grew cautious, and her voice lowered an octave. "What do you know of the gnomes?"

"I observed you visiting with them along the trail," he replied.

She set her hands on her hips. "You spied on us!"

Niccolo fought laughter. "Of course I did. How else could I have followed you here? Though I must say I find your choice of companions peculiar."

"The gnomes are my friends and they protect me," she burst out.

"No doubt," he conceded drolly, glancing about them. "And are the odd little fellows here with you now?"

She waved a hand. "Certainly not. There are no gnomes here, as any dimwit can see."

"Then to whom were you just speaking?"

She paled.

Reveling in her discomfiture, Niccolo spoke in a low, deliberately suggestive tone. "Did you come here to meet a lover, milady?"

Aghast, she backed away from him. "Nay! I came here to meet no one!"

"Aha!" he cried. "Then I have caught you in a most telling admission. You were talking to no one . . . or do you converse with the dead?"

She eyed him warily. " 'Twould be heresy."

"*Sì*, so it would, milady." He pointed toward the statue. "And yet this is a shrine, is it not?"

"It is," she admitted cautiously.

"Are shrines not, generally speaking, holy places erected to honor the dead?"

"Yea," she answered warily.

"Then you were conversing with ghosts?"

Again she did not respond, twisting her fingers together and appearing terribly ill at ease.

Niccolo edged even closer to her. "Come now, milady. Either you were conversing with spirits, or you were talking to yourself. And that would be even worse."

"Would it?"

So close to her now that he could smell her sweet scent and see the gentle rise and fall of her bosom, Niccolo reached out and plucked a leaf from her hair, wondering at the silken smoothness of her raven tresses. Delighting to her bewildered look, he murmured, "*Sì*, 'twould make you a witch, milady."

She gasped, backing away.

He followed. "For that high crime, you would surely be burned. Especially if the superstitious Ospreyans should ever hear of your heresy—or even of your speaking with gnomes. The peasants would surely roast you ere nightfall. 'Twould be a pity, no?"

"Yea," she concurred solemnly, "especially for me."

Niccolo chuckled at her wry humor. Reaching out with his large hand, he cupped her jaw, fighting a wave of tenderness at the baby-softness of her skin. "Are you a witch, milady?"

He watched her dark eyes fill with turmoil, watched her lovely lips tremble. Just as he was ready to relent and stop ruthlessly tormenting her, she shoved his fingers away.

"How dare you threaten me, knight!" she raged, like a vengeful lioness. "I am princess here! I have the right of high justice, and I could order you beheaded! I could cut out your insolent tongue, and carve out your black heart!"

Niccolo whistled, amused by her show of bravado. "What crime have I committed, milady? And how can you blame me, without exposing your own greater guilt?"

He observed the stormy struggle on her face as she tried to deal with his outmaneuvering—something he guessed had not oft happened to this spoiled, spirited princess.

"Are you a witch, milady?" he pressed. "Surely you can confess your sins to me. After all, I have already seen you conversing with gnomes—evil little fellows who are greatly feared in these parts, I hear. 'Tis not so great a leap to speak with the dead, eh?"

She blinked at him angrily. "You are despicable, knight! I shall go now. You have insulted me quite enough. Do not dare follow me again, or I shall order you flogged!"

He grabbed her arm. "Not so quickly, milady. We must yet settle up accounts, you and I."

"What accounts?" she demanded, trying unsuccessfully to twist her arm free.

Niccolo grinned. "You must offer me an enticement to keep me from telling the others of your witchery."

In her outrage, she stamped her slippered foot. "Oh! I have never heard of such arrogance!"

"And you will not dissuade me with your tantrums," he continued confidently. "You are a witch, milady, and thus you have much more to fear from the man who knows your secrets than he has to fear from you."

That remark gave her pause. She eyed him narrowly, and at last asked, "What would you have?"

Eyeing her petulant face, her shapely bosom, which heaved slightly as she waited for his response, Niccolo was powerfully tempted to blurt out, *All of you. Now.* She looked so adorably indignant that he suddenly ached to seduce her, to sweep off that gossamer gown, to kiss the pout off those tempting lips, to suckle those lush breasts and bury his face in her silken hair. He was stunned by his own overwhelming desires. Certainly his goal was to ruin the princess, but he had never expected to anticipate the ravishment so much! What before had been an obsession for revenge now promised to be a journey of delight. This troubled him, for he feared any softening of his feelings might defeat his purpose.

Nonetheless, he flashed his most beguiling smile. "A kiss, milady," he whispered seductively. "I must have a kiss to keep my silence."

To his surprise, she did not protest, did not swoon in horror. Instead she eyed him boldly, her gaze traveling slowly up his body in a manner that made his loins harden painfully.

At last her impertinent gaze settled on his rigid mouth. She licked her bottom lip in an unconscious invitation that made Niccolo's blood roar, and murmured demurely, "Very well."

Niccolo was so stunned, so delighted, his heart unexpectedly soared. He felt amazed that this minx could make him, a dark, ruthless knight, feel vulnerable. He was further captivated when the princess closed her eyes and stretched on tiptoe to present him with her mouth. She looked ravishingly lovely and so young, even uncorrupted, her cheeks bright, her expression dreamy. Awestruck, he leaned over to press his lips on hers, touched her incredible warm softness, tasted her honeyed flavor—

At once, both of them moaned, and Niccolo pulled Aurora into his arms, molding her warm curves against him. She smelled of the copse, of honeysuckle and rose. Her heavenly mouth felt as if it belonged on his, making him ravenous to know all of her secrets. She was so delicious, and he ached to savor her, arouse her, devour her—

They both pulled back as if touched by lightning, breathing hard, staring at each other, overwhelmed by the emotion flaring between them. Niccolo could not believe how one taste of this woman had set him reeling!

" 'Tis true then, milady," he whispered huskily. "You are a witch, and this is a place of enchantment. Have you bewitched me now with your kiss?"

"Have I?" she responded with a smile.

He stroked her lush mouth with his fingertip. " 'Twas quite some enticement you offered."

She drew herself up to regard him proudly. "Do not think I kissed you to bribe you, knight. No amount of threats could have coerced my favors."

"No?" He laughed. "Then why did you kiss me, milady?"

She shrugged, but a deepening blush gave away her own excitement. "Because your countenance is pleasing, knight, and because I was curious about kisses."

Niccolo felt charmed by her honesty. "And now, milady? Are you more curious still?"

She wiggled nearer, again eyeing him boldly. "Mayhap a little."

Enchanted to his soul, Niccolo slowly shook his head in mock reproach. "Oh, milady. You should not tease a man so."

"And why not?" she inquired saucily.

All at once, Niccolo could barely breathe. He had

never expected such unabashed temptation from her. He had expected to play the jaded seducer ravishing the quivering virgin, but instead she was enticing him. Desire pounded in his veins as he raked his hot gaze over her.

Intensely he whispered, "You may not have come here to meet a lover, milady . . . but you may find one ere long."

She regarded him raptly, and Niccolo could not bear it. He caught her close and leaned over, kissing her with tender insistence. When she tried to catch her breath, he could not resist the lips that had opened in unwitting invitation. He pushed his tongue inside her hot, velvety mouth, and he felt a wild shudder wracking both of them without even knowing its source. He felt as if he had just plundered a virgin, and yet the ravishment was so sweet, it set him spinning and turned his blood to fire. When she trustingly coiled her arms around his neck and clung to him, the emotion was unbearable, making his chest ache . . .

At last he drew back, staggered by his own response, terrified he would reveal himself and his true motives, that he would pour himself, and all his pain, into this willing girl who was his enemy. He stared at her. Her cheeks were bright, her lips wet and slightly parted, her eyes confused yet glowing with passion.

"Commune with your spirits—and your gnomes—milady," he said softly. "I will keep your secret . . . at least for now."

Before he could lose his resolve and bed her there on the forest floor, Niccolo turned and left the copse. His heart pounded and his limbs quivered from unassuaged passion. He felt confused, at war with himself. He had wanted to think of Aurora as cold, heartless, and conniving, not as a woman who chatted with gnomes, played with a fawn, picked wildflowers, communed with the dead, and kissed him with such trusting innocence. She might be a schemer, but she was also an enchantress. Now their remembered kisses and the entire meeting were wreaking havoc with his conscience, his feelings, and all his well-laid plans. He felt like a scoundrel for plotting to deflower her. Guilt gnawed at him for taking her guileless kisses while he harbored such malice in his heart.

How could she feel so virtuous in his arms when he knew her soul must be corrupt? How could he allow himself to be fooled again? Mayhap Aurora *was* a witch, for he felt himself becoming entranced, in danger of losing his own will, just like before with Cecilia. He bucked up his determination to ruin her quickly, before this weakness she stirred threatened his obsession to seek revenge.

Yet how could he be so ruthless when the memory of her kisses still made him tremble?

Back in the copse, Aurora felt shaken, beset with turmoil as she stood before the altar. She had asked the spirits for an answer and then Niccolo had appeared. Was he her one true love? Or had she just admitted evil into her very own Garden of Eden?

She still did not trust Niccolo, but oh, she felt powerfully drawn to him. Especially when he had enticed her kisses. She sighed dreamily, remembering the emotions he had stirred. His arms had been a welcome, strong refuge, and his body had felt hard and powerful against her own softness. His mouth had felt wondrous—wild, hot, and sweet on hers. She had gone feverish, weak, dizzy all over, and even her belly had ached oddly but pleasurably. When he had pushed his tongue inside her mouth . . . oh, never had she known a man could kiss a woman so intimately, and stir such a riotous, ecstatic response! An incredible, torrid thrill had shot straight through her, leaving her weak, consumed with longing. Her heart pounded even now at the memory, and she placed her fingertips over her breast, awed by the strong thumping.

What was this mad response? Why had Niccolo stirred her so? She was not certain, since she had never before been kissed this way by a man.

She did know the man who had kissed her could not be entirely ruthless; there was a tenderness in him that belied his brutality, that had proven devastating to her. There must be some goodness buried in him somewhere. Possibly he was her true love, to appear when he did and steal her first kiss, even if he had tried to coerce her cooperation.

But what if she was wrong? Would Niccolo betray her feelings, expose her secrets? If she chose him in error, she would surely die, and condemn her ancestors to forever haunt the countryside with her. How could she be sure?

She smiled. She must ask the spirits. Yea, that was the only answer.

Aurora went to kneel at the altar. Assuming an attitude of prayer, she whispered fervently, "Tell me, spirits, is Sir Niccolo my one true love?"

Silence was her only answer.

Seared by frustration, Aurora implored, "Spirits, pray, favor me with your wisdom. You know the heavy choice I face, and how your fates are tied in with mine. I am your one remaining chance to be free. If I fail, we shall all be trapped forever in this place. Pray, then, tell me of Sir Niccolo. Is he the one I have waited for?"

Another long silence strained Aurora's overburdened nerves. Then at last the breeze began to stir, to shiver over the flowers and rustle the tree leaves. After a few moments, Great-Aunt Beatrice's low, eerie voice whispered:

> His countenance is fair and bright,
> His soul as dark and grim as night.

Aurora gasped, horrified by the dire pronouncement. "But, spirits," she pleaded, "the man who kissed me must possess some gentleness in his soul. If Niccolo is not my one true love, then why do I feel so drawn to him?"

There was another long pause, as the spooky wind whistled through the copse. Then Aunt Phoebe ominously intoned:

> Beware the barbs of passion's path,
> Seeds of lust sow fruit of wrath.

Aurora felt sobered indeed.

FIFTEEN

Beyond that mellow place, in the Valley of the Boulders, Ignatius, the royal constable, wended his way slowly down a narrow path clogged by large rocks, twisted roots, and brave dandelions. Supporting his weight with a crooked staff, he hobbled toward the large man who awaited him on a wooded rise at the edge of the valley.

Basil, King of Ravenia, stood holding the reins of his large gray destrier. As always, the sight of the king washed a shudder over Ignatius. Basil was rough-featured, with a surly disposition to match. His greasy hair was a dull orange in color; his features were uneven and battle-scarred—fleshy lips, a crooked nose, battered cheeks, an irregular brow, and beady eyes. He was dressed in a hauberk and leggings, a broadsword sheathed at his side.

"You are late!" he called belligerently.

"I beg your pardon, Sire," answered Ignatius, creaking on. "These old bones will not cooperate."

"I care not about your bones, man!" scoffed Basil. "I pay you well to meet me at my ease. What tidings do you bring?"

At last the old man paused before Basil, catching a labored breath. He fought back a grimace at the king's body odor. "No additional knights have arrived at

Falconia Castle since we last spoke, Sire. Not since the Castilian arrived bearing his bride's chest."

" 'Tis a relief to hear," replied Basil, sneering a laugh. "The ones Artemas has dispatched thus far have plagued my army enough. How goes the contest?"

Ignatius shook his head. "All of the knights are eager to prove their prowess in battle, and also fawn over the princess each eve like slobbering pups. They woo her with poem and song. And she still contends she will wed the knight who defeats you."

Basil's expression turned ugly. "That will never happen. I shall continue to attack Falconia Castle until the princess surrenders—to me!"

"I fear she will not do so any time soon," Ignatius fretted. "Princess Aurora is a stubborn woman, Sire."

"And I am a determined man!" Basil retorted, his green eyes gleaming with ire. "On the day Aurora first cruelly spurned my suit, I vowed I would have her. I even pressed my cause with her glutton of an uncle, but that wily scoundrel would not cooperate." He waved a hand in his anger. "They think they are better than us, those arrogant Falconians. Well, I shall have the woman, by damn, even if we must first do battle until the cursed trolls bubble up from hell!"

Ignatius groaned. He had heard Basil rant and rave this way many times before. "I am certain you shall prevail. How may I continue to serve you, Sire?"

The king shrugged. "Merely watch and listen. And try to bring more useful tidings next time."

Ignatius eyed the other man in suspicion. "You will pay me now, Sire?"

"Pay you?" scoffed the king. "But you have provided no real intelligence to warrant your traitor's portion."

"I have tried to aid your cause," protested Ignatius. "I have offered you advice—"

"Worthless babble."

"But you could win the war so much more quickly, Sire, if you would take the princess by stealth," Ignatius implored. "I could admit you and some of your comrades into the castle under cover of night."

"Bah!" scoffed Basil. "My superstitious warriors will not breach the castle through your tunnels. They fear the darkness, and the forces of evil hidden beneath the earth."

As do you, Sire, thought Ignatius, though he did not dare voice aloud such an insulting truth. Like the rest of the Ravenians, Basil was riddled with superstition—fearing darkness, storms, the terrors of the black forest, and the creatures that lived beneath the earth.

Ignatius tried a different tack. "Then take the princess by daylight. I sometimes spy her leaving the castle through the sally port. You could dispatch several knights to lie in wait for her in the forest."

"Nay, my knights will not wait for her in the forest," Basil grumbled with a dismissive gesture. "Not after three of their numbers were slain by gnomes—those evil fellows who eternally protect their princess."

"The gnomes do not threaten me," asserted Ignatius.

Basil laughed derisively. "You are Falconian, and assumed to be a servant of the crown. Besides, you are so hunched and ugly, the little rascals likely mistake you for one of their brethren. Not even a cursed gnome could fear a broken-down wretch such as yourself."

Ignatius retained his patience with an effort. "I still contend there must be some way to kidnap the princess."

Basil set his arms akimbo and glowered. "Nay, I have made up my mind to storm the castle gates until Aurora surrenders and accepts me as her husband. Mayhap much later, if she still will not cooperate, we shall consider taking her by duplicity." With a sneer of disgust, he took a gold coin from his purse and tossed it at the man. "Take your Judas portion and be gone, wretch. Bring me better information next time, or I shall slit your worthless throat."

Ignatius greedily pocketed his coin and kept his silence, while musing that Basil was a stupid, ignorant fool. With some clever plotting, the princess could surely be his for the taking. But, proud as he was witless, Basil was determined to continue his demented siege. He was like a rutting boar who knew only how to charge for his target straight on.

SIXTEEN

THE NEXT MORNING AS HE FINISHED BREAKING HIS fast with the knights and Christian in the great hall, Niccolo was astounded to note that the siegers still had not appeared; he did not hear the usual bang of the ram, nor the whoosh and crash of the catapults, coming from the castle gates.

"The enemy is late this morn," he remarked to Sir Galen.

"Methinks Basil and his knights will not appear at all today," responded the captain of the Guard.

"And why is that, Sir Galen?" inquired Sir Edgar.

" 'Tis the Holy Day of the Cricket in Kestrel, the peasant village of Ravenia," explained Sir Galen. "No Ravenian knight will do battle on such a day."

"The Holy Day of the Cricket?" scoffed Niccolo. "Are the Kestrellians as dim-witted as the Osprey-ans?"

A grinning Christian spoke up. "The peasants be-lieve the cricket brings good luck. The Kestrellians fear storms and floods, and crickets have for centuries appeared in great numbers to warn of such calamities. Thus the cricket is revered in Kestrel. Indeed, the last peasant who stepped on the sacred insect was placed in the public stocks for three days."

As laughter rang down the table, Niccolo was too flabbergasted to comment.

Once the chuckles abated, Sir Edgar patted his stomach and remarked, "Well, men, since we have this welcome respite, I suggest we spend the day honing our battle skills in the bailey."

"Hear, hear!" agreed Christian, raising his cup, while several other warriors added their own lusty endorsements.

After the meal, all of the knights, save for Niccolo, went to mass. The warriors then gathered in the bailey, several men practicing their archery or tilting at quintains. Sir Edgar and Sir Rafael engaged in a mock joust on horseback. As several peasant children watched and cheered, Christian trained his falcon to pursue a lure attached to a long piece of twine that he twirled about him. Niccolo, joining in the mood of camaraderie, challenged several knights to mock sword tourneys.

Aurora also ventured outside to watch. She sat on the steps of the keep with her ladies-in-waiting, watching Niccolo engage the Genoan, Sir Cesare. Dressed in chain-mail tunic and pale hose, her dark knight appeared magnificent as he advanced, muscles rippling, leaping toward his opponent, striking and parrying with the proficiency of a master. The Genoan put up a valiant defense, but was forced to give ground again and again. Aurora found Niccolo utterly splendid and ruthless; his strength, skill, and vitality powerfully drew her to him. Obviously he was as skilled with the sword as he was with his kisses. That last thought made her pulse quicken as a memory of their magical tryst yesterday roused high color in her cheeks.

Was it his tenderness then or his fearsomeness now that excited her the most? Whatever the source of his magic, watching him she felt a palpable hunger, a craving for more of his kisses, even though, if the spirits' warnings were correct, such urges might well defeat her!

Soon Niccolo knocked the sword from Sir Cesare's hand and pressed the tip of his wooden weapon to his heart. Several other knights cheered, and Sir Cesare conceded defeat with a nod and backed away.

Aurora watched in building amazement and admiration as Niccolo then defeated Sir Baldric and Sir Olaf. When Niccolo challenged Christian, Aurora's heart jumped into her throat in wild fear that her precious half brother might be harmed. The fight was fierce, since Christian's skill was almost equal to Niccolo's; several times Christian put Niccolo on the defensive, forcing him to duck, spin, or back away. Yet Niccolo proved the stronger competitor, finally using a mighty blow to knock the sword from Christian's hand. As her half brother conceded defeat with a grin and a bow, Niccolo raised his own sword high over his head amid new cheers from the other knights.

Then he walked over toward the keep, knelt, saluted Aurora, and grinned up at her arrogantly, his face glowing with sweat, his bright blue eyes mocking her. As Aurora's ladies tittered, she felt her heart thumping with mingled exhilaration and fear.

Niccolo's message was clear. He was claiming her. He would become her champion, her prince, her lover. The prospect thrilled Aurora deeply, but daunted her as she again remembered the admonitions of her ancestors . . .

Late that morning, Aurora slipped away from the others and left the castle through the sally port. Within moments, she was safely in her copse, amid the sweetness of midday, the chirping of birds and buzzing of bees. Tansy bounded up to her, and Aurora knelt and played with the fawn not far from the shrine, petting her and feeding her some cabbage she had taken from the kitchen stores.

Glancing about her as she scratched the fawn's ears, Aurora mused that the spirits seemed unusually quiet today; so far, they had not intoned their usual dire messages. The breeze barely stirred, though the air was moist, slightly cool, and heady with nectar.

"Good day, milady," she heard a voice call.

Like yesterday, Tansy perked her ears, then dashed away. Frowning, Aurora rose and turned to see Niccolo standing at the edge of the copse. Excitement stormed her nerve endings at the sight of him. He had changed into a wool tunic and tan hose that hugged the fine muscles of his powerful thighs and strong calves. His thick, gleaming yellow hair fell about his strong shoulders. She remembered the shocking sensations he had stirred within her as she watched him at the tourney, and she felt her insides warming once more.

Still, her pride railed out at his invading her sanctuary. "Why have you come here—again?" she demanded.

"Why not?" he countered, striding toward her.

Feeling threatened as well as tempted, Aurora gathered her courage. Niccolo only increased her chagrin when he paused before her, filling her senses with his vibrant masculinity. He crossed his arms over his chest and grinned at her arrogantly, as if he had every right to be here.

"I thought it was agreed you would leave me in peace," she declared, feeling daunted by her new feelings. "I thought I had persuaded you."

"You persuaded me to return, milady," he teased. He glanced toward the altar. "What—you are not talking to yourself again today? Or do you hear voices?"

Refusing to be baited, Aurora took an offensive tack. "Why are you not attending to your own affairs? I thought you were making war games with the other knights."

"I was, but I bested them all," he drawled lazily, then winked at her. "Which means I shall make quick work of making you mine, Princess."

Aurora struggled against a new surge of excitement at his confident words. "You are too cocksure of yourself, knight. You cannot win me unless you first best Basil."

He gave a shrug. "From what I have seen, defeating such a dimwit will be easy."

Curious, she asked, "Why do you call him a dimwit?"

Niccolo laughed. "You yourself find him repulsive, do you not, milady? And I find your enemy's tactics less than ingenious—attacking with each day, and fleeing with every sunset. Methinks a page could come up with more clever strategies."

Aurora fought a smile. "You still have not told me why you are here."

"Why, because I want to be here," he responded. "I enjoy this place—and your company, milady."

She tossed her curls. "Mayhap I do not crave your company, knight."

Edging closer, he whispered wickedly, "But you have no choice but to tolerate me . . . if you want me to keep your secret, no?"

Ire churned in Aurora. "You are threatening me yet again, knight? And after I gave you your . . ."

He raised an eyebrow and waited eagerly. "My what?"

She blushed crimson. "Your enticement!"

Chuckling, he stared boldly into her flushed face. "As I have already explained, milady, the enticement only made me hungry for more."

To hide the guilty smile that at last won out over her embarrassment, Aurora turned and strolled off—quickly pursued by Niccolo. Eyeing him with resentment, she gestured toward a clump of bright yellow jonquils. "You are a nuisance, knight, like the bees that pester the flowers."

He grabbed her arm and pulled her toward him. "And you are sweet, milady, like those lush blossoms, especially when you spread your pretty petals."

Catching a sharp breath, Aurora was not certain how to interpret his remark, or what "petals" he meant. She suspected he was referring to her lips, and their kisses, and mayhap to something even more shocking.

She gazed up at him in challenge. "Did you come to coerce more kisses from me?"

"Would it please you if I said yea?" he taunted.

His response piqued her temper. "You have answered my question with a question, knight."

"So I have. There can be wonder in the mysterious, can there not, milady?"

Aurora found Niccolo's response struck a common chord in her, especially as they paused before the steps of the shrine, which represented such mystery in her own life. "Yea," she murmured, and crossed herself.

He inclined his hand toward the steps. "Sit with me, milady?"

"You are offering me a choice, knight?" she asked with feigned incredulity.

"I am not leaving . . . but *sì*, I asked, did I not?"

Eyeing him askance, she sat down on the steps, and he joined her. For a moment they sat quietly, almost companionably, watching the light sift through the tree branches and dance across the flowers and the pond, hearing the soft, musical rustle of the wind and the rush of the stream, smelling the heady scent of greenery.

After a moment, Niccolo turned to Aurora and took her hand. She was left wondering why she did not protest, could not seem to resist, as his strong fingers confidently held hers, and she reeled at the hot thrill that shot through her at his warm, firm grip.

His expression was one of near reverence as he gazed about them. " 'Tis truly a marvelous place, milady."

"I am unaccustomed to sharing it," she confessed with a smile.

"Do you so mind sharing it with me?"

Regarding his sincere countenance, Aurora at last shook her head. "Nay, 'tis agreeable enough having you here, methinks."

Her words encouraged him more than she had intended. Releasing her hand, he stared into her eyes and slipped his fingers under her mane of hair, gently caressing her nape. She shuddered. His bold touch sent wild shivers streaking up and down her spine, yet again she could not seem to summon the will to resist him.

"What else will you share, milady?" he asked softly.

Watching Niccolo's ardent face descend toward hers, Aurora felt panic encroaching in the wake of her own desire for him. Gathering her fortitude, she braced a palm against his solid chest. "You take too many liberties, knight."

Eyeing her flushed, uncertain countenance, he dropped his hand. "It is my nature as a warrior to be aggressive."

"And never tender?" she asked.

He grinned. "I have kissed you tenderly, milady . . . and will gladly do so again."

As he would have demonstrated, she shoved both hands against his shoulders. "Nay, you would corrupt me."

He chuckled.

"Besides, methinks I have already given you enough kisses," she continued saucily.

Undaunted, he cupped her chin in his large hand. "And I think we have only begun, milady . . . especially as much as you seem to be enjoying this."

"Oh!" she cried.

Over the roar of her own heartbeat, Aurora watched him once again lean closer. Still fearing she would not be able to stay him, she flinched when she felt a nudge against her knee. She looked down into her fawn's huge brown eyes. Never had she felt so grateful to see her pet!

Pulling away, she flashed Niccolo a tentative smile. "Tansy is here."

Niccolo glanced, puzzled, at the little animal. "You do not wish to kiss me in front of the fawn?"

"Verily, you well know we should not kiss here at all," she scolded primly. " 'Tis a holy place."

"Holy or haunted, milady?" he teased.

Aurora struggled against another smile but did not answer, instead stroking Tansy's soft ears.

Watching her, Niccolo snapped his fingers and whistled softly. To Aurora's delight, Tansy moved over to him and nudged his knee. He petted the top of her head.

"She takes to you!" cried Aurora. "She has always refused to come to anyone but me!"

Niccolo scowled. "But how would you know that, milady? You said you never share this place."

Guiltily her gaze darted away from his. "Verily, almost never. Sometimes the gnomes will pass through the copse and speak with me. They always spook poor Tansy."

"No doubt," agreed Niccolo ruefully.

"And Christian has also visited the shrine with me . . . but Tansy runs from him, as well."

"So you have shared this copse with others," Niccolo said softly, but with an underlying menace. "Then you lied to me before."

"I did not truly lie," she responded uneasily. "I have never been here before with . . ." Her voice trailed off and she colored.

He stared her in the eye. "A lover?"

She avoided his question, nervously petting the deer.

Niccolo reached out, grasping Aurora's face in his large hands. "A lover, Princess?" he repeated, insistently.

Aurora stared up at him in rapt uncertainty. Unnerved by his look of intense yearning, she could not reply, though a sweet aching twisted through her, and a little sigh burst in her. That breathless sound was evidently all the encouragement Niccolo needed. She caught a brief glimpse of the triumph lighting his eyes, and then his face was covering hers, blotting out the sun, his lips claiming her own. The pressure of his mouth on hers was hot and firm, yet passionate and seductive, too. She was shot through with such a tingling warmth that all of her trembled. Instinctively she curled her arms around Niccolo's neck and clung to him, fearing otherwise she would be swept away on this wave of dizzying pleasure that surged through her so powerfully, demanding a release that frightened her even more.

At last they pulled apart, staring at each other spellbound, and breathing raggedly. "You have stolen another kiss, knight," Aurora blurted.

Niccolo gathered her closer and spoke roughly. "Do you really think I will *ever* take my fill of you, milady?"

Aurora eyed him in helpless yearning. Niccolo leaned over and recaptured her lips, caressing her back with his strong fingers. A little moan escaped her, and she did not protest when he eased his tongue inside her mouth, the taste of him heady and seductive. Her toes curled in delight. Niccolo was wooing her with such gentle intimacy, yet wild currents of longing jolted her, making her feel as vulnerable as a leaf in a storm.

She was the leaf . . . he, the storm.

All at once, Tansy sprang forward, pressing her forelegs on Niccolo's knees and using her small head to nudge the lovers apart. Niccolo and Aurora separated, laughing as they regarded the wide-eyed fawn.

"She is jealous, no?" Niccolo asked, winking at Aurora and petting the animal.

Feeling rattled, her breathing labored and her cheeks hot, Aurora gathered her composure. "Mayhap she is. She will see to it that you behave yourself, knight."

He smiled and caressed her bright cheek. "Not likely, milady."

Still fighting her own response, Aurora stroked Tansy. "She is a magical fawn, you know."

"And how is that?"

"She came to me soon after I first . . ."

"First what, milady?" Niccolo encouraged. "You can tell me."

Awkwardly she glanced away. "After I first became a woman. 'Twas four summers past. Tansy was small then . . . and yet she has never grown, not even an inch."

He scowled and ran his hand over the fawn's smooth back. "She is remarkable indeed."

"She likes you, Sir Niccolo Campioni," Aurora went on. "So you cannot be all evil."

He glanced up, amusement glittering in his eyes. "What makes you think I am evil?"

Laying a finger alongside her jaw, she regarded him assessingly. "You are very different from the other knights. Darker, more complex. Sometimes I do not know what thoughts lie behind those beautiful blue eyes—"

"You find my eyes appealing, milady?" he asked with obvious relish.

"I would like to have them," she admitted frankly. "They are quite attractive."

"Your eyes are lovely, as well, milady," he replied.

"I like it when they look on me with pleasure."

"But they are dark." She studied him more closely. "With eyes as pure and clear as yours, I should be able to see into your soul, knight. But I sense you still hide your real self from me. I am not sure I can trust you, or your motives."

"But of course you can trust me," he protested. "Have I not sworn to become your champion, to defend you to the death?"

Ruefully she replied, "Mayhap you will be my champion, but I sense you will never truly be my friend. I fear you want me only for what I can bring you."

He frowned. "I thought you have no dowry, Princess."

"I have my castle and fief, the rents from my tenants," she protested with a wave of her hand. "All told, what I offer is not inconsiderable. Enough to tempt a man like you, surely."

He fell silent. "Mayhap you mistrust what you do not know, milady."

She considered his remark with a frown, then nodded. "Then let me know you, knight. Tell me more of yourself."

She was surprised to watch his countenance darken, his shoulders stiffen. "What would you know?"

"I would know of your life before you came here."

He picked up a twig and tossed it aside. Tansy bounded after it. "My life would only bore you, milady."

"I think not. I would know."

He breathed a great sigh. "Very well, then." Scowling as if to gather his thoughts, he began. "I was the only son of a wealthy Venetian shipping family. I have one younger sister, Caterina. As a young man in Venice, my life was good. I was tutored by monks, and completed my education at Naples. When I returned home, I joined my father's shipping enterprise, and also became a member of the prestigious fraternity *Compagnia della Calza,* for which I won the privilege of wearing bright red hosiery around town to impress all the fair ladies."

She giggled.

Somberly he continued, "My father died not long after I reached manhood, and left me heir to his various enterprises."

"I am sorry you lost him," she murmured. "But you still have your mother?"

"*Sì.* Mamma is wonderful." With unaccustomed wistfulness he added, "You would like her, I think."

"I am certain I would," she assured him. "And it seems we have much in common, Niccolo Campioni."

"How is that, Princess?"

"I, too, had a wonderful childhood," Aurora confided. "But as I have mentioned already, I lost both of my parents to a fever two summers after I reached womanhood. Thus I became heir to the throne."

He nodded. "Then our backgrounds are somewhat similar."

"Tell me of how you became a knight."

"The men in my family have been knights for the Republic for many centuries," he explained. "Like my father before me, when I turned eighteen, I was inducted into the order of *Cavalieri di San Marco,* eventually becoming grand master. After war broke out against the Turks, I accepted my *condotta* as captain general of the Venetian forces and led an expedition of state galleys to the Far East. Eventually I returned home . . ." His voice trailed off, and his countenance hardened.

"What happened?" she inquired, noting his anxious expression.

Tightly he related, "I came home to find that my

business affairs had languished, and my wife had died."

"You were married!" she gasped, astounded.

He nodded, and broke a twig. "I suppose I neglected to mention it. Does it bother you that I am a widower?"

"I am not certain," she admitted honestly. "Did you and your wife have children?"

"No."

"Did you love her?"

Niccolo's words were hoarse with bitterness. "Our marriage was arranged, but *sì*, at one time, I loved her. I prefer not to speak of it, milady."

"Then 'tis still painful?" she asked gently.

"*Sì*."

Aurora was silent a moment, lost in thought, wondering if the tension she spotted in Niccolo's face bespoke that he still loved his bride. "Is that why you are so different from the others? Because you lost your wife?"

He flashed her a stiff smile. "Do you find me so unusual, milady?"

"Verily, I do. For one thing, you have no faith."

Harshly he replied, "After one sees knights blown apart by cannonball, or roasting in their own armor soaked with Greek fire, one must wonder if prayer before battle has any true benefit."

Aurora blanched. "Do you enjoy killing other men?"

He scowled. "Why would you ask that?"

"You seemed to relish besting the others today."

"*Sì*, very much."

"And Sir Galen told me of how you shoved the attackers from the parapets," she continued tensely. "He told me you dispatched the siegers quite pitilessly."

"I am surprised to hear of Sir Galen using such an intelligent word," Niccolo commented cynically.

Aurora was not swayed by his humor. "Did you take joy in killing the attackers?"

"*Sì*, there is triumph in defeating an enemy."

"You are ruthless, then."

He reached out to toy with a strand of her hair and spoke softly. "Very."

Her eyes went wide. "And do you truly want me to increase your own fortunes?"

"You think the others are not equally mercenary, Princess?" he scoffed.

"I think they are far more chivalrous than you, sir knight!"

"Then you are sadly deluded, milady."

Aurora slowly shook her head. "You have no true feeling for me, yet you think you will make a fitting husband for me?"

"I *know* I will." His gaze slid down her comely body. "And do not assume I have no feeling for you."

"Then why do you not revere me more?" she challenged.

Deliberately taunting her, he leaned over to pluck a bloom from the grasses, then placed it behind her ear. "What makes you believe I do not revere you?"

Petulantly she replied, "You do not court me as the others do . . . and you torment me terribly."

Niccolo threw back his head and laughed. "You are complaining because I do not compose lofty verse exalting your beauty, or kiss the rushes as you pass?"

She nodded. "Methinks if you truly respected me as your future bride, you would honor me as do the other knights."

Niccolo touched the tip of her nose. "You are wrong, milady."

"Why?"

A sardonic smile curved his lips. "I shall never worship you from afar, Princess, never exalt you with verse and song, because I find the entire concept of courtly love to be flawed."

"Why flawed?" she asked, frowning.

Leaning closer, he confided provocatively, "Because it ignores the entire matter of physical passion, which must be strong for a marriage to endure."

She glanced away, her face hot. "You know of what you speak?"

"Indeed I do, milady."

She dared to look at him, remembering Aunt Phoebe's grievous warning. "And you have such feelings for me, knight?"

He grinned. "Shall I demonstrate?"

She shook her head. "I believe you."

"Good." He gathered her into his arms.

Caught off guard, she stiffened in his embrace. "B-But how can you know whether what you are feeling is love, knight, or merely the lure of passion?"

Fighting a smile at her sober query, Niccolo slid his strong hand beneath her hair, and kneaded the tense muscles there. "I suggest more kisses so you may decide, milady."

Shocked and secretly thrilled by his words and touch, Aurora tried to protest, but Niccolo's determined mouth captured her open lips, melting her protest into an ecstatic moan. He nestled her closer, kissing her at first hungrily, and then, as she softened against him, with exquisite tenderness. He tormented her with the sensual rub of his lips and the tantalizing flicks of his tongue. Aurora felt a trembling heat suffuse her, warming her face and breasts and pulsing between her thighs, as if Niccolo were exploring her intimately, even there. She dug her fingers into his spine and winced with the overwhelming desire she felt.

At last he pulled back, his expression triumphant as he studied her dazed face. "You say I have no feeling for you, Princess?"

" 'Tis—'tis only passion," she panted.

"I am not so sure," he murmured, and cupped her breast with his large hand.

Aurora squirmed, her nipple tingling at the bold contact, even through her gown. Defensively she placed her fingers over his, although she could not bring herself to shove his hand away as she knew by all rights she should. His touch simply felt too good, arousing decadent, forbidden urges in her.

"Are you afraid, milady?" he asked.

"You—you must remove your hand," she stammered.

"Move aside yours, milady," he urged huskily, "and let me pull down your bodice and kiss you there. Let me suckle that sweet little bud that already feels so tight and hard against my palm. You know you want me to."

She gasped.

His bright gaze smoldered into hers, turning her blood to fire. "Let me," he whispered hoarsely, "and then perhaps you will know whether what you feel is love or lust."

Wide-eyed, Aurora shook her head. "Nay—nay, we must not."

But heedless of her protests, Niccolo kissed her lips again, his tongue swirling deeply in her mouth, his fingers kneading her breast with a skilled, insistent pressure . . . Clamping an arm at the small of her back, he nudged her down beneath him on the wide step, his huge body crushing her, his mouth devouring hers.

"Aurora . . . sweet Aurora . . ." he whispered, and possessed her lips once again.

Aurora did not know what was happening to her! Was it magic? Had Niccolo bewitched her? For she was sinking into a sensual abyss, losing herself to him, her insides aquiver and tendrils of desire pushing deep inside her belly . . . 'Twas surely enchantment, she thought achingly. For why could she not stay him, nor halt the potent urges consuming her?

All at once, she flinched as she heard a soft, eerie voice whisper, *Beware the barbs* . . . She froze in alarm. Was it the voice of the spirits? Or merely the wind?

When the ominous voice repeated, *Beware the barbs*, Aurora's doubts surged into panic. Verily, she could *feel* Niccolo's barb against her now—part of her ached to be pierced by it, yet it might well bring her to ruin!

Abruptly the erotic spell Niccolo had cast about her shattered. Gathering all her fortitude, Aurora shoved him away, steeling herself against his look of angry bemusement. She stumbled to her feet—

"You are confusing me, knight!" she cried. "You will surely doom me!"

She fled the copse, while Niccolo stared after her in consternation, the taste of her still on his lips, the scent of her haunting his senses. Why had she fled so abruptly? What had her words meant? Had she already guessed the dark motives he harbored in his heart?

SEVENTEEN

Aurora spent the balance of the day in her solar, alternately pacing about or lying on her bed, trying to sort out her overwhelming feelings for her dark knight. Endlessly she relived their passionate interlude in the copse, remembering how wonderful it had felt to be held in Niccolo's strong arms and ardently kissed by him. When he had boldly caressed her breast, she had felt tempted to surrender all of herself to him. Only the spirits' warnings had given her pause.

Now she was in a terrible quandary. Although she felt more drawn to Niccolo than ever, it seemed the more she learned about him, the more doubtful she became that he was the one she had waited for. Verily, he had lost a cherished bride. He must still love his deceased wife, which would explain his sometimes aloof behavior toward her.

Yet he had kissed her with such fervor, even tenderness. Was there truly goodness in him, or was she becoming captivated by the skills of a master of seduction? Much as he moved her, she feared what he felt for her might always be lust and never love.

And lust, as she well knew, could prove deadly for her!

To make matters worse, she now knew that Niccolo

had suffered financial reversals while off fighting the Turks. She suspected he truly was a soldier of fortune, out to win her castle and lands. If this was true, how could he possibly be her one true love? He seemed determined to wed her, and if her misgivings proved correct, his self-serving designs would instead doom her.

He had also confessed to having lost his faith, which explained his ruthlessness. 'Twas daunting indeed for Aurora to face the prospect of falling in love with a man who lacked both pity and hope!

Yet he alone, out of the seven men her uncle had dispatched, fascinated and attracted her. Mayhap she should give the others more of a fair chance. After all, the eternal fate of her ancestors—and her very soul!— were at stake here.

That eve after dinner, Aurora sat on her dais surrounded by her ladies, Christian, and her royal staff; her hounds dozed at her feet. She tried to restrain her gaze from straying toward Niccolo, who sat at the knights' trestle table, watching her intently, his eyes bright as blue fire. He might be wrong for her, she mused, but oh, he was potent temptation—so handsome, so virile, radiating such coiled strength. A strolling minstrel sang a poignant ballad of unrequited love that further chipped away at her resolve as she again relived her passionate moments with Niccolo in the copse.

She was pleasantly distracted when Sir Mortimer stepped forward, bowing before her dais. "Milady, the other knights have implored me to inform you they have gifts to present you in honor of the lull in the battle. I hear they all traveled to Osprey today, to the village fair."

Aurora smiled. "I am pleased by the thoughtfulness of my knights. Do ask them to come forward."

Mortimer bowed, slipped away, and spoke with Sir

Edgar. A moment later, he strode up to the dais bearing a magnificent gold, bejeweled chalice. Elegantly he bowed on one knee before the princess. "Milady, I present you this cup, made by the finest goldsmith in Osprey. May it be a small token of my great regard for your beauty, which outshines even gold."

As Aurora's ladies emitted ecstatic oohs and aahs, she reached out and took the dazzling goblet. "Thank you, Sir Edgar," she declared regally. "You may kiss my hand."

The Englishman grinned his happiness, took Aurora's hand, gently kissed her fingers, then backed away.

Next, Sir Gilbert came forward carrying a hammered silver necklace with a medallion of Cupid and Psyche. Going down on one knee, he extended the glittering chain and intoned, "Milady, I present you with this necklace from the finest silversmith in Osprey. Exquisite though 'tis, 'twill never gleam as brightly as your eyes."

With her ladies again tittering ecstatically, Aurora smiled brilliantly, accepted the gift, and also allowed Sir Gilbert to kiss her hand as he lavished additional compliments on her. 'Twas not so unpleasant, she mused, being the center of so much male adoration! If only Niccolo would come forward to woo her so! She stole a glance across the room, and caught his dark expression. He appeared in a foul humor, and she felt a perverse thrill at the possibility that he might be jealous. Yet he doubtless would not bring her gifts or compliments this eve, she thought with a twinge of disappointment.

Then she became distracted as Sir Rafael came forward . . .

Across from Aurora, Niccolo indeed felt tortured as he watched the other knights woo the princess. Sir Rafael now stood before her, one hand extending a handsome volume of poetry, the other pressed over his heart as he eloquently described Aurora's many virtues. Niccolo could barely contain an urge to storm across the room and tear the man away from the woman he coveted.

He felt angry, bemused, outsmarted by the others. It had never occurred to him to rush off to the village today during the lull to buy gifts to lavish on the princess. But then, Niccolo Campioni was not a thoughtful man, not the type to woo a lady with trinkets and flowers. Aurora obviously preferred his more chivalrous competitors, and her flirtation put him in enough of a temper to want to strangle her—indeed, to throttle her and her suitors, as well. She was all shameless coquette—just like Cecilia!

The intensity of his passions stunned him. Why should he care if the princess was a coy temptress? Why should it matter to him if she granted so many others her smiles, or even her body? The last thing he wanted was to feel possessive of Aurora, to be tied to her emotionally. Indeed, he preferred to feel for her nothing at all—for any softer, amorous emotions could threaten his mission.

But today in the copse she had enticed him, charming him with her smiles, exploring his heart with her questions. She had gotten him to admit much more about his past than he had intended. She had probed too close to his own pain, even tempting him to spill out his torment to her, to find his ease—rather than his revenge—in her sweet arms. Her trusting kisses had set his blood on fire.

He felt in a terrible quandary. He had sought to entrap and ruin Aurora . . . Now he felt increasingly troubled by the possibility that he would not be able to complete her seduction before becoming totally captivated himself.

Oh, *Dio*, what would he do? He could not afford to lose his heart again to a woman who would ultimately betray his love as Cecilia had. He must keep his mind on winning his revenge—and on winning alone.

His thoughts scattered as he observed Sir Rafael backing away from the royal dais, then watched Sir Cesare advance with dark eyes glowing ardently, presenting the princess with a huge bouquet of white roses. Niccolo gripped the edge of the table with his fingers, watching Aurora extend her hand to take the lovely bouquet, smiling radiantly at the Genoan ...

That guileless encouragement given to another stabbed Niccolo like a lance in his heart. Too furious to contain himself, he surged to his feet, causing the bench to scrape loudly against the floor. He was pleased to watch a startled Aurora drop the bouquet the Genoan had just handed her.

Niccolo glared about the table. "Men," he announced, "enough of this folly."

As the knights murmured ominously to one another, the Genoan glowered at Niccolo. "Are you jealous, Venetian, because we woo the princess so skillfully and you have no such finesse?"

"Forget the princess for now," Niccolo retorted, and heard a gasp ripple over the room. He noted that even Aurora appeared stunned—

Surging to his feet, Christian waved a fist and called angrily, "Knight, you insult my sister!"

Sir Rafael also bolted up indignantly. "*Sí, señor,* you malign our princess! Retract your dishonorable words, or I shall challenge you to the death!"

As several other warriors added their own threats, demanding that Niccolo make amends to the princess, he groaned and tried to rein in his surging temper.

With great restraint, he turned to Aurora. "I meant no disrespect, Princess," he muttered.

"None taken, knight," she called back sweetly.

Seething with frustrated anger, Niccolo managed to turn calmly to Christian. "Sir Christian, I ask your pardon, as well."

Christian nodded curtly and resumed his seat.

Holding on to his patience with an effort, Niccolo turned back to the warriors. "What I am trying to say, men, is that it seems foolish for Lady Aurora's knights to be wooing her night after night like fawning troubadours when she is still so greatly threatened by her enemies."

"What are you suggesting?" asked Sir Gilbert.

Niccolo waved a hand. "Does it not strike you as odd that we all sit here at the castle, day after day, like witless ninnies, and let the Ravenians attack us?"

"But we always repel the siegers," put in Sir Galen defensively.

"Simply repulsing them is not enough," argued Niccolo. " 'Tis time for us to seize the offensive and defeat the Ravenians decisively."

The knights consulted among themselves for several moments, then Sir Edgar nodded for the group. "What would you propose, Venetian?"

Niccolo scowled. "We need to discuss strategies, but we cannot do so here." He turned and forced a benign smile, nodding to Aurora. " 'Twould surely bore and displease our lady."

On the dais, Niccolo saw Aurora smirk at him, causing hostility to churn anew within him. Behind him, he heard the knights muttering their agreement.

Niccolo stepped away from the table and bowed to Aurora. "Princess, if you will excuse us, the other knights and I have tactics to discuss in the barracks war room." He inclined a hand toward Christian. "Sir Christian, we would be honored to have you join us, and favor us with your wisdom. Afterward, we must all hie to bed early, to see our plan triumph."

"Very well," called the princess imperiously, while laughter shone in her eyes. "You may all be excused." She nodded to her brother. "Christian, do go with them."

"Yea, sister."

Heaving a sigh of relief, Niccolo led the knights from the chamber.

On the dais, Aurora petted Bink, a secret smile curving her lips. At Lady Flora's giggle, she turned and raised an eyebrow at her friend.

"Milady, methinks you have made your dark knight jealous," confided Flora with obvious relish. "Sir Niccolo seemed in a frightful choler."

Ruefully Aurora nodded. "Methinks you are right."

As Lady Flora turned away, Aurora relived Niccolo's magnificent show of temper. She knew she had stirred a possessive response in him tonight, and it pleased her inordinately to have such power over him.

Then she frowned. As much as she was enjoying herself, she was still playing a reckless game—toying with a knight who was clearly dangerous, who was likely not her true love—and trying to seize a victory that could ultimately hasten her own death . . .

EIGHTEEN

AT DAWN, NICCOLO AND ALL THE KNIGHTS, INCLUD-
ing the Royal Guardsmen, were gathered in the forest
on horseback, lying in wait for the enemy. The warriors numbered over threescore, with Niccolo and
Christian at their head. A tense silence gripped their
ranks, save for the occasional soft scrape of metal on
metal as one of the men shifted slightly in his saddle,
and the neighing and stamping of the spirited war-
horses. The morn was cool, a slight fog hanging in the
thicket, a delicate breeze bearing the tangy essence of
the conifers and the sounds of birds singing. Niccolo
spotted a red-tailed hawk flying over, and hoped
'twould prove a portent of his company's ferocity this
day.

Niccolo was warm inside his plate armor, and even
on this chill morn, he expected to be scalded by his
own roaring blood ere the battle ended. He had been
up for hours, Lorenzo helping him strap or buckle on
the various pieces of his white armor, from breast and
back plates to *faulds* and bascinets. Lorenzo had
begged to come along on the mission, but Niccolo had
forbidden this; his squire was much too old, his heart
too weak for dangerous combat.

Niccolo was prepared for battle save for the lowering of his visor. In one hand was gripped his deadly

steel lance, in the other his iron shield, emblazoned
with both his family coat of arms and the lion of San
Marco. Even Nero was prepared for the fray, his
handsome mane braided and gleaming plate armor
protecting his breast and muzzle, a colorful robe
draping his flanks.

The other knights were similarly readied, fully armored and bearing lances, swords, shields, maces,
and axes. A few feet ahead of the small army stood
three heralds with their trumpets and two pages bearing the royal banner with its red and gold colors and
fearsome coat of arms of the falcon. Beyond the heralds at the edge of the trees were hidden several archers on foot with crossbows.

During the strategy session last night, Niccolo had
suggested they surprise the Ravenians in this manner.
He had argued that they must take the offensive and
cease passively waiting for Basil and his knights to
appear to besiege the castle daily. After some spirited
discussion, the other warriors had agreed to give Niccolo's plan a try.

An excited young page now galloped up to join
them. Breathlessly he announced to Niccolo, "Milord,
the enemy comes over yon hillside just beyond the
castle green."

Niccolo nodded to the page, then turned to address
his army. "Men, let us move a bit closer to the archers,
but stay well within the trees so as not to give away
our position. As soon as the enemy has fully arrived
on the castle green, I shall order the bowmen to aim
for their lead horses. Afterward, the rest of us shall
charge."

The men trotted their destriers into position near
the fringes of the sheltering trees. Soon the enemy began to appear over the rise—first the heralds, then
pages bearing the Ravenian colors, followed by
knights on horseback, bowmen on foot, some of them
leading hacks that pulled the small field catapults.

Once the entire enemy army had arrived on the green about a hundred yards from the castle gates, Niccolo gave the signal to the archers. Lethal arrows whizzed through the air, and the hysterical screams of horses could be heard as the bowmen's missiles met their targets. Instantly the shrieks of men joined the wails of the animals as several horses tumbled to the earth with hooves flying wildly and riders pinned beneath them.

Niccolo signaled the heralds and lowered his visor. At the sound of the trumpets, the Falconian knights charged out of the woods and onto the battlefield, their weapons and armor screeching as they moved, the hooves of their horses thundering on the loam.

The enemy was already in wild disarray, several knights down with their mounts while other horses had spooked at the scent of blood, causing their riders to fight to rein them in. One hapless rider ended up far afield, his mount tossing him into the lake. Several Ravenian knights tried to take charge, shouting and waving their arms. At last horses were wheeled about, lances and swords readied, crossbows cranked to the proper tension, longbows drawn with arrows.

The Ravenian reaction came woefully late. Even as Basil's knights would have attempted a charge, the Falconian army swarmed into their ranks with harrowing battle cries, swords and lances flashing, maces swinging, and axes chopping. Shrieks of metal scraping metal and high whinnies of hysterical horses rang out, along with the groans of Ravenian knights being unseated, the howls of those unfortunate ones who fell beneath the lethal hooves of the rampaging horses.

With the heat and excitement of battle surging in his blood, Niccolo unseated one knight with his lance, then quickly discarded the weapon for the close-quarters fight. He unsheathed his broadsword and swung mightily, beheading one hapless knight, run-

ning through another. As a third Ravenian knight
charged him with a roar of rage, he blocked the warrior's ax with his shield, then felled the man with a
thrust to his gullet.

Flipping back his visor and shaking sweat from his
face, Niccolo paused to reconnoiter the battle, and
was pleased to note that around him, his comrades
were meeting with equal success. He watched Sir Edgar chop an arm off a howling Ravenian, saw Sir Cesare wield his mace to dispatch a bowman. Grim
satisfaction welled in him.

Then he yelled his triumph as he watched the enemy begin a panicked retreat . . .

Up on the allure behind the parapets, with Christian's falcon on her wrist, Aurora watched the battle
below. When none of the knights had appeared to
break their fast in the great hall this morn, and she
had seen but Christian's falcon alone on its perch, she
had summoned the bird, then gone outside to the bailey, where a sentry had informed her that Christian,
Niccolo, and the others had left the castle fully armored before dawn. Her curiosity had spurred her to
climb high into the battlements.

Now, with awe and admiration, she observed the
fray below, watching the clash of bright colors,
shields, swords, and armor, hearing the screams of
horses and shouts of men in agony. She was pleased
to note that Christian was holding his own against the
enemy, wielding his mace like a master. But her gaze
soon became riveted to a huge knight on a magnificent black destrier, a knight she was certain was Niccolo. He was utterly fearsome and ruthless, swinging
his mighty broadsword, dispatching every luckless
knight who crossed his path.

Aurora smiled. So this was the strategy Niccolo had
discussed with the others last night—an ambush of
Basil's forces before they even reached her castle

gates. She had to admit his plan was inspired, that he was clearly emerging as the mightiest and most clever knight vying for her. In time, he would no doubt prove himself her champion and claim her hand—

Yet he remained a man she could not trust, a knight without mercy, a warrior without a soul. How could there be an ounce of real tenderness in a man who savaged his enemies so brutally?

Still, Aurora had to admit that his barbarism also treacherously stirred her. Verily, the sounds of battle were nearly drowned out by the fierce pounding of her own heart, and she felt swept by wave after wave of dizzying excitement. Oh, this could not be love! she thought achingly. Only lust could bring such staggering longings in the face of her suitor's cruelty. Surely the spirits had spoken the truth there.

Even as she struggled with these daunting realizations, Basil was routed, his knights fleeing into the woods, the green littered with his casualties and abandoned catapults. Niccolo and the others waved their swords, shouted their victory, and gathered their captives.

Aurora climbed down from the parapets to greet the victors. The army rode triumphantly into the bailey, using their weapons to prod along the six battered and frightened prisoners who staggered along ahead of them. Aurora arrived in the midst of the knights soon after they had dismounted. At once the falcon flew off her wrist and over to Christian. Holding the bird aloft as she flashed her wings, her brother grinned at her, and she smiled back, delighted to see him unharmed. Then her gaze shifted to Niccolo, who stood but a few paces beyond her, looking splendid in his gleaming, close-fitting armor, and staring at her so intently!

"Milady, we have won the day for you!" announced an exultant Sir Gilbert.

"So I have seen," she replied happily.

A beaming Edgar strode up to the princess. "We caught Basil totally by surprise! We captured several of his fleeing knights, and the craven even abandoned his trebuchet and ballista on the field!"

"How splendid!" she declared.

Aurora stepped closer to Niccolo, who was still quietly watching her. She could smell his sweat—and the scent of the enemy blood that streaked his armor and mail mittens. Again she wondered why she could summon no revulsion, no outrage. To the contrary, his strength, his ruthlessness, set her aquiver.

"For all of this, we must thank Sir Niccolo—is it not so?" she asked.

While Niccolo nodded modestly, Christian called, "Yea, sister, 'twas Sir Niccolo who mapped out this brilliant strategy. We are clearly in his debt."

"Hear! Hear!" shouted the other knights, waving fists and cheering Niccolo.

Niccolo addressed his comrades. "We have accomplished much today, knights, but the war is hardly over. Basil will surely not give up after only one route. He will return." He gestured contemptuously toward the prisoners, and continued without passion. "I suggest we torture the captives for information, gouge out their eyes and apply hot coals to their feet. Then, mayhap after we draw, quarter, and disembowel them, we shall gallop through the village of Kestrel with their heads on our lances. When Basil hears of the fate befalling his men-at-arms, he will think twice before trifling with us again."

Niccolo's words were met with gasps of horror on the part of the Falconian knights, while the captured Ravenians fell to their knees in sick fear and began to babble incoherently, begging Niccolo for mercy while he arrogantly ignored their plight. Aurora was appalled; she could not believe Niccolo would so calmly suggest such unspeakable torture!

Sir Edgar, his expression deeply dismayed, spoke

up for the others. "Nay, Sir Niccolo, we cannot possibly commit such a sacrilege. 'Tis against the rules of chivalry to torture a knight."

"Bah!" scoffed Niccolo.

"A knight may only be ransomed," argued Christian. "To deal with a man of chivalry in such a barbarous manner is unheard-of."

"*Sí*, señor, what you suggest is dishonorable," declared the Castilian haughtily.

"I care not for honor," retorted Niccolo, "but only for winning."

Aurora fought a shudder as she recalled Niccolo bespeaking precisely the same ruthless attitude toward *her*. As he and the other knights continued to bicker over the captives, Sir Galen stepped up to her.

Behind his hand, he confided, "Milady, it falls on you to settle this. You alone have the right of high justice in Falconia."

With the prisoners still pleading miserably, Aurora gathered her courage. Staring straight at Niccolo, she announced, "Knights, I must agree with my brother. We shall imprison the captives in the dungeon, and ransom them according to tradition. 'Tis wrong to so abuse men of chivalry."

Niccolo shot her a hard look. "Do what you will, Princess," he retorted, tearing off his mail mittens and tossing them down. "I am trying to help you win this war . . ." He paused, scornfully regarding the other knights. "But I cannot save you from your own foolishness. Nor can I lead men who call themselves warriors but possess hearts of women!"

Niccolo turned and stalked away, and a relieved sigh rippled over the bailey . . .

"Who is this devil knight?" demanded Basil.

That afternoon, Ignatius and the King of Ravenia were again conspiring, this time on a hillside not far from Ravenia Castle. Basil was pacing about the small clearing in a rage, furious about the ambush his forces had suffered at the hands of the Falconians that morn. Ignatius had already grown weary just watching him storm about.

"Your antagonist is Niccolo Campioni, of Venice," Ignatius explained. "He is the one who planned and led today's attack. Indeed, Sir Niccolo and the other knights were in the barracks war room plotting their treachery until well past midnight."

"Had I been riding at the fore today, he would have slain me!" Basil roared.

"Mayhap so, Sire."

Like a raging dragon, Basil sputtered in his fury. "That son of hell lost me three of my best knights— and six others are now captive."

"You could likely ransom them, Sire—"

Basil waved a hand angrily. "These trees will turn to stone ere I pay one penny in tribute to the Falconians. Let Aurora feed my knights as they rot in her dungeons. We shall simply gather more men-at-arms from among our villeins."

Ignatius stifled a frustrated groan. "Then you intend to keep besieging the castle in the same manner, Sire?"

Wearing a fearsome scowl, Basil continued to march about, muttering under his breath. "If we return on the morrow, they shall lie in wait for us again, methinks."

"I agree, Sire," said Ignatius wryly.

Basil nodded. "We shall delay a day or two, let them grow complacent. Then we shall smash them like ants beneath a rock." He pounded a fist against his palm in emphasis.

"Yea, Sire, an inspired strategy," agreed Basil, while musing that the King of Ravenia was a feeble-minded dolt.

Basil shot Ignatius a suspicious glance. "Is this Nic-

colo Campioni as successful in wooing the princess as
he is on the battlefield?"

Ignatius chuckled. "Nay, Sire. Princess Aurora ignores Campioni each eve as the other knights sing her
praises like giddy troubadours. And I have heard she
is quite displeased with him now, for wanting to torture your men taken captive today."

Basil laughed cynically. "Campioni is a man who
thinks much as I do. 'Twould be better we had him
on our side, eh?"

Ignatius kept his peace, while musing that Basil
could never touch Niccolo Campioni's brilliance. But
Ignatius knew voicing his true thoughts would not
secure him his coveted bribe, the fat gold coin Basil
now tossed his way ... which he eagerly pocketed.

NINETEEN

THAT AFTERNOON, NICCOLO JOINED AURORA NEAR the shrine. She was sitting on its steps when she spotted him walking toward her through the wild-flowers. Tansy trotted over to greet him, and he paused, hunkering down to pet the little fawn. Aurora shook her head. To see him now—his blond hair gleaming in the sunlight, his handsome face lit with a smile as he cavorted with her pet—one would never guess this seemingly gentle man had brutally unseated at least ten knights this morn, then argued that the enemy captives should be horribly tortured and cruelly slain.

After a moment, he rose and walked over to her, his stride easy and confident. He sat down beside her and leaned over to kiss her. Despite the thrill of his nearness, she held up a hand and eyed him mutinously.

"Do not try to kiss me, knight," she scolded. "I am displeased with you."

He appeared stunned. "But I won the day for you!"

"Yea, but your thirst for blood was not assuaged," she continued reproachfully. " 'Twas brutal, the way you suggested tormenting our captives."

"And you do not think it is brutal for Basil to attack

your castle day after day, trying to force you to wed him?''

She fell silent, her expression turbulent. ''What made you so ruthless, knight, that you would suggest abusing others so savagely?''

Frowning, Niccolo picked a stalk of grass, then cast it aside. He could not speak to her of the true cause of his rage and bitterness, the betrayal that had driven all compassion from his heart.

Instead, he chose a less revealing explanation. ''Milady, you do not wish to hear details of what I saw and did in battle.'' He flashed her a cajoling look. ''And why pout so? Do you think a knight who kills with brutality cannot kiss a woman with tenderness?''

Feeling uneasy, she arose. ''I—I do not know. You confuse me. I wish you would leave me be.''

He stood to face her resolutely. ''You do not. Whatever your protests, you welcome me here.''

''I do not!''

But Niccolo only gently took her hand and raised it to his mouth. Holding her captive with his bright eyes, he brushed his lips sensuously over her soft skin. Aurora winced with yearning, his skilled wooing again decimating her defenses.

He knew. Niccolo grinned and slowly drew her into his arms, raking his fervid gaze over her. Even though she pressed her hands on his chest to hold him at bay, Aurora felt her heart skidding at his strength, his warmth, his enticing scent. Her lower lip trembled as she struggled to hang on to her pride, her resolve, in the face of his overwhelming charm and masculinity.

''Your arms welcome me, milady,'' he murmured seductively, ''as do your honeyed lips, your lovely body.''

''Nay,'' she denied hoarsely.

''Yea,'' he taunted back. ''Come, now. Give me but

one kiss . . . one sweet kiss to reward your champion. Am I not deserving of a prize after winning the day for you?"

She rebelliously shook her head. "Nay, you have enticed enough kisses, knight."

"Have I?"

She nodded, but without conviction.

Aurora's heart roared as Niccolo leaned over, his breath warm on her lips as he repeated, "Have I?"

Aurora was not sure just how it happened, but this time, her lips claimed *his*. Longing jolted her, for the contact was sweet and staggering. She heard Niccolo's groan of pleasure, felt his arms tighten about her, his tongue sliding inside her mouth in a wanton caress. Her senses in chaos and her lie exposed, she curled her arms about his neck and clung to him. Distantly she knew she must fight him, fight her own weakness, yet it felt so good to give in to the marvelous feelings he alone stirred. Seeing him triumph over her enemies today had roused her terribly, she realized.

Finally she managed to push him away and move on, her limbs, her voice, quivering. "We must stop."

"No."

"Yea," she retorted. "You think you have the right to steal my kisses, knight, but you do not!"

"I have not stolen, milady," he chided. "You kissed me."

Embarrassed, she stammered, "But—you stormed my defenses."

"And you surrendered," he added wickedly.

She glanced away, coloring.

His hand firmly grasped her shoulder. "Why do you fight me, milady?"

She turned to him in uncertainty. "Because I do not trust you, knight."

He blanched. "I have fought for you, risked my life for you, routed your enemy this morn, yet still you say you do not trust me?"

She sadly shook her head. "You do not tell me who you really are, what you really are about. You are locked up inside yourself, knight."

He said nothing, his expression brooding.

She stepped closer, her bright gaze challenging him. "Did you come here today because you want me, or because you want to win?"

Appearing for once ambivalent, he reached out to caress her cheek with his fingertips. She felt a rush of heat at his merest touch.

"What if I said I come for both—and I shall win both, milady?" he asked solemnly.

Her face growing hotter still from his words, she backed away from his tempting touch. "I must take great care with the choices I make in love . . . or I could die."

Appearing alarmed, he seized her arm. "What do you mean, you could die?"

Confronted by his formidable frown, Aurora hesitated, not sure whether she should share her dire legacy with him. She so often suspected Niccolo was only toying with her, that wooing her was a game to him. Mayhap he needed to understand that the game he played was life or death.

She faced him boldly. "Remember when you first spied me here, and accused me of talking to no one?"

"*Sì*, milady."

She lifted her chin another notch. "Well, I was talking to someone. To the spirits of my dead ancestors."

"What?" he cried, backing away and eyeing her askance. "Then you are a witch—or a heretic!"

She lowered her gaze. "You do not believe me."

He pondered this for a long moment, and finally seemed to relent. "Tell me, and I shall try."

She stole a glance at him, and decided his expression seemed sincere. "Almost a century ago, one of my female ancestors spurned her one true love, and was later cursed by him as he died. Ever since that time, every female in the royal line who has married for less than true love has died within a year."

His brow knitted fiercely. "All, milady?"

"Yea, all."

"But how?" he asked.

"Some in childbirth, some from strange maladies." Aurora paused to shudder. "My grandmother went mad and threw herself from a tower."

Niccolo's hand closed over hers. "I am sorry, milady," he said sincerely.

Touched by his gesture of comfort, she inclined a hand toward the altar. "The shrine is dedicated to all my female ancestors who died so young. Three of their spirits still haunt this copse. That is why you thought you heard me talking to no one, for the ghosts are here and they have spoken to me ever since the advent of my fertility."

Niccolo had been listening to the account with an expression of amazement. "So you do hear voices."

"Yea."

"They haunt you? But why?"

"Because I am the last remaining female in the royal line," she continued passionately. "If I marry for less than true love, I, too, shall perish, and shall be doomed to roam the countryside for all eternity with my ancestors. I am their last hope for breaking the curse and freeing their trapped spirits."

Niccolo stared at the shrine, perplexed.

"That is why the choice I make in matrimony is so critical," Aurora finished soberly. "If I choose wrongly, then I will die ere long."

Stroking his jaw and glancing from the statue back to her, Niccolo seemed to mull this over. Then a suspicious look settled over his features. "But if you believe in this curse, why would you vow to marry the knight who proves himself your champion?"

"For a long time, I planned to marry no one, so

badly did I fear the curse," Aurora confided. "But soon after you arrived in Falconia, the spirits decreed that I must have a contest for the knights. They told me my own true love will emerge as my champion."

A smile tugged at his lips. "They said that, did they?"

She nodded. "And they warned me about you, knight."

"They warned you?"

Aurora gestured toward the statue of the Angel of Wisdom. "They said your soul is black, and what I feel for you is lust, not love. As I have already informed you, if I marry for passion, then I shall be doomed."

Having said her words and exposed her secret, Aurora waited tensely for Niccolo to respond. He paced about nearby, scowling.

"Well, knight?" she challenged. "Do you believe me?"

Turning to her, he shook his head. "No. You speak convincingly enough, milady, but ultimately I cannot give credence to such nonsense. I believe curses are the product of an overly active imagination—or of madness."

"Then you do not believe I will die if I choose the wrong husband?" she asked with an edge of hurt.

"No, I do not believe it," he replied bluntly.

Bitter disappointment washed through Aurora. She should have known the jaded Niccolo would scoff at her story. She felt betrayed, especially after the intimacies—both physical and emotional—they had shared.

She eyed him accusingly. "I never should have trusted you with the secrets of my heart."

Appearing contrite, he stepped closer and laid a hand on her shoulder. "Mayhap I spoke too harshly."

"Mayhap," she agreed petulantly.

With his fingertips, he raised her chin. "But I refuse

to believe in any curse that warns you against me."

She fought a treacherous smile.

"However, I will concede that, whether the curse is real or not, you do seem to believe it."

"Thank you," she returned stiffly.

Gravely he went on, "I also fear that, believing in the curse, you could succumb to it. You could well become your own worst enemy, milady."

"The curse is my enemy," she countered adamantly.

He glanced again at the shrine, a calculating smile drifting over his handsome features. "Even if the curse is real, could you not outwit it?"

"Outwit it?" she asked, intrigued. "How?"

His expression cynically amused, Niccolo curled an arm about Aurora's waist and trailed his fingertips up and down her spine, raising shivers. Impaling her with his passionate gaze, he whispered, "You could have a love affair with me, milady."

Wide-eyed, she jerked away from him, pressing a hand to her pounding heart. "Without benefit of marriage?"

Eyeing her scandalized countenance, he chuckled. "*Sì*, milady. Then you could know all the sweetness of passion, and exorcise all the treacherous lust you feel, without risk of reprisal."

Aurora felt confused yet wildly titillated by Niccolo's bold suggestion. To try to circumvent the curse had never even occurred to her! Oh, he was wicked to suggest they commit such brazen sin!

But had he spoken with a grain of truth?

"I am not certain a curse can be outwitted, knight," she replied, frowning. " 'Twould be dangerous."

Appearing emboldened by her words, Niccolo pressed a hand to the small of her back and began backing her toward a nearby tree. "But worth the risk. 'Twould it not be far more dangerous to let yourself continue to feel this passion that could destroy you?"

She frowned up at him. "What makes you think I feel passion for you, knight?"

His earnest expression reproved her. "Milady . . . I can see it in your eyes, feel it in the way you tremble against me." He pressed his mouth against her temple, touching the vein that throbbed with sensual awareness. He spoke in a deep, seductive tone that mesmerized her. "You gave yourself away when you pressed your soft lips to mine. Darling Princess, you know you want this. You can safely vent those feelings with me."

"I—I am not sure," Aurora stammered, reeling at his nearness. "You confuse me again."

Niccolo pinned her against the tree and nuzzled her ear with his mouth. Seared by the heat of his lips, his breath, she moaned in helpless torment.

"Let me convince you, milady," he whispered. "Let me make love to you."

Aurora's cry of longing was swallowed up by Niccolo's passionate kiss. By the time his tongue stole inside her mouth, she was frantic with hunger. Incoherent moans of abandonment escaped her. Pressed against the tree as she was, she could feel his heat, his incredible strength, the hard pressure of his muscled chest crushing her breasts. Their bodies were tightly, provocatively melded together; Aurora could feel his hard member pressing into her pelvis, both shocking and thrilling her. When he reached behind her to cup and knead her bottom, tilting her into his burgeoning manhood, she feared her heart would burst in her chest, so fierce was the desire storming through her.

"I can feel you wanting me, Aurora," he whispered roughly, arching against her erotically. "You cannot deny that you yearn to take me inside you . . ."

"Pray, do not say such things," she implored, digging her fingernails into his shoulders.

"I must, Aurora," he continued hoarsely, his gaze burning into hers. "I must have you. Tell me, have you ever imagined making love with a man?"

Her eyes went wide. "Nay, never!"

He chuckled, tracing his thumb over the swollen outline of her nipple until she winced with desire. "Admit the truth, milady. I think you *have* imagined it."

"Well ... mayhap," she gasped, sinking rapidly.

His mouth hovered close to hers. "Mayhap you have imagined it with me, no?"

His breath mingling with her own, their faces pressed so close, Aurora implored Niccolo with wide, desperate eyes until he took mercy on her and kissed her again ... When his hand curled about her breast, excitement swamped her and she arched shamelessly into his touch.

"Are you frightened?" he asked gently, between soft kisses. "Do you fear I shall hurt you?"

"I ... I do not know."

His lips roved down her throat, raising gooseflesh. "Do not be afraid, milady. 'Tis beautiful, you know, two beings joined as one. Lay aside your pride and your fear, Aurora, and give yourself to me."

Indeed, Aurora could not deny the fierce hunger that gnawed at her so insistently, demanding release. But Niccolo's bold fingers, tugging insistently at her skirts, soon reminded her that the potential price of assuaging her lust was simply too great!

"Pray, you must not," she implored. "Stop, or you shall doom me!"

"Then stop me, milady," he rasped. "Stop me, or I shall have you, now."

At last, with a fevered cry, Aurora managed to shove Niccolo away and break free, running out of the copse, fleeing her own overwhelming desires ...

Niccolo stood behind in the grove, breathing hard to control his passions and watching her flight. Then, remembering her ardent response, and how close she had come to surrendering, he smiled.

Niccolo returned to the castle, his thoughts exultant. He knew he would soon have Aurora within his grasp. If he held steadfast and refused to allow his own desires to defeat him, he could surely use her belief in the curse to bring her around—

Of course, he gave no credence to such nonsense himself. Curses and hearing voices! Surely the princess was simply prone to flights of fancy, as young ladies her age tended to be.

He frowned, unease washing over him. The alternative was, of course, unthinkable. For if the curse was real, then he would be toying not simply with Aurora's future but with her very life, making his actions not just self-serving but depraved.

Surely the curse was not real.

Still, a doubt niggled, especially as he recalled the sweetness of her kisses, and imagined her dead within a year, her lovely smiles, her lilting laughter, lost to him forever. Unexpectedly, the prospect ate at him like bile . . .

Angered by his own weak thoughts, he soundly scolded himself. The princess was a wily enchantress, a schemer who had surely contrived with her duplicitous uncle. Her latest claims were doubtless just a ruse to gain his sympathies. He must not give up his determination to win the revenge due him, and to punish her as she so richly deserved . . .

As Niccolo neared the sally port to the castle, he spotted a furtive figure in the distance. He stopped in his tracks and ducked behind a tree, peeking out to have a look at the person.

'Twas Ignatius again! The hunched little man stopped near the lichen-encrusted steps, pulled out his purse, and opened it. He gleefully held up a gold coin to the light, then replaced the coin in his purse, his expression smug as he descended toward the door.

Niccolo scowled. So the little man was a traitor, after all. There was much more to be feared in these woods than gnomes, ghosts, and curses.

Then guilt assailed him as he realized he was no better than Ignatius as he, too, plotted the princess's downfall . . .

TWENTY

AT DINNER IN THE GREAT HALL, NICCOLO WAS AN-
noyed to see Sir Edgar and Sir Cesare sharing the
royal dais with Aurora, Christian, Aurora's ladies-in-
waiting, and other favored members of her royal staff.
Although Edgar, busy carrying on a spirited conversation with Lady Iris, seemed more interested in her
than in the princess, the despised Genoan and Aurora
had their heads together throughout much of the
meal. Niccolo could hear their laughter, could see Aurora's treacherous smiles and Cesare's idiotic grins.
He ground his teeth as Cesare offered to refill Aurora's goblet, or to slice her another serving of mutton.
And Christian, he noted to his irritation, was not protecting Aurora as a loyal brother should; busy fawning all over Lady Flora, he seemed oblivious to the
fact that his sister was being enticed by the wily Cesare.

The fact that Niccolo still had not been invited to
Aurora's table both angered and bemused him. 'Twas
a deliberate affront, and they both knew it. How
could she kiss him so sweetly in the copse, then flaunt
her charms to all his competitors? He chided himself
for ever allowing himself any softer feelings toward
her, for ever thinking of her as anything but a faithless
coquette.

179

Yet he wanted her even more fiercely than he had
ever wanted his own traitorous wife! For Aurora had
responded to him in the bower today as Cecilia never
had. When he remembered Aurora's flushed cheeks,
her breathless sounds, the way her mouth had melted
into his, and how her fingernails had dug into his
shoulders in betrayal of her passion . . . the tormenting memories made him mad with jealousy as he
watched her tempt another now. He burned to take
her into his arms and seduce her with his kisses until
she was compelled to look only at him. Today in the
copse she had given him such a feeling of heady
power . . . Now she had cruelly forsaken him, leaving
him powerless.

His exasperation only heightened when yet another
cavalier appeared that eve to take up Aurora's cause.
Aurora had moved from her table to her throne chair,
and Niccolo was sharing a dessert of custard and
spiced wine with the other men, when a very agi-
tated-looking Mortimer ushered in a tall, red-haired
knight dressed in a skirt of Highland plaid, with a
matching colorful sash slung over his doublet, and a
saber in a jeweled scabbard strapped around his
waist. The man's rough-hewn, freckled features were
set in a noble scowl; in his arms he bore a length of
bright green wool.

Before the royal dais, the seneschal wrung his
hands and proclaimed, "Milady, I present Sir Duncan
of Scotland."

As all waited in rapt silence, the huge man bowed
on one knee before Aurora, and spoke in a heavy
Scottish brogue. "Princess, I be Sir Duncan Cartwright
of Clan MacDougal, grand master of the Order of Dal-
mally. I've helped our good King James route the
English from our homeland's southern borders. I
present ye with this fine length of Highland wool to
keep ye warm, and in tribute to yer royal loveliness.
You see, Highness, I've been dispatched by yer uncle

to save ye from yer enemies and to claim yer hand in holy matrimony."

Upon completion of Duncan's pompous speech, several of the knights guffawed, and even Aurora struggled not to snicker as she reached out to accept the Scot's gift. "Thank you for your fine tribute, sir knight, and welcome to Falconia," she declared regally. "However, if you have come to save me, I reckon you had best wait your turn with the others."

As the Scotsman glanced about him in consternation, the knights roared with laughter. Furious, Sir Duncan bolted to his feet, unsheathed his saber, and charged the knights' table. Under the men's astonished eyes, he vented his spleen on a boar's head, skewering it to bits.

"I dinna come here to be mocked!" he yelled, waving his sword.

A hush fell over the gathering, some of the most fearsome knights appearing daunted. Understanding the newcomer's chagrin and admiring his spirit, Niccolo stood. He noted that the Scot was so enraged that his face had darkened by several shades and veins stood out on his stout, sunburned neck and broad forehead.

Niccolo flashed the man a sympathetic smile. "We are not mocking you, Sir Duncan. Believe me, we jest much more at ourselves."

The Scot sheathed his weapon and faced Niccolo forbiddingly. "I dinna understand. Who are ye, sir, and what are ye babbling about?"

Squelching a grin, Niccolo replied, "I am Niccolo Campioni of Venice, grand master of *Cavalieri di San Marco*—and I am trying to explain that you have become another unfortunate victim of the Count of Osprey's chicanery."

As the Scot blinked uncomprehendingly at Niccolo, Aurora called imperiously, "Sir Niccolo, will you kindly explain to our guest what has transpired, and see that he is provided food and drink?"

His expression cynical, Niccolo bowed to Aurora. "Of course, Princess." He inclined a hand toward the Scot. "Sir Duncan, if you will have a seat, I shall attempt to explain to you about the . . . er . . . sudden proliferation of royal bridegrooms in the Kingdom of Falconia."

Duncan sullenly joined the others. After the stewards brought the newcomer wine and food, Niccolo and the others tried to explain to Duncan about Artemas's ruse. The Scot went through the predictable stages of rage and disbelief. He bellowed furiously that the treacherous Artemas "should be drawn and quartered for all to see!" When several knights endorsed the bloodthirsty suggestion, Niccolo, glancing toward the dais and noting Aurora's wan expression, pointed out wryly that first the man must be found.

After much pontification, the Scot finally acknowledged that he had been duped. Niccolo explained to him about the contest, and he listened with a massive scowl. He asked a number of shrewd questions about the war with Ravenia. When Niccolo outlined the shift in strategy he had suggested, and told of how Basil had been routed that very morn, Duncan replied cagily, "Why dinna we go one step further and go steal this rascal from his bed, then hang him from our parapets? 'Twould bring his mischief to a swift halt, no doubt."

Silence fell in the wake of that aggressive suggestion, although Niccolo again felt a sense of grudging respect toward the Scot.

"But 'twould not be chivalrous," argued Gilbert at last.

"*Sí*, señor, 'twould be dishonorable," echoed Sir Rafael.

"Aye, but 'twould be expedient," laughed the Scot, lustily waving a fist. "I'm fer whatever quells the enemy, whether it be lopping off his head in battle, or disemboweling him while he sleeps."

Listening to the man, Niccolo was given pause, realizing that at last a knight had arrived at the castle who was as ruthless as he was. Could Sir Duncan prove himself Aurora's champion and thwart his own plans?

His anxieties only increased when the Scot rose from the table and approached the princess, again bowing on one knee. With a hand over his heart, he spoke earnestly. "Princess, yer uncle has done me a terrible wrong. But I've made the journey now and I fully believe you innocent of yer kin's treachery. I shall not be discouraged from my goal. I offer myself as yer champion, and swear I shall defeat your enemies and win yer royal hand."

To Niccolo's amazement, Aurora smiled at the Scot and extended her hand. "You may kiss the hand you covet, knight."

The Scot, appearing delighted, grinned at Aurora, took her hand, and kissed her fingers slowly and reverently. Meanwhile, several knights mumbled to one another in irritation, while Niccolo churned in fury.

And thus the knights vying for Aurora rose from seven to eight.

Later, Aurora sat in her solar near the window, looking out at the misty courtyard below. Behind her, Flora was quietly brushing her hair.

She did not spot Niccolo galloping about the courtyard this eve, though she reckoned he was in a fine temper. She had caught his menacing looks tonight, and they had washed many a chill down her spine. She knew she had made him and the others jealous by allowing Sir Duncan to kiss her hand. She had piqued the ire of all the knights by granting favors to the Scot so quickly. Yet she felt so confused, and some devil in her had wanted to incite the men . . . particularly to incite Niccolo.

Oh, he had bewitched her so . . . especially today in the copse. Shivers consumed her at the memory. Niccolo's words, his kisses, had been so passionate, so persuasive, and when he had argued that the curse could be outwitted if they had a love affair . . . she had been powerfully tempted, especially when she had felt his hard desire thrusting against her, prompting a scandalous corresponding ache deep inside herself.

Yet she could not trust him, could not trust his motives. He refused to believe in the curse, and that chafed badly at her pride. Was there any goodness in him, or was he all cynical mercenary? Her intellect argued that he could be playing her falsely, yet her emotions became more tied to him with each passing day. She feared those feelings might soon defeat her.

With whom could she share her intimate quandary? She dared not consult Christian regarding Niccolo's designs, for her brother would become infuriated and would surely challenge any knight who tried to steal her chastity prior to marriage. Verily, she had the spirits to consult, but they had already denounced Niccolo as her true love. As for her dark knight himself . . . she might just as well make counsel with the devil!

Hearing her lady humming a love ballad, she glanced upward and caught the expression of serene happiness on Flora's face. For a brief moment Aurora's anxiety faded in the rush of gladness she felt to see her lady so joyously in love with Christian. She had noted the two had eyes only for each other during the meal tonight. She could always consult dear Flora regarding her own dilemma of the heart, but she must take care. As heir to the throne, she was held to a very high standard.

As if she had sensed Aurora's thoughts, Flora

ceased her humming. "Milady, you appear troubled. Are you unwell?"

Aurora smiled at her friend. "Nay, I was only spinning wool in my mind."

"About what, milady?"

Aurora hesitated. "Flora, how can a lady know her true love is really true?"

Flora frowned. "Well, I am not sure, milady. Of which knight do you speak?"

Suddenly feeling impish, Aurora replied, "Were I you, I would be speaking of Christian, would I not? I saw you and my brother exchange many an adoring look tonight."

Flora blushed deeply, her hands pausing in Aurora's tresses. "Milady, does it trouble you that Christian and I . . ."

"Nay, you both have my blessing," Aurora reassured her. She winked. "Will you soon be consulting Father Mark about the reading of the banns?"

Flora shyly shook her head. "Nay, Christian and I have agreed that the war, and the matter of your husband, must be settled first, milady."

Aurora laughed. "You may not wish to wait too long, or you may both turn to stone. Basil appears as stubborn as ever. As for the question of my husband, many have come to court me, but only one may have me."

"And that is why you have staged the contest, milady?" Flora inquired with a frown.

"Nay, I did so because the spirits so directed me," Aurora replied solemnly. "They told me my champion will be my true love."

Wide-eyed, Flora crossed herself. "Milady, take care when you speak such heresy," she urged hoarsely.

"I am sorry, I forgot," Aurora murmured, reaching upward to squeeze her friend's hand.

"Pray, do not apologize," fretted Flora. "Just practice caution. One never knows when Martha or another of your servants may overhear. You know how fearful they are of the curse."

Aurora nodded and decided to change the subject. "Tell me, what do you think of the newcomer, Sir Duncan?"

Carefully plaiting Aurora's hair, Flora laughed. "He is full of fire and bluster, that one. I reckon he will serve you well, milady, but I am not sure I trust him completely."

"I am not certain I trust any knight completely," concurred Aurora ruefully.

"And especially not Sir Niccolo?" asked Flora.

Aurora laughed, looking up to meet Flora's amused gaze. "Then you know he is the one who stirs me most?"

Flora nodded. "I can see it in your eyes, milady."

"But is he my true love?" Aurora asked, again serious. "You know the risk I take . . ."

"Yea, milady, I know," whispered Flora, shuddering.

"Then is Niccolo my true love?"

Flora sadly shook her head. "Milady, all I can tell you is, choose wisely, and take your time. Do not allow any knight to rush you into making a choice that could mean your death."

"You are saying I must give a fair chance to all the knights?"

"Yea, milady." Flora laughed ruefully. "Mayhap 'tis a blessing your uncle dispatched so many, eh?"

"Mayhap," agreed Aurora with a frown. "But how can I know for certain which man I must choose? The spirits say my champion will be my true love . . ." She helplessly clenched her fists. "Oh, 'tis so confusing."

Flora gently touched Aurora's shoulder. "I know, milady, and I wish I could advise you more. But I cannot, not with so much at stake. I am no expert in matters of the heart—"

"But you know Christian stirs your heart?"

"Yea, I know," the lady admitted with an expression of wistful pleasure. "But one cannot measure or test true love. 'Tis simply felt, I reckon."

"I suppose," agreed Aurora.

In an obvious attempt to lighten the mood, Flora added, "Narcissus searched for love in a pond, but became enamored with his own reflection. The road to true love can be treacherous, eh, milady?"

"Yea," agreed Aurora, feeling more conflicted than ever.

TWENTY-ONE

DAYBREAK FOUND NICCOLO, CHRISTIAN, SIR DUN-
can, and the rest of the knights hidden in the woods
not far from the castle. Niccolo was hoping they might
again rout Basil before he reached the castle walls.

Yet the enemy did not arrive, not even when the
sun pushed well into the skies. The company waited,
the horses impatiently stamping the loam with their
hooves, the men mumbling to one another and rest-
lessly shifting in their saddles. Each knight's armor
became a miniature oven as the day grew warmer. Sir
Duncan in particular grew peevish, cantering his
horse about the area and threatening to give away
their cover. When Niccolo cautioned Duncan that he
was creating too much of a clamor, the Scot yelled,
"Whose addlepated scheme was this in the first
place?"

Niccolo glared back.

After another hour trickled past, Sir Rafael spoke
up to Niccolo. "Señor, it appears we have dissuaded
the enemy from attacking us."

"Do not be fooled," Niccolo replied, scowling. "I
have an instinct Basil will hold back for a time. He
likely knows we will be in the woods waiting to ambush him again. Thus he will surely forestall, hoping

we will grow complacent and he can later storm our gates with impunity."

"What would you suggest we do, Sir Niccolo?" asked Christian.

Niccolo pointed about the area. "I suggest we retreat back to the castle, but post a number of sentries in the woods and over yon rise. That way, if Basil is spotted, we can be alerted and can cut him off again before he reaches the castle."

Several knights within earshot of Niccolo consulted among themselves and nodded—except for Duncan, who had listened in stormy silence.

"Why do we not cease this folly, go to Ravenia, and seize the bloody scoundrel?" the Scot demanded.

Niccolo ground his jaw. Although at first he had admired Duncan, the man's hotheadedness was beginning to grate on his nerves. "To mount such an intrigue demands great planning—"

"Then why are we not about it?" cried the Scot in exasperation.

"How would you suggest we gain entry to Basil's castle?" Niccolo asked patiently.

Sir Duncan merely shrugged. "Surely we can bribe a servant to give us admittance through a sally port. We have castles in Scotland, so I know of such matters."

Hearing murmurs of agreement from the others, Niccolo snapped, "We shall discuss this later. For now, we must assign sentries and return to the castle. We are accomplishing naught here."

"Aye," Duncan replied with a meaningful gleam in his eyes. " 'Tis true we are all wasting our time, Sir Niccolo."

As several knights chuckled at this barbed comment, Niccolo turned and barked orders to the men-at-arms, all the while itching to throttle the arrogant Sir Duncan.

The knights galloped back to the castle and as-

sumed defensive positions high in the parapets. By
noontide, when Basil still had not appeared, Niccolo
recommended that the warriors again practice their
combat skills in the bailey while waiting for news
from the sentries stationed in the woods and beyond.
Niccolo's suggestion was greeted with enthusiasm by
the restless men, who quickly shed their armor, except
for their mail shirts. In the bailey, while peasant children watched and cheered, the knights practiced their
archery, charged one another with blunt-tipped
wooden practice lances, and locked wooden swords.

Conducting a sword tourney with Sir Baldric on
horseback, Niccolo was bemused to spot Aurora once
again sitting on the steps of the keep with her ladies-
in-waiting. She was laughing with her companions as
all of them watched the practice. He wondered why
she was lingering about the castle, when normally in
the afternoons she slipped away to the copse. The
sight of her unsettled him so that he momentarily lost
his concentration, and Baldric was able to strike him
in the side through his chain mail. He bellowed with
pain and glared at his opponent, even as his well-
trained destrier whinnied and instinctively back-
stepped.

Niccolo wheeled his horse and returned his attention to the tourney, charging aggressively at Baldric,
battering his opponent's weapon as both chargers
pranced and shrieked, maneuvering for the optimum
battle position. Despite the rigors of the contest, the
pain in Niccolo's side, and the sweat trickling into his
eyes, he found his gaze straying again and again to
lovely Aurora. And yet she did not even seem to note
he was there. *Dio,* she was watching Duncan lock
swords with Edgar! When Duncan drove the usually
formidable Edgar to his knees, she cheered and stood
with her ladies.

Niccolo's blood boiled. Totally distracted and angered, he groaned as Baldric took another swipe at

him, this time grazing his arm. Niccolo cursed under his breath and charged anew.

Seconds later, Niccolo was alarmed to watch Duncan approach the castle steps and bow before Aurora. He heard titters breaking out among her and the other ladies, then Aurora rose and swept down to his side. The two strolled away from the others.

Niccolo was so enraged that this time he swung brutally at Baldric, knocking him off his horse. He looked down at his dazed opponent—flat on his back on the ground, a stunned expression on his face—and realized what he had done.

He hopped off his horse, lifted Sir Baldric to a seated position, and pounded his back to restore his breath.

The Bavarian knight gasped, coughing violently. "Are you trying to murder me, Venetian?" he demanded hoarsely.

"You have merely lost your wind—you will recover," said Niccolo gruffly. "I did not mean to unhorse you."

And leaving Baldric to sputter furiously, he strode off.

Niccolo trailed Aurora and Duncan to the far side of the bailey, his fury becoming blinding as he heard their laughter. He continued to stalk them, grimacing at the sight of Aurora's pale blue, jewel-trimmed skirts trailing in the breeze. At last he stepped up to join the couple, and both turned to eye him in perplexity.

Niccolo spoke straight to the point. "Sir Duncan, I would speak with the princess alone."

Duncan colored. "I am speaking with her now; 'tis plain to see. Leave us be, Venetian."

"You are needed elsewhere," Niccolo said coldly.

"Bah!" scoffed the Scot.

"Your page is looking for you."

"Balderdash," the Scot blustered.

Niccolo smiled nastily. "He says your destrier has gone lame."

Duncan paled, glancing in uncertainty from the princess to Niccolo. Then he stormed off.

Niccolo watched the knight's retreat, only to turn at the sound of Aurora's laughter. She stood there with mischief in her eyes and her lovely lips twitching with amusement, making him want to shake her—or kiss her senseless.

"What is so amusing, milady?" he asked with soft menace.

"You!" she replied. "Sir Duncan is going to be furious when he discovers you have lied."

"The devil with Sir Duncan," Niccolo retorted, moving an aggressive step closer and regarding her forbiddingly. " 'Tis you with whom I have a bone to pick."

She merely shrugged and strolled off. He followed her, grinding his jaw when she leaned over to pluck a daisy from a garden plot, as if she had not a care in the world.

"What is this bone, knight?"

Niccolo was blinking rapidly, eating the ground with his angry strides. "Why are you encouraging Sir Duncan?"

"I was not encouraging him, merely being hospitable," she protested.

"Then explain your most commendable hospitality," he sneered.

"Oh, I do not know," Aurora replied with a scowl, twirling the daisy in her fingers. "There is something about the Scot that commands respect. He is very direct."

Niccolo grabbed her arm and pulled her toward him, sending the bloom spinning away. "So am I, milady," he replied roughly. "Direct enough to give a coquette her comeuppance, you may be certain."

She faced him haughtily. "Release my arm."

Cursing, he complied, but shook a finger at her. "You had best understand I will tolerate no more of this mischief—"

" 'Tis not mischief and I am not a coquette," she retorted. "Furthermore, you, sir, have no right to dictate to me!"

Niccolo stepped closer to her, so close that he could smell her intoxicating scent, which only made him more insanely jealous than ever. Eyes gleaming with passion, he demanded hoarsely, "Yesterday when your breast was cupped in my hand, when your nipple puckered at my touch, had I no right?"

Obviously flustered, she glanced away. "I—I have now realized you have taken unfair advantage in the contest to win my hand. I merely wish to grant equity to the other knights."

"Equity to Sir Duncan?" he roared.

She swallowed hard. "Yea."

Niccolo was quickly losing all patience. "If you wish the contest to be fair and equal, then why do you not rendezvous with the other knights in the copse, as you do with me?"

She eyed him in challenge. "Are you saying we must cease our meetings, milord? Or should I invite the others, as well?"

Niccolo cursed so violently that Aurora actually flinched. He seized her by the shoulders and shook her soundly. "Invite another man to *our* copse and I will throttle you! Is that clear?"

Not waiting for her reply, he wheeled about and stormed off.

Aurora watched him, feeling shaken, confused, and angry with herself. Why had she so provoked Niccolo? Now he would likely never again come to meet her in her copse, a prospect that filled her with aching sadness. For the truth was, she wanted him much more than all the others . . . even as she feared in her soul that she had already strayed far down the road to disaster. After all, 'twas not as if she had only her-self—her own desires and her own destiny—to con-sider. There was her ancestors' fate, and the fate of the royal line, which would die out with her unless she chose wisely.

She watched Niccolo stride back toward the center of the bailey, watched Sir Duncan advance toward him angrily, shouting and waving his arms. Niccolo paced on, ignoring the outraged Scot. In his fury, Duncan kicked over a slops bucket. Then he spotted Aurora in the distance and started toward her.

Aurora dashed behind a cottage and wended her way back toward the keep. The thought of being with Duncan suddenly left her cold.

Niccolo joined in the war games with renewed vigor, locking swords with Olaf and Cesare. He re-mained furious at Aurora for tormenting him so. She was just like Cecilia, he realized—a heartless conniver who liked to twist apart the hearts of men in her cruel little hands. Could it be that she had guessed his darker motives, and this was her subtle way of tor-turing him . . . kissing him so sweetly, then favoring so many others with her breathtaking smiles?

Yet even as enraged as he was, he still wanted her more. When he imagined her sharing their special copse with another—especially Sir Duncan—he grew so blinded by rage that he swung brutally with his sword and sent Sir Cesare flying into a wall with a sickening thud.

Niccolo dropped his sword and cursed. As much as he held the Genoan in contempt, 'twas not a pretty sight, watching Cesare's eyes roll back in his head, seeing the insensible body crumple to the ground. He fetched a cup of water and tossed the cold liquid into the Genoan's face to revive him. Apologizing gruffly to the coughing, sputtering man, he hauled Cesare to his feet and helped him limp back to the barracks.

TWENTY-TWO

At midafternoon Aurora went to the shrine, forlornly hoping Niccolo would join her. The spring air was heady with nectar. The spirits were silent today, and even Tansy seemed subdued. Aurora waited and waited, strolling aimlessly about the copse, picking wildflowers and pulling weeds around the steps of the shrine. Still Niccolo did not appear.

After a while she settled herself on a boulder next to the small, rippling pond that fed off the mountain stream. Tansy dozed at her feet. Glancing at her own reflection in the pond—her sad eyes and wistful expression—Aurora wondered if she would be doomed like Narcissus, to be forever alone, perhaps even mesmerized by her own reflection . . .

Then a flicker of motion danced across the waters, and she started slightly at the sound of bells jingling.

"Milady?" called a small, shrill voice.

Aurora glanced up and was pleasantly surprised to see the gnome Francis standing before her with a bouquet of wildflowers in his hands. He was dressed in a green jacket and yellow tights, a striped knitted cap that drooped over his wrinkled forehead, and pointed shoes with bells.

She smiled at the little man. "Good day, Francis. Are those for me?"

"Yea, milady." His gamin face twisting into a smile, he extended the blooms.

Aurora took the bouquet. "Thank you; 'tis thoughtful of you to pluck these," she murmured, inhaling the sweet scent of the flowers. She eyed him curiously. "Where are the others—Farley, Findley, Finn, Fiske, and Frey?"

"They are in the hills, about the royal business, of course," replied Francis importantly.

"And how goes the royal business?" asked Aurora.

"Splendidly as always, Princess."

"I am pleased to hear it."

The two paused as Tansy stirred, staring wide-eyed up at the gnome. Francis grinned at the little fawn and stepped toward her, holding out his small, gnarled hand and making a clucking sound. But despite Francis's friendly overture, the little animal struggled to her feet and bolted away.

Francis flashed Aurora a woebegone look. "She does not like me."

But she adores Niccolo, Aurora thought wistfully, slanting Francis a sympathetic look. "How long have you been here watching me?" she asked.

"For some time, milady." A somber expression gripped his wrinkled features. "I fret about you. Especially today. You seem so forlorn . . . That's why I picked the blooms."

"They are lovely," she agreed, twirling the stems in her hands.

Francis settled himself on a large rock, crossing his stumpy legs. "If you are feeling droopy like the daffodils, Princess, I shall brew you up some of my magical herbal tea to perk you back up."

Aurora laughed. "I am not a flower, Francis, and my impediment is not of the body, but of the spirit."

"Are you sad because the blond giant has not come today?"

Aurora gasped. "You have spied on us!"

"I have seen you here with him," Francis admitted. "I have always guarded you, milady."

"But to watch us—"

The little man held up a hand. "Nay, milady, I do not linger . . . not when the two of you kiss and such. 'Twould be unseemly, even for a gnome."

Aurora smiled, a guilty blush stealing up her face. "You are a wicked fellow."

The little creature cackled. "We gnomes are known to be so." He studied Aurora's countenance closely. "You do look dejected, milady."

Aurora's expression was indeed poignant as she stared at the beautiful blooms—blue jonquils and yellow daisies, small white roses sweet with dew. "He would never pick these for me," she confessed quietly.

"And that is why you are so sad, Princess?"

Aurora sighed. "I am sad because there is so much I do not understand . . . and especially not about him. He woos me because he wants what I have to offer. He is charming and oh, so clever, but there is no love or tenderness in him, methinks."

The gnome drew himself up proudly. "If the giant ever hurts you, the others and I shall cheerfully slay him."

Aurora smiled. "You are too good to me."

"As you know, it has been our charge for centuries to guard the royal family." He glanced toward the shrine in the distance. "I only wish we could have saved the others."

Aurora followed Francis's somber gaze. In a small voice she asked, "Do you ever hear their voices, Francis?"

The little man blanched. "Nay, Princess," he replied, waving a hand nervously. "One time I thought mayhap there was a whisper . . . but nay, 'twas only the wind, methinks."

Aurora restrained a smile. She could tell, by the

way Francis was suddenly avoiding her eye, that he was prevaricating. "Verily, 'twas good of you to come check on me."

"Yea . . ." Francis stood and brushed off the back of his jacket. "Princess, I had best go now, find the others, and make certain they are about the royal business. When left to their own devices, Farley and Fiske fight like badgers, and Finn and Fiske chase rabbits."

Aurora nodded. "Yea, you must go ensure they are not into mischief."

The little man bowed. "Good day, Princess."

Francis left in an echoing of bells, and Aurora lingered by the pond with her solitary thoughts. By late afternoon, she knew Niccolo would not come, and her tears flowed freely. Yea, she had ruined things with him . . . ruined all with her pride, her fear.

She was about to give up, to leave the copse, when yet another reflection joined hers in the water—a handsome visage she knew so well—

Exultant, she rose, dropping the flowers in her excitement. Niccolo stood there, magnificently tall and handsome, regarding her intently. Her heart pounded in delight and new tears flooded her eyes. Then, blessedly, she was in his arms, crushed close to his pounding heart.

"Niccolo, you came! You came."

His arms trembled about her. "I did not want to," he admitted hoarsely, "but I could not help myself, milady."

She stared up at him, her expression one of heartfelt joy. "Then your heart is more genuine than you have admitted, sir knight, for it brought you here to me. You do want me."

"Heaven help me, I do," he murmured achingly.

"You must know I would never share this place with anyone else, save my brother and mayhap the gnomes," she assured him. " 'Tis our special place."

He regarded her in uncertainty. "Do you truly mean that, milady?"

"Truly, I do."

"Oh, *Dio*." He leaned over, his lips capturing hers. "You smell of flowers, and the sweet earth."

For a moment they clung together, kissing hungrily, Niccolo roving his hands over her back, Aurora reaching upward to caress the strong muscles of his arms and shoulders.

At last they moved apart slightly, and Niccolo stared at the mound of discarded blossoms at their feet. He scowled, and his voice took on a hard edge. "You say you would never share this place with anyone else."

"Yea," she admitted warily.

His accusing gaze flashed to her. "Then who brought you the flowers, milady? Or did you pluck them yourself?"

A guilty grin lit her face. "Francis the gnome brought them. He watches over me here—and everywhere, methinks."

Niccolo frowned. "He spies on us?"

Aurora giggled. "Nay—not when we kiss and such, or so he claims."

Niccolo was still glowering. "If he ever spies on us when we kiss, I shall skewer him alive and roast him over an open pit."

Daunted by his ferocity, she bit her lip. "Francis says if you ever hurt me, he and the others will slay you."

His response surprised her, for instead of being cynically amused as she would have expected, he grew utterly solemn. He reached out to brush a wisp of hair from her eyes, and regarded her in a stark, intense manner. "Should I ever hurt you, milady," he whispered, "mayhap I would be deserving of the wrath of the gnomes."

Aurora regarded him in confusion, not certain what

he meant, or why she seemed to detect a hint of self-reproach in his tone. "Do you wish to harm me, knight?"

He did not answer immediately, again glancing at the discarded blossoms. When he spoke, his voice was rough with anger. "Had Sir Duncan brought you flowers . . . had you trysted with him here, in our place . . . *Dio*, I might not have been able to restrain myself."

Studying his impassioned features and clenched fists, Aurora swallowed hard. "Is that why you stayed away today? Because you thought Sir Duncan was here with me?"

"Can you blame me after you encouraged the Scot this morn?" he demanded.

Feeling perturbed, Aurora strolled away from Niccolo, toward the shrine. Hearing him following her, she spoke with frustration over her shoulder. "You are not being fair, knight. 'Tis a very heavy burden I carry . . . the royal curse and its terrible ramifications. How can I not be confused and uncertain? What choice do I have but to be elusive, to test the mettle of every knight I meet until I find my true prince? Sometimes I know not what to do."

Aurora continued toward the shrine, only to gasp as, from behind, Niccolo caught her against him, his arms tight at her waist. For a moment she froze, mesmerized by his strength and heat, the scent of him, the hard, scandalous desire she could feel pressing against her bottom.

With his mouth against her hair, he whispered, "I think you lie, milady."

Outraged as well as weak with excitement, she turned in his arms. "You dare to call me a liar, knight?"

"Yea, I think you lie about the curse," he replied stubbornly. "I think no curse exists, that 'tis merely your excuse to toy with the hearts of so many men."

"Why, that is outrageous! I do not toy with hearts!"

"Indeed you do, milady!" he exploded.

"Including yours, knight?" she challenged, feeling rather pleased to have incited his ire.

He chuckled, deflating her sense of victory. "Yea, milady. Especially mine. You have chosen me to torture so much more than the others."

" 'Tis not true!"

" 'Tis true. You love exercising your power over men, making them subservient to you. Can you deny it?"

Aurora stared up at him, intrigued, for she had relished that part of the contest. "Mayhap I enjoy it a little."

"You savor it a lot," he retorted. He gathered her closer, until her breasts ached pleasurably against his hard chest. "And you consider not the risks you are taking."

Stealing a glance at his determined, intense visage, Aurora felt panic encroaching, though the sensation was delicious in its way. "What risks, knight?"

"That a man like myself will call your bluff and give you a coquette's just deserts."

From the way his hand roved intimately over her spine, his intent was clear. "You will release me!" she commanded.

"Nay."

She shoved her hands hard against his shoulders, then stopped when he winced. "You are hurt!"

He glowered. "Today at combat practice, I was watching you watch the others. I dropped my guard, and Sir Baldric struck me hard more than once."

She giggled.

"What is so amusing?" he demanded.

"We were about the same purpose, knight."

"And how is that?"

Mischief in her eyes, she confessed, "I watched you, knight . . . when you were not aware."

He made a growling sound. "Oh, you are a minx, intent on driving me mad! But you will pay a price for your game—"

"Will I?" she asked flippantly.

He seized her by the shoulders. "You love exercising your power over men, do you not, Aurora? Admit it, damn you!"

No longer struggling, she regarded him with bravado. "Mayhap I do."

He groaned as if someone had punched him. His hands slid off her shoulders to curl at her waist. His mouth moved to her ear. As she waited in breathless expectation, he whispered huskily, "Feel my power over *you*, Princess."

And he tumbled her to the ground with him. It happened so quickly, amid a whirl of bright sunshine and dappled foliage, that at first Aurora could not react. Within seconds, she lay pinned beneath Niccolo on the ripe, grassy earth, the air about them heady with dew and flowers. He appeared glorious above her and very sensual, the sunlight striking the beauty of his ardent face and shining in his thick blond hair. He felt huge and crushing, his strength and heat further decimating her defenses.

But when his insistent fingers tugged at the bodice of her gown, exposing the tips of her breasts, she struggled.

He pinned her with an imploring glance. "Nay, love, lie still," he coaxed, and leaned over to place his hot mouth on her nipple.

Aurora writhed, but this time with incredible pleasure. Never had she felt any sensation so exquisite, so intimate. Niccolo's lips skillfully suckled her, and his hot, rough tongue flicked to and fro to torment her deliciously . . . Torrid shivers racked her, and helpless sobs rose in her throat. Her fingernails dug into his spine. She felt truly a part of him, her pride and fear destroyed. She yearned to be joined with him in every way.

"So lovely," he murmured in awe.

Seeming to sense her response, he planted slow, sensuous kisses all over her breast, then trailed his lips over the valley between her soft mounds and repeated the tender ritual on the other. Aurora thrust her fingers into the thick silk of his hair and held him to her.

A moment later, he slid up her body and kissed her deeply. Aurora could not bear the rapture. She tugged at the cloth of Niccolo's tunic, and he pulled back to aid her in removing it.

For a moment they stared at each other ardently, searchingly, both naked to the waist. Awed by the play of muscles across his beautiful chest and shoulders, Aurora stroked her fingertips over the warm, satiny flesh. When he grimaced as she kneaded his bruises, she stretched forward and pressed her mouth lovingly to the very aching spots . . .

For the first time in memory, Niccolo Campioni felt tears burning his eyes at this trusting girl's utterly sweet, tender gesture. He caught her closer and claimed her soft lips. He felt her tight nipples tormenting the flesh of his bare chest, and his loins hardened in response—

His heart thumped as if it might burst inside him. Half-dizzied by the savage need consuming him, he pressed his mouth to Aurora's soft cheek and caught a rough, convulsive breath.

"Oh, Niccolo, you feel wonderful against me," she whispered.

He drew back, smiling down at her flushed face. "As do you, milady. You feel as if you belong in my arms."

Niccolo kissed her again, while grasping and raising her skirts. At first she resisted, but when he whispered soothingly at her ear, tugging at her sensitive lobe with his teeth and teasing her with his tongue, she soon melted again.

Niccolo continued lifting her skirts while exploring her with his hands, caressing her smooth calves and silky, firm thighs. He slipped his hands beneath her and squeezed her shapely bottom. She squirmed, only further stoking his desires. He hiked her skirts high about her waist.

Incoherent sounds rose in her throat, and he pulled back to stare into her panicked eyes.

"Niccolo—" she panted. "Pray—"

"Easy, milady," he soothed, and moved his fingers to stroke her.

She froze, locking her thighs about his hand, but still he managed to insinuate his fingers into her feminine cleft. She was tense, but she made no real move to thwart him.

He buried his lips in her silky hair. "Do you like me touching you there, milady?"

A huge sigh escaped her, and she nodded solemnly. "Then open yourself to me," he urged.

She relaxed the tiniest bit, and his powerful thighs did the rest, smoothly prying her open. She tossed her head and breathed in sharp pants. Kissing her more insistently to distract her, he explored her with his fingers. Ah, she was slick and hot, ready for him! He probed more insistently, penetrating her slightly, and was rewarded by her sharp teeth sinking into his underlip.

Dio, she was a virgin, so tiny and tight! He rejoiced in his good fortune. Despite all her flirting with the others, he would be her first lover, the man to breach her maidenhead. His head swam with lust for her, and his trembling fingers moved to free the manhood that throbbed so painfully against his hose.

When his stiff erection touched her soft inner thigh, he felt her resistance. "Relax, love," he murmured into her mouth. "Let me inside you. Let me touch you there . . . Like this."

He demonstrated with a deep, provocative kiss. He heard her softly moaning, felt her quivering against him, and then she kissed him back with equal abandon. He pressed into her again, only to feel her tensing once more—

Gasping, she caught his face in her hands. "Niccolo, pray wait—"

"Why?" he demanded, agonized with desire for her.

"Because I must know what lies in your heart!" she cried. "I must know what tortures you, what drives you . . . and what you feel for me. I cannot give myself to you unless I am certain you are the one."

Shuddering with frustration, Niccolo buried his face against her throat. "I cannot tell you what you want to know, milady. I only want to lose myself in you, to pour myself into you, to forget . . . Do you not understand that?"

She nodded and clutched him tightly. "I do. Sometimes I would even forget that the curse exists! But I must be sure. If I chose wrongly, 'tis not just my soul at peril."

Niccolo gazed down at her, so vulnerable beneath him, her turmoil-filled eyes imploring him. *Dio*, she truly did believe in the curse. And was not his soul at peril also, if he took her for all the wrong reasons, and perhaps compelled her to succumb to her own self-defeating superstition? Seducing her and making her suffer was one thing, but damn it, he did not want her death on his conscience!

Then, even as he struggled between self-doubt and desire, the greenery about them stirred and rustled, blowing the essence of the grass across them, and Niccolo could have sworn he heard an eerie voice whispering a warning—

Uncertain of what he had heard, he shook his head.

Nay, surely 'twas only the wind! Then why was Aurora tensing beneath him, her features filling with fear?

"Did you hear that?" he asked.

She nodded.

"What did you hear?"

"I—I dare not say," she replied.

With a groan of exquisite frustration, Niccolo rolled off her and righted his clothing. As she watched in confusion, he straightened her bodice, yanked down her skirts, and pulled her to her feet.

"What is wrong?" she cried.

His voice trembled. "Go! Go now, milady!"

She regarded him in hurt and confusion, tears spilling from her eyes. "I . . . no longer please you?"

Niccolo would have laughed had he not been in such agony. He grabbed Aurora's hand and pressed her moist palm to the painful bulge in his hose. She did not flinch or try to retreat, and their eyes met starkly. The touch of her, the heat flashing up her cheeks, the dazed look of desire on her lovely face, almost had him relenting and dragging her back to the ground.

Breathing hard, he pulled her fingers away. "You think you do not please me? Leave this very instant, milady, or you will have an answer that may well doom you!"

Aurora eyed him in confusion, then fled the copse. Niccolo glanced about the landscape in bewilderment, then exploded with curses.

Niccolo was still consumed with frustration—both physical and emotional—as he returned to the castle. Every inch of him burned to be back in the copse, with beautiful Aurora naked in his arms, his mouth locked on hers, his manhood buried inside her.

Dio, he had come so close! He had coaxed her surrender. She had opened to him, and he had anticipated the glory of claiming her. He had had the princess within his grasp, like a bird in his hand, and he had let her go!

Why? Why should he, a cold, ruthless knight, succumb to weakness simply because of an eerie tone on the wind? Why had he all at once felt as if he were the murderer of Aurora's entire future? What was happening to his courage, his obsession for revenge? The princess was clearly penetrating his facade, chipping away at his resolve. She was affecting him on every level—physical, emotional, spiritual. She was wreaking havoc with his desires, his thoughts, his conscience. Why could he not simply seduce her and betray her as she so richly deserved? Instead, he was surely becoming the helpless pawn of yet another treacherous woman, allowing her guileless smiles and eager kisses to seduce and enthrall him, to blind him to her wiles.

He had better regain control of himself or he was doomed!

He reentered the castle through the sally port, his irritation only increasing when he could not find a torch and was compelled to grope his way through the slimy corridor and then the dungeon passageways. Near the kitchen, a servant, backing through the doorway, collided with him, splashing him with a bowl of hot soup.

Niccolo bellowed in pain and shook the burning liquid from his legs. The terrified little man jerked away, dropping his bowl in his agitation, and splashing Niccolo again.

"*Santa Maria*, are you trying to murder me?" Niccolo roared. "Why must every servant in this benighted castle go through doorways backwards?"

Trembling in fear, the bearded servant blinked at Niccolo in the scant light. "Your pardon, milord. I was merely taking soup to the Ravenian hostages in the dungeons. I had no idea anyone else was about."

"If you would look where you were going, you would know, fool!"

"Your pardon, milord, but 'tis forbidden to go through a portal any other way."

Niccolo flung a hand outward in exasperation. *"Madre del Dio!* I have traveled the world, but a stranger place, I have never seen! Peasants with iron crosses on their doors, servants wearing garlic necklaces, gnomes roaming the forests—"

At the mention of the gnomes, the servant sucked in his breath and quickly crossed himself.

"Not to mention, a fawn that never grows up . . ."

The servant regarded Niccolo in consternation.

Niccolo stepped closer and glowered murderously at the little man. "Tell me of the curse."

At once the servant fell to his knees, all but babbling incoherently. "Oh, nay, milord, nay!"

"Tell me!" Niccolo bellowed.

The frantic servant laced his fingers together and murmured entreaties to the saints. "Pray, milord, do not press me," he pleaded. "The royal curse . . . No commoner in Falconia may speak of it. To do so is to die!"

For once, Niccolo did not respond. He walked off in a daze, his features white.

Aurora lay curled up on her bed in her solar, still atremble from unassuaged desires. Her belly ached, yearning for Niccolo's heat deep inside her, and her nipples still tingled where he had so passionately suckled her.

She felt confused and vulnerable. How she wished she could understand Niccolo. He had almost given her his passion in the copse, but he still withheld his heart. She had wanted him desperately, had been prepared to give herself to him, yet again the spirits had cautioned he was not the one. Had Niccolo heard the warnings, as well? Was that why he had suddenly pulled away, insisting she leave? Had he done so to protect her?

She sat up on her bed, smiling. If this was true, then there *must* be some goodness in her dark knight, after all! If he could consider her welfare above his own desires and designs, then he must possess a noble heart. The possibility endeared him to her and only intensified her craving. He had let her go . . . Now she wanted him more than ever.

And Aurora's instincts argued that a time might soon come when Niccolo would *not* pull away, when the two of them might well become lovers. Verily, if he took her in his arms again, she feared she could no longer resist! She might be headed for disaster, on the verge of giving herself to a man who was not her true love . . . yet she desired Niccolo so much, she was not sure she cared.

She had learned one bitter lesson, however. She would not try to rouse Niccolo's jealousies again. In toying with him, she had punished herself even more. She had spurred his anger and deprived herself of his coveted company. Why she had ever thought 'twas enjoyable manipulating men, she did not know! The consequences of her flirtation were rueful, 'twas sure . . . just as her longing for him now was bitter-sweet.

He might yet doom her, she thought with a shudder. But she could not seem to help herself. She was no longer in charge of her own emotions, or her own fate . . .

TWENTY-THREE

LATE THAT NIGHT, NICCOLO PACED THE SMALL CELL he and Lorenzo shared. He felt as if he were losing his mind. Whenever he was alone with Aurora, especially when they were at the copse, something magical happened between them. She melted the ice encasing his heart and crumbled his determination to gain revenge.

He could not believe what had happened today. First, she had blatantly encouraged Duncan, again demonstrating she was untrustworthy, a coquette. Although furious, he had ultimately followed her to the shrine like a sniveling puppy. She had kissed him with a tenderness that had torn at his heart, and he had been poised on the brink of deflowering her, only to lose his nerve when he *thought* he had heard some ominous voice warning of a curse.

What ailed him? Had he gone daft? Was he hearing voices now? Never in his life had he yielded to superstition, nor had he been daunted by any force he could not actually see. Where was his ruthlessness, his steely resolve to make Aurora suffer? If he did not take greater care, soon he would become her helpless pawn, his heart hers for the breaking. And he had no doubt she would do so.

How could she seem so perfidious, and yet so guile-

less? Was she a wily enchantress like Cecilia, or was
she genuine and warm? Niccolo was not certain, but
he did know he could not risk giving his heart
again . . . he could not! After being abused and hurt
so grievously by Cecilia, he could never endure the
pain. On some elemental level, he also recognized that
in order to accept love back in his life, he would first
have to give up the hatred consuming him, to forgive
Cecilia and Cosimo. And this, he could never do.

He must think of Aurora as false . . . He *must*. Otherwise, he would soon be lost . . .

The presence of Sir Duncan also plagued him. Tonight during dinner, Duncan had again shamelessly
charmed Aurora, bringing her a pair of bejeweled pat-
tens he had purchased for her in the village. Niccolo
mused grimly that if he did not take great care, Duncan would make quick work of defeating Basil and
would win Aurora's hand, as well.

Thus he must follow through with his plans to win
revenge before it was too late. He must strengthen his
resolve, ransom Aurora to her enemy, before she utterly defeated him . . .

"Master, what ails you?" called a sleepy voice.
"You are all but shaking the floor with your pacing."

Niccolo glanced apologetically at Lorenzo, who had
just sat up on his cot and was regarding his master
with an expression of bewilderment. "I did not mean
to awaken you. Go back to sleep, old man. I will pace
the bailey."

Lorenzo regarded Niccolo shrewdly. "You are a
man in torment, your soul in agony."

"Well put," agreed Niccolo ruefully.

"You are still plotting the downfall of the princess?" Lorenzo reproved.

"I do not think you want to know," Niccolo replied
tightly.

The old squire crossed himself. "Master, this is

wrong. 'Tis evil. A lady must always be treated with respect, with honor and chivalry—"

"And what if the lady has no honor?" Niccolo cut in bitterly. "What if she is a heartless coquette?"

Lorenzo's wise gaze chided Niccolo. "Master, 'tis not fair you judge the princess by Cecilia."

"Does the princess not flaunt her charms to the others just as Cecilia did?" demanded Niccolo.

Lorenzo waved a frail hand. "Verily, she must choose from all the suitors dispatched by her uncle."

"She need not enjoy herself!" exploded Niccolo.

Eyeing his furious master, the old squire shook his head. "My son, you must learn to forgive. Your hatred is like a bile gnawing at your entrails. 'Twill destroy you."

"I know not how to forgive!" countered Niccolo in fury.

Lorenzo heaved a great sigh. "Master, we must leave this place, while there is yet time for you to redeem yourself. I am no longer equal to the task of attending to your salvation. The way matters are proceeding, I shall never rejoin my beloved Marta."

Niccolo sighed heavily. "Sleep, *amico mio*. I shall trouble you no more tonight."

But Lorenzo eyed his master ominously and shook a finger at him. "Niccolo Campioni, heed my warning: You are bound on the road to hell."

Throwing his squire an anguished look, Niccolo slipped from the room, muttering under his breath, "Verily, I am already there."

The following morn the Falconian forces, including Niccolo and Lorenzo, again gathered in the forest, waiting for Basil and his knights to appear on the castle green. This once, Niccolo had allowed his squire to join the mission, but only after gaining Lorenzo's promise that he would remain in the woods and not try to participate in the battle, should Basil actually attack.

Within minutes after the Falconians assumed their positions, a sentry burst through the trees, yelling, "The enemy is in sight!" Excitement stormed over the ranks, archers tensioning bows, knights lowering visors and gripping lances.

Sir Duncan waved his sword and called out lustily, "Follow me, men! Let's ride out and slay them in their tracks!"

Before Niccolo could protest, the rest of the knights roared their agreement and followed Duncan's lead, storming out of the trees on their chargers.

Only Niccolo and Lorenzo hung back, exchanging a rueful glance. Niccolo knew Duncan's plan was folly. He realized that in some ways, the Scot possessed more pluck than good sense, and he was relieved to see signs of flaws in his rival—

For surely any idiot knew that the Ravenians would spot the approach of the Falconians and would likely flee unscathed.

After waiting a few moments, Niccolo and Lorenzo rode onto the green to reconnoiter the action. They skirted the edge of the lake and continued on toward the west. At the top of a rise they paused, both chuckling at the sight below them. The Falconians, led by Duncan, stormed into the valley just as the enemy was appearing over the next knoll. The startled Ravenians dropped their colors and fled to a man. Despite a vigorous pursuit, the Falconians swiftly lost sight of the enemy knights as they scattered into the forest.

Niccolo threw back his head and laughed.

"Sir Duncan possesses more courage than wit," commented Lorenzo. "He needs to think before he charges like a mad dog."

"Indeed," agreed Niccolo.

He was still grinning as he and Lorenzo turned

their mounts back toward the castle. How he savored his small victory over the arrogant Duncan!

That afternoon Niccolo debated whether or not he should go to the copse to find Aurora. He feared what might happen if he met her there. He was desperate to see his plans for revenge realized before he lost all his resolve.

He was in the bailey when he spotted the constable, Ignatius, trudging painfully toward an outside door to the cellar. The little man glanced about covertly, then slipped inside.

Niccolo decided to follow him. He had spotted Ignatius behaving suspiciously several times before—and today he would determine what the constable was truly about.

Niccolo pursued the man, stealthily entering the cellar, proceeding past the kitchen, the well, and the dungeons. As Niccolo would have guessed, Ignatius headed straight for the secret passageway. Touching his waist to make sure he had his sword and dagger, Niccolo continued to trail him through the secret passageway.

Ignatius exited the sally port and crept down the dappled trail through the woods. But over the next moments, the constable made plodding progress at best. Growing impatient with the man's slow, creaky movements, Niccolo seized his quarry from behind and pressed his dagger to his throat. His captive gasped and froze in fear.

"Pray, sir, do not harm me!" Ignatius cried.

"Where are you going?" Niccolo demanded.

"I—I am the royal constable, on business for the crown," the little man replied shrilly. "Pray, sir, release me!"

"Only when you confess to the treason you are really about this day!"

"Pray, sir, I cannot see your face!" the man cried.

"You do not need to!" Niccolo tightened the grip of his dagger. "Now, tell the truth or I shall make quick work of your worthless throat. And mind you, if you lie, I shall only kill you more slowly."

Niccolo could feel the man gulping and shuddering. "I—I merely was on my way to the village to gather rents from the princess's tenants—"

"You lie!" shouted Niccolo. "There is no reason to carry out such routine business in stealth. I shall give you one final chance to tell the truth—and if you fail, I shall disembowel you before your very eyes."

"Very well, sir!" the man shrieked. "I go to meet King Basil!"

With a contemptuous curse, Niccolo shoved the man away. Ignatius crashed to his knees with a grunt of pain. At once he struggled to his feet and stood cowering before his tormentor.

"You!" he cried, regarding Niccolo in wild-eyed fear.

"*Sì*," replied Niccolo nastily. "So you have been conspiring with the Ravenians against your princess, have you, Constable?"

Ignatius shook his head. "Nay, sir! I—'tis true I have been meeting with Basil, but I swear I always meant to inform the princess as soon as I could find a way to use Basil's designs to her royal benefit."

"You are a very poor liar indeed," sneered Niccolo. "What are Basil's intentions?"

The man hesitated.

Niccolo unsheathed his sword and pointed it at the man's chest. "Tell me or I shall run you through!"

Ignatius shuddered and spoke in a cracking voice. "Basil desires to learn your strategies so he may better defeat you. He wishes news of the contest for Aurora's hand, and to know of all goings-on at the castle."

Niccolo laughed. "Where are you planning to meet him?"

Again Ignatius hesitated.

Niccolo pressed his sword to the man's chest. "Where?"

Ignatius stood his ground with bravado. "If you are going to slay me in any event, sir, what reason do I have to tell you?"

Niccolo smiled cruelly. "So you will die quickly instead of slowly?"

Though trembling badly, the constable continued to balk. "Nay, sir, 'tis not sufficient incentive."

Niccolo's irritation was such that he considered dispatching the miserable wretch there and then. But he knew this would not help him accomplish his goal. Finally he snapped, "You will tell me where you are meeting Basil, and then you will walk away from this kingdom, with no more than the tunic on your back. If you ever again appear in Falconia, I vow I will expose you as a traitor and personally slit your throat."

The constable's mouth fell open. "But, sir, to simply walk away from all my duties and possessions! You must allow me to prepare."

With the tip of his sword, Niccolo touched the money pouch hanging from the constable's waist. "It appears your purse is full, no doubt due to your traitorous endeavors. Consider yourself lucky to escape with your ill-gotten gains . . . and your life."

"You drive a hard bargain, sir!"

"I wield an even more ruthless sword." Niccolo pressed the point to the constable's neck, his captive wincing when the sharp tip drew a spot of blood. "Now, speak and give me detailed directions to your rendezvous. My patience has reached its limit."

An hour later, Niccolo was waiting for Basil. He crouched hidden in the foliage at the edge of a clearing on a rise overlooking Ravenia Castle. In the valley beneath him, the yellow walls and square keep of the fortress jutted up sharply at the edge of a small lake. The overall layout was similar to Falconia Castle, yet here the curtain and donjon were ordinary in design, sharing none of the fanciful lines and majestic beauty of the Falconian stronghold.

He smiled as he watched a tall, bulky man stride into the clearing and scowl at the deserted area. The man wore a plain wool tunic and hose; a broadsword was sheathed at his waist. Studying Basil, Niccolo found his countenance displeasing: greasy, orange hair; rough, irregular features; pockmarked skin; and small, beady eyes. He had a sullen, shifty, untrustworthy air about him.

No wonder Aurora found the man repugnant! This one glimpse was enough to make Niccolo dislike and distrust the King of Ravenia. He was tempted simply to leave, then decided against the rash instinct. He could not miss this opportunity to get to know his enemy—

But what then?

The large man prowled the clearing, obviously searching for Ignatius, and growing impatient. As soon as Basil's back was turned, Niccolo drew his sword and stepped out into the glade.

"Good day, my friend," he called softly.

Basil whirled, drawing out his own weapon. "Who goes there?"

"I have business with you," said Niccolo.

"Who are you?" snarled the king.

"My name does not matter," said Niccolo. "Ignatius has sent me in his stead—to conspire with you, not to fight you."

The ugly giant hesitated. "Where is Ignatius?"

"On his deathbed," Niccolo lied. "He ate some poisonous mushrooms quite by accident, and he is writhing in agony even now. The physician assures us his demise is imminent. Thus, you must deal with me now."

"And I ask again, who *are* you, sir knight?" Basil demanded.

"I am Niccolo Campioni, of Venice."

Basil laughed, and Niccolo grimaced as he viewed the man's stained teeth. "So you are one of the fools Ignatius told me about—one of eight knights who came here, duped by Artemas, thinking you had secured Aurora's hand in marriage?"

"I do not consider myself a fool, sir!" Niccolo snapped. "Nor am I at fault because the Count of Osprey is a thief and a liar! Do you desire my assistance or not?"

Basil scowled at Niccolo for a tense moment. At last he sheathed his sword, and Niccolo followed suit.

"Ignatius's death will prove inconvenient," muttered the king. "As for Artemas, I have known about that rascal for years and can understand your frustration. I even tried to bribe him into turning Aurora over to me, but he refused to accept my offer."

Good for Artemas, Niccolo thought grimly. To Basil he said, "It seems many men want to win the hand of Princess Aurora."

"Yea," said Basil nastily, "including all the knights that keep arriving in Falconia and interfering with my own plans." He eyed Niccolo shrewdly. "Why do you wish to betray the princess?"

"Because she betrayed me!" Niccolo responded bitterly. "I desperately needed her fortune to save my own enterprises back in Venice, and then I arrived here to discover I had been duped."

Basil studied Niccolo. "The others were duped, as well. Yet they do not wish to betray her."

"The others have faith and chivalry in their souls," Niccolo scoffed. "I have none."

Basil grinned, once again revealing his blotched teeth. "That I like, knight. Yea, I like it very much. You will help me then, as Ignatius would have done?"

"*Sì*," responded Niccolo. "But first I will know something. Why do you wish to wed Aurora?"

Basil's beady gaze narrowed. "Has she told you she and I were childhood friends?"

"No," Niccolo lied.

"We were, and I always coveted her as my future bride, beauty that she was. Yet when I grew to manhood, she cruelly spurned me." Basil's features contorted in rage. "When I tried to kiss her, she laughed at me. She told me I smelled worse than a pig and she found me physically repulsive. I swore on that day that I would have her, and shape her into an obedient bride."

Niccolo hesitated to even think of how Basil might go about molding Aurora. "You wish to punish her, then?"

Basil shrugged. "She will suffer only until she accepts me as her rightful husband."

"That is why you lay siege to her castle?"

The king held up a fist. "Yea—and I will continue to do so until she and Falconia are mine!"

Niccolo laughed scornfully. "The way you are proceeding, you shall not attain her soon."

Basil mulled this over with a scowl. "What is your purpose coming here today, knight?"

Niccolo shrugged. "To assist you in achieving your goal. Indeed, were I you, I would have attained the princess long before now."

"You think yourself more clever than I, eh?" Basil sneered.

I know I am, Niccolo thought, though again he was wise enough not to voice aloud such an insulting sentiment. "I am only contending there is a much simpler way to secure Aurora."

"How?" Basil demanded.

"I will ransom her to you for ten-thousand ducats, and deliver her into your hands."

"Ten thousand!" Basil cried, aghast.

"I will not bargain," stated Niccolo vehemently. "This is my only offer."

"Then choke on it and die!" yelled Basil, drawing his sword.

The violent response was not unexpected to Niccolo. Basil was strong and brutal, but Niccolo was quicker, unsheathing his own weapon in the twinkling of an eye. Even as Basil swung at Niccolo aggressively, he skillfully blocked each stroke. The two men danced about, thrusting and parrying, filling the pristine clearing with the shriek of steel striking steel. Again and again Niccolo blocked skillfully, frustrating his opponent, prompting the king to grow careless. His features contorting with rage, Basil charged Niccolo with a great yell. Niccolo only increased his opponent's ire by laughing and leaping out of range, causing Basil to crash into a tree. Wheeling about half-drunkenly, Basil barely had time to lift his sword before Niccolo charged, swinging, thrusting, and banging until he knocked the broadsword from his enemy's hand. Ruthlessly he pressed the tip of his own weapon to Basil's chest, while the King of Ravenia gulped at him in white-faced horror.

"Pray, spare me!" cried the frightened man.

"Do you agree to my terms?" demanded Niccolo.

"Yea—yea!"

Breathing hard, Niccolo spoke with explosive rage. "Draw your sword on me again, man, and I will make a eunuch out of you! Is that clear?"

"Yea! 'Tis understood!"

Grimly Niccolo sheathed his sword. "Then listen well, for I have a plan. We must proceed carefully to convince the princess that the war has ended. Then, when the time is right—and my price is paid—I shall turn Aurora over to you . . ."

Returning to the castle late in the afternoon, Niccolo seethed with anger, frustration, and self-recrimination. His turmoil was such that he could have felled trees with his bare hands.

He had made his devil's bargain with Basil. The two men had agreed to stage an end to the war; Basil would send word of truce, and Niccolo would be declared the victor in the contest. But before Niccolo and Aurora became formally betrothed, Niccolo was to arrange another meeting with Basil, who would tender the required payment. Afterward, Niccolo would turn Aurora over to the Ravenian king.

Now Niccolo was at war with himself, more confused than ever, because he realized he could not fulfill his end of the agreement and give Aurora over to her loathsome, bellicose enemy—a man who was almost certain to beat and abuse her. She would surely be cursed then, if she was not already.

The truth was, he could no longer bear the prospect of Aurora wedding anyone else, because he craved her desperately for himself. Perhaps he should marry her, after all. Mayhap he could turn the tables on Basil, using their bargain to defeat him, and then claim the princess for his own.

Mayhap he could punish her that way . . . punish her by making love to her until she could not move, by filling his mouth with those ripe breasts, gripping that soft bottom in his hands, holding her to him until he sated his ravenous hunger for her . . . if he ever could.

And what of her fate if he claimed her? He frowned as he remembered the words of the servant, his warning about the curse, and the ominous voice he had heard in the copse, his own inexplicable panic afterward. Even if the curse was not real, Aurora believed in it, and he knew he was not her true love. Indeed, with his own soul so blackened, he would be no better for her than Basil. Either alternative would likely doom her . . . and doom him! Did he truly want her death on his conscience?

He cursed under his breath, amazed he was even confronting such a dilemma. What had happened to

him, his ruthlessness, and all his fine plans for revenge? Why could he not bring himself to betray her?
Had he truly become bewitched?

Mayhap he had. He simply wanted her so desperately that thoughts of having her overwhelmed all
other ambitions. Yet if he wedded her, he would torture himself, not her. He would become so tempted
to love her, to make himself vulnerable, to let her
break his heart.

He may as well throw himself on his sword!

Then as he neared the castle, he practically collided
with her as their two paths converged. She looked
ravishingly beautiful in a gown of purple silk embellished with pearls, feathers, and a gold-laced girdle.
The bewildered look on her face jarred him deeply;
the scent of her aroused him.

"Niccolo!" she beseeched, her voice full of hurt.
"Why did you not come to the copse today?"

He stared at her in anguish, hating himself, yearning to take her into his arms even though he had just
plotted her ruin. "I cannot come there again, milady,"
he said hoarsely, and started past her.

She grabbed his arm. "Why? I missed you, Niccolo!"

"Do not say such things!" he cried. "You do not
know what kind of man I am!"

Tears filled her eyes. "I know I wanted you there
. . . you, and no one else."

"You want me?" Desperately close to losing control, he seized her by the shoulders. "What if I pressed
you to the forest floor this minute, milady, and raised
your skirts? What would you do then?"

She stared at him achingly, and whispered back, "I
would give myself to you."

"Oh, *Dio*," he groaned, releasing her and striding
away, not trusting himself to remain.

TWENTY-FOUR

ON A HILLSIDE OVERLOOKING RAVENIA CASTLE WERE gathered Niccolo and all of the Falconian forces. Just past dawn, the knights waited to mount a sneak attack on Basil and his knights according to a plan Niccolo had presented to the Falconian warriors in the barracks war room last night.

The morning was mild and quiet save for the whistle of the slight breeze stirring the tree leaves and rippling the glistening surface of the lake, the singing of warblers in the foliage, and the harsh cry of a sparrow hawk as it swooped down into the grasses near the lake and soared off with a rodent in its talons. The castle appeared placid, except for the ravens swirling about the parapets, and several sentries who prowled the battlements, their iron helmets glinting in the sunlight.

Despite the lack of activity, Niccolo fully expected the enemy forces to emerge at any moment. Basil had no knowledge of this surprise attack, although he had agreed to permit his forces to be routed. After the king sent word of truce, allowing the Falconians to assume the war was over, Niccolo was to arrange to turn Aurora over to Basil within a fortnight.

He already knew he could never perform the foul deed, never let Basil have her. But at least he had

bought himself some time . . . time to figure a way out
of this muddle.

What should he do about Aurora? She had become
his torment, his obsession, the subject of his every
waking thought. Could he truly destroy her? Would
he not destroy himself if he even tried? Had Lorenzo
been right all along that, beneath all his hatred, he
possessed a pure heart?

Heaven help him!

Perhaps 'twould be best if he abandoned this mad
scheme and returned to Venice as soon as possible,
he mused grimly. After all, he had never possessed
conclusive proof that Aurora was a party to her uncle's intrigue . . . Mayhap he had tried to punish Cecilia through her. If he remained, his passion to make
Aurora his might well bring them both sorrow, for he
would never trust nor give his heart again. In the
meantime, perhaps 'twould be best to steer the princess toward one of the other knights—Duncan, who
possessed great valor even if his bluster irritated Niccolo, or perhaps Edgar, both stalwart and honorable,
whom Niccolo had come to admire . . .

The distant creaking of the drawbridge roused Niccolo from his thoughts and caused a tense stirring
among the knights. He held up a hand to stay their
excited whisperings. "Wait until all of the knights
have crossed the moat," he ordered, "and the drawbridge has been retracted. That way, 'twill be much
more difficult for them to retreat."

Murmurs of agreement flitted over the ranks, and
even Duncan offered Niccolo a nod and a grin of respect.

The waiting was excruciating for Niccolo and the
others as the enemy troops plodded over the bridge,
including knights on horseback, archers on foot, and
men-at-arms pulling the catapults. Once the forces
had cleared the moat and the drawbridge was being

raised, Niccolo held high his own hand, then dropped it to signal the attack.

The knights hesitated only long enough to lower their gleaming steel visors, then the company thundered down the hillside toward the enemy. At the pounding of hooves, the stunned group of Ravenians momentarily froze in their tracks just beyond the moat. Then their leaders yelled and gesticulated, and the heralds furiously blew the trumpets. The Ravenian men-at-arms scrambled into action, knights wielding swords or lances, and archers frantically cranking their bows.

But the Falconians swarmed down on the enemy before the Ravenians could fully prepare a counterattack. Aiming his lance well, Niccolo charged straight for an unsuspecting Basil, who was busy barking orders to his captains-at-arms. Amid a shriek of metal scraping metal and a groan from Basil, Niccolo struck the king on his side, knocking him off his destrier. With a mighty splash, Basil landed in the lake.

In the wake of the king's cry of mingled shock, outrage, and pain, Niccolo smiled in vengeful pleasure. He wheeled Nero about and tightened his grip on his lance. Around him, men yelled and the battle roared, the metallic odor of blood filling the air. Niccolo watched with grim satisfaction as Sir Gilbert impaled a man-at-arms before he could load a rock in the trebuchet, and Sir Edgar swung his sword, dispatching an archer.

Hearing a shout of rage, Niccolo spied another Ravenian knight charging him with lance readied. Niccolo spurred Nero, and the destrier leapt forward with a high whinny. The two knights stormed toward each other in a clamor of hooves. Niccolo lunged in the saddle to avoid his opponent's lethal lance, while driving his own weapon home. He heard the man's harrowing scream and watched him fly backward off his horse. Niccolo's lance still imbedded in him, the doomed knight did a sheer flip in the air before he tumbled into the moat.

Noting that the waters near the moat were turning a sickening red, Niccolo quickly turned his mount and unsheathed his broadsword. His heart pounded with the excitement of the battle, and sweat trickled into his eyes. Glancing about him through the slats in his visor, he noted that the Ravenian sentries had succeeded in lowering the drawbridge, and additional men-at-arms were pouring out from the bailey. Pride surged in him as he watched the Falconians stand their ground, the warriors fiercely hacking and bludgeoning at Basil's knights until the latter were forced to give way and begin retreating over the moat. Locking swords with an enemy knight, Niccolo groaned in frustration as he spied an archer help Basil stagger out of the lake and over to the drawbridge. He had really hoped to kill the bastard!

As the Ravenians continued their retreat, men-at-arms high in the parapets began working the catapults, hurling chunks of rock and iron down on the Falconians to discourage them from trying to scale the walls or penetrate the bailey. Hearing a loud crash, Niccolo winced at the sight of Sir Olaf being knocked from his destrier by a chunk of rock. Watching additional shrapnel shoot off the battlements, he realized they had accomplished as much as they could here, and the time had come to order a retreat. He waved his arms and whistled to his company. The Falconians hastily began gathering their weapons and their wounded. Niccolo frowned at the sight of Sir Olaf's squire hoisting his limp body over a horse. Within seconds, the company wheeled about and rode off. A few Ravenians followed, soon discouraged by the Falconian archers and a couple of knights wielding maces.

As soon as the last Ravenians retreated and the Falconians cleared the next rise, a great cheer went up from all the knights. Niccolo flipped back his visor and grinned at Edgar, who rode beside him.

"Bravo!" cried the Englishman. "A brilliant strategy this morn, Sir Niccolo."

Christian galloped up to join the men, his visor raised, his face gleaming with sweat and excitement. "On behalf of my sister the princess, I thank you, Sir Niccolo. Now Basil will surely think twice before he tries to storm our gates again. He deserved such a trouncing for trying to force my sister's hand."

"Agreed," said a grinning Niccolo.

Christian nodded toward the ranks behind them. " 'Tis a pity about Sir Olaf, however. I helped his squire pull off his helmet in the nick of time, though 'twas not easy. I fear his brain is already swelling."

"He is a fine man," agreed Niccolo. " 'Twill be a pity if we lose him."

"But there is no greater glory for a knight than to give his life for a cause he believes in," put in Edgar solemnly.

Although Niccolo appeared skeptical, Christian eagerly nodded.

"Good work, Sir Niccolo!" called Duncan from deep in the ranks.

"Thank you, Sir Duncan!" Niccolo yelled back.

"But I still say we should kidnap the bloody bastard from his bed!"

The other knights shouted with laughter, and even Niccolo chuckled, enjoying the triumph and camaraderie more than he would have expected. Although in the end they had retreated, the victory was clearly theirs, and with only one serious casualty. The enemy had been cut off at his own castle gates; after two years of being subjugated by Basil's forces, the Falconians had seized the upper hand.

* * *

"Princess, we have won the day!" cried Sir Baldric.

Aurora stood inside the bailey, watching the triumphant knights gallop back in with Niccolo at their head, her dark knight appearing resplendent in his gleaming armor. She was pleased to note most of the men appeared unharmed as well as exuberant, and they bore only a few wounded.

She walked up to Niccolo's horse, which was well lathered, stamping and snorting, still high-spirited from the battle. Niccolo's face shone with exhilaration. Her heart tripped with excitement as he smiled down at her. Was he having second thoughts after spurning her yesterday? Or was his vitality only evidence that he had taken pleasure in slaying others? How she hoped the glow he radiated was for her, since she had missed him terribly.

"What has happened?" she asked him.

" 'Twas like the men said," he replied. "We gave Basil a taste of his own by storming his gates even as he and his knights emerged from the bailey this morn."

She clapped her hands in glee. "Oh, that is so clever. Whose strategy was this?"

" 'Twas Sir Niccolo's," called out Sir Gilbert proudly.

As Niccolo and Aurora regarded each other raptly, meaningfully, Duncan bellowed, "Do not be thinking, Campioni, that the rest of us will allow you to claim you have bested us and won the contest. There is no evidence Basil has been decisively defeated."

"Is this true?" Aurora asked Niccolo.

Niccolo gave a shrug. "*Sì*. Although I knocked him from his destrier into the lake, unfortunately, King Basil survived to limp back into the castle."

Aurora giggled, then frowned as she watched two squires carefully remove the battered, insensible Sir Olaf from his steed. "What has happened to the Viking?"

Niccolo sighed. "I am afraid he was pelted with a large rock from a trebuchet. Even though he wore his helmet, he took a terrible blow, and his brain is swelling badly. It looks dire, milady."

She nodded soberly. "How terrible. I shall have my personal physician attend him at once."

"That is good of you, Princess."

Brightening, she flashed him a smile. "Otherwise, if this victory is as decisive as it seems, we must celebrate."

"*Sì*, milady," said Niccolo.

But Aurora noted his expression was abstracted as he dismounted his horse and strode away.

TWENTY-FIVE

THE NEXT MORNING, INSTEAD OF AN ENEMY ATTACK, a Ravenian herald appeared before the gates of Falconia Castle with a banner of truce in hand. The sentries shouted the news to men-at-arms in the bailey, who quickly relayed the tidings to the princess and the knights.

Great excitement gripped the bailey as everyone—from Princess Aurora, to the knights, to peasants and children—assembled in the ward just beyond the portcullis. Niccolo joined the others just as the iron gate was cranked upward, admitting the herald.

A hush fell over the crowd as the man dismounted and approached the princess. Bowing on one knee before her, he announced, "King Basil sends you tidings."

Aurora nodded gravely. "Arise, herald, and speak."

The man rose. "My king is willing to end the hostilities between you—if you will pledge your agreement, and release our hostages."

A great cheer sounded out in the bailey, with knights pounding one another across the shoulders, peasants shouting their joy, children jumping up and down.

Appearing pleased though cautious, Aurora held

up a hand to quiet the clamor. She addressed the herald. "This is unexpected news. What has caused King Basil's change of heart?"

"He is weary of combat, eager for a truce."

"He is willing to surrender?" asked Aurora.

"Nay," the man answered awkwardly, shifting from foot to foot. "But he is willing to end the siege."

As ominous murmurs flitted over the crowd, Sir Duncan strode up to Aurora. "Do not believe him, Princess! Insist on an unconditional surrender! Otherwise, this shabby trick is meaningless!"

Aurora glanced at Niccolo. "What say you, Sir Niccolo?"

Niccolo moved toward her. "I suggest we give the truce a try, wait and see if Basil is sincere in his willingness to end the hostilities. If so, we can always release his hostages once he demonstrates his trustworthiness."

She frowned for a moment, then nodded. "Yea, I think you are right."

"But, Princess—" pleaded Duncan.

Motioning him to be silent, Aurora turned back to the herald. "Tell King Basil we agree to the truce. The hostages will be released in due course, if he keeps his word and does not attack us."

"Yea, milady," answered the herald.

With the crowd again erupting in triumph, the man mounted his horse and galloped away. Duncan sneered at Niccolo. "You were foolish to suggest the princess trust Basil, Venetian. His tidings of peace are likely only a ruse to make us grow complacent. He will surely regroup his forces and mount another offensive. By damn, we routed the bloody scoundrel yesterday and we should move in for the kill!"

As Aurora listened with a frown, Niccolo only shrugged. "What have we to lose by giving Basil a chance to withdraw from the conflict with his pride intact?"

Christian stepped up to join them. "I agree with Sir Niccolo. Do you not, sister?"

"Yea, I do," she replied, gazing at Niccolo meaningfully. "Although we must take care to ensure Basil does not intend to trick us, methinks to demand his complete surrender will only provoke him. 'Tis likely he is defeated, and we have Sir Niccolo to thank."

Amid renewed rooting from the spectators, Niccolo smiled stiffly at Aurora, guilt gnawing him due to the truth he alone knew.

Over the next few days, Basil did not again attack. Although hope grew that the war might truly be at an end, the mood among the knights was cautious enough that Niccolo went through the motions of stationing sentries at numerous points outside the castle and in the woods. He saw Aurora only when others were present, and he dared not meet her again in the copse, despite the reproach he oft spotted in her eyes. Turmoil assailed him at the realization that she might soon declare him the victor and expect him to wed her. He did not know what to do.

Four days after the battle, the unfortunate Sir Olaf succumbed to his brain injury, never having regained consciousness. On a gray, misty morn, most of the inhabitants of the castle, as well as a number of paid mourners from the village, gathered near the steps of the chapel for the funeral. The royal priest, Father Mark, solemnly pronounced the Mourning Office. Then the procession began to the burial grounds outside the castle. The monks bearing the black-draped bier were followed by the priest and the mourners.

As Niccolo strode along, carrying his candle with the others, Aurora surprised him by stepping up to join him. She wore a traditional black crepe gown and high headdress with short, wispy veil.

"Why have you not met me in the copse?" she

whispered tensely. "We have important matters to discuss."

Sensing just what those important matters were, Niccolo glanced away. "I cannot meet you, Princess. Other duties command my attention."

Her voice rang with anguish and accusation. "What other duties? Basil no longer attacks us! He has sent tidings of truce. You could meet me if you wanted to."

Niccolo hated himself for causing her confusion. " 'Tis true the threat seems over for now, but the lull could still be a ruse. I do not fully trust Basil, and feel 'tis imprudent for us to continue to meet. And 'twould be best if you did not wander off on your own, Princess."

"Why not?" she retorted. "No one knows about the shrine except you, Christian, and the gnomes—who also watch over me. Do you think I would ever tell another of our own special place?"

Niccolo's fingers clenched about his candle. Hoarsely he said, "Princess, 'twould be best you no longer think of me as your suitor."

Appearing alarmed, she grabbed his arm and pulled him out of the ranks of the mourners. "You are withdrawing from the contest? But most everyone agrees that you have proven yourself the best in combat. You appear to have won!"

"You do not understand!" he replied fiercely. "If I win, you will lose." He glanced ahead to see several of the knights frowning back at them. "Let us proceed on. The others are staring at us."

"Nay!" she denied, still gripping his arm. "You must explain this change of heart. All along, you have wanted nothing more than to win the contest. Now, with victory within your grasp, you are giving up and casting me aside. Why?"

Confronted by the intense bewilderment and hurt reflected on her lovely face, Niccolo was in hell. But how could he answer her without admitting his terrible designs and mixed feelings . . . thus making matters much worse?

"Princess, we cannot speak of this now." He turned, following the others.

Aurora stared after Niccolo in consternation. Why did he keep avoiding her? Did he no longer want her? But that made no sense . . . not after he had all but made her his in the copse.

What had he meant by his odd comment that if he won, she would lose?

She smiled. Had he truly come to believe in the curse? Did he fear his feelings for her could doom her?

Yea, that must be the answer! she thought exultantly. Again she remembered him pulling away from her in the copse, and asking her if she had heard something. He *must* have heard the dire warnings just as she had! And he had sent her away to keep her safe!

The realization spread awe through Aurora. If this was true, then she and her dark knight shared a bond she had never before known with another human being. If Niccolo could commune with her ancestors just as she could, then was he not likely the one, despite the spirits' warnings? And had he not protected her and proven himself her champion . . . more proof that he was the one?

She frowned, still uncertain. Yet she knew she must convince Niccolo not to forsake their love. In an ironic sense, his pulling away from her had sharpened and clarified her own feelings. She thought of him every moment, craved him whether they were together or apart. Verily, she wanted him so much, she no longer cared if what she felt for him was love or lust; she no longer cared if she was doomed! Yea, she was even prepared to sacrifice herself for him. She wanted Niccolo, and she would have him!

By now the group had arrived in the cemetery on the side of a hill, and were gathered by the bier. As Father Mark blessed the grave, the wind picked up, blowing moisture across the mourners and dousing most of the candles. Lightning lit the dark heavens, and thunder boomed out.

Aurora tried to catch Niccolo's eye, but he studiously avoided looking in her direction. He stood gazing at the bier, his hair blowing about his handsome, impassive visage.

At the end of the ritual, Aurora felt a firm hand gripping her elbow, and she turned to look into Christian's kindly brown eyes. She regarded him quizzically.

"Come, sister," he whispered. "The blessing has ended and the others are departing." He glanced at the ominous heavens. "We had best follow suit before the skies open on us."

Looking upward, Aurora felt a cold, fat raindrop splashing her nose. "You are right, brother."

Trailing the mourners and holy men, the brother and sister left the cemetery. Aurora glanced back to see Niccolo still standing by the grave, holding his extinguished candle as the diggers shoveled out mounds of earth.

"Aurora, is something troubling you?" asked Christian.

She sighed. "Yea, 'tis Sir Niccolo."

"What about him?"

"He has proven himself the fiercest in combat, has he not?"

"Yea, he has."

"He appears to have won the contest, yet he refuses to claim his prize," Aurora confessed morosely.

Scowling, Christian glanced back at the knight. "That is odd. All along, Sir Niccolo has struck me as being an utterly ruthless man who places winning above all else. Do you think mayhap he will not claim victory until he is certain Basil is fully committed to peace?"

"Mayhap," conceded Aurora. She gripped her brother's arm to stay him. "Christian, I must ask something of you."

He nodded. "You know 'tis always a great honor to serve you."

"Then listen well," began Aurora. "If the truce endures and Basil does not attack again within the next week, I shall declare Sir Niccolo the victor. You, as my only attending male relation, must speak with him regarding our nuptials."

Christian went wide-eyed. "Nay! You cannot ask me to act against your own best interests!"

"Why would you say that?" asked Aurora.

Christian's features tensed with anxiety. "Because I am not certain I trust Sir Niccolo."

"You are wrong," she countered. "You do not know him as I do. I think there is goodness in him."

"What goodness?"

She mulled over his question. " 'Tis difficult to describe, but I know he has considered my welfare above his own. Moreover, the spirits have told me my champion will be my true love, so he must be the one."

Yet Christian appeared skeptical. "Aurora, I find accepting the counsel of ghosts to be a risky way for you to choose a husband. Besides, it falls to our uncle alone to arrange your nuptials."

"But 'tis Uncle Artemas who placed us in this dire predicament," argued Aurora. "God only knows when he may reappear . . . if ever. 'Twas I who challenged the knights to the contest, and you yourself have conceded that Sir Niccolo has won."

Christian distractedly wiped moisture from his brow. "That is true, but I still doubt Niccolo Campioni is the right man for you. Pray wait a while, sister."

"Nay, I shall have him," she declared proudly.

Christian gripped her shoulder. "Sister, you could die if you choose wrong."

But she vehemently shook her head. "I shall honor my word and give Niccolo my hand . . . and you, as my brother, are bound to support me in this."

Christian hesitated for a long moment, then at last sighed his defeat. "Very well, sister. I shall honor your wishes, however much it grieves me to do so."

Even when the cold, hard rain began to fall, Niccolo lingered in the cemetery, his thoughts as dark as the muddy pit the diggers were carving out for poor Sir Olaf.

He hated holding himself apart from Aurora, but did not know what else to do. This woman had turned all his fine plans to ashes. Now, if he proceeded to claim his prize, instead of ruining the princess as he had initially intended, he would be the one defeated.

For he did not doubt that if he took Aurora in his arms again, he would lose his heart and soul to her. Even being near her was torture, so powerful was his urge to close the distance between them, to make her his.

Ah, he was enchanted by her! But he could not risk loving again, becoming vulnerable once more to emotional devastation. And even if Aurora never betrayed him as Cecilia had, he could not give her the love she needed to sustain her and shield her from the curse.

More and more he felt he had been wrong about Aurora, that she had likely never conspired with her uncle, that she was, after all, a good and worthy woman. The truth was, she increasingly reminded him not of his traitorous wife, but of his mother, who possessed such strength and courage, and his sister, who was filled with innocence and joie de vivre. Just as he would never allow Caterina to marry a soulless infidel such as himself, so Aurora clearly did not belong with him.

He did not know which way to turn. Should he leave Falconia? But what of Basil? He would surely attack again, once he figured out his bargain had been betrayed. Could he leave Aurora possibly vulnerable to that repulsive lout?

Niccolo tarried with his grim thoughts until the rain faded into a dreary mist, long after the diggers had lowered Sir Olaf's casket into the grave, shoveled dirt over it, and left. 'Twas then that he was startled by the sound of a shrill voice calling out from birch trees beyond him. He jerked to attention at once.

"Sir Niccolo! Pray, come nigh! I must speak to you!" called the voice.

Drawing his sword, Niccolo whirled in the direction of the noise. "Who goes there? Show yourself or be slain."

To his amazement, he watched Ignatius step tentatively from the woods. The hunched little man wore a drenched gray robe and dripping cap. He trembled in fear as he regarded Niccolo.

"You!" Niccolo cried in rage. "I told you to leave these parts! I should slay you now!"

"Nay, sir!" pleaded the man, holding up a gnarled, trembling hand. "Pray, hear me out. I have a message from King Basil."

Niccolo strode closer with sword still in hand. "Explain yourself, then. Why are you still here, and conspiring with Basil?"

The man gulped. "I have gone over to the side of the Ravenians."

"Judas!" cried Niccolo. "You defied my orders!"

As Niccolo advanced, Ignatius jerked backward. "Pray, sir, I had no choice but to remain in Ravenia! I ask you, what chance would I have had, proceeding through the Alps on foot, with barely enough coin for the tolls? I am a citizen of Kestrel now, and I swear I shall never again set foot in the princess's domain."

Niccolo hesitated for a long moment, glowering fearsomely. "Well, you had best not appear in these parts or I shall see you hung!" He sheathed his sword. "What is your message?"

"King Basil will meet you at sunset at the rendezvous point overlooking the lake."

"Why?" demanded Niccolo.

Ignatius coughed awkwardly. "He thinks you have betrayed your agreement."

"So Basil told you of our arrangement?"

"Yea, and he has asked me to act as emissary. Will you come to the meeting, sir?"

Niccolo regarded the sly little man narrowly. "How do I know this is not a trap?"

" 'Tis not, I assure you, sir," insisted the man nervously. "But King Basil says if you do not appear, he disavows your bargain."

Niccolo cursed, causing Ignatius to cower anew. "Very well, tell Basil I shall come," he snarled at last. "But give him a message for me. I shall leave behind in Falconia instructions that if I do not return, or if any harm comes to me, Princess Aurora is to be wed to one of her own knights as soon as the banns can be read. Thus, if Basil betrays me, he will never become her husband. Is that clear?"

Ignatius nodded earnestly. "Yea, sir, I shall pass along your message."

The sun emerged mercifully late in the afternoon, the aftermath of the rain leaving a cloying sweetness in the air. With the gilded light of eventide emblazoning the lake beneath him and highlighting the curtain of Ravenia Castle with shades of umber, Niccolo waited for Basil in the clearing along the hillside.

All day he had dreaded this meeting, which reminded him of his own perfidy, even though he no longer intended to betray Aurora and ransom her to

Basil. But at least the meeting might buy him more time . . . if he smoothly lied and convinced Basil that he did intend to fulfill their bargain.

He soon spotted the bulky man trudging up the trail, his gait painful. Basil limped into the open area, an ugly snarl gripping his features as he spotted Niccolo standing there.

Regarding Niccolo with anger and loathing, he spoke straight to the point. "Cursed Venetian! You betrayed me!"

"I did nothing of the sort," Niccolo retorted, standing his ground.

"Liar!" shouted Basil. "You deceived me from the beginning, telling me Ignatius had died—"

"I told you he was on his deathbed. And who cares what happens to that weasel?"

Basil waved a fist. "You attacked my castle and unhorsed me. Damn it, you broke three of my ribs. My physician said that had your aim veered a flicker, 'twould have been my heart you impaled. And you knocked me into the lake, badly spraining my hip, and making a fool of me before mine own men!"

"I gave you but a glancing blow on purpose," Niccolo snapped. "Consider yourself fortunate."

"Fortunate!" Basil's face was turning a nasty shade of red, veins standing out on his forehead. "You attacked my castle!"

"I told you your defeat had to appear decisive."

"I will not be made jest of this way!"

Niccolo smiled cruelly. "Do you want to win the princess?"

Basil glared, breathing with an effort.

"Well, your only hope now is to follow our plan," Niccolo continued coldly. "If you do, I shall turn Aurora over to you before we are formally betrothed, as we agreed."

"Why not give her to me now?" demanded Basil.

Anger and revulsion consumed Niccolo at the very

thought. "I shall soon, but 'tis complicated," he hedged. "I must choose the right moment."

"You are trying my patience!" roared the king, waving a fist.

Niccolo faced down the bellicose man with equal menace. "I would advise you to guard your meager patience, prepare the recompense as we agreed, and await word from me. You must not deviate from our plan, or you shall never win the princess. If you break your vow, I promise I shall see to it that she weds another at once."

For a moment, Basil hobbled about the clearing, muttering curses and running his fingers through his greasy orange hair, his features purpling with ire and frustration as he seemed to realize Niccolo had the upper hand.

At last he whirled on Niccolo and sneered, "How do I know you will not betray me . . . again?"

Niccolo spoke with chilling violence. "I have not betrayed you, *idiota* . . . and you had best remember it."

Niccolo turned on his heel and left the clearing, while Basil glared after him in rage.

TWENTY-SIX

WHEN SEVERAL MORE DAYS PASSED AND THE TRUCE was not broken, Aurora ordered the Ravenian captives returned to their homeland, and decreed that there would be a great three-day-long festival in Falconia, to celebrate the royal victory. The princess promised that free food and drink would be offered to every citizen on the castle green. Heralds with banners, along with jongleurs with trumpets, were sent into Osprey to proclaim the good tidings. At the castle, servants busied themselves rolling out barrels of wine from the cellars, preparing vast quantities of mutton, capon, veal, rabbit, fruits, wafers, and cheese for the banquet. Outside on the castle green, carpenters assembled tables for the feasting, guildsmen constructed a large platform for the miracle plays, and a number of villagers built booths where they would sell their foodstuffs and wares during the festival.

Niccolo felt uneasy regarding the imminent merrymaking. Although the castle remained in a defensive mode, he feared Aurora had assumed Basil was now totally defeated—and, of course, he could not inform her otherwise without revealing his own duplicity. Now he would be expected to claim Aurora as his bride. The prospect put him in a panic. He still felt tempted to leave Falconia, but could not bear the possibility of Aurora ending up in Basil's evil clutches when the king inevitably took the offensive again.

On the morn before the festival, Christian sought him out in the bailey. The young man strode up grinning, his fierce falcon perched on his wrist.

"Sir Niccolo, pray come hunting with me and several of our knights. We must snare additional grouse and pigeons for the feasting tomorrow."

Knowing 'twould be an insult to decline, Niccolo bowed. "Thank you, Sir Christian, I would be honored."

Christian escorted his guest to the royal mews, where the huntsman, Sir Gar, handed Niccolo a leather glove, then ducked inside the small, noisy rookery, emerging with a huge, fierce peregrine falcon, which he carefully transferred to Niccolo's hand. Staring at the fearsome bird of prey perched on his gauntlet, her talons and beak lethally sharp, her dark, beady eyes darting about rapidly, Niccolo felt somewhat daunted. When the huge bird flashed her brilliant wings and gave a bloodcurdling scream, he kept his arm—and his nerves—steady with an effort! Not since his youth had he handled a falcon, especially not a huge peregrine readied for the hunt, unhooded and unleashed. Thankfully, after a tense moment or two, the awesome bird folded her wings and perched docilely on his hand.

Several other knights soon joined them near the mews to select falcons or hawks of their own. Moments later, the small party left the castle on horseback, Niccolo and Christian joined by Sir Gar, Sir Galen, Sir Edgar, Sir Rafael, and Sir Gilbert. The knights were preceeded by half a dozen pages who walked along bearing large sticks.

During the brief ride, Niccolo's peregrine remained perched on his wrist, her sharp eyes peering about in all directions. When they approached an expanse of marsh grasses near the lake, she grew restless again, chewing at her talons and his glove, and he sprinkled her with water to soothe her.

At Christian's signal, the knights halted their mounts. The pages tramped through the boggy areas, yelling and beating the rushes with their sticks. Amid a loud flapping of wings and a cacophony of harsh cries, a number of pheasants, grouse, pigeons, and cranes were spooked from their lairs.

Feeling his falcon's talons tense on his wrist, Niccolo raised his arm. Emitting a high screech, the magnificent peregrine sailed away, soaring briefly on her huge, brilliant wings, then diving for a pheasant, catching the fat bird in her deadly talons and quickly killing it with swift, hacking strokes of her sharp beak. By now, the other falcons and hawks were also busy performing their deadly work, attacking grouse, pigeons, and cranes. The air resounded with the shrieks of predator and prey, with myriad flashes of furiously whirling feathers. On the sidelines, the hunters cheered their birds on and congratulated one another on the successful kill. Even Niccolo felt exhilarated, remembering the idyllic days of his youth, when he had hunted thus with his father.

Within seconds, the melee ended. Once the pages had bagged the slaughtered fowl, and the knights had retrieved their birds of prey, the group started back for the castle. Ahead of Niccolo, several of the knights passed around a small flask of wine and sang a bawdy song.

After a moment, Christian turned his mount and galloped back to join Niccolo. "Sir Niccolo, I would have a word with you," he said solemnly.

"How may I be of assistance, Sir Christian?" Niccolo politely responded.

The young man grinned. "You have already been of ample assistance to us all here in Falconia. This hunting expedition would not have been possible had it not been for your skilled strategies against my sister's enemy. You have won the day for Falconia—and especially for Aurora."

Niccolo frowned. "I may have led the princess's knights to an important victory, but I can hardly share your sanguine view regarding the overall conflict, my friend. Despite his sending tidings of truce, I think Basil is not yet finished with us."

Christian shook his head. "And I say you are being far too modest. Aurora and I have agreed that the war is ended and you have won the contest."

Suddenly alert with tension, Niccolo did not reply.

"Now, I wish to speak to you on behalf of my sister, since her uncle is not presently in the kingdom," continued Christian.

Niccolo was feeling extremely discomfited. "Of what do you wish to speak?"

"Why, of your marriage to my sister, of course," replied Christian. "I must admit I have had my doubts about you, Sir Niccolo. But as Aurora has pointed out, you have won the day. Since you have proven yourself the greatest champion of all the knights, my sister wishes to have Father Mark perform your betrothal ceremony on the final night of the festival. The wedding will be arranged as soon as the banns can be read."

Niccolo felt as if the breath had been knocked from him. He had never expected Aurora to act so aggressively, nor so quickly, or to make plans through third parties this way . . . although he supposed it was all very proper.

"Well, what say you, Sir Niccolo?" prodded Christian. "For a fellow who has just won the princess's hand, you seem rather hesitant."

Niccolo shifted the falcon on his wrist. "I . . . I must have time to consider this. I had not expected to win so soon—"

Christian chuckled. "Come now, my man. One gen-

erally expects a blushing bride . . . not a timid bridegroom."

"I . . ." Niccolo gave a groan. "I am simply not prepared to take this step."

Christian regarded Niccolo in anger and disbelief.
"You are saying you will break your word? You will
actually consider spurning my sister, royal princess of
Falconia?"

Niccolo spoke through clenched teeth. "I tell you, I
am not convinced I have truly and fairly won the contest!"

"My sister is convinced, sir," Christian replied
proudly. "And I shall die ere I let *any* man insult her
honor. I expect your consent by day's end . . . or a
much better explanation of why you will not keep
your word."

Watching Christian gallop off, Niccolo cursed his
frustration. What was he to do now? Marry Aurora
when he knew he could not love her, when his motives were not pure, when he would only bring her
pain?

He shook his head at the terrible irony. He was a
champion who was unwilling to claim his prize . . .
not even the long-coveted trophy of his revenge.

When the knights galloped back inside the bailey,
she was there with her ladies, looking too beautiful
for words in a gown of gray silk so pale and fine, it
resembled silver. She and the other ladies greeted the
knights with waves and laughter as the men brandished gunnysacks bearing their prizes of slain fowl.

She strolled up to Niccolo's horse, eagerly gazing
up at him as he held his falcon. "Well, Sir Niccolo,
did one of Christian's birds serve you well this
morn?"

His expression grim, Niccolo carefully dismounted
and handed his falcon to a page. He firmly took Aurora's arm. "I would speak with you, milady."

She smiled pleasantly, only increasing his exasperation. "Certainly, Sir Niccolo."

"This way," he muttered gruffly, leading her away from the others, toward the courtyard fronting the keep.

She eyed him curiously. "Did Christian speak with you?"

"Indeed he did," Niccolo replied. "Was that not the entire purpose of this little hunting expedition?"

She laughed. "Why are you acting so churlish, Niccolo? Of course I asked my brother to speak with you. You have won the contest . . ." She paused to eye him dreamily. "And now it appears you have won me."

He glowered, fighting back the rush of tender feelings her guileless expression inspired. "And you, milady, have no idea what you are doing."

She lifted her chin in challenge. "Are you still afraid I fancy the others?"

"Do you?" he asked intently.

Fervently she replied, "I want *you*, Niccolo, you alone . . . and you want me."

Niccolo helplessly clenched his fists. "You do not know anything about me, Aurora. You do not know what kind of man you are dealing with." *A man who has plotted your ruin.*

"I know I would risk death for you," she whispered.

He stared at her. Sweet Christ, she appeared utterly sincere! She was gazing at him with utter trust and adoration, her expression tearing at his conscience.

She lightly touched his shirt with her fingertips. He felt as if he had been scorched. "Is that not why you hesitate?" she asked gently. "Do you fear I shall succumb to the curse? Well, I shall gladly risk its vengeance to know your love, so you need not worry anymore."

"I need not worry?" he cried, blinking at her in disbelief.

"Nay," she replied, thrusting herself into his arms.

A tortured groan escaped Niccolo. Holding her incredible sweetness against his hungry heart, he felt agonized by her willingness to give of herself so completely, even to make the ultimate sacrifice . . .

He pulled back, regarding her in turmoil. "Aurora . . . my God, woman, do not be a fool! Why would you even want a man who is incapable of loving you?"

Her expression grew petulant. "I do not believe that. You have won the contest, and I want us to be wed, to be together always."

"*Dio*." Niccolo spoke hoarsely. "And what if you do not have an always, milady?"

"What time I have left, I want to spend with you," she declared passionately.

He held her apart from him with fingers that trembled. "Somehow I must save you from yourself."

Niccolo left her, haunted by the look of confusion he had spotted in her eyes. What was he to do? How could he possibly retrieve himself from this muddle?

She wanted *him*, him alone, or so she claimed. He had craved those words from her lips ever since he had arrived in Falconia, but now that she had spoken them, instead of crowing his triumph, he was writhing in hell. Never had he expected his victory to betray him, to flay him with guilt and agony. He knew he was wrong for Aurora, that the war was far from over. But he was bound to give Christian his answer by day's end, or Christian would feel honor-bound to challenge him.

Mayhap he should allow the lad to slay him and be done with his miserable life!

He climbed high into the parapets and sat there for hours, brooding, until at last a possible solution dawned. Day was fading by the time he rushed back down the many winding steps to the bailey. He sought out Sir Edgar, and finally found him in the barracks playing chess with Sir Rafael. "Edgar, I must have a word with you."

The Englishman scowled up at the man who had just burst into his cell. He gestured toward the table. "Can you not see I am occupied?"

"It concerns the princess. 'Tis urgent."

"Very well, that is different."

At once Edgar rose and left the barracks with Niccolo. The two men walked together near the stables. "What may I do to help the princess?" Edgar asked solemnly.

Niccolo laughed. "You may wed her, sir."

Edgar stopped in his tracks and grabbed Niccolo's arm. "What are you saying, man?"

"This morn Christian told me the princess has decided I have won the contest. She wishes to have our betrothal ceremony on the third night of the festival."

Edgar's features twisted in confusion. " 'Tis not unexpected news that she would declare you her champion—"

" 'Tis plenty unexpected to me," confessed Niccolo ruefully. "And I am unprepared to proceed."

Edgar shook his head in mystification. "But why would you give up your prize now, when it appears you are indeed our lady's champion? And why would you say you wish me to wed her when you have won her fairly?"

Niccolo groaned at Edgar's pronouncement. If this noble knight only knew of the dire motives Niccolo had harbored in his heart, how he had plotted with Aurora's enemy, he would run him through—and deservedly so.

Gravely he said, "I want you to wed her because I am not worthy of her hand. As we both know, I am not a Christian. I have watched you, Edgar, and you are a good man—your heart is pure. I want you to have her."

Edgar scratched his bearded jaw. "But how can this be? She has not chosen me."

Taking a deep, steadying breath, Niccolo said, "I want us to tell her the plan for routing Basil was made by you, not me. That you are the greatest knight, not me."

Edgar appeared incredulous. "You would have me win her hand through a lie? 'Tis impossible, and a desecration of my knightly vows."

Niccolo gestured his frustration. "But do you not understand? I shall be bad for her, no better than a heathen."

Fighting a smile, Edgar laid a hand on Niccolo's shoulder. "Then you must either recover your lost faith, my friend, or find your own way to withdraw from this obligation. I cannot be a party to your deceit."

Niccolo stood in helpless confusion as Edgar strode away. He was beginning to fear there *was* no help for him.

He was making his way back toward the keep for dinner when Christian again confronted him, stepping in front of him on the path.

The lad eyed Niccolo proudly and spoke straight to the point. "Knight, do you consent to the betrothal?"

Niccolo heaved a heavy sigh, wondering if Christian knew about the curse and the true threat to his sister. Should he tell Christian he feared he would doom Aurora? But how could he, without confessing his true motives? Christian was obviously primed for a duel, and any untoward comment about his sister might set him off. He had best take care with his words.

Earnestly he replied, "Christian, I am not the right man for her."

The lad's determined expression did not waver. "Mayhap you are not, but Aurora is convinced otherwise, and I cannot dissuade her. Are you saying you will dishonor her by renouncing your word?"

"I am simply contending I shall not make the best husband for her," Niccolo asserted. "Surely there is a knight more worthy of her, a man with the faith and chivalry I lack."

Christian's dark eyes gleamed with indignation. "I think you are only making excuses, knight. The contest has ended and my sister's choice has been made. Do you give your consent or not?"

"I cannot," Niccolo replied miserably.

His jaw set in fury, Christian unsheathed his sword and drove the tip into the ground near Niccolo's feet. "You have besmirched the honor of my sister, knight. I challenge you to the death."

Staring at the sword, Niccolo was in agony. There was no doubt in his mind that he could slay Christian—and there was no doubt that he never would. Mayhap he *should* sacrifice his own life. But if he did, where would that leave his mother and sister? No matter what, he had to try to help them, even if it meant going back to Venice and hiring himself out as a *condottiere*.

Sighing his defeat, he nodded to Christian. "I agree to the betrothal, on the condition that it is not announced until the actual ceremony is performed on the third night of the feast."

Christian eyed him suspiciously. "Are you trying to evade your responsibility?"

"Nay, merely giving the lady a chance to change her mind," replied Niccolo tightly.

"She will not," said Christian adamantly, "but I shall agree to your condition. I see no harm done, and Aurora will like the idea of surprising everyone."

* * *

In the great hall that night, Niccolo observed Aurora smiling radiantly at him from her dais. *Oh, my poor angel*, he thought achingly. *Have you no idea what you have done? You have placed yourself in Satan's hands* . . .

Of course, Satan would devour this woman, would ruthlessly ply her lovely flesh and bury himself in her silken depths. Even though Niccolo felt agonized by guilt, his traitorous lust for Aurora was stronger than ever, especially since tonight she did have eyes *only* for him. But he knew his soul was corrupt, that he was incapable of giving her the love and devotion she truly needed . . . and likely deserved, as well.

'Twas all his own fault. Through concocting his rash scheme to win revenge, he had engineered his own defeat . . . and likely hers.

Aurora felt exultant as she looked down at Niccolo. His handsome face was a study in stark anguish, but she vowed she would soon make him smile again. Tomorrow during the festival, she would find a way to take him aside and explain to him that his marrying her would bring her no harm. She was not quite sure she believed this herself, but somehow, she must reassure him.

For now, she had Niccolo's consent to the betrothal, and 'twas all that mattered! Three days from now, the ceremony would be performed, and there would be no turning back. Ere long, Niccolo would become her husband, and she would know the bittersweet ecstasy of giving herself to him. They would know such joy together, be it only fleeting . . .

TWENTY-SEVEN

At DAYBREAK NICCOLO AND LORENZO WERE AWAK-
ened by a loud banging at the door to their small cell
in the barracks. Niccolo yelled irritably, "Enter!" and
a bearded manservant carrying a candle slipped inside.

"Sir Niccolo, I bring a message from the princess.
She asks that you meet her by the stables to do her
royal bidding."

Stifling a yawn, Niccolo sat up on the side of his
cot and ran his fingers through his hair. Why was
Aurora summoning him at the crack of dawn? To the
servant he muttered, "Tell Her Royal Majesty I shall
join her shortly."

The servant slipped out, and Niccolo hastily
dressed, while Lorenzo sat up in bed, yawned, and
regarded his master in reproachful silence.

Finally Niccolo turned to the old man. "Why do
you stare at me that way, as if I have just murdered
a dozen children?"

"You well know why," replied Lorenzo. "You are
surely about the devil's business this morn."

"According to you, I am forever about the devil's
business."

Lorenzo nodded soberly.

Niccolo rolled his eyes. "The princess has requested

my services. What choice do I have but to oblige her?"

Lorenzo only shook his head, and Niccolo, buckling his scabbard, left the room and slammed the door.

Outside the barracks, the brisk morning air greeted him. He strode quickly toward the stable, as pigs oinked around him and cackling chickens scurried out of his path. He spotted Aurora standing near the gray stable doors. As beautiful as daybreak, she wore a luxuriant blue velvet cape trimmed with fox. Her rich raven hair fell to her shoulders, and she wore a small, fur-trimmed hat. Near her stood a stable hand who held the reins to two large brown horses; on each steed was tied a basket and a cask of wine.

At his approach, she smiled. "Milord."

"Milady," Niccolo greeted, bowing to her. "You summoned me?"

"Yea." She stepped closer and dimpled winsomely. "I would have you ride with me on an errand."

"What errand?" he inquired with a scowl.

"Do not argue with me, knight," she countered saucily. "I have a small mission to perform and I need an armed escort. You will do nicely, methinks. And we must be about our business quickly and return ere long, for the feast will begin at nooning."

Aware the young groom was watching them both curiously, Niccolo realized he was trapped. "Very well, milady, 'twill be an honor to serve you."

As the groom assisted Aurora up onto the side-saddle, Niccolo mounted his own steed. They rode out of the bailey amid the curious stares of both peasants and knights. In particular, Niccolo noted Sir Duncan glancing at them with resentment as he practiced swordsmanship with his squire.

They crossed the lowered drawbridge out onto the castle green, where they were greeted by incredible activity. Servants were arranging long trestle tables and benches, laying out loaves of bread and casks of wine. Guildsmen from the village were busy setting up booths to sell everything from gold and silver jewelry, to fine cordwain slippers and leather boots, to candles, tapestries, hats, and foodstuffs of every variety. Actors in costumes—including several angels and a ghastly-looking Beelzebub—were practicing a miracle play on their wooden platform. Once again, everyone stared at Niccolo and Aurora in pointed curiosity as they passed.

Just beyond the green, Niccolo turned to the princess and raised a brow. "Now that you have made a royal spectacle of us, milady, where would you have us go?"

She laughed, leaned toward him, and whispered, "To the gnomes' village."

Niccolo raised an eyebrow. "The gnomes have a village?"

"Of course," she replied. "Did you think they live in burrows in the ground?"

He chuckled. "Is that not where gnomes normally live?"

"Not in Falconia."

Niccolo stroked his stubbled jaw. "Actually, I had not given any thought to the accommodations of those nasty little fellows."

"How do you know they are nasty?"

Niccolo gave a shrug. "I have heard such about them."

"You have no proof, knight."

"True," he admitted ruefully. "But why would you go visit them, on the day of the royal feast, no less?"

She nodded toward the baskets and casks strapped to their steeds. "Why, to take the gnomes food and wine for the feasting. They cannot join the rest of us, since the Ospreyans fear them, and would likely roast them up with the pheasants. Do you not agree?"

Niccolo broke into a reluctant grin. "I suppose. And you are an odd one, Princess."

"But 'tis unjust the gnomes are not allowed to participate in the celebration," she contended.

Niccolo beseeched the heavens. "Far be it from me to argue with you regarding the care and feeding of gnomes." He glanced ahead toward the forest, and scowled. "Where do these gremlins live, anyway?"

"They are not gremlins, and you must follow me. The route to their village is complicated."

"No doubt," he agreed, musing that only Aurora would go on such an outlandish mission of mercy.

They rode into the forest in companionable silence, Aurora leading Niccolo through a maze of endless twists and turns. Amid the chirping of birds, the spicy scent of the woods, and the dancing of light through the trees, they traveled up well into the foothills, far from the castle and village.

"Are you certain you are not getting us lost, milady?" he called out to her.

"Nay, the gnomes are merely well hidden, as they have been for centuries. Otherwise, the villagers would seek them out, burn their cottages, and slay them."

At last they entered a dappled clearing sheltered by lofty black firs, where Niccolo was amazed to see six miniature wattle-and-daub cottages arranged in a semicircle. Each cozy house sported a thatched roof as well as tiny wooden doors and shutters. At the edge of the small village stood a shed, with sacks and tools strewn about it. In makeshift corrals and wooden cages were confined a few chickens, piglets, and rabbits.

"Remarkable," muttered Niccolo.

He halted his horse, dismounted, and went over to assist Aurora to the ground, placing his hands squarely on her slim waist and slowly lowering her. She murmured a thank you, and he stifled a groan as her tormenting curves brushed against him and the scent of her, dusky and floral, filled his senses. For a moment they regarded each other breathlessly.

"Pray, untie the baskets and casks from our horses, knight," she directed him at last.

"Yea, Princess."

As Niccolo went about his task, Aurora stepped up closer to the huts, cupped a hand around her mouth, and called, "Francis! Come out, pray! I have come to visit, and I bear gifts!"

After a moment, one of the small doors creaked open, and a wrinkled face peered out. "Who goes there?" demanded a high voice.

Aurora moved closer. "Francis, 'tis I, Princess Aurora, along with Sir Niccolo. Pray, come out and speak with us."

Francis peered at the baskets and casks of wine that Niccolo had piled at the center of the clearing. "A moment, Princess, and I shall join you."

The tiny door slammed shut. A moment later, the little man emerged wearing his traditional colorful costume. He shot a suspicious glance at Niccolo, then bowed to Aurora. "Good morrow, Princess."

"Good morrow, Francis." Aurora gestured proudly toward the heaped goods. "I have brought a feast for you and the others."

Francis's gamin face lit up with pleasure and he rubbed his small, gnarled hands together. "Thank you kindly, Princess. You are most generous, and 'tis a most pleasant surprise." He stepped closer to Aurora and slanted a dubious look toward Niccolo. "But tell me, Princess, this escort of yours . . . is he trustworthy?"

Aurora glanced toward Niccolo, laughter in her eyes. "Mayhap. He shall shortly become my prince."

The little man gasped, glancing from Aurora to Niccolo. "He shall?"

"Yea. He has won the day for me, defeating Basil.

Would you not think that makes him trustworthy?"

The gnome scowled up at Niccolo for another moment, then turned back to Aurora, whispering intently, "But will he not give away our hiding place?"

With amusement, Aurora regarded Niccolo. "Will you, sir knight?"

Niccolo glanced at Francis. "Believe me, sir gnome, I could never find my way to your village again, not if my life depended on it."

Francis beamed his relief, and Aurora smiled.

"Now, rouse the others, Francis," she directed. "Thanks to Sir Niccolo's efforts in defeating our enemies, we are having a great feast at the castle . . . and you deserve to celebrate just like the others. I only regret that, for your own safety, I cannot welcome you and your kinsmen on the castle green."

Francis bowed. " 'Tis understood, Princess, and your generosity is most appreciated."

The little man backed away, then went dashing about the semicircle of huts, pounding on doors and calling, "Farley, Findley, Finn, Fiske, and Frey, get your lazy bones out of bed. Your princess has come bearing gifts!"

As Niccolo watched in sheer amazement, the rest of the gnomes soon swarmed from their cottages in a cacophony of jingling bells and shrill voices. They greeted their princess with bows and effusive smiles, then fell on the feast she had brought. Niccolo and Aurora sat down together on a large tree stump at the edge of the clearing, chuckling at the sight of the little men squatting on the ground beside the baskets, swilling wine and tossing about food—bread, cheese, ham, cooked capon, grapes, nuts, and wafers. Two of the gnomes even fetched three white pet rabbits to join them in the frolic and feasting. The fluffy animals bounded about, nibbling on scraps.

Niccolo felt awed by the magical scene. "I never

would have believed it, had I not seen it with my own eyes," he muttered.

" 'Tis a joyous sight," Aurora agreed.

Francis dashed up to them, a loaf of bread tucked beneath his arm, a cask of wine gripped in one set of stubby fingers, a chunk of cheese in the other. "Princess, we must not forget to honor you," he said, handing her the cask.

Aurora took the bottle and handed it to Niccolo. "Thank you, sir gnome. I am not hungry, but mayhap Sir Niccolo has not yet broken his fast."

The little man grinned, placed the bread and cheese in Aurora's lap, and dashed back to join his cronies.

Watching Aurora break off a chunk of bread, Niccolo wiped the lip of the cask with his jerkin, then offered the wine to her. When she shook her head, he took a sip. "This is undoubtedly the strangest breakfast I have ever had in my life."

Her face lit with amusement, Aurora handed him the piece of bread. "Here, eat this. I did not give you time to take nourishment before we left." She boldly eyed the downy gold stubble along his jaw. "Or to shave."

He grinned and tore off a bite with his teeth. "Ah, but when one has starving gnomes to attend to, that is a true crisis, no?"

She giggled and handed him a bit of cheese. "You are a patient man to indulge me in this, Sir Niccolo."

"Am I?" Looking her over, he teased, "Mayhap I wanted to get you alone."

"For what purpose?" she asked guilelessly.

"Mayhap to question you."

"Regarding what?"

Hearing a shriek go up from the little men, and watching them gleefully toss scraps of bread to the scampering rabbits, Niccolo shook his head. "To begin with, who are these gnomes and what purpose do they serve for the crown of Falconia?''

"I cannot say," she murmured demurely, delicately chewing on a crust of bread. " 'Tis a royal secret."

Niccolo fought amusement at her droll reply. "You say the gnomes have lived in these hills for centuries. But where are their wives, their children?"

She chortled. "You are a silly man, Sir Niccolo."

He glowered magnificently. "How dare you say I am silly!"

She waved a hand. "But you are absurd to assume gnomes would have families. Francis and the others are far too grumpy to have wives, and besides, they are like children themselves."

In consternation, Niccolo stared at the little men, two of whom were chewing capon, two tossing nuts and grapes about, two others chasing down the rabbits. "But if the gnomes have no families, how can they have lived in this forest for centuries?"

She gestured toward the little men. "You misunderstand me. 'Tis these same six who have lived in the Falconian hills for hundreds of years."

Niccolo was flabbergasted. "Nay."

"Yea."

"Princess, you are jesting!"

She solemnly shook her head.

Niccolo gaped at the creatures. "But no man can live for centuries."

"They are not mortal men."

"Then they are . . ."

"They are eternal, like Tansy," Aurora murmured. "Some things live forever in Falconia . . ." She sighed, her expression poignant. "And others die far too young."

Deeply affected by her words, Niccolo reached out to cup her chin in his hand, and tilted her troubled countenance toward his. With utmost sincerity he whispered, "Princess, pray reconsider our betrothal . . . or at least, postpone it."

He watched turmoil and pride fill her lovely dark eyes. "Nay. I have made up my mind, knight. I want you."

At the fierce possessiveness in her tone, Niccolo had to smile. "Do you, now?"

She nodded.

His hand fell to his side. "I will not be good for you, you know."

She looked him over mischievously. "You appear plenty good to me."

He closed his eyes and clenched his fists. "I cannot love you, Aurora."

"I do not believe you."

He opened his eyes and shook his head at her adorably determined expression. "Have you always been this way, milady, playing with gnomes and fawns, communing with spirits . . . and believing only what you *want* to believe?"

She chuckled. "And are you so jaded, so cynical, knight, that you denounce it all?"

He glanced at the gnomes. "I cannot denounce what I can see with mine own eyes."

Her hand touched his. "Then why can you not love?"

He stared at her in anguish.

She held his gaze earnestly. "You can laugh with me, Niccolo. You can share my joy. You can woo me. What makes you think you cannot love me?"

He groaned. "We are different, Aurora. In our hearts, we are different. Despite this curse you claim to believe in, your soul is bright, while mine is black as midnight."

She clutched his fingers. "I can lead you out of the darkness."

He gazed at her ardent, sincere face, and felt as if

his gut had been punched. What if she could? Could he ever open his heart again?

"You are mine now, Niccolo," she whispered.

His reply was edged with sadness. "So it appears, milady."

"Then you will honor your word to my brother, and your obligation to me?"

"Of course I shall honor my word."

"Good," she replied, brightening. "Will you kiss me now?"

Oh, he was tempted, so guilelessly had she asked.

"Will you?" she pressed.

"In front of the gnomes?" he teased. "And what if I become swept away by your charms, milady?"

She blushed. "Methinks there will be time enough for that later, then."

"When there are no gnomes to scandalize?"

Her lips twitched. "Mayhap we should ride back to the castle. My villeins will doubtless arrive early to pay their rentals . . . and to seek my justice." She eyed him meaningfully.

She looked so earnest, Niccolo could not resist taunting, "Does that mean if I refuse to honor my word, you will order me hanged?"

"Nay, not hanged." She wrinkled her nose at him. "Mayhap drawn and quartered, though."

Laughing, they took their leftovers to Francis, and all of the gnomes heartily thanked Aurora for bringing the feast. As the couple headed back to their horses, Niccolo caught Aurora's arm.

"Princess, why did you ask me to accompany you this morning?"

She regarded him wistfully. "Because I reckoned you had never before been on a gnomes' picnic."

His voice trembled. "You reckoned correctly."

With pride, she dusted a crumb off his doublet. "And because you are my affianced now, and I trust you."

He caught her hand and kissed it. "You should not."

She moved closer, pressing the flats of her hands to his chest, looking up at him frankly. "Nay, Niccolo. I shall give you my trust . . . and you shall prove yourself worthy of it."

Niccolo's heart crashed in his chest. She was utterly precious and so sincere, giving him her trust even though he did not deserve it, tempting him to have her. Their dilemma—and the gnomes—momentarily forgotten, Niccolo pulled her close and kissed her with devastating tenderness. She gave herself freely, molding herself to him, opening her mouth wide and pushing her own tongue past his teeth, deeply into his mouth. *Dio*, she was so eager, and she tasted so delicious. Desire stormed through him with staggering intensity and he nestled her closer still . . .

Only when the gnomes began to hoot and cheer in the background did they pull apart, laughing, and hurry back to their horses.

TWENTY-EIGHT

BACK AT THE CASTLE, NICCOLO RETURNED TO THE barracks and dressed for the celebration, donning a gold brocaded tunic, pale hose, and an elegant black velvet cap. When he emerged on the castle green, the festival was fully engaged. While servants busied themselves laying out the feast on trestle tables, villagers thronged the various booths, haggling with merchants who sold everything from hats, jewelry, pottery, and fabrics, to dried fruits, pickled fish, live eels, and caged birds, amid a carnival atmosphere of roving acrobats doing leaps and handsprings, jugglers tossing colorful balls, spoons, and plates, minstrels strolling with their harps and lutes. Niccolo noted to his amusement that a number of the Ospreyans wore their clothing inside out, and that talismans known to ward off evil—frogs, garlic, forks of rowan wood, and pouches of rosemary and nutmeg—sold briskly at the booths. Small children, some with cats or dogs in tow, raced about gleefully. A potpourri of smells laced the air, the enticing aromas of fresh bread and hot kidney pies mingling with the more pungent odors of the pickling vats and freshly tanned leather goods. Around the perimeter of the green and in the woods beyond were stationed numerous sentries to ensure that the celebration was not curtailed by an unexpected attack, evidence that King Basil's vow of truce was still not completely trusted.

Off to one side, Niccolo spotted Aurora sitting on a dais covered by a yellow silk canopy. Wearing her blue velvet gown, she was holding court, meting out justice to a long line of peasants and villagers who had lined up to hear their princess settle disputes and judge the validity of various complaints. Niccolo stood listening, amused, as two peasants bickered over ownership of a large goose, which they had brought along with them on a leash. The little vignette was truly comical as the peasants ranted and waved their hands, and the goose honked. But Niccolo was most intrigued by Aurora's expression of utter gravity as she patiently listened to the harangue, for this was a side to her he had not seen before.

But then, he was learning much about his princess this day. Who would have thought that a lady who picnicked with gnomes would perform her royal duties so earnestly? He chuckled when he heard her pronounce her verdict, that the two peasants must slaughter the goose together, then both of their families should partake of it. He continued to listen as she sentenced a petty thief to a day in the public stocks, and ordered a ten-year-old boy who had acted a bully to spend a week mucking out the royal stables. Niccolo found himself admiring Aurora even more for meting out justice with a hand that was firm, wise, but not cruel.

Not far from Aurora, at a small wooden table, sat her royal bailiff with his quill and account book. Before the bailiff's table stood another long line of peasants who were dutifully paying their royal rents. No coins changed hands, as the villeins proffered everything from sacks of oats and rye to goats, pigs, and chickens, to reimburse the princess for the privilege of farming on the lands she had allotted them. Those found short on their rents were ordered to spend time working the royal fields, or to chop wood or harvest grapes for the princess.

As the morning stretched on, additional townsfolk, minstrels and jongleurs, jugglers and acrobats, appeared, and a number of the knights engaged in mock jousts, melees, or tourneys. By noon, Aurora had finished holding court and had moved to the brocade-draped head table for the feast. All of the knights and ladies joined her as servants circulated with huge plates of mutton, capon, fish, and jugs of wine. Roast boars' heads and peacocks cooked in their feathers were brandished on ornate trays for effect, while minstrels strolled, singing ballads, and magicians and acrobats performed additional feats.

A respectable distance away from the royal table, the town burghers and their families ate from common tables packed with dishes from the royal kitchens—boiled eggs and kidney pies, apples and nuts and pickled pigs' feet. Many of the peasants sat nearby on the ground, eating grouse or mutton with their fingers, and throwing scraps to the many roving dogs.

Niccolo sat across and slightly down from the princess, and frequently their eyes met. He regarded her with helpless anguish, while she looked at him with secret pride, happiness glowing in her dark eyes. Observing the trust on her lovely face, Niccolo felt filled with self-loathing and near panic. If he could not find a solution, he and the princess would be betrothed in two more days. What would he do?

He wondered if the other knights already knew of the coming betrothal. Had Edgar told them? They seemed to know the contest had ended, for they no longer wooed the princess. Indeed, he spied Sir Edgar pouring wine into Lady Iris's goblet, while Sir Rafael offered a tray of wafers and dried fruits to Lady Violet. Christian, too, seemed unconcerned over his sister as he wooed Lady Flora with courtly lines from

the romances of Chrétien de Troyes. Did not any of
them recognize how utterly unworthy he was to win
the princess's hand?

The wine flowed freely, as did the laughter, and
soon even Niccolo was feeling much more mellow.
When a strolling minstrel began playing a lively May
song, Sir Edgar popped up to address the princess.
"Milady, let us all join in a carole!"

"Why, of course, Sir Edgar," Aurora replied. "If
you will lead us."

The ladies and knights, including Aurora and Niccolo, left the tables, and, at Edgar's instruction,
formed a circle together and joined hands. The group
whirled and danced as the minstrel played his spirited round again and again. Townsfolk gathered to
clap and cheer, and a number of children formed their
own circle nearby to mimic the adults. Even a few
dogs joined in, barking and racing about.

Staring at Aurora, who danced across from him, her
lovely cheeks gleaming with high color and her dark
curls bouncing as she moved, Niccolo was again
struck by how adorable, how utterly innocent, she
looked.

He remembered the wonderment of the gnomes'
picnic. How could she be so full of life when she was
convinced that death shadowed her fragile, precious
existence? Mayhap believing her days could be numbered, she seized what joy and sweetness she could.
He shuddered at the thought of her being consigned
to his jaded hands.

When he saw her thus, his old angers, his bitterness, seemed almost alien to him. But he still feared
the love that could make him vulnerable once again.
The wounds of his hurt still festered somewhere deep
inside him.

Abruptly his thoughts scattered as an ominous
hush fell over the group. The knights and ladies
ceased dancing and looked toward the south. The

minstrel's tune faded away, and even the dogs grew silent.

Turning with the others, Niccolo was astounded to view a familiar stranger riding into view, trailed by two guides. At first Niccolo blinked in disbelief at the man, then he cursed in angry recognition.

'Twas no other than Artemas, Count of Osprey, decked out in a bejeweled tunic and elegant turban, and trotting his fine horse onto the green as if he had not a care in the world!

Angry rumblings spilled forth from several other knights who spotted the newcomer. Niccolo glanced at Aurora to see that she had gone pale. She must surely fear for her uncle's life, he realized, and he felt filled with dread for her sake. The count was a madman to appear here!

Indeed, within seconds, Sir Duncan and Sir Cesare unsheathed their swords and rushed toward Artemas with cries of "Villain!" and "Thief!" Niccolo was relieved to note that the rest of the knights lingered behind, appearing uncertain, obviously struggling between their indignation and their innate chivalry. Christian tore after Duncan and Cesare, yelling at them to stop. Niccolo grimaced as he watched Duncan spin about and knock the lad to the ground.

Niccolo caught a brief glimpse of Aurora's horrified face before she, too, raced off. He hurried after her, intent on protecting her and aiding Christian, but uncertain as to what else he should do. Artemas surely deserved to be publicly hoisted on a hook for his misdeeds, but the thought of Aurora seeing her uncle executed sickened him.

In the distance, he spotted Duncan and Cesare hauling the corpulent count down off his horse. Villagers converged onto the scene in an angry mob, quickly catching the contagion of bloodlust, yelling, "Hang him!" and "Draw and quarter him!" As several villeins encouraged the knights with cheers and demands for vengeance, other peasants pushed a hay cart beneath a tree, and tossed the end of a rope over a high branch. Duncan and Cesare hauled Artemas toward his makeshift gallows; the condemned man appeared ashen-faced, in a state of shock.

At last, Niccolo caught up with Aurora and grabbed her arm. "Milady—"

She turned to him in despair, tears spilling from her eyes. "Stop them, pray. I must help Christian. I know you despise my uncle like the others, but pray—"

"Of course, milady." Niccolo dashed off, thinking this was the least he should do for her. Granted, Artemas did deserve his fate, but Aurora would suffer even more for it, and this, he could not abide.

He broke through the ranks of the howling crowd just as Artemas was being shoved up into the cart. The Count of Osprey was shaking badly and babbling incoherently, he noted with some satisfaction.

Niccolo grabbed Duncan's wrists as he would have slipped the noose over Artemas's neck. "No, you must stop!"

Duncan glared back. "Stand aside, Venetian. This man deserves to hang."

"He duped and embezzled us all," added Cesare.

Even as the crowd clamored for a hanging, waving fists and hooting jeers, Aurora stepped through their ranks, along with Christian, who appeared dazed and was rubbing his jaw.

Forbiddingly, Aurora faced down Sir Duncan. "How dare you strike my brother, Scot! And I forbid you to execute my uncle."

Duncan had the grace to appear somewhat abashed. "Your Majesty, I meant no harm to Christian. But you both must stand aside. This is a debt of honor and we men will settle it."

"No, you will not," argued Niccolo. "Only the princess has the right of high justice in Falconia. And you will be violating your oath of chivalry if you try to seize that right from her." He turned to Edgar, who, along with Gilbert and the others, had stepped up to join them. "Is this not so?"

Edgar nodded, his expression grave as he confronted Duncan and Cesare. "I know you are angered. But Sir Niccolo has spoken the truth. We are holy knights, not a lynch mob. We cannot hang a man who has not been properly tried and sentenced."

"Sir Edgar speaks the truth," agreed Christian. "Only my sister may judge our uncle."

"But the princess will not give us justice," the Scot retorted, hurling an accusatory glance at Aurora. "She will not condemn her own uncle."

A grim silence fell as everyone looked to Aurora. She glanced at her terrified uncle, then thrust her chin up proudly. "You are right, Sir Duncan. I shall not condemn my own flesh and blood. But I shall do my best to see that my uncle makes reparations to you all."

Cesare and Duncan grumbled to one another, obviously considering her words and wavering.

At last the condemned man spoke up from the cart, his voice trembling. "Men," beseeched Artemas with a crooked grin, "I realize I have wronged you terribly, but have things not turned out for the best? When my escorts and I rode through the village, a peasant informed us the war has ended. You have all won the day for my niece. Actually, although I regret my own duplicity, I had no choice but to act as I did, in order to raise an army of champions to save the princess." He waved a quivering hand. "And look how laudably all of you have performed."

Niccolo waited tensely for the knights to respond. At last, muttering his disgust, Duncan flung down the rope and stalked away, and Cesare followed suit. Artemas heaved a huge sigh and clambered down from the cart. Niccolo smiled his relief, watching a shaken, teary-eyed Aurora rush over to embrace her uncle.

Christian joined them, hugging first his sister and then Artemas.

The scene of familial intimacy tore unexpectedly at Niccolo's emotions. He waited a respectful moment, then stepped up. The three turned to eye him—Aurora radiant, Christian relieved, Artemas wary.

Niccolo nodded to Artemas. "Well, signore *il conte*," he murmured ironically. "We meet again at last."

Artemas blinked rapidly in betrayal of his agitated state. "*Grazie*, Sir Niccolo; I owe you my life."

"You owe all of us more than your life," Niccolo retorted. Watching Aurora blanch, he continued with less venom. "You will do well to remember, sir, that I intervened today on Aurora's behalf, not on yours."

" 'Tis understood," stated Artemas heavily.

"Then understand this, as well," said Niccolo. "Even though the crisis has been averted, do not think for a moment that any of the honorable men you have defrauded have forgotten your deceit."

"I do not expect otherwise," acknowledged Artemas humbly.

Christian stepped toward Niccolo, grinning and clapping him across the shoulders. "Bless you, Sir Niccolo. You have served our family well today."

Niccolo nodded gravely.

"Yea, thank you, Niccolo," added Aurora, flashing him a tremulous smile.

"Milady," he acknowledged.

Aurora gripped Artemas's arm. "If you will excuse us, I must see to my uncle."

"By all means," Niccolo agreed, turning away.

Nearby in the crowd stood a hunched, arthritic figure in a heavy, hooded mantle. Ignatius cackled to himself as he watched the princess move off toward the castle with her still shaken uncle.

Ignatius had come to the Falconian celebration to

spy for his new lord, King Basil. So far, the day had
proven amusing as well as enlightening. The return
of the Count of Osprey had been a welcome diversion.
Ignatius only regretted that Artemas was saved from
the gallows by Sir Niccolo, for he had never liked the
princess's wily uncle.

Verily, he was not shocked that the Falconians were
celebrating their presumed victory over Ravenia, for
Basil had cautioned him to expect this. Otherwise, the
news he would convey back to his lord was not good.
Basil was already fuming because Sir Niccolo was
stalling in the fulfillment of their bargain. The king
would surely become enraged to learn that his coveted princess might soon be forfeit to Sir Niccolo, for
Ignatius had overheard several knights gossiping
about the betrothal ceremony that would be performed ere the festival ended. From what he had as-
certained, Sir Niccolo planned to proceed with the
ceremony and had no intention of turning Aurora
over to Basil first, as agreed.

Now it fell to him to inform Basil he had been betrayed by the very knight he had conspired with. Ignatius shuddered at the prospect. He dearly hoped
the king was not inclined to slay the messenger of ill
tidings . . .

TWENTY-NINE

ONCE THE CROWD ON THE VILLAGE GREEN BEGAN TO settle down, Niccolo headed back toward the castle. He remained concerned about Aurora, and hoped he might catch her alone after she saw to her uncle's needs. He was still hoping to convince her to revoke or postpone the betrothal, perhaps for the sake of her just-arrived uncle. Granted, Artemas deserved no special deference, but Aurora clearly remained devoted to him, and at this point Niccolo was willing to resort to any ploy to save her from her self-defeating decision to wed him.

In the courtyard not far from the keep, he was intrigued to spot Aurora and her uncle strolling together. Curious as to what they might be discussing, he paused within earshot, shielding his presence at the side of the barracks. Their conversation drifted over to him . . .

In the courtyard, Aurora was intently scolding her uncle. Considering Artemas's brazen conduct, first in defrauding the knights, then in appearing here, she mused he was very lucky to be alive at the moment. Thank God Niccolo had intervened and convinced the other knights to spare her uncle!

"I cannot believe you were so foolish as to return here to Falconia, Uncle Artemas," she admonished.

"How did you expect the knights to behave after you deceived and robbed them? Did you think they would hold a banquet in your honor?"

Not at all appearing like a man who had narrowly escaped death, Artemas chuckled, his beady eyes glittering. "But, my dear, I could not leave you to face the lions alone."

Aurora made a sound of outrage. "You have done so long enough, not appearing here until now, the eleventh hour! Moreover, you owe me an explanation for your despicable conduct. Why did you dispatch eight knights, each of whom you convinced he had contracted to become my future husband?"

Artemas avoided his niece's eye. "My purpose was to protect you—"

"Your purpose was to pad your own purse, and you well know it!" she cut in. "Furthermore, you left me to deal with the consequences of your foul deeds—and having no knowledge or forewarning of your intrigues! Have you given a thought to the position you placed me in, having to deal with *eight* disgruntled suitors?"

Artemas acknowledged her point with a gesture of resignation. "Yea, you are right, niece, and I admit my own transgressions. I have always been far too roguish for my own good. But I am here now, am I not? And has it not all turned out for the best?"

She appeared mystified. "If it has, 'twas no thanks to you! How could you send me so many suitors, fully knowing I am cursed?"

He paused to regard her solemnly. " 'Tis because you are cursed, niece, that I knew I must send you a wealth of potential husbands to choose from, to increase the chances that you would find the right one."

She considered his words with a skeptical frown. "I have made my choice."

"What choice?" asked Artemas tensely.

Aurora faced her uncle with pride. "After six of the

knights arrived here, I challenged them all to a contest for my hand."

"You did what?"

"I had to find some way out of the morass you had mired me in!" she exclaimed, waving a hand. "Thus I vowed that the knight who proved himself my greatest champion, the man who defeated Basil, would become my prince. Now I know that knight is Niccolo Campioni, since he led the successful campaign that routed Basil and compelled him to send tidings of truce. Sir Niccolo and I shall be betrothed on the third night of the festival."

Artemas frowned. "You have decided to betroth yourself to the Venetian? Without gaining my consent?"

"Christian spoke with Niccolo on my behalf," she asserted. "Besides, you have neglected your duty, doing your worst by me already!"

"You are wrong, niece," contradicted Artemas. "Your father left to me the obligation of choosing your husband. You are cursed, and I shall not see you wed in haste. We know very little about this Niccolo Campioni—"

"We know he is the knight who defeated Basil— and saved your worthless hide! We know that, after the way you have abused my good graces, you have little right to dictate to me now!"

With obvious reluctance, Artemas nodded. "I understand your anger, niece, but I shall not be browbeaten into acting contrary to your best interests. Truth to tell, when I met Sir Niccolo in Venice, there was something about him that gave me pause . . . a potential for violence and ruthlessness, mayhap. I remember sensing much anger in him . . . Indeed, I seem to recall his saying he was betrayed once before. I know I did not completely trust him."

For a moment, Aurora regarded Artemas in stormy silence. Then she flung a hand outward in exasperation. "Who are you to speak of trust, uncle? Whether you had doubts about Sir Niccolo or not, you duped him and accepted his purse readily enough, did you not?"

"True," Artemas conceded with a guilty smile. "What can I say, niece? I am surely a wicked man, and mayhap I shall burn in hell for my waywardness. But that does not mean I will see you betrothed to the devil. Moreover, how can we be certain the war with Ravenia is completely at an end? Despite the apparent truce, Basil has always been a shifty scoundrel. I may have been self-serving in some ways, niece, but I shall not risk your life. Therefore, we must wait a time before announcing your betrothal, to ensure Niccolo Campioni is the right husband for you."

"Nay!" cried Aurora. "I have made my choice and I shall wed Niccolo!"

Artemas raised a thin, dark brow. "You will defy my wishes, niece, and violate the dictates, indeed the memory, of your dear departed parents?"

Aurora churned in turmoil, at war between her determination to have Niccolo, and her honor, the nagging voice of her conscience. She soon realized that ultimately she could not so dishonor her parents' memory or their wishes. True, Artemas had behaved disgracefully, putting her in a frightful predicament. But her father *had* left to Artemas the task of choosing her husband, and she must now abide by her uncle's decision, much as it rankled. Now that he was here, she would have to gain his blessing and consent before she could wed Niccolo.

To him she conceded wearily, "Very well, uncle, I shall abide by your wishes for now, and delay the betrothal for a time. But I tell you this—either you will make reparations to the knights you have wronged, or I shall do so on your behalf."

Artemas fell silent, scowling . . .

Still listening nearby, Niccolo felt extremely unset-

tled about what he had overheard. For he knew now
with a certainty what his conscience had argued all
along—that Aurora had never been a part of her uncle's intrigue. His heart welled with tenderness
toward her, and his gut clenched with self-
abhorrence. How could he have misjudged her so
grievously?

Even more astounding, Artemas obviously believed
in and feared the curse. Thank God the man possessed enough wisdom to insist Aurora postpone the
betrothal . . . and enough shrewdness not to trust *him*.

'Twas truly ironic. The man who had originally betrayed him had now delivered him . . . but even more
important, Artemas had saved Aurora.

That night the merrymaking continued, as fresh
food and drink were laid out on the trestle tables, and
numerous candles and torches provided illumination.
As servants circulated with wine, a harper plucked his
instrument, and a storyteller told tales of the Crusades
of old; in the background, fireworks lit the sky.

At the royal table, Artemas sat between his niece
and Christian, gaily visiting with both. Niccolo again
sat across and down from Aurora; several times he
caught her staring at him wistfully. He yearned to
hold her, but feared he never could again. He prob-
ably should return to Venice, he mused, before he succumbed to temptation . . . much as he suspected it
might break his heart to leave her, and much as he
would still worry over her safety, her future. But
would he not ultimately do her more harm if he
stayed?

The feasting stretched on well into the night, long
after most of the villagers had returned home. Soon
several of the knights nodded off, snoring with their
heads on the table. Other knights and ladies seemed
in an amorous mood: Christian and Flora sat gazing
into each other's eyes; Sir Edgar and Lady Iris whis-

pered with their heads together; Sir Rafael and Lady Violet slipped away from the table together and walked off toward the woods.

After Artemas also fell asleep, his heavy head resting on his plump forearms, Niccolo could again feel Aurora staring at him. He glanced over to see her smiling; when she got up and left the table, he followed her.

She glided across the green, her lovely form illuminated by fireworks exploding off the parapets; near the woods, he caught up with her, taking her arm. "Where are you going, Princess?"

She glanced back at him. "Pray, I must speak with you alone, Niccolo. 'Tis urgent."

She headed on among the darkened trees. He followed. Soon she turned, looking exquisitely beautiful as the moonlight struck her lovely face. He pulled her into his arms, and they kissed hungrily, deeply. She tasted so sweet and felt so warm, so soft, in his arms that Niccolo ached to have her. He wondered if ever again they would share such a poignant moment.

As the kiss ended, she rested her cheek against his chest. "Oh, Niccolo, I have missed you so."

He caressed her back. "I have missed you, milady." *And shall likely miss you for the rest of my life.*

She met his eye earnestly. "Thank you for saving Uncle Artemas."

He nodded stiffly. "Again, I must emphasize that I intervened for your sake—not for his."

"I realize this." She gazed up at him in sorrow, her eyes glowing. "And I must tell you . . ."

"What, Aurora?"

She heaved a breath of frustration. "My uncle will not allow us to be betrothed as yet."

His expression painfully resigned, Niccolo drew her close again, tucking her head beneath his chin. He pressed his lips to her silky hair and inhaled its enticing, dusky scent. Fresh yearning suffused him.

"I know, milady," he said hoarsely. "I heard."

Alarmed, she backed away. "You heard?"

"Earlier, when you and your uncle spoke in the courtyard, I overheard you."

"Oh!" she cried, indignant.

"I apologize for eavesdropping," he continued, "but 'tis good to know what Artemas is about, why he has returned here."

Reluctantly she smiled. "I suppose you have reason to distrust him."

"Indeed. But I must allow the man has rather astounded me."

"In what respect?"

"Artemas may be a wily rogue, but he seems devoted to you in his way. After all, he returned here, risking his life, to see after your welfare."

She nodded, but a slight frown furrowed her smooth brow. "True . . . but that does not excuse his perfidy."

"I agree, milady. But I must say your uncle was right to insist we postpone our betrothal."

Her expression grew petulant. "I do not wish to wait . . . but my uncle insists he does not trust you."

"You should not trust me, milady," Niccolo said ruefully.

"Why do you keep saying that?"

He caressed her soft cheek with his fingertips. "Mayhap because, in my own way, I may be as much a scoundrel as your uncle."

"I do not believe that!"

"You are too trusting, milady, too loyal." He cupped her lovely face in his hands and regarded her sympathetically. "Aurora, you know I feel we must not rush into matrimony. After all, Basil could attack again."

"You do not want me," she accused.

"Nay, milady, 'tis not true," he denied huskily. "I

want you more than ever. Especially now that I
know . . ."

"Know what?"

Letting his hands fall to his sides, he smiled at her
tenderly. "That you had no part in your uncle's intrigue. Forgive me, Aurora, but for a time I did doubt
you. I promise I never will again."

Confusion filled her eyes. "If you are finished
doubting me, then why do you say I should not trust
you? Why will you not wed me?" As he would have
replied, she pressed her fingers to his lips. "I know
why. You fear your desires will doom me, do you
not?"

Niccolo regarded her in mingled surprise and concern. "After what I heard today, how can I not fear
for your future? Your uncle believes in the curse—"

"I know, but I no longer care," she cut in recklessly.

A shiver of alarm shot through him. "What do you
mean, you do not care?"

Aurora wrapped her arms tightly around Niccolo's
waist. He clenched his fists as the ripe curves of her
breasts pressed against his chest.

" 'Tis true, my dark knight," she whispered, touching her lips to his tunic. "I am willing to risk anything
to make you mine, even the wrath of the curse. For
what I feel for you is so splendid, so strong, that it
must be love. But even if I am wrong, even if we are
both fooled by the barbs of passion, I shall gladly
chance death to know the sweetness of these wondrous feelings, just once."

Niccolo groaned, agonized anew by her willing
self-sacrifice, a sacrifice he in no way deserved. He
grasped her shoulders and regarded her sternly. "Aurora, you do not know what you are saying."

Undaunted, she stretched on tiptoe and pressed her
lips to his throat. "I know I want you. I know I want
to give myself to you."

"Aurora . . ." His defenses staggering, he clutched

her tightly to him. "You must understand, dearest, I am wrong for you. I have no faith, no heart!"

"You have a heart! 'Tis beating fiercely for me now!"

Indeed it was! Niccolo was in hell, wanting Aurora so badly, he felt he might die of it, while knowing all the while that to take her now could well mean her own destruction. "Darling, I shall surely doom you."

She pulled back to look at him. "I do not believe it! I will not!"

And she stretched upward to kiss him.

A mighty shudder shook Niccolo as her warm, honeyed lips inflamed his desires. He molded her softness against him and kissed her back with all his heart. They stood there clinging together until they seemed one soul, one body, one heartbeat . . .

At last both pulled back, breathing hard, regarding each other with wonder. Nodding toward the duskier trees beyond them, Aurora extended her hand to Niccolo and smiled in unreserved invitation—

When a burst of fireworks illuminated the sheer trust, the utter devotion, on her lovely face, Niccolo could not bear it. She was so good, so pure . . . and the monster of his own unworthiness rose again to confront him. He was not the one she had waited for, her one true love, her noble knight in gleaming armor. He simply was not!

Holding up a hand to stay her, he stared at her in torment. "Listen to me, Aurora! We cannot do this! 'Tis wrong! 'Tis over!"

She blinked at tears, her expression shattered. "Nay."

"*Yea*, Aurora." Hating himself, he drew a shaky breath. "Come back with me now."

But she proudly turned away. "Leave me."

"Aurora . . ."

"*Leave me!*" The words came choked.

While he still possessed the strength to do so, Niccolo turned away.

A moment later, Aurora emerged from the forest, her emotions raw, her face stark with tears. Again she had offered herself to Niccolo, sharing her heart and her feelings with him, telling him she would gladly risk death to be with him. And he had spurned her once more.

Oh, she had been so wrong. Niccolo could not possibly want her as much as she wanted him. If so, he would never call their love wrong, nor turn away as he just had!

Even she had pride. And she had just abandoned that pride, offering him her heart, her soul, even her life . . . and still he had forsaken her.

Sobs choked her, and her throat ached with sorrow. Was she doomed never to find her one true love? If she could not have Niccolo, there was no man left on this earth whom she wanted . . .

In the Kingdom of Ravenia, Basil and Ignatius were meeting in the darkened courtyard of the royal castle. Above them, sentries prowled the battlements and a flock of bats sailed over.

Once again, King Basil was pacing about in a rage. "That traitor Niccolo Campioni! He vowed he would turn Aurora over to me before the betrothal ceremony. Now he seeks to betray me, to wed the woman he promised to deliver into my hands?"

"So it appears, Sire," agreed Ignatius anxiously.

"Well, I shall attack the Falconian fortress again, capture Aurora, and carve out Sir Niccolo's perfidious heart in her very presence!" Basil declared.

Ignatius cleared his throat. "Sire, mayhap you should not attack just yet, at least not until the festival is concluded. Methinks there are too many sentries stationed about the castle and in the woods."

"But Aurora may soon wed the Venetian!" thundered the king.

"Mayhap so, but I think not posthaste," argued Ignatius. "Her uncle has returned now, and as I recall, her parents left to him the task of choosing her husband."

Basil sneered. "You are referring to Artemas, the dimwit who has already betrothed her to eight knights?"

Ignatius nodded. "Yea. Even if the princess and Sir Niccolo should proceed with the betrothal, you can still stay them before matters proceed too far. 'Twill likely be weeks before the banns can be posted, the wedding arranged. Let me continue to watch and listen, Sire. If the nuptials are announced, I shall so inform you at once. Otherwise, 'twould it not be best to wait a bit, and allow the Falconians to become careless and complacent?"

The king made a growling sound, kicking a rock out of his path. "We shall see. My patience has all but reached its limit!"

THIRTY

Niccolo was in a foul humor the following morning, hating himself for rejecting Aurora, when she had offered herself to him so selflessly . . . and yet knowing he had chosen the only right course. He knew he must return to Venice, but decided he would wait until after the days of feasting, when his departure would be less conspicuous—

Of course, his decision had nothing to do with his aversion to leaving her . . . or so he tried to convince himself!

The merrymaking continued. On the vast castle green, Niccolo participated in several mock jousts, hoping the physical activity would lesson his turmoil and frustration. On the field, he was ruthless. As Aurora and her court, as well as many of the townspeople, watched from the sidelines, he unseated first Duncan, then Baldric, then Cesare. The crowd cheered him on, especially when no other knights came forward to challenge him; as he dismounted, Aurora stepped up to offer him a garland. She looked especially festive today in her gown of green velvet; but spotting the anger, hurt, and confusion in her dark eyes, he hated himself all the more. He offered her a conciliatory smile.

In response, she hurled the garland at his feet,

turned on her heel, and walked away. Niccolo stood
thunderstruck, his face darkening by shades as the
spectators began to snicker, then howl with laughter.

He charged after her into the crowd, only to be de-
tained when Cesare stepped into his path. "It seems
you have not won the princess after all, have you,
Venetian?" the Genoan sneered. "Then what we have
heard from Edgar is not true!"

Hurling the man a blistering glare, Niccolo shoved
his way forward.

He caught up with Aurora by the drawbridge and
grabbed her arm. "What was the meaning of that display?"

She turned to him, eyes gleaming with outrage.
"You can ask that, when you make a mockery of my
feelings before the entire village?"

"How have I done that?"

Her voice vibrated with hurt and reproach. "By
proving yourself my champion, over and over, even
though you spurn my feelings."

"What would you have me do?"

"Leave!" she cried. "Go back to Venice, and cease
torturing me!"

Niccolo groaned. "I really do not mean to torture
you, Aurora. Actually, it may be best that I go, as soon
as the feast ends."

Not commenting, she shook loose of his touch and
moved on.

He charged after her, falling into step beside her.
"Aurora, please know I never meant to hurt you—"

"Spare me your lies!"

" 'Tis true! I only wish I could make you understand—"

"But I do not understand!" She turned to him, eyes
bright with tears. "I do not understand you, Niccolo.
Did you not accept my gauntlet? Do you not need my

hand in marriage, my castle and my lands?" Choking
on a sob, she finished, "Do you not want my body?"

He hauled her close. "Aurora! Of course I want
you!"

She shoved him away. "Nay, you do not! Or you
would take me."

She might never know how close he came to doing
so, even then. Standing there so full of hurt and defiance, her eyes bright and her bosom heaving, she
had never looked more proud, more desirable to him.
He had never so hungered to wipe the look of heartache from her beautiful face. Every inch of him
burned to grab her and take her off, to claim her body
in the nearest haystack. But even as he stepped closer,
she held up a hand.

"Go, and leave me in peace!"

"I will leave as soon as the festival ends."

"Why linger until then?" she asked defiantly.

"I shall leave tomorrow."

"Splendid!" she declared, blinking at tears.

Niccolo watched helplessly as she stormed away.
With heavy heart, he started back toward the castle
green, only to watch an angry Lorenzo step into his
path.

"What have you done to the princess?" the old man
demanded. "By heaven, if you have brought her
harm, I shall choke the life out of you with my bare
hands!"

Niccolo had reached his limit. "I have done *nothing*!" he retorted, clenching a fist in frustration. "And
that is the entire problem. Pack our belongings, old
man. We leave on the morrow!"

Lorenzo watched in consternation as his master
stalked away.

Niccolo could barely endure the remainder of the
day. He felt desperately alone, even amid all the ac-

tivities. The trading fair continued, with jugglers, jongleurs, minstrels, and acrobats entertaining the townsfolk as they went from booth to booth. An animal trainer with his dancing bear proved a particular diversion. On the wooden platform, a succession of miracle plays was performed by the various guilds, the selections including the Creation, the Birth of Christ, and the Resurrection. A number of the knights mingled freely with the townsfolk and peasants: Sir Edgar taught a group of small children how to play knucklebones, while Christian entertained several older boys with a display of falconry. Even Artemas joined in, delighting onlookers as he performed sleight of hand, removing his huge turban to release three pigeons. Niccolo mused that the chicanery suited him well.

The hours of the feast that eve proved even worse punishment for Niccolo, as once again, he sat not far from Aurora. Being so close to her was killing him. Occasionally he caught her eye. She no longer appeared angry, but rather deeply saddened, very hurt, her gaze dark and morose, her features pale, her vitality and laughter absent, as if her very soul had left her. Her anguish was devastating for him, especially since he knew he was the cause of it. Although he could have accepted and understood her outrage, he found her pain impossible to bear, and he ached to glimpse again that joy in her eyes that could light up even his dark soul.

Her earlier words kept haunting him: *If you wanted me, you would take me.* He no longer seemed to care about his own doubts, about what was wrong and what was right. He just wanted to see Aurora smile again.

Once the fireworks began, she arose and strolled away from the tables toward the trees. Mesmerized, feeling as if his will were no longer his own, Niccolo followed her.

He found her standing beneath a tree at the edge of the forest, her back to the festivities. He came up behind her and wrapped his arms about her waist. He heard her soft shudder of mingled surprise and pleasure. She felt heavenly against him, warm and pliant, and he cupped her breasts with his hands, feeling the nipples tighten through her gown. His manhood responded in a tortured throbbing. She shivered and nestled her bottom close to his heated loins in a trusting yet very provocative gesture. His blood roared in his ears.

He leaned over and nibbled at her soft throat, raising gooseflesh. He heard her soft sob of pleasure, and his control disintegrated. He would have her now. He must, or he would die.

He pressed his mouth to her ear and whispered roughly, "Go to the copse, milady. *Now*."

She slipped out of his arms and walked into the woods without looking back.

Niccolo moved like a man possessed, racing for the castle, and to the stables, feverishly saddling Nero. All his logic, all his doubts, seemed decimated in his overwhelming desire for Aurora.

He was just galloping across the drawbridge when he again spied Lorenzo on the green. The squire waved his arms. "Master! Where are you going?"

"For a ride in the moonlight!" Niccolo called arrogantly as he sped past.

Maneuvering his destrier into the trees, he ducked branches and smiled to himself. No doubt Lorenzo was suspicious of him now, but even that would not sway him. Every second away from Aurora was hell.

His heart tripped with joy as he galloped into the copse and spotted her standing near the steps of the shrine, her beautiful form awash in moonlight. He trotted Nero toward her and scooped her up before him on the saddle as he passed. Cradling her tightly against him, he rode on.

"Oh, Niccolo, Niccolo!" Her voice was thick with tears of joy, and he felt her shivering against him.

"How did you know 'twas I who came up behind you?" he whispered against her hair.

"No one has hands like you do," she whispered back, touching his strong hand as he worked the reins.

"You know you are mine now," he told her fiercely. "You know there is no turning back."

Her voice broke as she replied, "There has never been any turning back for us, Niccolo . . . I think not from the moment I first saw you."

They galloped on through the moonlit trees, deep into the night. Owls hooted and shadows danced across their huddled figures.

"I wish I could take you away with me and never bring you back," he whispered. "Mayhap I shall yet."

"Take me where you will," she murmured.

He brushed his lips against her ear. "To Elysium, milady . . . this very night."

All at once they both gasped as a brilliant flash of light streaked over the trees. "Look, Niccolo, a shooting star!" Aurora cried. "Make a wish quickly!"

He leaned over and kissed her with all his heart as they both shared one fervent wish. With the taste of her still on his lips, Niccolo looked up to find the star gone, and anguish seared him. Would their love beam so brightly yet die so quickly?

He halted his horse in a downy clearing, where the forest floor was thickly lined with pine needles and leaves. He helped Aurora slide to the ground and then dismounted beside her, pulling her into his arms, pressing his lips to hers and possessing her honeyed mouth with his demanding tongue. She was so incredibly eager!

Around them the forest throbbed with sounds— tree frogs croaking, nightjars calling, furry creatures scurrying about. They fell to their knees on the soft earth, kissing and caressing. Niccolo roved his hands over Aurora's smooth back, her rounded buttocks. He thrilled to the small sigh rising in her throat as she snuggled closer to him, brazenly inviting more caresses. She clung tightly to his neck and buried her fingers in his thick hair. Niccolo pulled down the bodice of her dress and leaned over, suckling each of her ripe breasts in turn; she arched her back in joy and dug her fingers into his spine. He nipped at the tight nipples, delighting at her frenzied cries.

Gently he eased her to the ground, while raising her skirts and gathering them high about her waist. His body covering hers, he looked down into her eyes, so filled with wonder, desire, and some uncertainty.

"Are you frightened, milady?" he asked huskily, brushing a wisp of hair from her eyes.

"Nay!" she replied, clutching him tightly to her. "Never!"

"You do not fear the curse?"

She regarded him with tear-filled eyes. "You do not curse me, Niccolo. You bless me. You bless me and make my spirit soar free."

"Oh, my love," he whispered back. "I shall pray your words prove true."

Hungrily he kissed her, and felt the paradise of her trust and love . . .

Indeed, Aurora was already floating in Elysium to have Niccolo's magnificent, hot body crushing her, to have his rigid desire pressing so insistently against her bared intimate parts. She caught the hem of his tunic and raised it, so she might feel the delight of his warm, muscular chest against her bared breasts; she sighed ecstatically as their heated flesh joined. He felt so heavy, so splendidly muscled; she wanted to feel the solid heat of him deep inside herself.

Niccolo slowly worked his lips down her soft throat, returning his attention to her breasts, tonguing the taut nipples and then sucking on them. Breathing raggedly, she leaned forward to kiss his hair, and kneaded the strong muscles of his shoulders and arms with her fingers. He responded with another searing kiss, while caressing between her thighs with his fingers, until she throbbed for him. Instinctively she slipped her hand between their bodies and stroked his stiffened manhood.

"*Sì!*" he encouraged, kissing her deeply. "Touch me there, my love, just as intimately as I am caressing you."

Encouraged, she unfastened his codpiece and explored him, awed that a shaft of flesh so rigid could also be so velvety soft. With untrained curiosity, she examined the satiny tip of him, and heard him seize a frenzied breath; she felt his swollen member pulse and harden even more as she curled her fingers about it. Oh, she ached to feel it inside her!

He knew. With feverish haste, he untied his hose. His strong thighs spread hers widely apart, and he pressed his hardness into her. She gasped as the tip of him pierced her, and he hesitated.

"I am hurting you," he said contritely.

Even though the penetration smarted, Aurora welcomed the tender invasion that would make them truly one at last. She reached down to stroke him again, and smiled up at him. "Your barb is sweet, milord. And wondrous large."

"Oh, *Dio*." Aroused past sanity, Niccolo pushed deeper, groaning as he felt another shock wave shudder over her. "I know it pains you, but 'twill become better in time, milady."

"Will we have time?" she asked poignantly.

Tears blinded Niccolo, but he was beyond stopping, burrowing himself into her as he covered her face with soft kisses. "I fear you may have doomed yourself now, milady. I have tasted you, and I may never

again be able to sate my hunger. Just try to keep yourself away from me—"

"I would never try—"

The rest of her words were drowned by Niccolo's
kiss. Unable to stop, he breached her maidenhead,
sheathing himself in her hot, snug vessel. She stiffened and cried out, and he clutched her tightly, whispering to her soothingly, slipping his hands beneath
her and kneading her buttocks, trying to relax her.
Reining in his own need was hellish, as the hot ecstasy
of her squeezed about him exquisitely, tempting him
to plunder her with unbridled passion . . .

Aurora felt filled to bursting with Niccolo's rigid,
throbbing desire. Yet Niccolo soothed her so tenderly.
His mouth on hers was a joyous caress; his fingers on
her bottom stroked boldly, urging her to release tight
muscles and accept his overwhelming presence deep
inside her, to feel the exquisite delight of his hot, demanding possession. Slowly he mesmerized her with
the flick of his tongue in her mouth, the touch of his
hands on her backside, the almost imperceptible pressure of his shaft pushing deeper still. As soon as she
stopped fighting the discomfort, he withdrew, then
pressed home again, transporting her with deep, intimate strokes. She moaned, feeling the rapture flow
through her in waves, building with relentless tension
toward a fiery explosion of bliss, a pinnacle of such
power that she half feared its intensity. Nonetheless,
she gave herself over to the feeling and to Niccolo,
trusting him to take her away . . .

Her surrender broke his own control. Clamping his
forearms at the small of her back, he possessed her
with quick, rhythmic strokes and kissed her with frantic need. Never had he really given himself to a
woman, he realized dazedly. Before, he had only
taken. Now *he* was being taken, being consumed,
heart and soul, mind and body—

Seconds later, he went rigid, breathing in agonized gasps as the paroxysm seized him. He lay buried in her to the core, shuddering violently and pouring himself into her as they were bound together in a moment of eternal union.

THIRTY-ONE

THEY DOZED FOR A FEW MOMENTS IN EACH OTHER'S arms. Niccolo awakened to stare down at Aurora's luminous face outlined in the quicksilver light. She appeared so innocent and trusting as she slept, and he cherished her so! He leaned over and kissed her brow. When she did not stir, he nuzzled his lips against her cheek, her chin, then her soft mouth.

She opened her eyes and smiled up at him. "You look beautiful in the moonlight, my shining knight."

"Not nearly as ravishing as you appear, my lovely lady," he replied, kissing her.

She moaned, her fingertips kneading his smooth shoulders.

"My love, we must leave," he said gently.

"Nay!" she denied, clutching him tightly.

Her possessive gesture battered his resolve. He forced a firm tone. "*Sì*, we must go back, before the others become suspicious, or even begin searching for us."

She sighed deeply. "I suppose you are right." Her expression turning almost impish, she wrinkled her nose at him. "But first kiss me again. Give me one last memory to savor ere we meet again."

Niccolo joyously complied.

He bore Aurora back toward the castle, holding her

before him on the horse. He thought of how everything had changed between them in just a few magical moments. However unworthy he might be, this
sweet girl had given her heart to him, had surrendered her body to him completely. Whatever the future might hold, he would always remember her
selfless gift.

At the edge of the forest, with the castle green
stretching beyond them, they shared a last, bittersweet kiss. Then Aurora slipped to the ground and
walked back to the festivities alone. Niccolo waited a
respectable period before riding out of the trees.

When Niccolo returned to the barracks, Lorenzo
shot him a look of blistering contempt, then attended
to his prayers, for once not inviting his master to join
him.

Sleep did not come to Niccolo for many hours as
he lay in the darkness, reliving the heaven of his moments with Aurora, wanting her again . . .

Aurora also found sleep elusive as she lay in her
big, cold bed, missing Niccolo and wishing he were
there with her. Her restless movements prompted
slight, half-pleasurable twinges between her thighs,
reminding her that she had given herself to him, that
she was a virgin no more. She felt no regrets about
surrendering to him, and the incredible pleasure he
had brought her was well worth bearing the brief moments of pain. She wanted to be with him for the rest
of her life, no matter how short that life, and regardless of the risks.

He had loved her so tenderly, so passionately, so
completely. He had loved her like a man of good
heart and noble designs. But was he truly hers? He
kept insisting his soul was dark, that he could not
love her. Yet their passion had shined so brightly tonight. Would it fade as quickly, like the shooting star?

These questions haunted her for the remainder of
the night.

* * *

The next morning, Niccolo passed Aurora in the courtyard. She looked so lovely, today wearing a gold brocaded gown and a wispy silk wimple fluttering over her dark curls. They shared a shy smile, and Niccolo struggled against an instinct to pull her into his arms.

"Good morrow, milady," he murmured, taking her hand and kissing her soft fingers.

"Good morrow," she whispered back. "I have missed you since last eve. Have you missed me?"

He stepped closer. "I hardly slept a wink for thinking of you."

She caught a sharp little breath. "Nor did I. Then you do not regret . . ."

He regarded her intensely. "Nay. I shall never regret it, milady. I only wish . . ."

"Tell me your wish."

He caressed her cheek with his fingers, gazing at her with great longing. "That I could make love to you by the light of day, in a real bed."

She smiled at him. "Remember the shooting star last night? Mayhap your wish should be granted."

"But how?"

Edging closer to him, she whispered conspiratorially, "This afternoon I shall slip away, telling the others I need a nap. There is a small inn on the edge of town. Meet me there."

Her suggestion left Niccolo wildly excited, but also skeptical. "Will you not be recognized?"

She shook her head. "Nay, I shall wear a heavy, hooded mantle. Join me at the hostelry, and tell the innkeeper you are there to meet your faithful wife, Margaret."

He grinned, savoring the prospect immensely. "And should I pretend you are my goodwife, milady?"

Mischief danced in her eyes. "You may pretend anything you like."

"And in the meantime, how will I keep my hands off you in front of the others?" he teased.

"I care not if you kiss me in front of everyone," she replied recklessly. "If you do, they will all assume we are to be betrothed, will they not?"

He groaned. "Mayhap we should take greater care, for the sake of fairness."

She made a sound of outrage. "You have bedded me, yet you speak of sharing me with others?"

"That is not what I meant," he retorted gravely. "I shall never willingly share you. I just want you to be very sure of the choice you make."

She set her chin at a stubborn angle. "I am sure now. I want you, Niccolo Campioni. But if you are unconvinced, mayhap I should not meet you, after all."

Having her tempt him with this tantalizing morsel, then threaten to snatch it away, was torture for Niccolo. "Fail to meet our rendezvous, milady, and I will come take you," he warned.

Her eyes twinkled with secret amusement. "Mayhap I should cross you, then. I loved it when you carried me off last night."

Niccolo pressed a finger to the tip of her impertinent nose and leveled a stern glance at her. "You will not savor it this time. For if you break your word to me, this knight will teach you a swift lesson in obedience."

"You would threaten a princess?" she asked impudently.

"A princess can be tossed over my knee as well as any saucy wench."

She smirked up at him.

He heaved a great sigh. "You tempt the devil, milady."

Still smiling, she looked him over slowly. "So it appears."

Niccolo had reached his limit. He pulled her close and pressed his lips to her hair.

"Meet me, love," he whispered. "I shall make you very glad."

Her arms wound around his waist in a trusting gesture that warmed his heart. "I am glad now."

They clung to each other for a poignant moment, then she slipped away. Starting back toward the barracks, Niccolo was grinning. Then he spotted Lorenzo standing outside near the door, glowering at him. How much had the old man seen? Overheard? How much had he guessed?

Niccolo could barely suffer through the morn, despite the liveliness of the continued merrymaking, the wrestling contests, the dancing and singing, the games for the children. His every thought was of Aurora, and his gaze was riveted to her throughout the hours. He burned with impatience as she gaily visited with her ladies, with Christian, with Artemas. When Edgar led them all in another lively carole, and Aurora joined her hand with Niccolo's, he could not bear being so close to her, yet unable to pull her close and savor her thoroughly. He was tempted to do as she had challenged, to kiss her in front of everyone. But then he would be announcing his intentions quite publicly and dramatically; then he and Aurora would be bound together irrevocably, a prospect that plagued him with guilt and confusion.

Certainly he no longer wanted to punish Aurora, to gain his revenge. But he was not worthy of her love, given the fact that his motives had been both self-serving and nefarious. And he still feared lowering his barriers, revealing himself to her as he truly was, subjecting them both to heartache when she realized he was not her perfect prince.

Yet he craved her so ... Despite all his doubts, heady anticipation coursed through him when at last he spotted her slipping away after the midday meal. He waited a respectable period, then fetched his horse from the stables and rode off toward town. He soon spotted the small Romanesque stone inn on the outskirts of the village; it stood sheltered beneath the limbs of lofty pines, its roof heavily encrusted with needles. He dismounted and tied Nero to the post. Approaching the steps, he noticed on the inn door the typical Ospreyan portents to ward off evil—a large iron cross and a fishnet filled with acorns. Shaking his head, he proceeded inside.

In the front counting chamber, he encountered a couple seated at a small, scarred table. A frowning, bearded man in a soiled tunic sat with his wife, a sallow creature in a food-stained surcoat and dingy house cap. The two were chopping beets and shallots.

"Good day," greeted Niccolo. "I am here to meet my goodwife, Lady Margaret."

"Upstairs in the front room," replied the man gruffly, gesturing with his grimy knife.

The woman eyed Niccolo mockingly. "Yea, sir, your *goodwife* is upstairs having a fine chat with the Holy Virgin herself," she informed Niccolo with a high cackle.

Fighting a grin, Niccolo strode off for the narrow steps. Although the innkeeper and his wife evidently harbored no illusions regarding this tryst, at least they had betrayed no signs of recognizing Aurora.

Upstairs, he wended his way down a bleak, dusty corridor to the door nearest the front of the house. He knocked softly.

Her voice came in a whisper. "Who goes there?"

"Niccolo."

"Come in."

He entered and found her sitting by the window, the hood of her mantle shielding her face. He caught a brief glimpse of a featherbed near the chair, and his loins hardened painfully. "Aurora?"

She stood, thrust back her hood, and smiled. "From the tone of your voice, milord, I fooled even you."

He chuckled, feasting his eyes on her lovely face. "Mayhap we have kept your identity secret, but the innkeeper and his wife seem to know we are here for a lovers' rendezvous."

"Then let us be about it," she whispered, crossing over and thrusting herself into his arms.

The feel of her soft curves against him racked Niccolo with desire. "Aurora . . . oh, Aurora."

"Niccolo."

Their lips met ravenously. Niccolo kissed her hair, her forehead, her cheeks, her throat. He pulled back and drew his heated gaze over her. "It feels like forever since we last touched . . . sheer torture. I have missed you terribly, milady."

"I have missed you, milord," she whispered fervently. "You have stirred in me a hunger I cannot seem to sate."

"Nor I."

Feeling inordinately pleased, Niccolo held her at arm's length. "But I shall try, milady. First, there is entirely too much cloth between us. Remove your garments. I would see you naked."

She did not flinch; indeed, she met his fiery gaze boldly. "Remove yours. I would see you."

Niccolo raised an eyebrow and grinned.

They both undressed, eyeing each other ardently, hungrily. After removing his tunic, Niccolo reached for the ties on his hose, only to pause as he watched Aurora's chemise slide to the floor. His mouth went dry, his heart thumped, and his eyes hungrily devoured her glorious nakedness. *Dio*, she was perfectly formed, with smooth shoulders, ripe, firm breasts, a flat belly, and long, beautifully shaped legs. He perused the downy joining of her thighs, then glanced upward at her beautiful face, the cheeks so flushed with desire, the lips lush and bright, slightly parted ... as another part of her would soon become, to receive his deeply thrusting organ.

His words came choked. "Milady, you are wondrous fair."

"As are you, milord." Her gaze slid downward. "Remove your hose."

He did so, shucking them with a grin, proud of the thick erection straining against his stomach.

Aurora saw that blatant proof of Niccolo's desire—and all of him—and her toes curled in delicious anticipation. Niccolo's shoulders were so big and powerful, his chest a masterpiece of chiseled muscles, his belly flat and trim. From just below his navel to his feet, he was covered in coarse golden hair. His thighs were massive and muscular, his knees and calves splendidly formed.

He was as beautiful as a god, so big and strong. The sight of him—and especially the sight of his bulging passion for her—made her weak.

"Come to me, love," he whispered, extending his hand.

"Mayhap I would have you come to me," she teased back.

With exaggerated gallantry, Niccolo went down on one knee, pressing a hand to his heart and smiling up at her. "Come take me, milady. I am yours."

He looked wondrous in that pose, his blond hair spilling upon his shoulders, his face nobly turned to her. She stepped closer. "You are not mine. You are teasing me."

He reached out and caressed the soft back of one knee, nudging her closer. "Teasing is something I intend to do much of." Easing her legs apart, he positioned one of her knees on either side of his raised leg. "Sit on my thigh, milady."

She eyed him quizzically.

He gripped her waist and guided her downward. "Do not be afraid."

"I am never afraid of you," she asserted.

"No?" he taunted. "Then show me."

Heatedly holding his gaze, Aurora sank down. She shuddered as her intimate recesses contacted Niccolo's rough thigh. Her knees did not reach the floor, only intensifying the pressure of his firm flesh against her. Niccolo pulled her closer and hungrily kissed her, and she sobbed her delight. Then his fingers slid between her thighs, stroking her and parting her so she would better feel the coarse texture of him. When she cried out, he looked at her, frankly, boldly, carefully gauging her response—

Aurora could not catch her breath, for the abrasion against her tenderest parts—and the seduction of Niccolo's bright eyes—were exquisite torment. Niccolo braced his hands at her waist and began to rock her gently, intensifying the erotic sensations throbbing and peaking within her. When he kissed her again with sweet violence, her joy was unbearable. He rubbed her against him until she learned the rhythm, then he placed his hot mouth on her breast, sucking deeply. Aurora dug her fingernails into his spine and sobbed. She was taken out of herself, tumbling over the precipice, riding him fiercely until she took her pleasure with a soft cry.

Seconds later, she fell limp against him, still straddling him, her inner thighs damp, her head on his shoulder.

Tenderly she bit him. "I think I am a shameless wench, milord."

His sensual chuckle rumbled forth. "I think you are wonderful, my love," he rasped, "and *sì*, most unafraid."

At his encouragement, her fingers slid downward to curl about his turgid shaft, and a groan of desire escaped him. Her lips sought his, and she whimpered.

"Niccolo, pray, pray . . ."

Wildly stirred by her touch, her plea, he lowered her to the rug, surging into her so powerfully that she cried out, startled, overwrought with pleasure, so full of him . . .

"I am sorry," he murmured, pulling back.

"Nay!" she cried, clutching his buttocks and pulling him into herself.

At her brazen surrender, a mighty shudder seized Niccolo and he lost control as he never had with a woman, plunging into her repeatedly, losing himself in his lady, barely hearing her cries over his own groans of ecstasy. He crushed her to him and quickly spent himself inside her.

A long time later, he drew back to regard her glowing face. "Milady, you quite took me away. I trust those sounds you made were of pleasure."

"They were," she confessed happily, then wrinkled her nose at him. "But I thought you wanted to make love to me in a bed, milord."

He smiled, leaning over to nibble at her breast. "That we shall do, my love. Many, many times."

Later, Niccolo went downstairs and fetched a bottle of wine and some glasses from the innkeeper. He returned upstairs and walked in as Aurora was stirring. She sat up on the bed, letting the covers gather at her waist, exposing her lovely breasts to him. The fading light drifting in through the window stirred auburn highlights in her raven hair, and she looked a totally fetching enchantress. Smiling at her, he set the tray on a table and poured them both glassfuls of wine. He returned to the bed and handed her hers.

He kissed her soft shoulder. "Drink this now, milady, then we must go. 'Tis getting late."

She stared at him frankly. "Will you wed me now, Niccolo?"

Frowning, he glanced away. "I think your uncle was right that we must not act in haste."

She grabbed his arm, forcing him to meet her bewildered countenance. "I do not understand. Do you still love your dead wife?"

His voice went cold. "No."

She reached out to stroke his tense jaw. "Did she hurt you?"

Niccolo spoke tightly. "More than I can say."

"Will you tell me?" she coaxed.

"No." As she flinched, he added almost helplessly, "I cannot."

She regarded him in outrage and turmoil. "I hate the thought of anyone hurting you."

Niccolo closed his eyes, his throat burning. She could say this, when he had wanted so badly to ruin her life, to make her suffer . . .

Her quiet voice roused him from his painful thoughts. "Do you miss Venice, your mother and sister?"

Relieved that she had changed the subject, he opened his eyes and regarded her wistfully. "I wish you could meet them. I know you would like them . . . and they would love you."

"I would like to meet them," she agreed eagerly.

He nodded. "I wish I could take you there."

"And if you did, what would you show me, Niccolo?"

He nuzzled his cheek against hers. "Oh, first I would take you to meet Mamma and Caterina, at my family's villa on the mainland. Then I would sweep you off for a long gondola ride along the Grand Canal. You know, my family once had a great palazzo there, before the reversal of our fortunes. The palace is there still, and the facade is *magnifico*, with its icons of the saints and its Gothic colonnades."

"It sounds wondrous."

He continued with gusto. "I would show you the

Ca' d'Oro, the Palazzo Bembo, the magnificent ware-
houses and bridges along the canal. I would take you
to see our glassmakers on Murano, our lace makers
on Burano. I would take you to San Marco to see the
Basilica, and to receptions at the doge's palace. Perhaps on Ascension Day, we could stand on the colonnade and watch the doge's gilded barge glide out
for the traditional marriage of Venice with the sea."

"How marvelous," she commented raptly. "You
must truly love Venice."

He nodded soberly. "*Sì*, my devotion runs deep. I
have risked my life for the Republic many times."

"I shall live with you there," she declared.

"What?" he cried, laughing. "And give up all of
this—your kingdom, the crown?"

She regarded him with utter sincerity. "You are my
kingdom now, Niccolo. You are my life—"

Niccolo pressed his fingers to her mouth. "Pray, milady, do not," he implored.

"'Tis true!" she insisted. "And I shall please you.
If you hunger to return to your homeland, I shall live
with you there."

He glanced away, a sad, faraway look in his eyes.
"Our being from different countries is not the only
impediment to our marriage, milady."

She blinked at tears. "You still will not love me?"

Her words tore at his heart, and he clutched her
hand to comfort her. "I wish I could love you, Aurora," he admitted. "There is something so magical
about you, so innocent and joyous. I feel that wonder
when I make love to you. I wish I could take your
magic into my heart."

"But you will not give your heart to me," she said
in torment. "Why, Niccolo? Is it because your wife
hurt you? Or do you fear the curse?"

He fell silent, thinking of how the curse now
seemed to symbolize all the darkness in his own soul.
"I fear you would never find true happiness with me,
milady."

"Why?" she pressed.

"I am not a man capable of giving it to you," he said stiffly.

Reaching out, she boldly stroked his manhood. "They pray, what did you give me just now?"

Although again Niccolo could not answer, his clenched features and labored breathing betrayed his inner turmoil and burgeoning desire.

"What of the passion we have shared?" she continued. "What if it brings a child, Niccolo?"

He tensed at the painful question. The thought of Aurora bearing his babe tore at his soul. Could he ever desert a child of his . . . or desert Aurora?

But was it even possible for him to plant a ripe seed inside her? "I am not certain I can give you a child, my love," he answered. "My wife never conceived."

She ran her fingertips over his muscled thigh. "You appear remarkably virile and potent to me, milord. I would think if there were an impediment, 'twould have been your wife's."

Niccolo shut his eyes, her caresses torturing him. Finally he said, "I would never desert a child of mine, if that is what you are asking."

She continued to stroke him, and he clutched her fingers.

In a small voice she asked, "Niccolo, why will you not share your heart with me?"

He regarded her in anguish. "I share what I can."

"But you do not give your love to me . . . only your passion."

"I give everything I can."

"Do you?"

Her words were an unabashed invitation, and Niccolo was not immune to them. His expression impassioned, he took her wineglass and his, and set them on the floor. Then he took his beautiful princess in his arms and gave her everything he could . . .

THIRTY-TWO

WHEN NICCOLO RETURNED TO HIS ROOM THAT NIGHT, Lorenzo stood to confront him angrily. "You scoundrel! You are having a love affair with the princess, are you not?"

Niccolo fell back a step. "Why do you think that?"

Lorenzo began to pace about and wave his arms. "Do not compound your sin by lying. You well know you can never lie to me. I have seen the two of you trysting together in the courtyard, and stealing off together, both yesterday and today."

Niccolo avoided the squire's reproachful gaze. "The situation . . . is complicated."

" 'Tis not complicated at all!" blazed Lorenzo, his eyes gleaming. "I always knew your soul was in hell, but never until this moment did I realize you are an evil man."

The well-deserved diatribe lashed Niccolo's conscience. "Lorenzo, please believe me. I wish the lady no ill."

"No ill? Do you still intend to ransom her to her enemy now that you have ruined her?"

"No!" Niccolo cried, thrusting his fingers through his hair. "Very well, I admit it. I met with her enemy. I conspired against her, staging the victory. I said I would turn her over to Basil, but found I could not do it . . . Now I know I never can."

Lorenzo waved a fist in righteous indignation. "Then your only recourse is to repent at once . . . then wed the lady."

"But I cannot," said Niccolo miserably.

"Why?"

Niccolo swallowed hard. "I cannot wed her because she is cursed."

Lorenzo went pale. "What curse is this?"

Niccolo explained, detailing how Aurora might die within a year if she chose the wrong husband, and how he was convinced he was *not* her one true love. "I think it is best we leave this place," he finished.

"Leave?" cried the horrified Lorenzo. "But you have surely doomed her now."

In anguish, Niccolo clenched his fists. "I have bedded her . . . but not wedded her."

"*Idiota!*" raved Lorenzo.

For the first time in memory, Lorenzo slapped Niccolo's cheek. Niccolo touched his stinging face and stared at his livid squire, too stunned to respond.

"So you think a curse can be outwitted, do you?" ranted Lorenzo. "Listen to me, my son! A curse can never be fooled! Your only hope now is to go to confession and repent, then marry the lady posthaste. You must banish all evil from your heart in order to become worthy, and to know the purity of the lady's love."

Racked by guilt, Niccolo spoke with desperate emotion. "You may have uttered the truth, *amico mio*, but I fear my soul is already doomed. I do not know how to forgive, how to banish black thoughts from my heart, or how to accept love and trust back in my life. Now I may have destroyed Aurora's life, as well."

Lorenzo shook a finger at Niccolo. "My son, you are consumed with false pride, and it will be your damnation . . . and likely the lady's death, as well."

Lorenzo's ominous warning haunted Niccolo all night long.

The next morning Niccolo went alone to the copse, still bedeviled by doubt and fear. Although the sun shone, a few dark clouds rumbled overhead; the grasses were thronged with blooming wildflowers and buzzing bees.

Tansy bounded up to greet him, and he petted her for a few moments before she scampered off after a rabbit. He went to stand before the shrine, staring up at the imposing statue of the Angel of Wisdom. For a reason unbeknownst to him, he crossed himself for the first time in many years.

He felt so confused. Was he truly beset by false pride as Lorenzo had argued? Should he marry Aurora at once, or leave her? Could he bring himself to repent, to stop hating Cosimo and Cecilia, to stop hating himself for letting them deceive him? Could he banish malice from his heart forever and accept love and forgiveness back into his life? Could he risk being hurt again, learn to trust once more? Could he ever become worthy of Aurora's love, or was her destruction certain if he remained?

Even as he struggled with his demons, he felt bemused as a strange, eerie wind began to blow. A darkness slid over the copse.

Then a haunting feminine voice whispered:

Dark knight bringeth plague and gloom,
Repent or seal the lady's tomb.

Totally unhinged, Niccolo backed wildly away, almost stumbling over a juniper. He glanced about frantically, searching for the origin of the voice, although he already knew the words had not come from any human source. There was absolutely no doubt in his mind that he had just heard a phantom speak!

Then he remembered what the specter had said!

"Oh, my God!" he cried, reeling. "The curse is real! 'Tis real! Oh, sweet Jehovah, what have I done?"

Repent or seal the lady's tomb, repeated the dire voice.

"No! No!" he shouted, pressing his hands to his ears to seal out the prophecy of doom. "You cannot take her! This is not her fault! Leave her in peace, pray. *Dio,* she is the only angel I have ever known on this earth. 'Tis I who have done this terrible deed to her! Take me instead!"

Repent or seal the lady's tomb . . . intoned the grievous voice for the third time.

"Oh, sweet Christ," muttered Niccolo.

Even as he stood consumed by self-loathing and terror for Aurora's plight, he heard her lyrical voice, calling his name. He whirled to see her standing at the edge of the copse in a wide beam of sunlight, his angel of light emerging on the fringes of his own darkness. She appeared more radiant than daybreak, and was smiling at him, the very instrument of her doom!

"Niccolo! So there you are!" Joyously she started toward him.

He held up a hand and backed away. "No, stay away from me!"

She laughed, her curls dancing as she bounded toward him. "Away? But why?"

"Because the curse is real!" he cried.

"Of course 'tis real!"

He continued retreating from her. "Stay away! Oh, holy saints, I have doomed you!"

Undaunted, she thrust herself into his arms. "And I do not care!"

He held her at arm's length and stared thunderstruck into her euphoric face. "What do you mean, you do not care? You *must* care!"

"Nay, I do not." Her eyes glowed with happiness. "I know I love you, Niccolo, that you are my one true love. But even if I am wrong, I shall gladly risk death to be with you—"

He pressed his fingers to her lips. "No! You do not know what you are saying!"

"But I do!" she argued. "I have never felt so alive as I have felt while with you! Even if I must die, I shall first savor the sweetest year I have ever known. I cannot miss one second with you."

"No, you are mistaken!" he insisted. "You must stay away from me! I am bad for you, evil."

Her lovely eyes gleamed with anger. "I do not believe that! I have never believed that." Tightly she embraced him. "I am not afraid of you."

"Oh, Aurora." Niccolo was trembling, kissing her brow, her cheek. "My dear girl. You are so brave, so strong . . . and I am the weak one."

"Nay!" she cried, staring up at him with utter love. "You are my champion."

Something broke in Niccolo then, just as a harsh cry escaped his lips. He kissed her, cherishing her against him as if she were his entire world.

"Make love to me, Niccolo," she beseeched. "Now, pray."

"Aurora . . . oh, Christ."

But she pressed her lips against Niccolo's throat and spoke soulfully. "Take me, my love. I want to conceive your child, now, today, while there is yet time. For even if I die, I shall have known the joy of suckling your babe at my breast. And I shall live on through him, and in your heart."

Her heartfelt pleas made Niccolo feel torn apart inside, terrified he was dooming her. But ultimately her need, and his own, proved stronger than his conscience. He buried his lips in her hair and clutched her tightly.

But when he felt her tugging him toward the ground, he glanced warily toward the shrine. "Nay, not here," he whispered, and swept her up into his arms.

He carried her away from the copse, to the bright circle of light where he had first spotted her. They fell to the sunbaked grasses together, amid blooming daffodils and a brilliantly flitting hummingbird.

Laughing her joy, Aurora nudged Niccolo onto his back and settled herself astride him, leaning over to mate her mouth with his, her fingers coiling in his hair. He slid a hand up her skirts, caressing her warm, silky thigh.

Then both of them tensed as fat raindrops began to fall. Exultantly she sat up and gazed at the sky. "Look, Niccolo, a sun shower." She opened her mouth and licked her lips. "Taste the rain."

Staring at her with her head thrown back, her expression enraptured, her lips eagerly seeking the cool droplets, Niccolo mused that this surely *must* be love. For no other emotion could bring such sweet pain. He watched the raindrops splash onto her flushed cheeks, her adorable nose, her bodice. In wonderment he observed the moisture spreading across the thin fabric, outlining her tautened nipples. Desire stormed through him. Never would he forget her this way!

"I prefer to taste you, my love," he murmured, leaning upward to suckle her through the fragile silk, tasting her and the rain.

She cried out in delight, and he lowered her bodice. Impatiently she pulled away, tugging off his tunic and running her lips over his smooth chest. Groaning his frustration, he slid her body forward, clamping his forearms around her hips, trapping her breast against his hungry mouth and bold tongue. A blissful sob escaped her.

Soon she was pulling at the ties to his leggings. Soon he was hiking up her skirts. She caressed his throbbing erection with her fingers as he found her wet, warm center, stroking and parting her, reveling in her frantic moans. He nudged her back to straddle him. Holding her gaze, he eased into her slowly, fully, savoring every glorious sensation, until his thrust was met by her sharp cry of ecstasy.

Her look of near-desperate abandonment made him smile. "You think you have tamed the beast, milady," he whispered ironically. "And then the beast takes you."

"I am not afraid," she repeated. "Do not hold back. Give me your seed, your child. Now, pray."

Niccolo did so, claiming her with thorough, unhurried strokes until she sobbed her pleasure, then compelling her on to the next riotous zenith. She fell on him, kissing him passionately as their coupling intensified. Gasping, she sat up and began to move with him, arching and swaying against him, her expression dazed with rapture as soft rain fell on them both. Her erotic movements sent him into a frenzy; he held her immobile against him and pressed relentlessly toward release—

When Niccolo burst inside her, when he heard her shattered cry as her body drank in his seed, he felt as if his soul had been ripped out of him. He caught her trembling body close and tenderly kissed her hair, whispering words of comfort. Would he plant new life in her womb, only to destroy her?

Gently he rolled her onto her side, his flesh still embedded in her flesh. She was asleep, as radiant and breathtakingly beautiful as an angel. An angel with the mark of the devil fresh upon her . . . He reached out and stroked her silken hair, then leaned over to kiss her smooth brow. His eyes stinging, he watched her slumber among the flowers . . .

Later, Aurora awakened alone. The rain had stopped, and a twinge between her thighs reminded her of the wondrous passion she and Niccolo had just shared.

Where was he? Why had he made beautiful love to
her, only to leave her?

She felt so lonely and bereft. Then she sat up and
stared at the ground where he had lain beside her,
and saw the bouquet of wildflowers he had left, their
bunched stems wrapped in a long stalk of grass.

She picked up the bouquet and smelled the heady
essence of the blooms. Tears blinded her. For the first
time, Niccolo had brought her flowers . . .

THIRTY-THREE

Back at the castle, Aurora walked through the bailey, hoping to find Niccolo. But a fearsome clamor greeted her in the yard, near the royal mews. Hearing the sounds of men's loud voices and observing a number of her knights huddled together, Aurora rushed toward the scene. A hunting party had evidently just returned, since the huntsman was present, placing falcons and hawks back in the mews.

She broke through the ranks of the men, into the center of the group. "What has happened?" she demanded, staring into the anxious faces of Niccolo, Duncan, Galen, Edgar, and several other knights.

A grim silence greeted her question, then Niccolo said gently, "Milady, your Captain of the Guard will explain. I was not present when . . . er . . . the calamity occurred."

"What calamity?" Alarmed, Aurora turned to Sir Galen. "Tell me what has transpired." Uneasily she glanced about the area. "Where is Christian?"

Several knights shifted their stances awkwardly, and a shamefaced Sir Galen could not meet his princess's eye. Staring at his shoes, he confessed, "I am afraid he has been taken, milady."

"What do you mean, taken?" Aurora asked, her voice high with fright.

His expression morose, Edgar stepped forward. "Milady, this morn, several of us went hunting with Sir Christian. Then, quite suddenly, we were surrounded by Basil's army."

Aurora gasped, flinging a hand to her mouth. "Basil has violated the truce? Was Christian harmed?"

"Nay, milady, he was not," Galen quickly assured her. "But rather than see us all slain, Christian offered himself as hostage to Basil . . . and Basil accepted."

"Oh, my God!" cried Aurora.

Galen continued. "Basil told us to convey a message to you—that he will release your brother, unharmed, if you will offer yourself in exchange for Christian. Otherwise, he vows he will execute your brother on the morrow."

Aurora did not hesitate. "I must turn myself over to him."

A clamor of angry voices filled the air as every knight, including Niccolo, shouted, "Nay!"

"Milady, you must not even consider such a rash act," argued Galen. "Basil is a coward whose word is worthless."

"He is a stubborn ox determined to win me," replied Aurora.

"But your brother does not want you to offer yourself," insisted Edgar. "As he was being led away, Christian yelled out to us to tell you not to surrender yourself to Basil under any circumstances, that he will gladly sacrifice his life to see you free."

Shuddering with emotion, Aurora wiped away a tear. "That sounds just like Christian." She gazed at the others in wrenching uncertainty. "Then what will we do?"

"Why, attack Ravenia Castle at once and retrieve your brother," suggested Sir Duncan brashly.

As several knights murmured agreement, Niccolo spoke up. "Such a ploy will never succeed."

Red-faced, Duncan turned on Niccolo. "Why not, Venetian?"

"Because as soon as we storm Basil's fortress, he will surely slit Christian's throat." At Aurora's cry of distress, he quickly turned to her. "I am sorry, milady, but we must speak frankly if we are to save your brother."

" 'Tis understood," she replied resolutely.

"If you are so clever, Venetian, then what would you have us do?" Duncan demanded of Niccolo.

Niccolo scratched his jaw. "I think Christian can be saved, but this is a matter calling for utmost delicacy and discretion."

Rumbles of outrage spewed forth from the men. "Are you saying the rest of us are untrustworthy?" Duncan thundered.

"Nay. I am merely pointing out that the fewer people who know about our actual strategy, the better."

"I think Sir Niccolo may be right," concurred Edgar.

"I also agree with him," proclaimed Aurora. "I thank all of you for your concern, but I shall speak with Sir Niccolo alone and hear of his strategy."

Several knights grumbled, but all obeyed Aurora's orders and took their leave.

For a moment, Aurora and Niccolo stared at each other in anguish.

He grasped her hand. "Milady, I am so sorry this has happened."

She nodded, bravely swallowing back tears. "We have all grown too complacent, hunting, celebrating, going on about our lives as if Basil did not exist, assuming he would not attack again."

"I am just as guilty as the rest, milady," replied Niccolo grimly. "I had not expected Basil to make a move again so quickly. I thought we would have more time."

She regarded him skeptically. "Why did you think

that, knight? Did you not warn me that Basil was likely not finished with us?"

Niccolo gave a shrug. "He has proven rather easy to discourage so far."

Aurora stared Niccolo in the eye. "As have you, knight."

He heaved a great sigh and glanced away.

"You left me this morning," she accused.

His expression grew contrite. "I left you flowers, milady."

She moved closer and whispered seductively, "Yea, and they were sweet. But having you there, knight, would have been far sweeter."

Niccolo clenched his fists and regarded her in turmoil. "Milady . . . You know what my feelings are—"

"Nay, I do not know!" she cut in angrily. "You will not share your heart with me!"

"Aurora . . ." Reining in his control with extreme effort, he said, "Should we not be thinking of Christian now, and not our own dilemma?"

She drew herself up proudly. "You are right. I shall give myself in exchange for him."

"Nay!" Grasping her shoulders, Niccolo shot her a look of steely determination. "I shall not hear this demented talk!"

"But is it not better that I give myself to Basil and become his queen, rather than see my brother executed?" she pleaded.

"Do not even suggest that!" Niccolo declared. "Galen is right that we must not trust Basil. And we both know what will happen if you give yourself to him. You will be signing your own death warrant, milady. Basil is not your true love—not by *any* means—and thus you will die within the year."

"You really do believe in the curse now, do you not?" she asked, awed.

"*Sì*, I believe," he replied, "and I am determined

you shall not succumb to it. Christian would never want you to sacrifice yourself for him. I shall rescue him for you, and that is final."

"But how?" she cried.

Niccolo clenched his jaw. "I have considered this already. I shall send a messenger to Ravenia Castle, and ask Basil to meet us at the vineyard outside Osprey at nooning on the morrow."

"But why would Basil meet you?" she asked, perplexed.

"Because I shall inform him we agree to his terms, that we are prepared to exchange you for Christian."

Aurora frowned in confusion.

Niccolo held up a hand. "Mind you, my message will be a ruse, and you shall not even leave this castle, milady. I shall have one of your pages or ladies dress up as you, and wear a hooded mantle. I shall then station bowmen in the trees near the meeting place. When Basil and I meet for the exchange, one of the bowmen will slay Basil. Without their leader, methinks the Ravenian forces will flee, and Christian will be saved."

"That sounds like a risky plan to me," Aurora put in skeptically.

" 'Tis sound, and I shall not, under any circumstances, see your life imperiled." With a groan, he pulled her into his arms. "Nor will I ever, *ever* let Basil have you. Is that understood?"

Aurora pulled away, eyes bright with tears. "No, 'tis not understood."

"And why not?" he demanded, exasperated.

Her voice was choked with emotion. "Because you will not claim me, either."

Helplessly he pleaded, "Aurora . . ."

" 'Tis true! Can you deny it?"

To his despair, he could not.

Wiping away tears, she forged on. "Why should I not go to Basil? I shall never have your heart, Niccolo.

You confuse me, and you torment me. My love is yours for the taking, but you will not have it. Do you want me to stay because you fear if I go, you will lose control of my castle and lands to Basil? But how can you take all I have, when you will not even wed me?"

Aurora's heartbroken words, her anguished expression, stirred hellish guilt in Niccolo, especially since, at one time, he had harbored such mercenary motives, and he knew he was now responsible for her pain and confusion. How could he convince her he no longer wanted anything from her but her love, that he wanted terribly to love her in return, but was not certain if he could, or even if he should?

Solemnly he replied, "Believe what you will, milady, but I shall put you in irons myself before I allow you to go to Basil."

"Why? Why would you hold me?"

"So you will live, milady."

Her gaze riveted him. "I shall never live if I do not have your love."

Exchanging looks of sorrow, they parted. Niccolo was in hell to have matters still so unresolved between them. Aurora's words lashed his conscience, making him feel more confused than ever. He wanted to go to her and heal the rift between them. But how could he, when he still did not know whether his love would doom or save her?

For now, he must see to Christian's rescue. First, he would find a herald to convey his message to Basil, then he would plan tomorrow's strategies with the knights he most trusted . . .

Aurora sought refuge in the chapel. She spotted Niccolo's old squire, Lorenzo, praying at the altar. She waited patiently until the old man was finished.

At last, with slow, awkward movements, he arose. He bowed as he spotted her. "Milady."

"I have seen you here before, old man," said Aurora, smiling. "You pray much, do you not?"

"Yea, milady, I have much to pray about," confessed Lorenzo ruefully. "Moreover, I just heard the tragic news about your brother. I am so sorry, Your Highness. I came here at once to make supplication for his safe return." He solemnly crossed himself.

"You are very kind." She inclined a hand toward the door. "Will you walk with me for a time?"

Again he bowed. "I should be honored, milady."

The two stepped out into the churchyard, pausing as several peasant children scurried past on hobby-horses. They headed slowly toward the keep.

Aurora smiled at the old man. "Lorenzo, tell me more of your master."

"What would you know?" he asked cautiously.

"I would like to better understand Niccolo, for I love him," Aurora confessed.

Lorenzo scowled. "I am sorry to hear that, milady."

"But why?"

He avoided her eye. "I fear my master may be incapable of love."

"He says the same thing!" She heaved a sigh of exasperation. "I know Niccolo has known betrayal . . . I know his wife hurt him. But he will not tell me how, or why. So you must."

"Nay!" denied the old squire, waving a hand in agitation. "I am bound to keep my master's confidences."

"But do you not understand that I only want what is best for him?" Aurora implored. "I sense he is tortured, and I want to help. How can he be so kind and caring one minute, then turn away from me the next? Why will he not share his true feelings with me?"

Lorenzo was quiet for a long, tense moment. "He has suffered much, my master."

"How?" she pressed. "Do you mean when he lost his wife?"

Grimacing, Lorenzo crossed himself. "She was the devil incarnate, that one."

"Why do you say that?"

He shook his head. "I cannot tell."

"You must!" she cried. "I command you to."

Lorenzo struggled for endless moments, mumbling to himself, his lined face a picture of helpless frustration.

"Pray, tell me," she pleaded, touching his arm.

At last, with a shudder, he conceded, "Mayhap 'tis best you know how things truly are, milady."

"Yea, 'tis best," she agreed gently.

A faraway look came to Lorenzo's fine eyes. "I have known Niccolo Campioni since he was a young man and first dubbed in the order of *Cavalieri di San Marco.* 'Twas then I became his squire. The lad was truly a glorious work of our Creator then. He was devoted to God, to his knightly order, and to the Republic. When he wed Cecilia, he fell deeply in love with her."

"So he *has* loved!" Aurora cried.

"Indeed. He loved far too much, especially since his bride did not return his feelings. She was a beautiful woman, but cold and uncaring, manipulative and coy."

"She died, did she not?" asked Aurora.

"*Sì,* though not from natural causes," came the grim reply.

Aurora went pale. "Explain, pray."

The old man cleared his throat. "While Niccolo was off fighting the Turks, he left his business affairs in the hands of a cousin, Cosimo, not knowing the man was a villain at heart. Cosimo bankrupted the Campioni family enterprises, and also committed adultery with Cecilia—"

"He seduced her?" cut in Aurora, aghast.

"She was hardly without sin," Lorenzo continued sternly. "Indeed, 'twas Cecilia's indulging in a love affair with her gardener that prompted the terrible chain of events that all but destroyed my master."

"Go on," urged Aurora.

"Cosimo found Cecilia in bed with her gardener. He went into a rage, slaying both of them, and then he turned the knife on himself."

"How terrible!" Aurora cried.

Lorenzo shuddered, his face stark with anguish. "Niccolo returned from battle soon thereafter, to face scandal and heartbreak. He was devastated by the betrayal of the two people he most loved and trusted, and horrified that his family had been so callously embezzled of its resources. His widowed mother and unmarried sister stood to lose everything."

"Oh, my God!" Aurora cried, her eyes alight with realization. "No wonder Niccolo is so bitter. 'Tis not surprising he cannot love."

Lorenzo nodded. "When he met your uncle, he was a desperate man. He mortgaged his mother's home to bribe Artemas, and then . . ." Lorenzo shook his head. "You know the rest, milady."

Indeed, Aurora's mind was whirling with these shocking disclosures. "Oh, holy saints! He endured unspeakable heartache, and then he was betrayed yet another time! How he must have hated me when he first came here!"

Uneasily Lorenzo glanced away.

"He did despise me, did he not?" she persisted.

"He was very angry, milady," Lorenzo conceded, staring at his feet. "At first, he was convinced you were a part of your uncle's perfidy."

"Of course he would think that, after the way his wife deceived him." She stepped closer, clutching Lorenzo's sleeve. "He wanted revenge, did he not?"

"I cannot say, milady."

"Yea, you can," she insisted. "I remember how charming he was to me. But even then, I sensed there was some inner demon driving him, that his motives were different from the others. And he could not have trusted me. He surely wanted revenge. What did he plan to do?"

"You must ask him, milady," said Lorenzo miserably.

"Nay!" Aurora retorted. "I am asking you, old man, and I shall have an answer."

Lorenzo drew a labored breath. "Very well, then, I will tell you. At one time, he sought to betray you, to ruin you, to ransom you to King Basil—"

"Oh, my God!" she gasped, reeling. "No wonder he refused to marry me! He wanted to see me destroyed!"

Distraught, Lorenzo touched Aurora's sleeve with his gnarled fingers. "Nay, milady. Mayhap he felt that way once, but I know his thinking has changed. Niccolo has changed. He cares about you now, and he will ne'er betray you."

Yet Aurora was beyond hearing him, already shattered by Lorenzo's disclosures. "He will never have to betray me . . . not now," she muttered woodenly, and walked away.

Blinking at tears, Aurora stumbled back toward the keep. She was utterly devastated, her throat burning with sorrow, her heart broken, her soul crushed. She felt like a fool for ever hoping Niccolo could return her love. Like all her ancestors, had she been tricked by passion, deceived by the fates into believing she had found her true love? And instead, had she embraced her own doom?

Yet even though Niccolo had betrayed her feelings, Aurora was still convinced that what she felt for him was love, even if unrequited. She realized that perhaps the ultimate cruelty of the curse was that it condemned the women of her family to love men who could never love them in return. She choked on a sob. Perhaps it was enough that she had experienced the wonders of love herself, just this once. If indeed her life was over now, what really mattered was that she save Christian. For surely if the obstinate Basil were given his long-coveted prize, he would at last end the war and free her brother.

Bitterness welled in her. In an ironic sense, she could now give Niccolo what he must have wanted all along—his own revenge, her own devastation and death.

Near the castle, Aurora encountered an alarmed, panting Artemas. "Niece, what is all this excitement? The loud voices awakened me from my nap." He scowled. "Why have you been weeping?"

"I am afraid I have dire news, uncle," Aurora responded, sniffing. "While Christian was out hunting with our knights, he was kidnapped by Basil. Now Basil demands I surrender myself to him in exchange for Christian's release."

Artemas patted his niece's back to comfort her. "This is horrible. Dear God, what shall we do? Certainly your turning yourself over to that brute is unthinkable. Shall we dispatch our knights to rescue your brother?"

Grimly Aurora glanced away. "Do not worry, Uncle Artemas. I have already determined a course for saving Christian."

As the two entered the keep, Artemas tried to ply his niece for additional details, but Aurora would say no more.

THIRTY-FOUR

NICCOLO SPENT THE BALANCE OF THE DAY PREPARING for the next day's confrontation with Basil, and discussing strategies with the knights he most trusted, Edgar and Gilbert. The two agreed that Niccolo's plan was inspired, and also acknowledged that 'twould be best to inform the rest of the knights and the archers of the battle plan right before the company departed on the morrow.

When Niccolo entered into the keep early the next morning, an incredible clamor greeted him. Overhead he could hear the thump of footsteps, the sounds of loud voices and doors slamming. Then two servants scurried past him in the corridor, calling out, "Lady Aurora!"

Niccolo was staring after the two in consternation when Artemas and a servant woman rushed up to join him. "Sir Niccolo, thank God you are here," greeted Artemas frantically. "You must help us. My niece is missing."

"Aurora is missing?" Niccolo cried.

"Unhappily, yes." Artemas nodded toward the woman. "Martha went in to attend to her shortly after dawn, and found her bed empty."

"Oh, *Dio*," muttered Niccolo. He turned to the servant. "Has she ever done this before?"

The woman shook her head. "Nay, master, I have ne'er known milady to leave the keep so early."

"Let us hope she has gone off alone to the forest," Niccolo muttered. At Artemas's raised brow, he explained, "I happen to know she goes there on occasion."

"Yea, but I fear she is not there now," fretted Artemas. "She told me yesterday of her great concern for Christian. As much as I tried to dissuade her from her folly, I sensed she was determined to exchange herself for him."

"Why did you not tell me this?" Niccolo demanded angrily.

Artemas offered the other man an open-handed gesture. "Aurora never admitted her plans to me. 'Twas just an intuition on my part. Moreover, I never dreamed she would steal off this early, informing nary a soul."

"Oh, Christ, what if you are right?" Niccolo asked, reeling.

Duncan and Edgar dashed by, skidding to a halt near the others. Both men appeared agitated and breathless.

"No sign of our lady in the upper stories," confessed Duncan, wiping his sweaty brow.

"None of the servants remembers seeing her as yet today," reported Edgar.

Niccolo held up a hand to gain everyone's attention. "Let us keep our heads here and not panic," he cautioned. "We shall rescue the princess, but first we must be certain of where she has gone." He turned to Edgar. "Pray, organize our lady's knights to search every inch of the bailey, and check the stables to see if her horse is missing."

"Very well," agreed Edgar, starting off again.

Niccolo nodded to Artemas. "Pray, get the servants to search every nook and cranny of the keep one more time."

" 'Twill be done," he promised.

"I shall look for our lady in the forest," Niccolo went on. At the astonished looks he received from Artemas and Duncan, he waved a hand. "Never mind, I shall explain later. Let us all move quickly, and meet back in the great hall as soon as possible, to discuss our progress."

The foursome parted company, and Niccolo headed at once for the stairway to the dungeon. He felt sick with fear over Aurora's plight. Dio, he should have locked her up yesterday, as soon as she mentioned her rash willingness to exchange herself for Christian!

In the corridor he encountered Lorenzo, who appeared most perturbed. "Master, what madness has seized everyone? Knights are racing around the bailey as if demons have possessed them."

"Lady Aurora is missing," Niccolo said.

"Oh, *Dio*," muttered the squire, crossing himself.

" 'Tis good you are here," Niccolo went on. "You can help the servants search the keep."

Niccolo started to race off, but Lorenzo implored, "Master, wait!"

Niccolo pivoted impatiently, scowling at Lorenzo's oddly wan face. "Why do you detain me? I have not a second to waste!"

"I fear I know where the lady has gone," Lorenzo confessed in trembling tones.

Thunderstruck, Niccolo stepped forward. "What do you mean?"

The old man bowed his head. "I am afraid I have sinned, master."

Exasperated, Niccolo was tempted to shake his squire. "Damn it, old man, quit talking in riddles and tell me what you mean!"

Miserably Lorenzo admitted, "Yesterday your lady sought my council. She wanted to know of the demons driving you."

"And?" Niccolo pressed, his voice rising.

Lorenzo shuddered and stared at his feet. "I am afraid I told her everything."

"*Everything?*" Niccolo shouted. "You violated my confidences?"

Forlornly the squire met his master's eye. "*Sì.* I told Lady Aurora of Cecilia and Cosimo, and . . ."

"What else?" Niccolo roared.

"Of how you conspired to destroy her."

"*Santa Maria!*" Niccolo pressed his palms to his splitting temples. "I cannot believe you of all people have betrayed me!"

Desperately the squire beseeched, "Master, I only wanted her to understand you—"

"To understand me?" Niccolo repeated in crazed irony. "You fool! Do you not know she despises me now? Oh, *Dio*, how could you have done this to me? Do you not realize you have driven her to Basil . . . and to her own death?"

The old man only shuddered.

Eyes gleaming with murderous anger, Niccolo drew his sword. "I shall kill you for this, you traitor!"

Lorenzo fell to his knees and crossed himself. "Master, pray, show me mercy!"

Niccolo swung back his sword, only to feel something snap in him as Lorenzo cowered and cringed from him. Appalled at himself, he dropped the sword, and it clattered to the stone floor.

"*Dio del cielo*, what am I doing?" he cried.

For a few moments there was only awful silence as the squire quivered before his master. At last Lorenzo dared a glance up at Niccolo, and viewed his shattered face.

"I am sorry," said the squire.

"As am I, old friend," replied Niccolo hoarsely. He offered Lorenzo his hand. "Get up, pray. I know you meant no harm."

On his feet, Lorenzo asked, "What will you do?"

"I do not know," came Niccolo's reply. He regarded the squire in terrible anguish. "Lorenzo, for the first time in my life, I am consumed by fear. If I lose her now, I do not know what I shall do."

The old squire laid a hand on his master's shoulder. "You know whence strength cometh, my son."

Niccolo stared at him and swallowed hard.

"You will save her," Lorenzo assured him. "I am certain. But first, you must confront and defeat the darkness in your own soul."

Niccolo nodded, and reached down to retrieve his sword. "I know. I must go now."

As he started off, Lorenzo called, "Godspeed, my son."

Muttering his gratitude over his shoulder, Niccolo rushed off.

He hurried toward the bowels of the castle and the sally port. He did not know why, but he had to go first to the place where they had loved . . . perhaps to relive one last time the incredible sweetness they had known, perhaps out of the desperate hope that she might somehow be there, waiting for him.

Within minutes, he emerged in the forest and raced to the copse. He ran through the wildflowers toward the shrine, tears blinding him—

She was not there. Emptiness seared him, making his heart ache, his throat raw. He paused, alone, cowed, before the altar.

"Where is she, spirits?" he cried. "Is she lost to me forever?"

The sun shied behind the clouds. For a long moment, silence mocked him. Then at last the wind stirred, and a familiar, haunting voice repeated the dire prophecy:

> Dark knight bringeth plague and gloom,
> Repent or seal the lady's tomb.

"I repent!" screamed Niccolo, fists raised to the dark skies. Then, utterly shattered, he fell to his knees. "I repent," he repeated helplessly.

For the first time in memory, this great Venetian knight found himself terrified. Niccolo realized he had known so many emotions before—love, hate, pride, jealousy—but never fear. Now he had truly lost his heart to Aurora, and life without her had no meaning. There was only this unspeakable terror, this desolate, wrenching emptiness.

She was the love of his life. She was extraordinary, full of virtue and courage. She was totally unlike the faithless Cecilia. For only a woman of pure heart would risk death to know the sweetness of love. Only a woman of great compassion and selflessness would sacrifice her very life to an enemy to save her half brother. The reality of losing her was unbearable.

Niccolo realized that Lorenzo was right. His one chance—Aurora's only chance—was to lay aside all his pride and hurt, to repent and try to rediscover his own lost faith.

There before the altar, for the first time in many years, Niccolo laced his fingers together and prayed, begging both for forgiveness and the power to forgive, summoning all his faith and courage so that he might save the woman he loved. He prayed that he might at last become worthy to be Aurora's champion, her one true love, and the man who would free her from the curse.

As he knelt there, Niccolo felt warmed. He felt light—incredible, beautiful light—flooding through his soul, chasing away all the darkness and shadows. He felt the wonder of love and forgiveness filling his heart. He felt joy and hope such as he had never known before, the intensity of it bringing fresh tears to his eyes.

He gazed up to see that glorious light shining down on him, and he knew he would carry that bright sun in his soul forever. He surged to his feet as if reborn, tall, proud, and unafraid. He stood in the light of faith, justice, and righteousness. He knew in that moment that he and Aurora were meant to be, that he was worthy to become her shining knight and the prince of her heart.

THIRTY-FIVE

Niccolo returned to the great hall to witness a terrible sight. Artemas and all of the knights were there, chasing down a troupe of six gnomes. The chamber resounded with knights bellowing curses, furniture being overturned, and the little men shrieking like banshees. Niccolo watched in amazement as Sir Baldric crawled under a table, pursuing one of the wily fellows, while Sir Galen played a rough and tumble game of hide-and-seek with two others on the royal dais, and got slammed in the forehead with a silver pitcher for his efforts. He was flabbergasted to view one of the little men racing along a tabletop, pursued by a red-faced, fist-waving Sir Duncan. He grimaced as another gnome tripped the portly Artemas, who crashed to the rushes with a sickening thud. Wide-eyed, he saw one of the little men viciously kick Sir Rafael in the kneecap, then climb a tapestry and swing himself from a hammer beam!

"*Madre del Dio*, what is going on here?" he cried.

At Niccolo's harsh shout, the vignette froze like a nightmarish *tableau vivant*. A split second later, one of the small creatures scurried up to Niccolo and skidded to a halt.

Wide-eyed, his gamin features contorted in fear, the gnome tugged on Niccolo's tunic with his gnarled fingers. "Sir Niccolo, we come to bring you important tidings, but the ogres would slay us!"

Three other gnomes dashed up to cower near Niccolo. "Protect us, pray!" one shouted.

"Do not let the villains murder us!" pleaded another.

"Save us!" implored the third.

Even as Niccolo glowered at the gnomes in consternation, several knights rushed up to grab them. Watching Galen seize one of the tiny men by the collar of his jacket, and Duncan raise his sword over another, Niccolo shouted, "Wait, I tell you!"

Again everybody froze and stared at Niccolo.

Niccolo rolled his eyes. "Now, one at a time, tell me what has happened." He pointed. "You first, Duncan."

With disgust, Duncan sheathed his sword. "Why, the bloody rascals rushed up to the castle gates, bold as brass," he declared.

Rubbing his bruised forehead, Galen took up the story. "The sentries dragged them into the great hall, but the termagants got loose. We were trying to capture them when you came in."

"They are most wily little devils, señor," declared Rafael, wincing as he clutched his battered kneecap.

"So now we know the cause of this fiasco," Niccolo muttered sardonically. He stared at the first gnome who had addressed him, and squinted as recognition dawned. "You are Francis, are you not?"

"Yea, sir."

"Why are you here, Francis?"

The little man spoke up shrilly, pointing to his comrades. "Because all of us saw Lady Aurora give herself over to her enemy."

Rumbles of trepidation poured forth from the knights.

"You are certain, Francis?" Niccolo asked tensely.

"Yea, milord."

"When and where did this happen?" Niccolo pursued.

" 'Twas shortly after dawn, at the vineyard near Osprey," Francis continued in a rush. "Basil had his entire army with him, and Princess Aurora rode right up to surrender herself to him."

"We would have arisen to protect our princess, except there were too many soldiers," said Farley. "So we came here for your help, milord, and to volunteer our services."

While Edgar and the others eyed the gnomes askance and consulted among themselves, Niccolo asked Francis, "Do you know where Basil took Lady Aurora?"

"They are bound back toward Ravenia, milord," answered the little man. "But 'twill take them some time, methinks, since they have their catapults to drag along with them."

Edgar and Gilbert exchanged looks of outrage. "Basil meant to ambush and betray us during the exchange today!" cried Edgar.

"Of course he did," concurred Niccolo.

Artemas hobbled forward to address Francis. "Is my niece unharmed, sir gnome?"

"Yea, sir."

"And what of Christian?"

"He, too, appears safe, but we heard Basil refuse to release him. It angered our lady very much."

"We must all be going, then," announced Niccolo.

Duncan grasped Niccolo's arm and whispered behind his hand. "Are you certain you believe these devils?"

Niccolo glanced at the six little men, waiting nearby so expectantly. "*Sì*, I am certain the gnomes have spoken the truth. They have protected the royal family for centuries now."

"Centuries?" inquired Duncan, raising a bushy brow.

" 'Tis a long story."

"No doubt." Duncan grimaced at the gnomes. "Well, if you trust the louts . . ."

"I do."

Duncan nodded. "Then we had best be about it. To your horses, men."

But all at once the gnomes let out a clamor, jumping up and down.

"We want to come, too!" shouted Francis.

"Yea!" yelled Farley, bouncing on his stunted legs. "We brought our bows and arrows with us, but the sentries took them away!"

Niccolo turned to the others. "Well, men, what do you say?"

"Nay!" cried a wild-eyed Sir Galen. "Our men-at-arms fear the gnomes!"

"As do the Ravenians," Niccolo pointed out. "If we take the gnomes along, we shall have a chance to overcome our own prejudice, and to thoroughly unhinge the Ravenians when they see the gnomes with us . . . no?"

The men again consulted each other, then Edgar nodded for the group. "Sir Niccolo is right. 'Tis the gnomes who spotted our princess in Basil's clutches, and we must take them along to point the way. I shall have my squire find them ponies."

Niccolo nodded. "Then let us go fight, men . . . and gnomes." He paused thoughtfully. "But first, let us all pray."

The others regarded Niccolo in openmouthed amazement. But when he fell to his knees and humbly crossed himself, they all—to a gnome—followed suit . . .

"Master, you have recovered your faith! *Dio* be praised!"

Moments later, back in the barracks, an exultant Lorenzo knelt by Niccolo, armoring his master, buckling on Niccolo's greaves to protect his calves. Niccolo had just told his squire about his spiritual rebirth at the copse, and the events that had transpired on his return to the castle.

"*Sì*, I shall need every bit of my faith if I am to rescue milady now," stated Niccolo.

"You shall prevail, master," declared Lorenzo with glowing eyes. "You have right and justice on your side."

Niccolo smiled. "You never gave up on me, did you, old friend?"

"No, signore," stated the squire as he fastened Niccolo's cuisses. "Your heart is good, milord. I knew you would eventually rediscover the faith of your youth. I knew this day would come. Now, *Dio* be praised, I can prepare to rejoin my Marta."

"Not yet," Niccolo scolded. "For I still need you. Hurry, now. I fret for milady."

"Let me go with you," beseeched the squire.

Gently Niccolo shook his head. "No, you can best serve me here, *amico mio*," he replied tactfully. "It would please me greatly if you will attend to Aurora's uncle. The count is quite worried about his niece. Moreover, he took a nasty fall when one of the gnomes tripped him."

Lorenzo glanced downward to hide a secret smile. "*Sì*, master, I shall attend the count as you desire, until your return. Do bring Lady Aurora home to us safely."

"With God's help, I shall," Niccolo vowed.

THIRTY-SIX

In the forest on the eastern border of Falconia, Aurora rode beside Basil. She churned in impotent fury; her wrists were tied to the saddle pommel, and she was livid at her captor. Behind them rode Basil's army, and somewhere in those ranks was poor Christian, whom Basil had struck.

Basil had betrayed her. Shortly before dawn, Aurora had left the castle and ridden to the vineyard to await Basil's arrival and to offer herself in exchange for Christian. Before the sun was high in the sky, the enemy army had appeared, Basil leading his forces. Aurora, spotting her half brother with Basil, had ridden boldly up to join them. Seeing her, Christian had yelled for Aurora to stop, and Basil had turned, slamming his fist into the younger man's jaw. As Aurora watched in horror, Christian had slumped over on his horse; he would have fallen had his wrists not been bound to the pommel as hers were now.

Events had proceeded from bad to worse. Before Aurora could contemplate a course of action, she had been surrounded by Basil's men and borne to his side. She had screamed at him, calling him a brute for hitting her brother, and demanding he release Christian at once—

But Basil had arrogantly refused to free Christian,

338

telling Aurora he intended to take both her and her brother back to Ravenia Castle, and he would not release Christian until Aurora was his bride. Over her protests, he had ordered his men to take Christian to the rear, out of her sight. Aurora had watched in agony as her brother, just regaining consciousness and still dazed, was led away on his horse. And then Basil had forbidden her even to look at Christian!

Defiantly she did so now, twisting in her saddle and glancing back, trying to catch a glimpse of him, then burning in frustration as her view was blocked both by massive fir trees and by row after row of armored knights and pages on palfreys pulling along the catapults.

"I told you not to look at him!" roared Basil.

She turned to confront her captor, whose features were clenched in an ugly snarl. "Burn in hell, enemy. I refuse to obey a man who is a liar and a brute."

Basil made a growling sound. "Your defiance, Princess, will be taken out of your dear brother's hide if you do not take care."

"Harm a hair on his head and I shall never wed you!" she asserted. "Moreover, I demand you bring Christian forward to join us at once, so I may satisfy myself that he is unharmed."

"Bah! He is fine," scoffed Basil. "I struck him not nearly as hard as I could have."

"When do you intend to release him?" Aurora demanded.

"I have already told you. When you are my bride."

Aurora shook her head in disbelief. "Why should I believe you when you have broken your word twice now?"

"If you value your brother's life, you will obey."

Glaring at him and heaving breaths of frustration, Aurora could not believe this man had once been the shy lad with whom she had frolicked. "What has happened to you?" she asked bitterly. "Remember when we were children, when we were friends?''

'' 'Tis you who have forgotten!''

"Nay, I have not!" declared Aurora. "You are the one who has changed, Basil, transforming yourself into a man I no longer know. You used to possess honor, chivalry—"

"We have been at war, woman!"

"A conflict you started through your own stubbornness," she retorted. "Furthermore, you have won, and have no reason to act so rancorously toward my brother. You gave your pledge that if I surrendered myself to you, you would release Christian. What has made you such a scoundrel that your word is worthless?"

Basil's eyes glinted with rage, and he shook a fist at Aurora. "You have driven me to it, woman! I loved you, and you scorned my feelings."

Aurora stared at him. His pain was evident, in his tense features and angry, wounded eyes. She caught a glimpse of the real Basil in that moment, and even a hint of the hurt child inside him. Though her ire toward him did not diminish, Aurora felt she understood him then, and could even grasp why he had harassed her for so long.

'' 'Tis not my fault that I did not love you in return," she declared.

"You encouraged me," he accused.

"I did not. I tried to remain your friend—until you insisted I wed you."

"And then you were my friend no longer," he retorted. "You thought you were too good for me, a king! But now you will be shown your rightful place. And if you do not wish to witness me lashing your brother's worthless hide, then you had best obey me and curb that impertinent tongue."

Aurora jerked her gaze away from his and continued riding in murderous silence. Oh, she had been such a fool! She should have known Basil would betray her. Instead of helping her brother, she had only made things much worse! At this point, even if she wedded Basil, she could not be certain he would ever release Christian.

She thought achingly of Niccolo. What would he think when he found her missing? Would he even care? Doubtless he would be furious that she had defied his wishes after he had forbidden her to give herself to Basil. But would he come to rescue her and Christian?

Yesterday, when Lorenzo had told her of Niccolo's past, of how he had sought to betray her, she had been so shocked, so hurt, that she had not actually considered the rest of the squire's words. But now his final statements drifted through her mind: "Mayhap he felt that way once, but I know his thinking has changed. Niccolo has changed. He cares for you now, milady, and I know he will ne'er betray you."

Had the squire spoken the truth? Did Niccolo indeed care for her now, and had she been too blinded by her own pain to see the truth?

Mayhap he would never truly love her. But if Lorenzo was right, surely Niccolo would come after her. She must pray that he would, for he was her and Christian's only hope . . .

Niccolo and the others were riding hard toward the east when one of the scouts, a young squire on a swift gray destrier, galloped up to join them. As his steed snorted and huffed, he informed Niccolo, "Sir, I have spotted Basil's forces just ahead of us. I hid in the trees, within feet of them as they passed. The princess is at their fore riding with King Basil, and Christian is held captive at the rear. The princess appears unharmed, though Christian appears beaten. They are all moving slowly due to the field catapults they are hauling. They will soon enter the Valley of the Boulders."

Once the squire finished, everyone, including the gnomes, started talking at once, offering various suggestions for routing Basil. Niccolo raised a hand and yelled over the clamor. "Silence!"

Everyone paused and turned to him.

"If we are to rescue the princess, we cannot spin in all directions like ninepins." He addressed the squire. "Do you think if we ride hard, we can attain the Valley of the Boulders before they do?"

"Yea, sir, if we waste no time."

Niccolo nodded. "Usually it is imprudent to divide up one's forces, but since we must rescue two hostages, I suggest we take a split approach." He pointed to Edgar. "You take half our company and attack from the rear, making sure you rescue Christian right off."

Edgar nodded grimly. "Yea, I shall have the bowmen pick off the knights riding closest to him."

"Good strategy," agreed Niccolo. "I shall lead the rest of our forces, ride ahead, cut the Ravenians off at the fore, and rescue Aurora. I shall try my best to whisk her away safely into the forest. Hopefully, if we attack the enemy from both directions at once, we shall squeeze him to death."

Niccolo's plan was met by enthusiastic hurrahs and waved fists.

"But wait!" cried a small voice.

Niccolo glanced down at Francis, who was perched on a small pony next to him. "You have a question?"

"What do you want us gnomes to do?"

Staring down at six small, wrinkled, expectant faces, Niccolo scratched his jaw. "Why do you not tag along at the rear with Edgar and help him pick off any of Basil's stragglers?"

"Nay!" protested Francis indignantly. "We want to help rescue our princess. Why do we not ride ahead with you, sir?" Gesturing toward his compatriots,

Francis grinned. "Then the six of us can hide among
the boulders with our bows and arrows, and spook
the Ravenians when they come riding through the
valley."

Niccolo chuckled, and heard several other knights
laugh, as well. "A brilliant suggestion, sir gnome."

"Thank you," replied Francis, beaming.

Niccolo raised his shield. "Then let us all ride!"

The group split up and galloped for their positions,
the gnomes riding with Niccolo's company. They
raced through the forest in a wide circle, safely skirting Basil's army, and soon arrived on the Ravenian
side of the Valley of the Boulders. While Niccolo and
the knights hid in the trees on the hillside, the gnomes
dismounted and scurried into the boulder-strewn valley, hiding among the large rocks with their bows and
arrows.

As the next agonizing moments trickled by, Niccolo
said a silent prayer that he would do his best to save
Aurora and Christian. Once again, he felt a peace and
courage he had not known in many years.

At last Basil's heralds emerged through the giant
trees. Niccolo tensed as he spotted the Ravenian king,
and Aurora riding beside him. Her wrists were bound
to the saddle pommel, and Basil held the reins to her
horse. Never had she appeared more proud, or more
vulnerable. His heart pounded with love for her, and
again he asked *Il Dio* for strength to keep at bay the
fear that could so easily defeat him.

He and the others waited anxiously as the Ravenians moved fully into the valley. Only then did the
gnomes act, popping up with bloodcurdling banshee
screams, shooting off arrows at the startled knights.

The gnomes were brilliant, and for a few seconds
Niccolo could only watch in fascination as the wily,
shrieking fellows totally unhinged the Ravenians.
Men shouted, horses whinnied, reared, and pitched
their riders. Other knights, trying to control their hys-

terical mounts, succeeded only in dancing about in circles.

Two of the gnomes pursued Basil, shooting arrows at him. With the shafts bouncing off his armor, the king dropped the reins to Aurora's steed, drew his sword, and charged the little men.

The split second Basil was distracted, Niccolo signaled to his men to advance. Amid the clamor of hooves, Niccolo lowered his visor and galloped straight for Aurora. Around him, his comrades were waving swords, aiming lances, and howling blood-curdling battle cries. Almost simultaneously, Niccolo spotted Edgar and his forces converging from the rear.

The Falconians roared into the valley, hacking and impaling the enemy. Already spooked by the gnomes, the remaining Ravenian forces panicked, scattered, and tried to flee the double assault.

Niccolo watched Aurora spur her horse and attempt to escape. But even as she galloped away, Basil charged after her, grabbing her reins. Niccolo cursed as he watched the king lead her into the forest. He followed swiftly on their heels, his horse's hooves thundering on the forest floor.

At last Basil noted his approach, violently wheeling his mount and again releasing the leads to Aurora's steed. He reined in his destrier and unsheathed his sword.

"Release her, you swine!" Niccolo yelled, charging the king with his own weapon drawn.

Basil advanced, and the two knights met in a terrible banging of swords. As their destriers screamed and pranced and maneuvered for position, they clashed, Niccolo thrusting, Basil blocking, both men striking and parrying in quick succession.

Just beyond them, Aurora watched in terror and helpless frustration as the man she loved battled her enemy. Never had she seen a more beautiful sight than her beloved champion, her knight in shining armor, galloping into the valley to save her. Niccolo was risking his very life for her and Christian. If only her wrists were not bound and she could help him!

Then she heard a piercing voice cry, "Milady!"

"Francis!" She watched in joy as her friend the gnome galloped up on his pony. "Pray, cut the bindings on my wrists."

The little man reined in his pony next to Aurora. Unsheathing his dagger, he stretched upward to cut her bindings. As she rubbed chafed wrists, both watched the two knights locked in deadly combat, amid the whirl of the horses, the flash of armor, and shriek of the weapons.

"Should I help Sir Niccolo?" asked Francis.

Aurora shook her head. "Nay, we cannot risk startling him now. Let us watch and intervene only if he gets into trouble."

Francis nodded. "Yea, milady." But the grim-faced gnome snatched an arrow from his quiver and drew the shaft through his bow.

Then, amid a mighty clamor, they both watched Niccolo knock the sword out of Basil's hand and send the king crashing off his steed. The horses froze; an eerie silence fell as Niccolo quickly dismounted and pressed the tip of his sword to Basil's gullet.

On the ground, Basil barely stirred.

"Enemy, on your knees!" Niccolo yelled.

Basil complied, struggling awkwardly to his knees and raising his visor. Aurora noted that the vanquished king appeared very shaken, his face pallid.

Raising his own visor and wielding his sword over Basil's neck, Niccolo shouted, "Milady, come see your enemy slain."

At Niccolo's ruthless words, a cold chill washed over Aurora, and she was suddenly fraught with terrible indecision. She stared at Basil, who was shuddering and mumbling incoherent prayers. Did she truly want him to die?

All at once she heard Christian's exultant voice, calling her name. Everyone paused to watch the young man gallop up to join them. Both brother and sister quickly dismounted and joyously embraced.

"Sister, are you unharmed?" asked Christian.

"Yea. And you?" she asked, eyeing him anxiously.

Christian rubbed his bruised jaw and winced. "Yea, albeit I am slightly battered."

"I am glad you are here, Christian," Niccolo called out. "Now both you and your sister can witness your tormentor's execution."

Christian and Aurora regarded each other in uncertainty, then both walked over to join Niccolo.

Aurora glanced from the terrified king to her grimly determined champion. She touched Niccolo's mail mitten. "Pray, do not slay him."

Niccolo appeared angry and incredulous. "But he held both you and Christian captive—"

"Yea, but he did not truly harm us." Glancing at Basil, she pleaded, "Pray, spare him, Niccolo. Although he has made mistakes, he is but a man who loves me. Show mercy to him, as a man who will never feel what he feels."

With his sword poised to swing at Basil's neck, Niccolo paused and stared at Aurora in awe. He remembered his long-ago vow never to give his heart to a woman, and never to show mercy to any enemy. Now his heart was totally lost to Aurora, and he felt humbled by his newfound love. He realized her feelings mattered to him more now than his own.

He smiled at her tenderly, and spoke in a voice choked with emotion. "You are wrong, Aurora. I do love you, and I shall show your enemy more mercy than he deserves."

"Oh, thank you, Niccolo," she whispered, smiling

back at him, deeply touched by his declaration of love
and his display of mercy.

Niccolo sheathed his sword and said gruffly to
Basil, "You may go."

Yet the King of Ravenia surged to his feet in anger
and pride. "Nay, this is not settled!"

Niccolo regarded him in amazement. "Are you a
complete fool? Your army has been routed. You are
defeated, man."

Basil turned aggressively to Aurora. "Do you know
this man conspired against you, that he met with me
to plot your defeat?"

Niccolo's and Aurora's gazes met for a long, meaningful moment—his filled with anguish, hers with
love and forgiveness.

"Yea, I know," she replied at last. "But he is my
champion and it no longer matters to me what he has
done in the past. I love him and I shall shortly wed
him."

Even as Niccolo gazed back at Aurora in intense
relief and gratitude, Basil shouted to her, "You are an
idiot!"

Infuriated, Niccolo drew his sword. "Bide your
tongue, man, or I shall yet run you through. Aurora,
pray, give me your blessing to slay him."

"Nay." She turned to Basil. "Do not be foolish. Go
back to Ravenia and forget about me."

"Nay!" he denied, eyes gleaming vengefully. "I
shall never give up until you are my bride. I would
sooner have the Venetian slay me now!"

"Well, Aurora?" Niccolo demanded.

"What would you have us do, Basil?" Aurora
asked, exasperated. "Slay you?"

Basil glowered at Niccolo. "I think you took unfair
advantage today, terrifying my men with your
gnomes. I think you and I should settle this between
us, Venetian."

"How?"

"I challenge you to a *joute à l'outrance*," said Basil.

At once, Aurora felt panic-stricken. "Nay, Niccolo!" she cried. "I shall not allow you to fight him to the death!"

Staring hard at Basil, Niccolo did not seem to hear her.

Aurora whirled on Basil. "And you! How can you even suggest such a thing, after I convinced Niccolo to spare you?"

"I do not need a woman's help!" sneered Basil. He glared at Niccolo. "Well? What say you, enemy?"

"I shall accept your challenge, on two conditions," Niccolo informed Basil coldly. "The joust will settle the war. The victor will be awarded control of both kingdoms . . . and Aurora's hand."

"Agreed," said Basil.

Aurora grabbed his arm. "Nay, Niccolo, I shall not allow you to participate in this madness!"

He eyed her solemnly. " 'Tis better he and I settle this between ourselves, than countless others continue to die."

"But I cannot risk losing you," she cried.

He smiled at her sadly. " 'Tis either that, milady, or I slay him now. Which will you have, Aurora?" He turned to her brother. "And you, Christian?"

As she struggled in terrible indecision, Christian stepped forward. "Niccolo is right, sister."

"Why?" she demanded.

"Sir Niccolo has been challenged, and is honor-bound to accept," Christian informed her. "Besides, something will die in all of us if he slays an unarmed man. A *joute à l'outrance* is the only fair way to settle this."

She fell into miserable silence.

"Good, then it is decided," said Basil. "Where shall we meet?"

"Tomorrow at nooning on the Falconia Castle green," replied Niccolo. "You may have your army stand behind you to ensure a fair fight, and I shall do the same."

Basil stiffly saluted Niccolo. "Until then, enemy."

He mounted his horse and proudly rode off, and Aurora fell into Niccolo's arms.

THIRTY-SEVEN

With Niccolo, Aurora, and Christian riding at their head, the triumphant Falconian knights galloped back into the bailey. The six gnomes rode happily at the rear. Peasants abandoned their garden plots, and servants emerged from the keep to view the magnificent sight.

Near the stables, just after Niccolo had dismounted and helped Aurora to the ground, Artemas rushed up, trailed by Lorenzo. Artemas stared at his niece and nephew in incredulous joy. "Aurora! Christian! Thank God you have been returned to us, unharmed."

Niccolo watched as Artemas hugged first Aurora, then Christian. He was pleased when Aurora turned to him, took his hand, and smiled at her uncle.

"We have Sir Niccolo to thank for our safe return," she informed Artemas. "He rescued us and routed Basil and his knights."

Artemas at once bowed to Niccolo. "I am in your debt, sir."

"In more ways than one," Niccolo replied with wry humor, and heard several knights behind him chuckling. "Although I cannot take full credit—milady's other knights and the royal gnomes performed every bit as brilliantly."

"We must have a grand celebration tonight in honor of Christian's rescue," said Aurora.

"And your own, sister," added Christian.

"Then the war is won?" asked Artemas.

Niccolo and Aurora exchanged a grim glance. "I am afraid not, uncle," she replied. "Even though Niccolo fairly defeated Basil, he challenged Niccolo to a *joute à l'outrance*."

"A joust to the death?" Artemas repeated in an awed whisper.

"*Sì*," responded Niccolo. "And I accepted the challenge. The joust will be held at nooning tomorrow on the castle green. This will settle the war decisively once and for all. Basil has agreed that the victor will be awarded control of both kingdoms, and the princess's hand."

"But is this not risky?" Artemas asked, his features creasing with alarm. "To gamble all—including my niece's future and the fate of Falconia—on a single bout?"

"Basil will never stop attacking us otherwise," stated Niccolo. "But do not worry. Right will prevail."

Amid a tense silence, Christian stepped up to Niccolo. "Why do you not allow me to battle Basil in your stead, Sir Niccolo? After all, 'twas I who put these dire events into motion by allowing myself to become kidnapped in the first place."

But Niccolo firmly shook his head. "You are a fine and righteous young man, but you are not the one challenged." He smiled at Aurora. "And, although I mean no offense, you are not our lady's champion. I am."

Aurora smiled back bravely, while several other knights cheered.

"Sir Niccolo," murmured Artemas with a scowl, "might we speak for a moment in private?"

"Certainly." He glanced at Aurora. "By your leave, milady?"

She nodded, and the two men slipped away, heading toward the courtyard.

"What is on your mind, signore?" Niccolo asked.

Artemas glanced balefully at Niccolo. "I remain concerned that you have risked the fortunes of my family and our kingdom on this joust tomorrow."

Stiffly Niccolo replied, "As I have already told you, I had no choice but to accept the challenge. And I know I shall prevail—"

"How can you know?" demanded Artemas.

"Because, thanks to milady, I have recovered both my character and my faith," replied Niccolo solemnly. "Such concepts may seem foreign to you, signore, but I assure you good *can* prevail over evil. Moreover, Basil is wrong to try to force Aurora into a marriage she does not want."

Frowning, Artemas mulled over Niccolo's words. "I must concede that your assessment of my character is in many ways justified. But let me assure you that when it comes to my family, I do have integrity."

"This said by the man who sold off his niece's future eight times?" posed Niccolo cynically.

The count of Osprey drew himself up proudly. "It appears my actions have been for the best . . . if you do not fail my niece tomorrow."

"I shall not fail!" declared Niccolo. "And afterward, I shall wed her."

Artemas nodded. "First prove yourself her champion."

"I shall," said Niccolo, turning and striding away.

Heading back toward the barracks, Niccolo encountered Aurora. They smiled at each other almost shyly.

"Meet me in the copse," she said plaintively, touching his hand. "We must talk."

"Of course," he replied. "Just give me time to change."

For Niccolo, an eternity seemed to pass by the time he returned to the barracks and removed his armor with Lorenzo's assistance. He sensed Lorenzo knew he was frantic to go meet Aurora, but this time the old squire did not scold him. Donning a tunic and hose, Niccolo rushed off to his rendezvous.

He spotted her as soon as he entered the arbor. She was standing near the shrine, with Tansy nearby. She saw him, too, and they rushed into each other's arms, kissing feverishly, clinging to each other.

"*Dio*, it is so good to hold you again!" he cried, kissing her silky hair.

"And you," she replied, looking him over with awe and love. "I did not know if I would ever see you again."

He drew back to regard her sternly. "You were foolish, Aurora, and you disobeyed my orders."

"I meant well."

"But you placed your life in jeopardy."

"You are angry with me now?" she asked.

He gathered her close. "No, because Lorenzo confessed that he told you everything, all about my past." He sighed. "I am sorry. I deeply regret that I ever intended to hurt you."

She pulled back and studied his face. "But when you first arrived here, you did seek to betray me?"

"*Sì*," he admitted. "When I learned I had been duped, I intended to forsake and ransom you."

She bit her lip. "You sought to destroy me because your wife and cousin had betrayed you?"

He nodded. "As a very young, unworldly man, I gave my love to Cecilia, then she carved the heart and soul out of me. When I came here, I was an embittered, cynical man, devoid of hope, trust, and faith. When I learned Artemas had deceived and defrauded me, it tore open a barely healed wound." He stared down at her contritely. "I blamed you without proof, and I swore you would suffer for it. But you changed all that. My plans to win revenge were quickly abandoned as I began to fall in love with you."

She almost smiled, then a look of doubt returned. "But you still held yourself apart from me."

"*Sì*, because even as much as you moved me, I did not know if I could ever trust or love again, or become worthy of your love," he confessed quietly. "Then, when I realized the curse was real, I feared my feelings could doom you. It took the prospect of losing you to bring me fully to my senses. Once I abandoned my pride, all fear and doubt faded away." In a breaking voice he finished, "You, my love, have given me back everything I lost—hope, trust, and faith."

She eyed him quizzically. "Faith, Niccolo?"

He smiled exultantly. "This morning, for the first time in years, I prayed before going into battle."

"Oh, Niccolo!" she cried.

"I prayed that I might become worthy to be your champion, your one true love. And I prayed for strength to save the woman I loved."

"Do you truly love me, Niccolo?"

"With all my heart."

She hugged him. "Oh, I love you, too."

For a poignant moment they clung together. "Will you forgive me?" he asked humbly, caressing her back. "Forgive all the dark thoughts I once harbored?"

" 'Tis done," she said. "Speak of it no more."

He felt as if a great weight had finally been lifted. "I will speak only of my love for you," he whispered. "And I do love you so. I love your spirit, your joy, your hope. I love the magic of you, how you commune with spirits and talk to gnomes. I love your courage and your pride, your warm, giving nature and your caring heart."

"Oh, Niccolo," she breathed, gazing up at him. "I love you, too. Your strength, your passion, your strong heart." She blinked at bittersweet tears. "Surely you are my one true love. You must be."

He embraced her tightly. "I shall hope so, my love.

I shall pray you are right. Then we can marry, and live happily for many years to come."

"Oh, yea, Niccolo!"

He drew back slightly to regard her solemnly. "And I want you to know that I want you alone, Aurora—not your castle or your lands. If you so desire, you can turn your holdings and responsibilities over to Christian, and come live with me in Venice. We shall be poor, but we shall be happy."

All at once, she blanched. "Not if you die tomorrow," she whispered.

"Aurora—"

Her anguished gaze implored him. "I did not wish to address this in the presence of the others, but I beseech you, Niccolo, do not fight Basil tomorrow!"

"Have you so quickly lost faith in me?" he admonished.

"Nay, 'tis not just a matter of faith. Even a holy knight is yet a mortal man. I cannot bear the thought of losing you."

He caught her close. "You are not going to lose me, Aurora. You must remember that a Christian knight must also have honor. I have been challenged, and I will defend you tomorrow. From this moment on, we must both live by faith—faith that right will prevail, and faith that our love will triumph over the curse."

She sniffed. "I will try to do as you wish."

He brushed away her tears with his thumb and smiled at her tenderly. "Promise me you will believe."

"I promise," she said.

"Our love will burn brightly this day," he whispered, "and shine in both of our hearts forever."

They kissed, their hearts and souls finally one. Niccolo drew Aurora to her knees beside him on the sweet earth, to consummate their love before the shrine, each not knowing if this would be their last time to share such rapture.

"I want all of you, Aurora," he murmured huskily against her throat.

"And I, all of you, milord."

"I want to take you into myself, into my heart, so you will be with me, tomorrow and always."

"Yea, my love, I shall be with you," she murmured back in a breaking voice, "and you with me."

Niccolo lovingly undressed her, caressing her with his hands, his eyes. She drew off his tunic and his hose, brushing her lips over his smooth chest and muscled arms, teasing his manhood with her fingertips until he caught her hand and pressed it to his warm, rigid length. Breathing raggedly, naked and unfettered, they curled up together in the soft grass.

"You are so delicious, milady," he whispered, trailing his lips down her throat to her breasts, tonguing and nipping the tight red nipples, delighting to her sharp moans. "I want to partake of every morsel of you."

"And I of you, milord," she repeated breathlessly.

Niccolo grinned and worked his lips down her body, kissing the smooth contours of her belly, then moving lower to the joining of her thighs. She tensed as he kissed her there.

"I would taste you there, too, milady. Would you stay me?"

She shook her head. "Nay, milord. When I am with you, I have no pride, no fear. I surrender all of myself to you."

Niccolo gloried in that surrender as he leaned over to take his fill of her, the sounds of her cries making his chest tighten with love. First he titillated, caressing her with his lips and tongue, teasing and retreating. Then he explored more deeply, holding her to him, keeping her on the frantic edge of madness . . .

Sweet tears filled Aurora's eyes at Niccolo's taking her so intimately, so brazenly. Lying there with the scent of the grass filling her senses, the sun warm on her naked flesh, and Niccolo's mouth shattering all her inhibitions, she felt reborn in their love. She writhed at the riotous sensations pulsing within her, unleashed by his warm lips and bold tongue. Never had she felt more vulnerable to him, never more willing to give all of herself to him. Spikes of rapture threaded inside her to twist and spiral, distend and explode . . . She cried out, half in desperation, half in delight, as she gave herself to the man she loved. Then Niccolo delved deeper, plundering her, and she bit a fist as the next pounding peak overwhelmed her . . .

At her wanton cries, Niccolo found his own desires too difficult to contain. But even as he surged upward to fill her with his heat, she pushed him over onto his back, and her passionate face loomed over his.

"I would know all of you, too, milord," she declared.

Niccolo groaned with pleasure as his lady drew her warm lips down his throat, all over his chest. She teased his male nipples with her tongue, and he clutched her to him. His fists clenched in unbearable torment as her sweet mouth moved lower. Then he felt her hot, velvety mouth latch on to the swollen tip of him—and she engulfed him, drawing him into herself . . .

"*Dio*," he cried, pounding a fist as she made love to him with wet lips and hot, flicking tongue. Within seconds he could endure no more and pressed his hands to her face, nudging her away. With much greater impatience, he rolled her onto her back, spread her thighs, and buried himself in her tight warmth. Her hoarse cry set his passions soaring free. He withdrew and surged again, and she eagerly absorbed all of him, curling her legs about his waist. He stared down at her flushed face, her vibrant hair spread out on the grass, her hands balled tight, fin-

gernails digging into her palms. Oh, he adored her so!
She was his life, his every breath!

He raised and kissed one of those lovely hands, un-
coiling the moist palm against his cheek, even as his
loins continued to devour her.

"Always remember I love you," he whispered.

"Always," she sobbed, clutching him tightly to her
as rapture swamped them both.

Afterward, as his beloved princess slept, Niccolo
gathered many roses. He patiently plucked the petals
and threw them on the pond, until the air was laden
with incredible sweetness, and the pond lay cloaked
in the velvety blooms.

He fetched Aurora, scooping her naked body up
into his arms. She stirred and smiled dreamily up at
him, curling her arms about his neck.

He carried his lady to the pond, and she gasped as
he stepped down with her into the cool, fragrant waters. She glanced about at the blooms, breathed
deeply, and then her bright gaze questioned him.

"I always wanted to bathe you in roses, milady,"
he whispered, claiming her lips as he lowered her further.

They cavorted there joyously, laughing, kissing, caressing, and splashing. Niccolo rubbed rose petals all
over Aurora's hair, her face, her glowing breasts. Aurora ran her tongue over his wet, gleaming skin. Soon
he lost all patience, pulled her into his lap, and thrust
himself into her once more.

Aurora tossed back her head as she felt Niccolo
possess her to her soul. She was in heaven, her senses
filled with the scent of roses, her body bursting with
his throbbing heat—

Mere days ago, Niccolo had brought her flowers . . .
Today, they both took the essence of the rose, and
their love, deep into their hearts. If tomorrow Nicco-

lo's honor took him away from her, cutting his sweet life brutally short, she would always have this moment to remember . . .

That night, a great feast was held in the hall. Minstrels strolled, acrobats performed feats, and even the gnomes added to the magic by racing about, cackling, juggling loaves of bread and meat pies.

Up on the royal dais, Niccolo sat with Aurora, Christian, and Artemas. Christian rose with his cup. "To Princess Aurora and Sir Niccolo, the future King and Queen of Ravenia!" he cried.

All those present stood to make the toast, with shouts of "Hear! Hear!" Niccolo stared at Aurora, and they exchanged a look of poignant longing and bittersweet love.

THIRTY-EIGHT

THE MOOD WAS SOMBER IN NICCOLO'S BARRACKS CELL
the following morning as his faithful squire, Lorenzo,
buckled and strapped on his master's armor.

Having attached his master's spurs, Lorenzo struggled to his feet and handed Niccolo his helmet,
plumed in honor of the tournament, and his shield
with coat of arms. "You are ready, master."

Niccolo nodded. "I find it odd that you do not scold
me regarding this joust, as all the others have done."

"You have regained your faith, my son, and I trust
you to do what is right," replied Lorenzo. "Moreover,
having been challenged, you must fight for your
honor, and your lady."

"I am glad you understand, old friend."

"I have always understood you, my son. I rejoice
that you are free at last from your terrible hatred,
your obsession for revenge . . . and that I may truly
rejoin my Marta."

Alarmed, Niccolo touched Lorenzo's shoulder.
"You would leave me so soon, my friend?"

Lorenzo smiled sadly. "My mission on this earth is
completed."

"But I need you!"

Lorenzo shook his head. "You do not, my son. You
have rediscovered faith and courage within your own

heart and soul. Now I must find my own peace."

"But, Lorenzo—"

The old man held up his palm. "Say no more, pray. The rest we must leave in God's hands."

Niccolo sighed. "You are right. Let us pray together, before I do my part for milady."

Lorenzo crossed himself, then wiped away a tear. "Master, I have waited so long to hear those blessed words, and they warm my heart."

When Niccolo trotted his magnificently blanketed destrier out onto the castle green, a scene of pageantry greeted him, along with a great cheer from those assembled. Every knight from Falconia Castle, and every burgher and peasant from the region, stood in the audience outside the castle gates. At the head of the crowd had been placed the royal dais, and there Aurora, Christian, and Artemas sat. Niccolo could see Aurora staring at him intently.

He glanced across the field and spotted Basil, in full armor and mounted on his blanketed destrier. He automatically gripped his lance and shield more tightly. Behind Basil stood his knights and other attendees from the Kingdom of Ravenia.

Niccolo trotted Nero past the crowd toward the royal dais, causing a great roar of cheering to rise from the spectators.

Before the dais, he halted his horse and smiled at his lady. Her visage was endearingly anxious and she looked exquisitely beautiful in a gown of saffron yellow.

In a gallant gesture, he touched his visor. "I salute you, milady, just as I fight for your honor and virtue this day."

She rose and walked down the steps of the dais, untying a silk scarf at her waist. Extending it up toward him, she smiled bravely. "I give you this for good luck. Godspeed, Sir Niccolo."

As Niccolo took his lady's scarf and tied it to his plume, another great hurrah went up from the assemblage. He smiled at her one last time and blew her a kiss, which she lovingly returned, much to the delight of the audience.

Niccolo turned Nero toward his waiting enemy. The heralds stepped forward and blew their trumpets. An eerie hush fell over the crowd.

Lowering his visor, Niccolo felt strangely free from fear as he focused every ounce of his concentration on the joust. He glanced over at Basil and saw his enemy was prepared to charge. He nudged Nero with his thighs. With a high whinny, his well-trained charger leaped forward, even as Basil's destrier sprang into motion across the field. Heads down, the horses ate the turf with their hooves, heading for the inevitable collision.

Niccolo clutched his lance and aimed it with deadly precision for Basil's breastplate. On the first pass, the destriers all but collided, causing an outcry to ripple over the crowd. Niccolo lunged sideways, and Basil's lance just brushed him, causing a shiver of pain across his left side. His own stroke was more successful, glancing Basil's left side and knocking him back in his saddle. Niccolo was pleased to hear his opponent's grunt of pain as he galloped past.

At opposite ends of the field, the warriors wheeled their steeds and prepared for the second charge . . .

On the dais, Aurora had watched with her heart in her throat. A wince of anguish escaped her when she watched Basil's lance glance off Niccolo. Yet her champion had done her enemy much more damage. She prayed Niccolo would unseat Basil on the next pass and they could be done with this madness.

Yet Aurora had to endure three more passes, as the knights repeatedly grazed each other without either knight becoming unseated. A terrifying moment ensued for her on the fourth pass, when Niccolo all but threw himself from the horse while lunging to avoid Basil's lethal lance. Still, her champion remained seated!

Finally, on the fifth pass, Niccolo managed to evade Basil's lance, while striking the king squarely in the midsection. Although Niccolo's lance snapped with a mighty crack, Basil went flying back off his horse and landed on the ground with a sickening thud. Even Aurora gasped at the sound.

Watching Niccolo turn his horse, gallop back to his fallen challenger, and dismount, Aurora felt her heart surging with relief, and she smiled at her uncle and half brother, who both grinned back. Yet her triumph quickly faded into renewed panic as she watched Basil struggle to his feet and unsheathe his broadsword. Niccolo quickly followed suit.

Mercy! Would the bellicose Ravenian never surrender? Aurora sat anxiously on the edge of her seat as the horrible banging and striking began . . .

On the field, Niccolo found himself fighting once again for his life. Basil was a formidable adversary, making up through sheer stubbornness and brute strength what he lacked in skill. The Ravenian fought like an enraged wild boar, charging, chopping, and striking. Endlessly Niccolo blocked and parried and leaped out of range, until he began to tire the mad beast attacking him. Once Basil became fatigued, he quickly grew careless, swinging wide and almost losing his balance, leaving himself open to Niccolo's powerful thrusts. As he had done yesterday, Niccolo struck a mighty blow, knocking the sword from Basil's hand.

A hush fell over the crowd. Niccolo lunged forward for the kill, but hesitated when Basil fell to his knees in a position of supplication.

Raising his visor, Niccolo took deep breaths and tried to calm his raging passions in the face of Basil's appeal. Frustration churned within him to see his enemy again begging for mercy, as he had done yesterday. Should he slay the man, as he had every right to do, or show compassion once again?

"Raise your visor, enemy," he ordered. "I would see your craven eyes!"

Basil lifted his visor. Eyes full of grim triumph met eyes filled with stark fear.

"Have you something to say before I dispatch you?" Niccolo asked.

Shuddering, Basil was silent.

"Are you asking for mercy, enemy?" Niccolo demanded.

"This is a fight to the death," came the quavering reply.

"*Sì*, 'tis, but the code of chivalry requires mercy to the weak, does it not?"

"I am not a coward, sir!" Basil retorted.

"No?" mocked Niccolo. "You cringe from me like one, after agreeing to a fight to the death."

"Then slay me!" Basil cried.

Niccolo raised his sword high overhead, and a gasp rippled over the crowd. Still he hesitated, beset by conflicted emotion, struggling between his honor and his desire to win. He remembered Aurora's pleas yesterday, and realized Basil's death would bring her no joy—

At last he lowered his sword. "Let not your pride and stubbornness make you a fool, enemy."

"What are you saying?" demanded the king.

"I am saying only a fool will die to prove a point, when he can live and prosper if only he will forsake his pride."

"Live and prosper?" repeated Basil bitterly. "When I have lost all? My kingdom . . . and the princess?"

"I shall offer to you a new bargain," declared Niccolo. "If you will vow this moment, before the peoples of both our kingdoms, that this war is ended, if you will promise never again to attack Falconia, or to try to force the princess's hand, then you may go in peace and keep your own holdings."

Basil hesitated a long moment, then glanced toward the royal dais. "Is this arrangement agreeable to the princess?"

" 'Twill be acceptable to her," replied Niccolo. "She wishes not to see you slain . . . and besides, I can speak for her now, as I am to become her prince."

At last, nodding, the King of Ravenia struggled to his feet. He spoke with dignity. "Sir, I accept your terms, which are generous under the circumstances. I would have you know, however, that I would have continued to fight for Aurora, except that now you have finally convinced me you will never allow me to get past you to her."

"*Sì*," replied Niccolo. "She is mine now, and you must accept that you can never have her."

Basil nodded. "When I first determined to wed her, there was no man in either kingdom who could have stood in my way. But now that man is here." Basil bowed from the waist. "I salute you, sir."

Niccolo nodded back, and the Falconians, recognizing that Basil had yielded, let up a tremendous cheer.

Basil turned to his own ranks, to the hushed, somber faces greeting him. "My people, the war is ended," he announced solemnly. "I have given my word to leave the Kingdom of Falconia, and Princess Aurora, in peace from this day onward. Let us return to our kingdom and prosper."

Basil limped off to his charger, and the Ravenians departed. Niccolo leapt onto his destrier and galloped toward the cheering crowd, the royal dais. Aurora rushed down the steps to greet her lord, her face gleaming with happiness and pride. He leaned over, scooping her up before him on the saddle. The Falconians went wild with joy, stomping, shouting, and cheering their future king and queen.

With Aurora in his arms, Niccolo rode trium-

phantly into the bailey as the Falconians threw gar-
lands in their path and showered them with rose
petals.

Several weeks later, all members of the Falconian
court gathered in the copse for a garden wedding.
Niccolo and Aurora stood before the shrine as Father
Mark intoned the wedding mass. Aurora was be-
decked in a gown of dazzling white silk. She wore
her royal crown with small flowers threaded through
its golden links; she held a bouquet of pink roses in
her hands. Niccolo wore a dark blue velvet tunic and
pale tights.

Staring at Niccolo with love in her eyes, Aurora felt
filled with pride that her champion was to become
her prince. She felt no fear, only joy. And she sensed
her ancestors approved—

Indeed, even as the priest droned on, she felt she
could see them for the first time, nebulous forms
swirling about the altar, like veils of gray lace floating
on the breeze. Aurora blinked in awe and wonder, but
yea, they were there—diaphanous phantoms curling
and spiraling about the stone shrine! She could even
faintly detect their hazy, smiling faces! At last she
heard Great-Aunt Beatrice's voice, for what she
sensed was the final time:

May our heavenly peace be your earthy token,
Live long in bliss, for the curse is broken.

Aurora stared, entranced, at the wispy spirits floating away toward heaven, then disappearing into the
clouds. Rapture sang in her heart. The curse was broken! At last 'twas broken, and the spirits of her ancestors were finally at peace!

In reverence, she turned to Niccolo. Had he seen?
Had he heard?

Niccolo smiled at Aurora as their minds communicated. Yes, he had seen, he had heard, and his joy knew no bounds. He knew that the curse was broken, the spirits were at rest, and the future happiness of himself and his lady was at last secured. He must thank his beautiful Aurora for leading him out of the darkness into the light of her everlasting love . . .

At the conclusion of the mass, the two turned, hands linked, to hear accolades from the court as the other smiling knights and ladies saluted them. Then Niccolo witnessed an amazing sight. Artemas swept toward them, followed by four gnomes carrying a bier with a large, ornate chest.

He turned to his bride and raised an eyebrow.

Mischief shone in Aurora's eyes. "My lord, your dowry cometh."

"My dowry?" he repeated, amazed.

As the gnomes set down their burden, a grinning Artemas paused before them and snapped his fingers. Francis flipped open the chest, and Niccolo gaped at the contents—gold and silver coins, plates and goblets, jewels more splendid than he had ever imagined.

In amazement, he turned to his bride. "You said there was no dowry!"

She eyed him contritely. "I wanted the contest to be a true test of honor—and I wanted to be loved for myself. Can you forgive me?"

Niccolo was still in shock. "But where did the treasure come from?"

"You must ask Francis," she said.

Niccolo turned to the gnome, raising a brow.

Grinning, the little man spoke. "For centuries it has been the duty of the royal gnomes to dig for silver in the Falconian hills."

"So that is why you always carry picks and shovels!"

Francis nodded. "The silver has been exchanged for other riches—and we, the royal gnomes, guard the treasure carefully."

Niccolo slanted his bride another look of reproach. "*Pray*, forgive me?" she pleaded.

He laughed and hugged her. " 'Tis done. Speak of it no more."

Artemas strode closer, grinning. "I, too, must tender my apologies—to you, Sir Niccolo, and to the others I defrauded." He cupped a hand around his mouth and yelled, "Fiske! Finn! Pray, come forward."

Two more gnomes marched toward the altar, bearing a smaller chest, which they handed to Artemas. Artemas flipped open the lid, revealing an interior filled with small sacks.

"To all knights I have wronged," Artemas announced, "I offer you each a sack of Falconian silver in compensation."

But as the seconds trickled by, no knight came forward. Edgar, Gilbert, Baldric, and Rafael merely grinned at one another sheepishly and shifted from boot to boot. And although Duncan and Cesare appeared more tempted, ultimately neither man approached the altar.

Artemas glanced at Niccolo. "Why do your comrades hesitate?"

Niccolo chuckled. "You do not understand their lack of greed?"

Artemas shook his head.

"Honor, my friend," he replied. "To perform with chivalry is reward enough. Despite your defrauding them, my comrades are reluctant to claim any material prize for having served your niece faithfully." He turned to regard his bride with love. "Just as I hesitate to accept Aurora's dowry."

"But, Niccolo," she argued, "we shall need the royal treasure for our future children."

"And do you not have family back in Venice who are in need of your assistance?" added Artemas.

Niccolo frowned. At last he conceded, "I shall accept part of the treasure, but only to help others, never for myself."

"Ah, but you shall accept one small gift for yourself, milord," insisted Aurora.

As he regarded her, bemused, she snapped her fingers. Francis leaned over, sifted through the treasure, then straightened and handed Aurora a golden crown, splendidly bejeweled with rubies, emeralds, and topaz.

Stretching on tiptoe, Aurora placed the ornate crown atop Niccolo's head. Proudly she declared, "I crown you Prince of Falconia."

In front of all the witnesses, a grinning Niccolo drew Aurora close, and with his lips crowned *her* the princess of his heart.

EPILOGUE

A YEAR AND SEVERAL MONTHS LATER, ON A COOL fall morning, Niccolo and Aurora returned to the copse. Autumn had dusted the leaves of the birches with a russet color that splotched the landscape in vivid contrast to the green pines and still-blooming wildflowers.

A baby's cry rose above the soft rustle of foliage, the whistle of the wind through the copse. Niccolo carried in his arms his beloved firstborn, six-month-old Lorenzo, named after his faithful squire who had passed away in his sleep a year ago and gone to join his beloved Marta. Niccolo patted the baby's back and whispered to him soothingly as the robust child struggled against his father's shoulder.

"You had best give him to me," scolded Aurora. "He is hungry."

Niccolo turned to raise an eyebrow at his bride, admiring, as always, the way motherhood had put a new bloom in her cheeks and had added a tempting ripeness to her figure. The love of his life had never looked more alive than she did now, three months after the curse should have taken her. What fierce joy he felt that she was his!

Niccolo transferred the squirming baby into her outstretched arms. "My son is always hungry," he complained. "Not that I blame him for making you his favorite."

Aurora laughed and smoothed down the baby's linen gown. They settled themselves on the steps of the shrine. Niccolo watched in wonder as his wife tugged down her bodice, exposing her full breast, its nipple already beading with milk. He chuckled with pride as his blond-haired, blue-eyed son rooted to his bride's nipple and nursed lustily while kicking his little feet in delight.

In a choked voice Niccolo said, "I am so proud of you for suckling him yourself, for refusing to give him to a wet nurse."

"Nor shall he ever be fostered," his bride added.

"We must take him to Venice and show him to Mamma," said Niccolo.

"Ah, yea, I would love to see Venice again," replied Aurora, beaming. "Caterina's wedding last fall was so beautiful."

"But not as wondrous as ours here in the copse."

They shared a joyous smile.

"I would love to see your family again, and introduce them to Lorenzo," added Aurora.

"We shall go soon, my love."

"Mayhap after winter," she murmured.

Tansy crept forward to join the small family. Niccolo regarded the fawn thoughtfully and stroked her soft ears. "I think I would like a girl child next."

"A girl like Tansy?" she teased.

He glowered. "Of course not. A daughter like you, my love, with your dark hair and eyes."

Aurora rolled those dark eyes. "Allow me to wean this one first, milord."

"Which will not be an easy task from the look of it," he taunted.

She laughed. "Oh, he will want to be free of his mother in due course, and out playing with toy swords, bows, and arrows."

Niccolo reached out to touch his son's soft foot. "He will be stalwart and brave, our son. But at least we can hope he will never have to go off to fight a real war."

Aurora nodded. "I am so glad the peace with Ravenia has endured. You have made a wonderful king, milord."

"I have savored every moment with you, my love," he agreed. "And I am even happier that we have triumphed over the curse."

"Oh, yea," whispered Aurora, glancing about in awe at the copse. She shifted the baby to her other breast and wiped away a tear. "On that day long ago when we conceived him here, I never knew if I would survive to see him grow. There is nothing dearer."

For a few moments they fell silent, while the baby continued to drink his fill. Staring about them, Niccolo asked, "Do you ever hear them anymore?"

Knowing just what he meant, Aurora shook her head. "Nay, milord, I know they are at peace."

Niccolo glanced toward the bright heavens. "I know they are watching over us, and blessing our happiness, just as Lorenzo is with his beloved Marta."

She touched his hand. "I know you miss him still, my love, but he died peacefully."

Niccolo nodded, swallowing the painful lump in his throat. "I shall miss him always, but he is happy now. And he did die content, knowing I had recovered my faith—and won you."

"I am the winner, milord," declared Aurora, "and you shall always be my champion."

"And you, the greatest prize of my life," he replied gallantly.

Aurora glanced down to see that Lorenzo had fallen asleep against her breast. She leaned over, kissing the baby's cheek. "We must go back now. Your son needs his nap."

"And I need his mother," remarked Niccolo meaningfully. "But first let us dally and watch him sleep, so he may fill his lungs with the sweet, fresh air."

The small family lingered there on the steps, the Angel of Wisdom sheltering them with her heavenly arms.

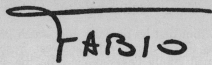

International Multi-Media Superhero
Champion of Romance, Fitness and Self-esteem, has an

Official Link to his fans—

THE FABIO INTERNATIONAL FAN CLUB

- *Have you wondered what Fabio is all about?*
- *Would you like a glossy photo of him?*
- *Want to know where to write to Fabio?*
- *Curious about Fabio's wants, needs, personal philosophy and future plans?*
- *Interested in collecting Fabio memorabilia?*

YES! Then the Fabio International Fan Club is designed for you...once you sign up, you'll receive

—an 8 x 10 glossy photo...
—newsletter "updates"...
—membership card...and much, much more!

For more information on how to join, write to:
FABIO IFC, P.O. Box 827,
DuBois, WY 82513